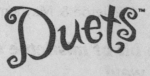

Two brand-new stories in every volume... twice a month!

Duets Vol. #39

"Colleen Collins is a real find," says *Under the Covers*, and there's no doubt Colleen is one of the funniest authors around. Joining her in this volume is talented Darlene Gardner, an Intimate Moments writer making her Duets debut with a hilarious story!

Duets Vol. #40

According to *Romantic Times*, Cara Summers "thrills us with her fresh, exciting voice... rich characterization and spicy adventure." Teaming up with Cara in this humorous Christmas volume is talented Lori Wilde, who has more than ten books to her credit.

Be sure to pick up both Duets volumes today!

A little bit of mistletoe sure goes a long way!

Shane fought to control his breathing. He looked at Jodie, expecting to find her embarrassed, angry even. Instead in her eyes was pure, unadulterated glee. Obviously noticing his confusion, Jodie let out a delighted chuckle.

"Aren't you upset about what that kid saw? The two of us necking like..." Shane's throat dried up at the thought of how far he would have *liked* to have taken the interlude. "Do you realize he thinks we're—"

"Lovers." Nodding, Jodie burst into a fresh wave of giggles. "Don't you see? I've been trying so hard to change my image in this town. I'm tired of being poor, predictable Jodie. And now they'll think that you and I, that we... Oh, I wish I'd thought fast enough to introduce you as the gardener."

"The *gardener?* Why would you want a gardener at this time of year?"

"So I could be *the* Lady Chatterley of Castleton, New York," she quipped. "After all, if people are going to talk, we might as well give them something to talk about...."

For more, turn to page 9

She'd caught Santa with his pants down!

Edie came to a halt at the storeroom door. She'd had no idea that Santa was so muscular, so manly, so gosh-darned sexy. And she hadn't expected to find him almost naked.

He snapped his head around, and deep sapphire eyes sliced into hers. "What is it?"

"I—I—" She forced herself to look at the floor.

"If you've gotten an eyeful, could you leave me in peace?"

"Why did you run in here and take off your clothes?" Edie asked

"*Fleas.* The suit had fleas."

"Oh, my, and I was giving you a hard time."

"Yes, you were. But before you go, could you scratch me right here?" He twisted his arm around his back.

Edie gulped. Until today she had never considered Santa the least bit sexy, but this man had changed all her preconceived notions about the Christmas icon!

For more, turn to page 197

HARLEQUIN DUETS

ISBN 0-373-44106-1

MISTLETOE & MAYHEM
Copyright © 2000 by Carolyn Hanlon

SANTA'S SEXY SECRET
Copyright © 2000 by Laurie Vanzura

Mistletoe & Mayhem

CARA SUMMERS

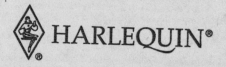

HARLEQUIN®

TORONTO • NEW YORK • LONDON
AMSTERDAM • PARIS • SYDNEY • HAMBURG
STOCKHOLM • ATHENS • TOKYO • MILAN • MADRID
PRAGUE • WARSAW • BUDAPEST • AUCKLAND

Dear Reader,

When my editor asked me if I wanted to set my romantic comedy in the holiday season, I jumped at the chance. After all, Christmas has got to be the most perfect time of year to fall in love.

The only problem was that my hero and heroine wouldn't cooperate. Jodie and Shane simply didn't have time to fall in love, let alone time to think about Christmas. They were much too busy trying to catch Jodie's embezzling ex-fiancé, who'd just escaped from jail. Only, they kept getting in each other's way.... And this led to a whole lot of mayhem... and many, many moments under the mistletoe!

I hope you have as much fun watching Shane and Jodie fall in love as I did bringing them together.

Merry Christmas!

Cara Summers

P.S. I'd love to hear what you think. You can write to me at: P.O. Box 327, Dewitt, NY 13214.

To Heather Smith Hanlon, my new daughter-in-law.
I always wanted a daughter, and I'm so lucky
to finally have one as nice as you.
Welcome to the family.

1

"I WANT TO BUY A GUN."

Jodie Freemont barely kept herself from wincing at the blunt way she'd blurted out her request. But the moment she'd actually seen the gun lying in the display case, the little speech she'd been working on all morning had flown right out of her mind.

Glancing around, she saw that everyone in Hank Jefferson's sporting goods store was staring at her, including the tall, handsome stranger testing a fishing pole. And Alicia Finnerty, Castleton's number one gossip, had stopped chattering to him in mid sentence.

In the sudden silence the music pouring out of the radio behind the counter seemed to grow louder. "All I want for Christmas is..."

"That gun." Jodie quickly pointed to the smallest pistol in the case before she could change her mind. "Could I hold it?"

"I can't sell you a gun." As if to emphasize his point, Hank moved forward and planted his hands, palms down, on the glass-topped counter.

Jodie peered between Hank's thick fingers, trying to keep the gun she'd chosen in view. *Visualize Your Goal.* In her mind, she pictured yesterday's motto of the day, one of many that her landlady Sophie Rutherford had been magnetizing to her refrigerator door over the past two months. She'd had plenty of time to practice her visualization skills last night while she'd listened to a prowler walk stealthily across the attic floor.

For just a second, the memory flashed through her—the creak of a board, the tension curling cold and tight in her stomach, the icy shivers shooting through her veins while she waited for the next sound…and the next.

Picturing a gun in her hand had helped her to keep the fear at bay.

But the one she'd imagined had seemed smaller, less lethal-looking than the one in the display case. How would it feel in her hand, she wondered? If she could lift it, would she actually be able to point it at someone and shoot it?

Raising her eyes to Hank's, she said, "If you're worried that I can't afford it, I have cash."

Hank leaned closer, pitching his voice low. "You've got every reason to be feeling a little low, losing your fiancé and your house all in the space of a few months. But what you need is a new young man, not a gun. Billy Rutherford isn't the only fish in the sea." Moving around the counter, Hank took Jodie's arm, patting it gently as he steered her up the aisle. "See that man at the cash register, the one with the fishing pole. He's new in town." Pausing, Hank winked at her. "And the Mistletoe Ball is less than a week away. Let me introduce you to—"

Jodie stopped short. "I didn't come here for an introduction." *Or a date!* She barely kept herself from shouting the words. Out of the corner of her eye, she could see the man with the fishing pole smile. He'd heard her whole life story and now he was laughing at her.

Next to him Alicia Finnerty had her mouth open like a guppy, absorbing the whole scene.

"My mother told me not to have anything to do with strangers," Jodie said and immediately bit her tongue. She sounded like a prude. When the stranger's grin widened, anger mixed with her embarrassment.

"That was good advice when you were young," Hank said, still keeping his voice low, "but you're a grown woman now, and you don't want to spend all your life pining away for a man who walked away."

Like your mother did. Hank didn't say the words out loud, but Jodie could hear them hanging in the air before she said, "I won't. I'm not. What I need right now is a gun."

"Well, I'm not going to sell you one."

"I can buy one somewhere else."

"I reckon you can, but whatever you might think right now, suicide is not the answer."

"*Suicide?* I don't want that gun to... You can't think that I ..." Jodie stopped because the concerned, pitying look on Hank's face revealed that was exactly what he was thinking. And one quick glance toward the front of the store told her that he wasn't the only one thinking it. The stranger wasn't grinning anymore. And Alicia Finnerty could hardly contain herself. Any minute now she would make a break for the door so she could pull out her cell phone and start blabbing the news.

"It's the holidays," Hank said. "Lot's of people get depressed around Christmas. What you need is something to look forward to—like a date for the Mistletoe Ball."

"Hank, I want that gun because last night there was a prowler in the attic."

"Did you call the sheriff?"

"I tried, but the phone wasn't working. Even if it

had been, the Rutherford sisters and I are alone in that house, and we're two miles from town. All we had to defend ourselves with was fireplace pokers.''

"Well, you go on over and tell the sheriff right now," Hank said. "Let him handle it."

Jodie opened her mouth and then shut it. She could try to explain to Hank that she and the Rutherford sisters might be dead in their beds before the sheriff or one of his men could even get to the house, but she wasn't going to change his mind. He was not going to sell her a gun. And if she read Alicia Finnerty's expression right, by tonight everyone in Castleton would know that poor Jodie Freemont was thinking of committing suicide.

"Fine," she said. "I'll just take some strong rope. Give me some of the stuff that they string sails up with."

As Hank's eyes narrowed, she hurried on. "I'm going to use it for...hauling a Christmas tree to the house." *It was a lie. If lightning was going to strike her, she might as well make it a good one.* "Sophie and Irene are putting up a second tree in the dining room so we're going to dig up a fresh one and replant it later."

"How much do you need?" Hank asked.

Pulling a piece of paper out of her pocket, she glanced down at it. "Thirty yards."

As Hank ambled off to the back of the store, Alicia Finnerty cleared her throat. "That's a lot of rope."

Turning to find the older woman at her elbow, Jodie couldn't resist saying, "The better to hang myself with, my dear."

"Oh, my. Oh, my. Oh, my." Her hand at her throat, Alicia Finnerty backed toward the door, pushed against it, and bolted out onto the sidewalk.

"She thinks you really intend to do it."

It was the stranger who'd spoken, and when Jodie turned, she found herself looking into the darkest pair of eyes she'd ever seen. Black smoke, she thought. The kind that blinded you. Though her gaze never left his, she was aware of dark hair falling below the collar of his blue work shirt, strong cheekbones, a square jaw, and lines etched around his mouth. Tall, dark and *tough*, not pretty. This wasn't a man you'd want to run into in a dark alley. Or an attic. She felt something curl in her stomach. Not the cold ball of fear she'd experienced last night when she was listening to those footsteps. No, this was something different, something warm…no, hot.

Then she watched, fascinated, as his lips curved in a smile and his eyes lightened to gray. This time he wasn't laughing at her, but with her, and the warmth inside of her grew. Quite suddenly, she felt as if she'd known him for a long time.

But she hadn't. Just as she hadn't really known Billy. Taking a step back, she said, "Maybe I do intend to do it."

"No." The man shook his head. "I don't think so. You're not the type."

"Not the type for what?" Hank asked, bagging the coil of rope and placing it on the counter.

"Nothing," Jodie said, grabbing the package.

"Where'd Alicia go?" Hank asked.

"She—" Jodie and the stranger spoke the word together. When she glanced at him, he was smiling again.

"Ms. Finnerty had a pressing engagement," he said.

Hank grinned at them. "With her cell phone, I'll bet. I take it you two have introduced yourselves."

"No."

Once again they spoke in unison. This time, Jodie kept her eyes on Hank and said, "I'll have to take a rain check on that introduction." She backed toward the door. "My lunch hour is nearly over. I've barely got time to meet Sophie and Irene before they head off to their meeting."

"You going to pay for that rope?" Hank asked.

"Oh." She could feel the heat rising in her cheeks as she said, "Just put it on the Rutherford House account." To the stranger, she managed a nod. "Another time. 'Bye."

She was halfway down the block before she remembered to breathe. The last thing she needed was to be introduced to another intriguing stranger. Especially one who made her feel hot one minute and icy cold the next. Strangers were dangerous, especially tall, attractive ones. Billy had taught her that.

SHANE SULLIVAN STEPPED out of the sporting goods store just as Jodie Freemont paused at the corner to wait for the traffic light. She would be getting her rain check sooner than she expected—in about fifteen minutes to be exact. That was when he'd agreed to meet Sophie and Irene Rutherford at Albert's Café.

It was just by chance that he'd run into Ms. Freemont in the sporting goods store. But then Shane believed in chance. It had always served him well in the past.

This time, too, he thought. It had given him the opportunity to assess Jodie Freemont before they were formally introduced. He made it his business to get to know anyone who might stand in his way. And right now, Jodie Freemont might be the biggest obstacle to his goal.

He'd come to Castleton, New York, because he had a hunch that she might know more about the five million dollars her ex-fiancé had embezzled than she'd told the police.

Narrowing his eyes, Shane studied Jodie as she stepped up on the curb and walked quickly and purposefully toward Albert's.

Now that he'd met her, he could see that the picture in her file didn't do her justice. It hadn't captured her smile or the light that came to her eyes when she laughed. Her hair was different, too. In the picture, it had fallen halfway down her back. Now, cropped short and framing her face, it made her look exactly like the homeless waif everyone in town thought her to be.

Shane frowned. Why was he so sure she wasn't just what she appeared to be? And why was he wondering again, just as he had back there in the store, exactly how she would feel pressed close against him?

His frown deepened. The only thing he should be wondering about was whether or not she was mixed up with her embezzling ex-fiancé, Billy Rutherford. In the six months since his arrest, the man had steadfastly maintained his innocence, refusing to reveal the location of the money. And not one cent had been found.

A quick gust of wind set bells jingling overhead, and Shane let his gaze sweep the street, decorated in picture-book fashion for the Christmas holidays.

The money was here. Shane could feel the familiar tingling in his fingers. Billy would make a break for it soon. Castleton was the perfect hiding place, and Jodie Freemont made the perfect cover. Who would suspect her of hiding five million dollars for the man who'd swindled her out of her home?

He did. He shifted his gaze back to Jodie as she ducked into Albert's Café. Or he had until he'd met her. Shrugging off the thought, he started down the street. This wasn't the time to start second-guessing his hunches. His job was to recover the five million, and he had just enough time to store his new fishing pole in his car before he joined the Rutherford sisters. Then he'd get his long-awaited introduction to Jodie Freemont.

"DID YOU GET the gun, dear?"

"No. Hank Jefferson flat out refused to sell me one," Jodie announced as she joined the Rutherford sisters at their regular table in the window of Albert's Café.

"It's for the best," Irene, the younger of the two sisters said as she patted the peach-colored curls that framed her face. "Guns make me nervous."

"Everything makes you nervous," Sophie declared. "And Hank Jefferson's an idiot." In her early seventies, Sophie Rutherford still dressed with military precision and wore her iron-gray hair pulled back and twisted into a neat bun. Sophie reminded Jodie of a tank, and she had a personality to match.

"It's your constitutional right to bear arms," Sophie added. "You could sue him."

"Hank would probably persuade the jury that he'd saved my life," Jodie replied.

Irene shivered. "Firearms *are* dangerous. An accident could happen."

"I don't think Hank was worried about an accident," Jodie remarked dryly. "He thought I wanted the gun to shoot myself."

Irene stared at her. "Why ever would you do that?"

"Because of Billy," Jodie said.

"What does he think you are? Some poor Ophelia pining away for her Hamlet?" Sophie demanded.

"He wanted to introduce me to a perfect stranger," Jodie said. "I think he was going to ask the guy to take me to the Mistletoe Ball."

"Well, Hank's got it all wrong. Billy's coming back to you, dear. He didn't desert you by choice," Irene said. "When the police came to the house, he tried to resist arrest. That shows how much he really cared for—"

Sophie set her teacup down with such force that it rattled every piece of crockery on the table. "When are you going to stop defending that good-for-nothing nephew of ours? It's thanks to him that Jodie lost her house, and we have to turn ours into a bed-and-breakfast!"

Irene clapped her hands over her ears. "I'm not going to listen to anything bad about Billy. He's innocent until proven guilty."

Jodie took one look at the expression on Sophie's face and hastened to intervene. "How are the preparations for the Mistletoe Ball going?"

Immediately a smile lit up Irene's face. "It's going to be the best one ever. Having it in Slocum Hall instead of the library gives us so much more room for dancing. It was Sophie's idea."

"You're the one who thought of having the caterers dress up as Dickens characters this year. People are going to remember that longer than they remember the extra dancing room, my dear."

Breathing a silent sigh of relief, Jodie leaned back in her chair as the two women continued to talk about the ball. For as long as she could remember, the Rutherford sisters had cochaired the Mistletoe Ball, an annual fund-raiser for the Castleton College Library. It was scheduled for the Friday before Christmas, and practically everyone in town would be going.

"Hank Jefferson could be right about one thing," Sophie said, turning suddenly to Jodie. "You really should have a date for the ball."

"Absolutely not," Jodie said. "No sympathy dates for me, thank you. Besides, attending the Mistletoe Ball is part of my job. I have to stand at my boss's side and make sure he knows the names of all the important contributors."

"It's time that Angus Campbell resigned from that job if he can't keep track of the contributors," Sophie said. "And you shouldn't let him intimidate you. Did you forget your motto of the day?"

"No," Jodie said. How could she, when Sophie tore them off a calendar and stuck them on the refrigerator door each day? According to the publishers of the calendar, if she incorporated them into her daily life, she was going to be a new person in just 365 days.

Privately, Jodie had her doubts about how effective a bunch of mottos was going to be in transforming her. The expression of pity she'd seen earlier on Hank Jefferson's face testified to the fact that they hadn't done much good so far. In the eyes of the residents of Castleton, she was still the same "poor Jodie" who'd allowed Billy Rutherford III to turn her into a complete patsy.

"Jodie!" Nadine Carter hurried toward them, a teapot in her hand. The pretty blonde had been Jodie's student assistant until she'd decided to quit college six months ago and start waitressing at Albert's. So far Jodie had been unsuccessful at getting her to go back to school.

"I've got this new herbal tea I want you to try. It's supposed to be great for pulling you out of depression."

"I'm not depressed," Jodie said, but she knew as she met Nadine's eyes that she had about as much chance of convincing her of that as she'd had of getting Hank Jefferson to sell her a gun.

"Just try it," Nadine urged. "I hear you're feeling a little down today."

Jodie stared down at the teapot Nadine had placed in front of her. It had bright-yellow daisies dancing all over it, mocking her. Alicia Finnerty had been busy, she thought. By this evening, everyone in town would know.

Suddenly, she'd had it. She glared down at the dancing daisies. "Take it away. I'm through with herbal tea. I'll have a...a cappuccino."

Nadine stared at her in exactly the same way Hank had when she'd asked to hold one of the guns in his display case. "But you...you don't drink caffeine."

"Well, today I'm just going to go for it," Jodie said, lifting the teapot and placing it firmly back in Nadine's hands.

Nadine opened her mouth, shut it. Finally she said, "I don't know—"

"On second thought, make that a double-strength cappuccino," Jodie said.

Sophie waited until the waitress had walked out of earshot before she reached over to pat Jodie's hand. "Atta girl. You *did* remember today's motto."

"Go for It," Jodie recited. "And I'm throwing over my herbal tea habit. Whoop-de-do," she muttered sarcastically.

"You tried to buy a hand gun, too. And Hank Jefferson had no right not to sell it to you. Did you tell him about the prowler?" Sophie asked.

"He told me to go tell the sheriff, and he patted me on the arm." Jodie frowned. People were always patting her—on the head, on the arm, on her back. Somehow she brought that out in people. She hadn't liked it at eleven and she didn't like it any better at twenty-six. "I don't think he believed me. He almost refused to sell me the rope." She gestured toward the package she'd carried into the café. "I'm sure he's worried that I might use it to hang myself."

Both women reached for her hands.

"You wouldn't," Irene said.

"You couldn't," Sophie said.

As Jodie looked into the eyes of the two older women, she smiled for the first time since she'd left Hank Jefferson's sporting goods store. "Of course not," she said.

She'd known the Rutherford sisters ever since she was a little girl. Born into a once affluent family of New York city bankers, they'd never married. And when the family had fallen on hard times, they'd moved into one of the Rutherford family's summer homes on Castleton Lake. Both women served on the board of trustees at the college, and they'd convinced the dean of the college to hire her as assistant librarian once she'd graduated.

Irene cleared her throat. "What *are* you going to do with the rope? If you don't mind my asking."

"Not at all," Jodie said. "It's Plan B. Sort of. Remember last Monday's motto—There's More Than One Way to Skin a Cat?"

Sophie shot a triumphant glance at her sister before

she turned to Jodie. "Those mottoes *are* starting to work. They're becoming part of you."

"I guess," Jodie said. The truth was that while she'd been working all morning at the library and trying to visualize the gun in her mind, she'd begun to have second thoughts about whether or not she'd have the nerve to actually use it. Pulling a paper out of her pocket, she spread it out on the table. "While I was helping one of the students do some research work on the Internet this morning, I came across this."

Irene frowned thoughtfully. "What is it?"

"A snare trap," Jodie replied. At the bemused expressions on the sisters' faces, she continued. "It's some kind of guerilla warfare thingamajig that they use in the jungles. Clyde Heffner, the student who downloaded it for me, is coming over this evening to help me rig this up in the attic. The next time that prowler starts poking around up there, he'll find himself hanging by his feet from the ceiling."

Leaning closer, the two sisters studied the diagram.

Sophie turned it upside down. "It looks very complicated."

"Do you think it will work?" Irene asked.

"They work out in the woods. Clyde uses them to trap game."

"I hope no one ends up hanging from their necks," Irene fretted.

"I say we go for it!" Sophie said. "I, for one, do not want to end up murdered in my bed."

"Well, I don't think we'll have to worry about that anymore," Irene replied as she began to refill her teacup. "And Jodie won't have to build that thingamajig, either, now that Mr.—Ouch!" Wincing, she broke off and shot her sister an apologetic look.

Jodie glanced from Irene to Sophie. "Why won't we need it?"

They stared back at her uncomfortably for a moment.

"We...that is...how about some lemon?" Irene asked, offering a plate.

"I'm not having tea," Jodie said. "Why don't we need my snare trap?"

"We were going to tell you this evening as a sort of surprise." Pausing, Sophie cleared her throat. "Irene and I have also come up with a Plan B."

"It's not nearly as complicated," Irene said.

Jodie pocketed the diagram and leaned back in her chair. "You had your committee meeting for the Mistletoe Ball today. And then you were supposed to be at the newspaper office placing an ad for a handyman. What else did you do?"

Irene beamed a smile at her. "We've taken in a boarder."

"But you've already got one—me," Jodie said.

"You're not a boarder. You're like family," Irene said. "And this is different. Mr. Sullivan's a carpenter and an electrician. When we got to the newspaper office, he was in line ahead of us, placing an ad to get work as a handyman. We got to talking, and we ended up hiring him. The best part is he needs a place to stay, and he agreed to accept room and board as part of his wages."

"It was fate," Sophie said. "We decided to go for it."

"You're inviting a perfect stranger to live under the same roof with you? Don't you realize how dangerous that is?" Jodie asked.

"He won't be living under the same roof," Sophie

explained. "We offered him the apartment over the garage."

Irene coughed delicately, then leaned forward and spoke in a low tone. "We explained to him that there was only one bathroom, in the house, and that until we add on another…well, there might be certain…lack of privacy issues. He said the garage would be fine with him."

"But he'll still be living on the property with you—with us—and we don't know anything about this man. He could be a serial killer!" Jodie said.

"I have references."

The voice. Jodie was sure she recognized it. What were the chances of two different strangers in town speaking in the same low, gravelly tone? *Absolutely none,* she decided as she turned and found herself looking into the laughing eyes of the man from Hank Jefferson's store.

"Jodie, this is Shane Sullivan, our new handyman," Irene said.

"I've been looking forward to this introduction, ma'am."

Shane? Oddly enough the name suited him. He looked like a lone cowboy, and he probably talked to his horses in just that tone, Jodie thought. Except this was Castleton, New York, not some fictional Western town she'd read about in seventh grade. "Your name is *Shane?*" she asked.

"Yes, ma'am."

"Pull up a chair," Sophie said. "We were just telling Jodie about you."

"See," Irene said as Shane snagged a chair and straddled it. "He doesn't look like a serial killer."

"Ted Bundy didn't look like one, either," Jodie said.

"Right you are," Shane said. "Everyone who knew him described him as charming."

"Except for the women he killed," Jodie pointed out.

Shane grinned at her as he pulled an envelope out of his pocket. "Right you are again. I can't blame you for being cautious. But these are the references I mentioned."

Jodie glanced at Irene and Sophie and read the determination in their eyes. It was going to be two against one, and it *was* their house. Reluctantly, she took the envelope from him just as Nadine arrived at the table.

"Your cappuccino will be right up, Jodie. Albert said to tell you he's having a little trouble foaming the milk. And what can I get for you?" Fluttering her hands, Nadine aimed the question and her smile at Shane.

"A cappuccino sounds great. I haven't indulged in one since I left California."

"Ooh my, California. I've always wanted to go there. I'll have to tell Albert we've got a connoisseur out here waiting to taste his cappuccino," Nadine said before she hurried away.

"There's only one letter in here," Jodie said as she unfolded it.

"I can get more," Shane replied easily.

Frowning, Jodie skimmed the paper. "The Kathy Dillon who signed it, is she the same Kathy who's married to Sheriff Dillon?"

Shane nodded. "She's a cousin. We haven't quite pinned down whether it's two or three times removed."

"Well, then there's no problem," Irene said, patting her curls. "If Kathy Dillon can vouch for Shane, we won't need those other references, will we, dear?"

Jodie stifled a sigh as Irene began to explain to

Shane their plans for the house. She would call Kathy, but she knew the Rutherford sisters had won the battle. Battle? Why was she thinking of it in those terms. She glanced at Shane Sullivan again, wondering what it was about him that had made her feel so...what? Hot and cold, all at the same time? She couldn't be...no, she really couldn't be attracted to him. That was just not possible. Lightning could not possibly strike one person twice, at least not in the same year.

She was just suspicious of him. That's what it was. Because he just didn't look like a handyman—unless it was the kind of "handyman" a mafia boss might hire as a bodyguard.

"Is there some reason you're staring at me?" Shane asked softly.

Jodie glanced quickly at Irene and Sophie, but they were heatedly debating the question of how many guest rooms they were eventually going to have.

"I wasn't staring," she said, leaning a little closer to him and keeping her voice low.

"It felt like staring to me," Shane said.

"Who are you really?"

"Shane Sullivan. We were just introduced, weren't we?"

"No one is really named Shane."

"What was that, dear?" Irene asked.

"Nothing," Jodie said, fixing a smile on her face as she turned her attention back to the sisters.

"Isn't it time for you to get back to the library, dear?" Irene said. "Mr. Sullivan will be all settled in by the time you get home from work."

Jodie glanced at her watch. She *was* due back at the college library in five minutes. Nadine arrived just as she rose and picked up her package.

"I brought your cappuccino to go," Nadine said, handing her the lidded paper cup. "I know you're never late." Then she turned to present a foaming cup to Shane. "I hope it's the way they make it in California."

As Jodie made her way through Albert's, she could hear Nadine's laughter blend with that of the Rutherford sisters. So Shane Sullivan was a comedian as well as a…what? Whatever he was, she was sure he wasn't a handyman. In the archway to the next room, she turned back. He was facing Irene and Sophie, and they were leaning forward, their attention riveted on him.

A strong sense of déjà vu moved through her and fear settled cold and hard in her stomach. Less than six months ago, she'd seen Irene and Sophie framed in the same window with their nephew Billy. When she'd come into the café, they'd waved to her to join them. That evening, they'd asked her to be their guest at the hotel for dinner. The rest had been history— one she didn't care to repeat. Nor was she about to stand by and allow the Rutherford sisters to be taken in by another smooth-talking charmer.

A quick glance at her watch told her that she could either be on time for work, or she could stop by the sheriff's office and ask him about his wife's two-or-three-times-removed cousin. Once out on the street, she took the lid off her cup of cappuccino, inhaled the cinnamon, and took a long swallow. It might only be a baby step, but she was changing. Perhaps those foolish mottoes were working, after all. Either that or she was learning from her mistakes. Whatever it was, she was going to get to the truth about Shane Sullivan. Turning, she headed down the street toward the municipal building. No one could really be named Shane.

2

THE DOOR WITH Sheriff Dillon's name on it stood open. Jodie paused, noting that the desk in the outer office was empty. That meant that his deputy, Mike Buckley, was either at lunch or working on a case.

"C'mon in. I'm here." The voice came from the adjacent room and Jodie headed toward it. Mark Dillon, who'd been sheriff for as long as she could remember, was indeed *in*—deep in a book, as far as she could tell. His back was to her, his feet propped on a nearby window ledge. The moment she entered the room, he dog-eared his paperback with a grunt, swung his feet down and swiveled to face her. A smile spread slowly across his face as he waved her into a chair.

Sheriff Dillon hadn't changed much from the first time she'd met him, except that his waist was a little thicker and his hair had started to thin. His smile was certainly the same, as was the shrewdness in his eyes. The kids at the college often underestimated him when they had the misfortune to cross his path, but he had a reputation for fairness among the students.

"I was going to stop by the library to talk to you." His gaze dropped to his watch, then met hers. "Shouldn't you be there right now?"

Good old predictable Jodie. The thought had her lifting her chin. "I'm going to be late. I doubt that the world will end."

"No, I guess it won't. I hear you had a prowler last night."

It occurred to her that she hadn't thought about the prowler once on her walk over. All she'd been thinking about was Shane Sullivan.

"And instead of reporting it," Sheriff Dillon continued as he flipped his notebook open, "you decided to ask Hank Jefferson to sell you a gun."

"Yes, I did."

Mark Dillon sighed and leaned back in his chair. "Buying a gun? That doesn't sound like you, Jodie."

"Well, maybe I'm tired of being like me! Do you have any idea what it was like to wake up and *know* that someone was in the house, walking around in the attic? I tried to call you and the phone wouldn't work. Irene left the extension in the kitchen off the hook. She swears not, but—"

"What time did this happen?" Dillon asked, pulling his notebook closer.

"Shortly after midnight. I hadn't been asleep for long."

"And you heard something that woke you up?"

Jodie frowned. "No. Sophie said she heard a muffled crash. But I must have slept through that."

Dillon nodded. "And then what?"

"I waited and listened. Then I heard floorboards creak in the attic. I was tracking the steps across the floor when Sophie and Irene opened my door. They were armed with fireplace pokers, and Sophie insisted we go up there. I couldn't talk her out of it. I shouted up the stairs that we were armed, and luckily, by the time we got up there, he was out the window and halfway down that old elm tree."

"Did you get a good look at him or her?" Dillon asked.

Jodie thought for a minute. "I'd say it was a *him*. He was tall and slender. We could see him run off toward the road."

"Was he carrying anything?"

Jodie shook her head. "He had to use both hands getting down that tree."

Dillon set his pencil down. "Don't you have a dog out there? What was he doing during all this?"

"Lazarus?" The dog was a stray she'd found nearly dead by the side of the road. "I don't know if he was ever much of a watchdog, but since Doc Cheney brought him back from the dead, nothing interrupts his beauty sleep—which is why I need a gun."

Dillon closed his notebook. "A gun isn't the answer. You don't know how to use one, so the chances are pretty good that a prowler could overpower you, take the gun away, and after that..." He met her eyes directly as he let the sentence trail off. "On the other hand, I can't do much besides send young Buckley out there to drive by every so often. Are any of those rooms in good enough shape yet to rent to a boarder?"

Jodie looked at him. "Funny you should suggest that. We've got a boarder, and that's what I came to talk to you about. I want to know all about Shane Sullivan."

"Shane? You've met him already?"

"Yes. Irene and Sophie introduced him to me *after* they'd already hired him on as a handyman and rented him the apartment over the garage. What do you know about him?"

"He's a distant cousin of Kathy's. He gave us a call a few days ago, said he was in the area. Seems he's quit his corporate job, and he's looking for a place to settle down. Kathy's convinced him to give upstate New York a try.''

"So he came here at Christmas? Doesn't he have a home or a family to spend the holidays with?"

"No," Dillon said. "Evidently his job has been keeping him on the move. He's never had a chance to settle down."

"What kind of job?" Jodie asked.

"Some sort of consulting business. Took him all over the place."

"Including California. He's got Nadine Carter dreaming of beaches and movie stars and a new way to get out of Castleton."

"I'm sure Shane can take care of himself," Dillon said.

"I'm more worried about Nadine. And I'm curious as to why Mr. Sullivan has all of a sudden discovered this deep-rooted desire to become a handyman."

"Kathy thinks it's some kind of midlife crisis. You know, come to think of it, this arrangement could be the answer to your problems. Ours, too. We don't really have room for him at the house with Kelly and David both home for the holidays. Shane must have realized that. And with a man living out there at Rutherford House, a prowler would have to think twice."

Jodie met Dillon's eyes squarely. "Pardon me, but the Rutherford sisters *had* a man living in their house six months ago, and thanks to him they lost their life savings!"

"I can vouch for the fact that Shane won't be conning them out of any more of their money."

"I'm not worried about their money. They don't have any left. The problem is that they're...he's..." Pausing, Jodie searched for the right words. "It's just that they seem to be every bit as charmed by him as they were by Billy, and I don't want them taken in and…hurt again.''

"I see." Dillon studied her for a moment. "As far as I know, there's precious little anyone can do to protect people from being hurt. But if you want, I'll speak to Shane, tell him to keep his distance."

Jodie sat still, thinking. What had she expected him to do? From his point of view, having Shane move into the apartment over the garage must seem like the perfect solution. But it wasn't. She was sure of it, as sure as…

"Has Billy tried to contact you?"

Jodie stared at the sheriff, surprised at the abrupt change of topic.

"Billy? No, I haven't heard from him since he…since they took him back to New York for the arraignment."

Dillon's eyes shifted over her head to the doorway. "Shane, come on in. We were just talking about you."

"I don't want to interrupt."

Jodie turned to see Shane filling the doorway to the office. He seemed larger than he had in the restaurant. Or perhaps it was just that the room seemed smaller because he was in it.

"Sit down. You might as well hear this since you'll be moving into the Rutherford House." Dillon paused until Shane had lowered himself into a chair. "Their nephew, who's been charged with embezzlement, may pay them a visit. I got a call this morning from the NYPD. It seems that Billy has jumped bail. They wanted us to know in case he shows up here."

Jodie concentrated very hard on keeping her expression neutral as thoughts swirled through her mind.

Billy had jumped bail? Would he really come back to Castleton?

"When did this happen?" Shane asked.

"The private security firm hired by one of the banks claims they lost him sometime yesterday afternoon. They're not sure where he's headed. Seems he used a credit card to buy a plane ticket to Florida *and* a train ticket to Chicago. They're still not sure which he took."

"The Chicago train would bring him this way," Jodie said.

Dillon nodded. "My deputy is checking at the Syracuse station."

"Why would he come back here?" she asked.

"It's almost Christmas, and Irene and Sophie are the only two relatives he has," Dillon said. "And you and he *were* engaged."

Jodie felt her hands tighten into fists. "Not anymore."

Dillon cleared his throat. "There's a third reason why Billy may show up here. The five million dollars he embezzled has never shown up. They traced it to a series of banks, and it was all withdrawn in cash before they were able to arrest him. There's a chance, a slim one, that he hid it while he was here last summer."

"Why would he do that?" Jodie asked.

"He's familiar with the area, and he had over a month to consider the possibilities. What I'm thinking is that he might need some help getting to it, and you or Sophie or Irene might feel sorry for him. I don't want you to do anything foolish like aid or abet a criminal. If Billy does try to contact you, I want you to let me know."

Jodie looked from Dillon to Shane. "And in the

meantime, Mr. Sullivan is supposed to spy on us and report back to you if we do anything suspicious?''

"Now, Jodie, that's not what I—'' The shrill ringing of the phone interrupted Dillon. Reaching for it, he punched a button. "Yes, Mindy Lou.... Calm down, I can't hear you.... What? No, no, I don't think you should call the fire department.''

"There's a fire at the library?'' Jodie asked. Mindy Lou had been her student assistant ever since Nadine had left.

Dillon shook his head. "No, Mindy Lou, you've called the right person. The fire department is made up of volunteers. I get paid to handle emergencies just like this one. And Jodie's perfectly all right. She's sitting in front of me right now. No, she doesn't look depressed to me at all.'' Pausing, he turned to Jodie. "Is that a rope you've got in your package?''

As Jodie nodded, she felt two bright spots of color stain her cheek. "For hauling a Christmas tree,'' she explained.

Dillon's eyes narrowed. "I drove past the house the other day, and I'm sure I saw one all lit up in the window.''

"We're putting another one up in the dining room,'' she said. If she told the lie often enough, she was going to start believing it herself.

As Dillon nodded and continued trying to calm Mindy Lou down, Jodie turned to meet Shane's eyes. They were filled with laughter, as she'd known they would be. But it wasn't the cold kind that you saw when someone was laughing at you. Instead, it was warm, just as it had been in Hank Jefferson's store, and it made her feel that he was inviting her to share in a private joke. For a moment, the two of them could have been alone in the room, and she was suddenly aware of how close they were sitting, close enough that she could reach out and touch him if she wanted to. And she did want to. More than that, she wanted him to touch her. The realization started a churning heat deep in her center.

Quickly she broke off eye contact with Shane, turning her attention back to the sheriff and forcing herself to listen to what he was saying.

"No, I'm sure she's not going to hang herself."

When Sheriff Dillon winked at her, she managed a smile. Every muscle in her face felt stiff.

"I can guarantee that she'll be fine," Dillon said. "She'll be there shortly.... I don't have any idea how a rumor like that got started."

Jodie heard Shane swallow a chuckle, but she didn't look at him. Instead, she rose the moment that Dillon hung up the phone. "I'd better get back. I'm never late."

"You'll remember what I said," Dillon said as she reached the door.

"Right. If Billy shows his face, you'll be the first to know." Jodie wanted in the worst way to run as she left the office. Only the thought that Shane Sullivan might look out the door and see her allowed her to keep her pace steady. And it wasn't the first time he'd made her want to run away. Why? Frowning, she stepped out onto the sidewalk and started up the street. She certainly wasn't afraid of him. But every time she was with him, he...stirred her up. In her whole life, she'd never before looked at a man and imagined him touching her. Nor had she ever before felt that kind of bubbling heat spreading outward, downward. Pressing a hand to her stomach, she glanced sideways and caught her reflection in a store window.

She didn't look any different than she had that morning. She was wearing her hair the same way. Running her hand through it, she watched it settle right back into place. Since she'd cut it off, it had developed a mind of its own. The winter coat was the same one she'd worn for the past five winters. So why did she feel so—

A warning bell sounded in the back of her mind. Billy Rutherford had made her feel *different,* too.

Billy had been all smoothness and polish. When she'd been with him, she'd felt special, noticed. Like Cinderella must have felt at the ball when Prince Charming had chosen her out of all the other women. Tightening her hands into fists, she jammed them in her pockets. She wasn't going to be that foolish again.

Not that Shane Sullivan was anything like Billy. Oh, he had a certain kind of charm all right—a surprising glint of humor in his eyes that hinted at…shared secrets?

Jodie's frown deepened as she turned and hurried toward the corner, quickening her pace even more once she rounded it. Whatever it was about Shane Sullivan, she had a hunch he'd never make a woman feel like she was Cinderella. No, he'd make a woman feel like…

Suddenly an image filled her mind. She and Shane, wrapped around each other, with very few clothes on…and…and they weren't even in a bed! Jodie felt an arrow of heat move through her, melting her insides. For a moment, she couldn't feel her legs or her feet. She wasn't sure she could take another step.

"Jodie! Jodie, are you all right?"

"I'm fine, Mindy Lou." Saying the words helped, but her voice sounded funny. Breathless. She cleared her throat. "Really, I'm fine."

"You look funny. Maybe you should take the afternoon off," Mindy Lou said as she raced down the library stairs.

"No," Jodie said.

"I'll fix you some tea...." Mindy Lou began.

"No," Jodie said again as she managed the first few steps. "I'm having a cappuccino."

"But...you never drink coffee," Mindy Lou said.

"I'm changing."

"AREN'T YOU GOING to say *I told you so?*" Dillon asked as Shane rose to close the door behind Jodie. "Rutherford bolted, just as you thought he would. And now he seems to be back in Castleton."

"You think he was the prowler at Rutherford House last night?" Shane asked.

"His aunts have a prowler the same night that their nephew jumps bail. He's my top suspect."

"The question is, did he get what he came for?"

Quickly, Dillon filled Shane in on everything Jodie had told him. "She says the man wasn't carrying anything. He needed both hands to climb down the tree."

"So they ran him off with fireplace pokers," Shane said with a grin. "He's lucky she didn't have a gun."

"Well, let's hope his luck has run out. I'd still like to know how you figured he'd show up here."

"When you've been hunting men for as long as I have, you get to know how they think. Castleton's a summer place he used to visit as a child. After a twenty-year absence, he suddenly pays a month-long visit to his aunts just before the sky falls on his head. It's a pretty big clue."

"This sure puts a hole in your theory that Jodie Freemont is helping him out."

"How do you figure that?"

"He wouldn't have to break in if she was."

"Maybe not." Shane glanced out the window just as Jodie came into view. When he found himself wanting to smile, he quickly stifled the urge. The truth was he hadn't quite made up his mind about Jodie Freemont. She was...different than he'd expected. She had imagination and an unexpected sense of humor. And then there was that passion that simmered just beneath the surface. He'd caught glimpses of it twice now in her eyes.

He watched her pause to look in a store window, then suddenly turn and hurry to the corner. Perhaps it was all that cool reserve laced with the promise of heat. It was the kind of contrast that would draw a man. The thought of it tempting a piece of scum like Billy Rutherford made him frown.

"You're wrong about Jodie helping him hide the money," Dillon said.

Shane turned his attention back to the sheriff. "I'm not so sure. She's smart enough to be putting on an act."

Dillon smiled. "Oh, she's smart all right, smart enough to come here to check you out. She doesn't buy your cover. She's curious as to why you're wandering around without a home to go to for Christmas. And she wants to know why a corporate executive would want to try his hand at carpentry. I told her it's a midlife crisis. Is it?"

"That's what we agreed you'd say."

"I'm asking for myself, now. You own a big investigative firm, and Billy Rutherford is small potatoes compared to some of the men you've hunted. Why not send one of your operatives?"

Shane studied the sheriff for a minute. Beneath the laid-back attitude there was a persistence and a shrewdness he admired. He decided to go with the truth. "I've been out of the field for a while, and I was feeling restless." *Empty* was the word he'd come up with in the wee hours of the morning to describe the mix of emotions he'd been experiencing lately. But it was much less disturbing to define them as simple restlessness. "Don't you ever miss it? Being in the field, I mean?"

Dillon shrugged. "In a town like this there's not much to miss. Anything exciting happens, I'm right in the thick of it."

The phone rang, and Dillon grinned. "And when my deputy is out, I get to double as my own receptionist during lunch hour. Never a dull moment."

While Dillon handled the call, Shane glanced out the window again, but Jodie had disappeared. Whether she was cooperating with Rutherford or not, he had a gut feeling that Ms. Freemont was the key to finding both the money and the man. His plan was to get close to her, and his job was going to be a lot more interesting and pleasurable than he'd first thought.

"One more thing," Dillon said as he hung up his phone. "I've known Jodie Freemont since she was a little girl. I promised her I'd tell you to keep your distance."

Shane's brows rose. "Does she think I have designs on her?"

"She's more concerned about Sophie and Irene— *being taken in by a smooth-talking charmer* was the way she put it. But I don't want her hurt again, especially by someone who'll be leaving town once he gets his man. Am I making myself clear?"

"As crystal," Shane said as he rose and walked to the door.

AT FIVE O'CLOCK on the dot, Jodie started her car. Two things were driving her as she shot it out of the parking lot: escaping from Mindy Lou's overbearing concern and building her snare trap in the attic. Clyde Heffner, the student who had downloaded the diagram, was going to drop by and help her string it up around eight-thirty, not a minute too soon.

It wasn't until late in the afternoon, when her boss Angus Campbell had been droning on about the contributors who would be attending the Mistletoe Ball, that she'd realized the significance of what Sheriff Dillon had told her. If Billy had come back to town, he could have been the prowler in the attic last night. And if he came back tonight, she wanted to have the trap all set! Catching Billy and turning him over to the sheriff would change her image in Castleton once and for all.

When she had to stop for the light at the corner, she turned the jazz music station she favored up full blast. Her car, a five-year-old red hatchback, was her one luxury. True, it wasn't the convertible she'd always dreamed of owning, but...

She lost her train of thought the moment she spotted Alicia Finnerty stepping off the curb with a group of women. Wasn't that just her luck? It would be too much to hope that the woman wouldn't recognize her car. Way too much, she thought, as Alicia glanced at her significantly, then turned to chatter to her companions.

One by one, the other women looked her way with varying expressions of concern and curiosity. Jodie was tempted to roll down her window, grab the rope lying on her passenger seat and wave it at them. Instead, she forced herself to smile as the light changed and she eased her car around the corner. Her impulsiveness had already gotten her into enough hot water today. And it hadn't helped her one bit. It had only contributed to everyone's notion that she was exactly like her mother, a woman who would never recover from the loss of a man.

No, if she wanted to change her image in the town, she was going to have to do something that destroyed the idea once and for all that she was the type of woman who would spend her whole life pining over a man who couldn't be tied down.

The moment she reached the village limits, she floored the gas pedal and watched the speedometer climb to fifty-five. When she automatically eased the pressure, she suddenly frowned. Why in the world did she always follow all of the rules?

Go For It! The moment the motto popped into her mind, she watched as the needle climbed to five, then six, finally seven miles over the speed limit. Not enough to get a ticket. Maybe she'd go for *that* tomorrow.

Tonight, she had bigger plans: catching Billy Rutherford. What had yesterday's motto been? Visualize Your Goal. Even as she smiled at the thought, she decided to give it a whirl. It couldn't hurt, could it?

In her mind, she pictured herself on the front page of the *Castleton Bulletin,* delivering Billy Rutherford to Sheriff Dillon.

Yes! She nodded her head in satisfaction. That one photo would truly be worth a thousand words. It would change her image in one fell swoop. With a jazz rendition of ''Jingle Bells'' pouring out of the radio, Jodie kept the picture clear in her mind until Rutherford House came into view.

The moment she turned into the driveway, she

stopped thinking about anything but the car that was parked in front of the garage.

It was in her space, but that's not why she skidded to a stop behind Sophie's station wagon and jumped out of her car. It was a red convertible, the kind she dreamed of owning one day. Circling to the driver's side, she peered inside. A two-seater with leather seats. Exactly what she wanted. Quickly she backed up to get a better view. Without any difficulty at all, she pictured herself behind the wheel, driving down the main street of town, her hair ruffled by the wind.

Perfect.

SHANE WATCHED Jodie from the shade at the side of the garage. She hadn't seen him yet, hadn't even glanced his way. It was the car that had held her attention since she'd arrived. He couldn't prevent a smile as he watched her circle it. He'd reacted much the same way the first time he'd seen it.

It suddenly occurred to him that the feeling he'd had more than once since he'd met her was one of... He searched for a word. Kinship? Recognition?

He found the thought both surprising and a little alarming. He had nothing in common with a small-town librarian. And he didn't want to have anything in common with her. A woman like that had home and hearth written all over her. She wasn't his type at all. He'd long ago decided that he wasn't the type of man who'd ever settle down.

Plus, she was his key to finding Rutherford and the money. Even if she wasn't Billy's accomplice, and he was beginning to believe that Dillon was right about that, she might still be the one person Billy might feel he could trust and turn to.

He'd seen evidence of her fierce loyalty to the

Rutherford sisters, and it might very well extend to their nephew. He couldn't fault that. In fact he admired it. Loyalty was rare these days. And it would draw a man back.

He watched her as she ran her hands over the hood of his car, slowly, hesitantly. Her fingers were short but slender, the nails tapered and unpolished. Her palms would be soft, and he couldn't help but wonder if she would have that same hesitancy the first time she touched a man. And how that might change when she was aroused, when that latent passion broke free…

With a frown, Shane reined in his thoughts. Clearly, Jodie Freemont was a distraction. But he didn't intend to let her interfere with his job.

If she *was* Billy's accomplice, she'd know where the money was. If not, she could be his key to finding it. In both instances, he had to get close to her, win her trust.

So you'll use her just as Billy did?

The thought left a bitter taste in his mouth he quietly stepped out of the shade.

"I think you're breaking one of the commandments," he said with a smile when he reached her.

Startled, Jodie snatched her hand from the hood of the car and whirled to find Shane at her side. "What? I wasn't going to steal it. I was just touching it."

"I was talking about the tenth commandment. 'Thou shalt not covet thy neighbor's goods.'"

"I wasn't…I was…" Pausing, she sighed. "I definitely was. You know, I've never understood that commandment. What's wrong with coveting as long as that's where it ends?"

"But usually it doesn't end that way. Coveting is a lot like lust. It doesn't go away. It just builds and builds until the temptation to reach out and take becomes so strong, you just can't resist anymore. Go ahead.''

Jodie found that while she'd been looking into his eyes, listening to his words, her throat had gone dry as dust. He was talking in theory, not about anything, and certainly not anyone, specific. But his eyes had grown so dark that the image of herself that she could see in them suddenly seemed swallowed up. And his tone of voice had been so intimate, so inviting that she wanted in the worst way to reach out and touch him the same way she'd felt compelled to touch the car moments ago. Was this the way a moth was lured into a flame?

"Go ahead and touch," Shane said.

Jodie blinked. Could he read her mind? No. No, he was talking about the car. Reaching out, she ran her hand over the shiny surface of the hood again. It felt hard and satiny smooth, but different somehow. Was she imagining that it felt warmer, as if it had been heated by the thin, wintery sun? Suddenly, the image filled her mind of what it would be like to touch Shane. *Visualize Your Goal.* The motto moved through her thoughts, mocking her as the heat moved up her arm like little spools of ribbon unwinding slowly. Her fingers felt singed when she finally found the strength to snatch them back.

"You want to give it a try?"

Jodie moistened her lips. "What?"

"You want to take it out for a spin?"

"Me?"

"Sure." Reaching into his pocket, he dangled the keys in front of her.

"I can't," she said backing a step away. "I don't know how to drive a shift. That's what it is, isn't it?"

"I could give you a lesson," Shane offered.

Immediately, she pictured the two of them riding in the car, and the image was much more potent than the one she'd pictured earlier. This time he was touching her, sitting close, his hand over hers on the gear shift.

She shouldn't. She couldn't. She needed some distance until she figured out how to handle the way she was feeling. There was something she had to do...if she could just think of what it was....

"Come on," Shane said.

"I can't. I have some work to do before dinner." Hurrying to her car, she lifted out the package of rope. When she turned, he was right beside her. She took a quick step backward. "And I...have to get the mail. I always stop at the mailbox when I turn in the driveway, but I got distracted."

"I'll walk with you."

Jodie took a deep breath as she started down the driveway. If he even brushed accidently against her... No. It wasn't going to happen. She concentrated on putting one foot carefully in front of the other on the hard-packed snow. By the time she reached the mailbox and emptied it, her breathing and her thought patterns were very nearly back to normal. Still, she avoided looking at him by sorting through the pile of Christmas cards, advertisements, bills... The moment she saw the handwriting, the letter slipped through her fingers. Shane was quicker than she was, and he grabbed it just before it hit the snow.

"It's addressed to you, and there's no stamp," he said. "It must have been hand delivered."

"It's probably from a student. They never have any money." Taking it from his outstretched hand, she tucked it quickly in her pocket and started back up the driveway. "Have a nice evening."

Shane waited until she disappeared into the house before he headed back to his car. She was as easy to read as a first-grade primer. That letter wasn't from a student. She hadn't even been able to look him in the eye when she said it. He was willing to bet his car that Billy Rutherford had contacted his ex-fiancée.

What he wasn't so sure of was whether she'd call Dillon or decide to help out her former lover.

3

THE SMELL assaulted her as soon as she opened the front door and stepped into the foyer. It was the same unidentifiable scent that filled the house every time that Irene cooked. Lazarus lay in a heap at the bottom of the stairs. He twitched his tail once in greeting, but otherwise gave no sign of life. Jodie could do nothing but sympathize. Dogs had a keen sense of smell, and no doubt he knew that he'd be going hungry tonight.

"I lost the coin toss," Sophie said in a lowered tone as she appeared in the archway to the dining room.

"What happened to your lucky streak?" Jodie asked.

Sophie shrugged. "It was bound to run out. What we need is a two-headed coin."

"What we need is to tell Irene she can't cook."

Sophie frowned. "She's having enough trouble trying to accept that Billy stole all our savings. I hate to disillusion her any more."

Setting down the mail and the package of rope, Jodie took the older woman's hands in hers. "I know. But when you open the bed-and-breakfast for business…"

Sophie sighed. "We'll sit down and have a talk with her after the Mistletoe Ball next Friday. She'll be basking in the glory of having brought it off, and that will cushion the blow."

Jodie squeezed Sophie's hands. "I wish I'd had a sister like you when I was growing up."

"Well, you've got me now," Sophie replied. "Why don't you ask Shane if he can get hold of a two-headed coin? He seems like an enterprising young man to me."

"You've known him less than a day, and you're on a first-name basis with the handyman?"

"Mr. Sullivan sounds a little formal when he's going to be joining us for meals."

The thought of Shane Sullivan sitting down to one of Irene's culinary creations had Jodie's lips curving. She doubted he'd be taking many of his meals with them in the future. Then wrinkling her nose, she asked, "What could possibly smell that bad?"

"She's calling it meat loaf."

Lazarus moaned.

Jodie knelt and ran a sympathetic hand over him, then when he turned, began to scratch his stomach. He'd been nearly dead the night she'd found him lying along the road, and Doc Cheney, the town vet, hadn't been sure he'd make it.

"What does that dog have to complain about?" Sophie asked. "If he doesn't like the meat loaf, he can eat his canned dog food. We're stuck." She glanced down at the pile of correspondence. "Anything interesting in the mail."

"No," Jodie said as Sophie began to sort through it. Thank heavens she'd stuffed the letter in her pocket. "Just some circulars."

"Oh, you're home," Irene said as she breezed into the foyer. Flour streaked her hair and seemed to hover in a little cloud around her. "You just have time to change before dinner."

"Change what?" Jodie asked.

"Your clothes. Shane is joining us for dinner."

"We have to dress up for the handyman?" Jodie asked.

Irene shooed her toward the stairs. "He's a guest, too. And he's worked very hard all afternoon. Haven't you noticed all the mistletoe he's hung?"

Jodie glanced up to see that mistletoe indeed now hung from the chandelier, as well as from every archway and door that led off from the foyer.

"We put it in every room," Irene explained. "There was quite a bit we didn't use for the ball, and we didn't want it to go to waste. What do you think?"

"Very...Christmassy," Jodie managed to reply.

Irene beamed a smile at her. "After you change, I could use your help in the kitchen. You could let me know what you think of my new gravy recipe."

"Actually, I was planning on starting on my snare trap," Jodie quickly improvised. "In the attic. Remember?" Grabbing the rope, she hopped over Lazarus and started up the stairs.

Once in her room, Jodie locked the door, set the rope down on her bed, then pulled the letter out of her pocket. It was Billy's handwriting all right. She hadn't been wrong about that. Staring at it, she sank down on the foot of her bed.

She hadn't lied to the sheriff. Billy hadn't tried to contact her after his arrest. But he'd given Irene a note for her shortly before the police had arrived at the house to take him away. In it, he'd asked her to believe in him, to believe in his love for her, and he'd promised she'd get her money back.

Even now, she could remember how much she'd wanted to believe him, how she'd clung for two months to her fantasy that he would keep his word. She'd checked the mailbox each day hoping for a letter until the day the bank had foreclosed on her house.

What did he possibly think he could say now? Tearing open the envelope, she unfolded the letter.

My dearest Jodie,

I haven't written to you before because I didn't want to put you in danger. But I'll have your money for you soon. Please don't tell anyone about this note. My life could depend on it. Yours, too.

I never lied to you about my feelings for you.

I'll be in touch.

Billy

Slowly, she lowered the note to her lap. Damn Billy Rutherford. What she wanted to do was rip his words into shreds. But she would keep the note because it would inspire her more than one of Sophie's calendar slogans ever could. She wasn't going to be that big a fool again. Ever. She glanced at the note again.

"My life could depend on it. Yours, too."

A ripple of fear moved through her. It was probably a lie. She doubted that Billy could tell the difference between the truth and a lie anymore.

Carefully folding the paper, she slipped it back into the envelope. It was only then that she recalled what Shane had noticed. It didn't have a stamp. Had Billy delivered it himself?

Rising, she began to pace back and forth. It meant that Billy was definitely back in Castleton. It must have been him in the attic, and he hadn't gotten what he was after. "I'll have your money for you soon." That meant he had to come back.

She was reaching for the phone next to her bed when she snatched her hand back. If she told the sheriff now, she could picture exactly what would happen. He'd have his distant cousin Shane watching her like a hawk, and she might miss the one chance she had of catching Billy by herself. She couldn't allow that to happen. Turning, she began to pace again. Catching Billy would allow her to kill two birds with one stone. She could change her image in the town forever, and she could get the money back that Billy had stolen from his aunts. They needed it. Because if they couldn't make their bed-and-breakfast work, they could lose Rutherford House.

Pausing, she sank back down on the foot of her bed. The money was probably in the attic. Otherwise, why go there? So she'd set the trap. In her mind, she pictured Billy swinging back and forth from the rope she was going to string up in the attic. Once he was in it, she'd make him cough up the money and then she'd call the sheriff.

"CLYDE, I can't thank you enough," Jodie said as she followed him out onto the porch. "I never could have figured out how to weight it properly."

"No problem, ma'am."

And it hadn't been. Jodie drew her coat more closely around her as she watched the skinny young man climb into his battered pickup truck and back down the driveway. In less than an hour, he'd adapted a trap designed for use in woods or jungles to something that would operate very efficiently in an attic. Clyde was a talented young man. What he needed was someone to give him a push into an engineering school; that just might get his mind off joining one of the militia groups he was always researching on the Internet. Tomorrow, she'd see his advisor at the college. And later in the week, she was going to have a talk with Nadine Carter and see if she could convince her to come back to school.

And tonight? Drawing in a breath of the crisp, cold air, she glanced up at the sky, polka-dotted with stars. Then crossing her fingers for luck, she wished on the biggest one. *Please,* let her catch Billy Rutherford III in her trap tonight.

But someone else might catch him first.

With a frown, she sank down on the top step and glared at the garage. In the moonlight, she could see that the space beside Sophie's car was still empty. The red convertible had disappeared shortly before Clyde had arrived.

Jodie resented the idea that, just because there was now a man about the house, he would be the one to nab Billy. It struck her how much she really wanted to be the one to turn Billy over to the authorities. How much she didn't want Shane to beat her to it.

Her eyes widened at the thought. Where had it come from? She'd never before thought of herself as the type of woman who had to compete with a man. And she wasn't. There were plenty of reasons why she wanted to be the one to turn Billy Rutherford over to the police—and they had nothing to do with Shane Sullivan. In fact, she was going to put him out of her mind.

Just then a car pulled into the driveway and the headlights pinned her. *Shane.* She could just make out the red convertible in the moonlight. The urge to get up and run was almost overpowering, but she couldn't bear the idea of him getting that look of amusement in his eyes at her expense. It wasn't until he parked the car that she noticed the top was down and Lazarus was sitting in the passenger seat.

Lazarus, the dog who could barely get himself out of a prone position except to eat? And who in the world rode around with the top down in the middle of winter? She was still staring as the man and the dog started toward her.

"How did you bribe him to go with you?" she asked when Lazarus plopped his head into her lap.

"He followed me to the car," Shane said.

"You never follow me to my car," she said, leaning closer to scratch the dog behind his ears. "And I pay your vet bills."

"Evidently, he prefers convertibles. There's no accounting for taste."

Jodie glanced up at him. "It's a taste for French fries that lured him into your car. I can smell them on his breath."

Shane grinned at her. "What can I say? We were hungry."

Her eyes narrowed. "How can you be? You ate two slices of Irene's meat loaf. I saw you."

"It's nice to know I'm not losing my touch."

Jodie's eyes narrowed. "What do you mean?"

"You only think you saw me eat two slices."

She studied him for a moment, intrigued. "What did you do with them? I know you didn't feed them to Lazarus. He draws the line at Irene's cooking."

"A little sleight of hand," Shane explained. "I worked my way through college as a weekend party magician."

"You did not!" Jodie said.

He raised a hand. "Scout's honor."

"You weren't a Boy Scout, either."

His smile widened. "No, but I really was a party

magician." Before she could move, he reached behind her ear and when he withdrew his hand, it was holding a French fry.

"How did you—" The scent of it had her mouth watering.

"Here," he offered.

She hesitated for only a minute. "Thanks," she said as she popped it into her mouth, then chewed slowly. Even cool and slightly soggy, it tasted wonderful.

"More?" he asked bringing a paper bag out from behind his back. "Lazarus indicated you preferred cheeseburgers."

She had reached for the bag before she could stop herself. But she didn't open it. "Dogs don't talk, and magicians don't really make things disappear. Where did you put the meat loaf?"

"Where you put yours—in the plant stand."

"You saw me?"

"Magicians are always looking for new tricks. Sophie ditched hers under her jacket."

Jodie couldn't prevent a laugh. Then tilting her head to one side, she studied the man standing in front of her. Though the moonlight was bright, it left his face shadowed, mysterious-looking. In another age, he could have been a powerful magician. A wizard, perhaps. Fascination warred with caution. She really didn't know anything about Shane Sullivan, she reminded herself.

Then she recalled the look on Irene's face when he'd taken that second slice of meat loaf, and in spite of her resolve, she felt something inside of her soften.

Just then her stomach growled.

"I think you better eat that cheeseburger," he said.

"Irene and Sophie were still up when I came out here. I don't want—"

"No, don't turn around," he cautioned. "They're watching us right now through the window."

"They... Do you think they saw the cheeseburger?"

"No. I think they're more interested in whether or not the mistletoe you're sitting under will work."

She glanced up, then back at Shane.

"It had to happen sooner or later. They pretty much had me booby-trap the whole house today."

Jodie felt the heat flood her face. "You think they want you...they want us to..."

"I think they feel guilty about introducing you to their nephew, but they're not willing to give up on matchmaking altogether."

The moment his hand closed around hers and drew her to her feet, something began to tighten in her center. Her gaze dropped to his mouth. *He was going to kiss her.* The heat in her cheeks suddenly burned through the rest of her body.

"So why don't you show me how to get down to the lake? Hank Jefferson says the ice fishing is very good, and I have a flashlight in the car."

He released her hand and turned away, but it was several seconds before she could make her feet follow after him. He'd had no intention of kissing her, yet for a moment, she'd wanted more than anything for him to do just that. She had to get a grip on herself. She had to...stop looking at him. Shifting her gaze to the car, she said, "You put the top down."

"It's one of the unwritten rules when you own a convertible," Shane said, extracting a flashlight from the trunk.

"But no one puts their top down in the middle of winter."

"Not true. Santa always has the top down on his sleigh."

Jodie laughed as she turned and led the way around the side of the house. "Okay. I guess I never thought of it that way."

Falling into step beside her, Shane said, "Lazarus isn't coming with us."

"He doesn't believe in exercise."

A few seconds later, Shane pointed his flashlight down a path that wound its way through the trees, and for a while they walked in silence.

"The Rutherford sisters are really into celebrating Christmas," Shane said as the trees pressed closer, blocking out the moonlight.

"Tell me about it."

"You're not quite as enthused, I take it?"

She shrugged. "Not the way most people seem to be."

"Rough childhood?"

"No. Nothing like that. I just always used to wish for one thing—that my father would be home on Christmas morning."

"Was he?" Shane asked, taking her arm as the path narrowed.

"Usually not. He'd always send a really wonderful gift and a note saying how much he missed us. But it wasn't the same."

"No."

Jodie glanced at him, but she couldn't tell anything from his expression. "I must sound ungrateful. Sheriff Dillon said that you don't have any family to spend Christmas with."

"That puts us in the same boat this year. And it

has to be especially rough for you—losing your house."

"Actually, the hardest thing about it was facing the fact that I'd been so stupid about believing Billy." She paused and glanced at Shane again. "I'm not sure how to explain it. That house meant everything to my mother. She needed the security. But to my father it was a prison. He could never stand to be in it for very long."

"He felt the lure of the open road," Shane said.

"Exactly. And I would have done almost anything to go with him."

"Yes."

She could hear the understanding in his voice. It prompted her to go on. "My mother would never agree. She said I couldn't until I finished school. Then he went off one day and didn't came back. When we got the news of his death, she never left the house again. She simply pined away until the day she died. Having the bank take the house over gave me a chance to get away from those memories. The day I moved out, I felt..."

"Free?" Shane asked.

"Yes." They had stepped out of the woods, and the snow-covered ground stretched in front of them to the edge of the lake. "Does that sound crazy?"

"No." Shane shook his head. "It's part of what your father felt every time he went off to seek adventure."

"You sound like you know what it feels like."

"In a manner of speaking. But I'm still curious as to why you're living with Irene and Sophie. Why didn't you just rent an apartment?"

"I figure I owe them."

Shane turned to her. "Why?"

"It's my fault they lost their life savings."

"You blame yourself because they trusted their nephew?"

"They only trusted him because I did. Before I mortgaged my house, they'd refused to give him any money. Paying them rent each month and helping them open their bed-and-breakfast is the least I can do."

Shane said nothing as they walked toward an old log that had fallen along the edge of the lake. When they reached it, he switched off the flashlight and sat down. "You better eat that cheeseburger before it gets any colder."

Joining him on the log, she fished it out of the bag and unwrapped it. It was still warm, and she could smell just a hint of onion. Her mouth was open when she paused.

"What's wrong?" Shane asked.

"I think I'm forgetting to Beware of Greeks Bearing Gifts," Jodie said. "There's got to be a catch to this."

"It's not poisoned. I promise."

She shot him a look. "Neither is the bait you'll use when you go ice fishing. But you won't be putting it on the line just because you think the fish are hungry. You lured me out here with food to pump me for information, didn't you? And so far, I've cooperated fully."

Shane threw back his head and laughed. The sound was rich and full. Jodie smiled as she bit into the cheeseburger.

"Why is it that you're so suspicious of me?" he asked.

"Because you're not what you seem to be." The

French fries were salty and tasted of grease. Wonderful.

"No one is what they seem to be," Shane said.

"Alicia Finnerty is," Jodie pointed out around another bite of cheeseburger. "And Sophie and Irene are. And Sheriff Dillon... Well, maybe he's not a good example."

"He's a good example of what I'm saying," Shane said. "And as far as Ms. Finnerty and Sophie and Irene go, I'll bet they have a side of themselves that they don't present to the world. Some secrets they're hiding. So do you, I'll bet."

Jodie thought of the letter from Billy that she was still carrying in her pocket and glanced at Shane. When he'd caught it and handed it to her, he'd noticed that it didn't have a stamp. Did he suspect she'd heard from Billy?

"Tell you what. If you'll tell me one of your secrets, I'll tell you one of mine," he said.

His eyes were dark and mysterious in the moonlight. It was even easier now to picture him as a wizard. She thought briefly of Merlin offering knowledge to Arthur. Of the snake in the garden offering much the same thing to Eve. She tucked the cheeseburger back into the bag. "I've already told you several."

Shane nodded. "Fair enough. It's your turn to ask," Shane said. "Ask me anything at all."

A breeze moved the branches overhead, shifting the shadows, and she could see the challenge in his eyes. The words were out before she could prevent them. "Is your name really Shane?"

"Yes," he said, shifting his gaze to the lakeshore.

"Were your parents big fans of the book?"

"They never said."

There was a flatness to his tone she'd never heard

before, but when he turned to her, he was smiling. "It was a tough name to grow into. It cost me several black eyes in grade school. Until I learned that it's hard for people to mock you if you turn the tables and laugh at yourself first."

"Some people never learn that lesson," Jodie said.

"They get a lot of black eyes. What about you? Is Jodie your given name or a nickname?"

Jodie wrinkled her nose. "It's my given name. My dad's name was Joe. Mom was Dee. But I never got in a fight over it."

"It sounds like your parents loved you very much."

When she looked into his eyes this time, she saw a bleakness that hadn't been there before. Then suddenly it changed to something else, something she couldn't put a name to. But it made her very aware of how close they were, so close that she could feel his breath on her skin. Her gaze dropped to his mouth. His lips no longer curved in a smile. All she had to do was lean forward, just a little, and she could know what they would feel like pressed against hers. Not soft. No, his mouth would be hard. And his taste as dark and mysterious as his scent. Her eyes widened at the drift of her thoughts. She couldn't possibly be thinking of kissing Shane Sullivan. But she was. She most definitely was. And the moment she shifted her glance to his eyes, she knew that he was thinking of kissing her, too.

And he was going to do it. He moved slowly to lay his hand along the side of her face. She had plenty of time to pull back, and in spite of the firmness of his hand, he might have let her. But she didn't move.

And then his lips brushed against hers, so gently that she barely felt them before they withdrew. The second time they lingered longer, but the pressure was still soft, so soft she felt herself sinking into it. The breath she'd been holding slipped out on a sigh as he slowly traced her lips with his tongue. She felt her arms go lax, her eyelids drift shut, as the pleasure seeped through her.

It wasn't at all the kind of kiss she'd expected from Shane Sullivan. It was exactly the kind of kiss she'd always dreamed about.

"Mmm," she murmured when he withdrew a second time. She had to have—

"More?" He whispered the question, and she felt his breath against her lips before his mouth at last returned to hers. A tremor moved through her, followed by a wave of heat that burned through her body right down to her toes. His lips continued to mark their magic as he coaxed hers apart with his teeth and his tongue.

This wasn't anything like her dreams. They'd never been this vivid, and the sensations had never been this intense. Each nip of his teeth on her bottom lip had her head spinning. Each quick flick of his tongue made her tremble. She felt as if she were burning up with a fever, inside and out.

His hand lay along the side of her face as his mouth moved on hers. He touched her nowhere else, and yet she wanted him to. She wanted his hands on her breasts, and even more, she wanted him to touch the heat that had settled at her very center and threatened to explode. Her fingers closed into fists as the greed built within her.

When he drew back, she stayed where she was. Not because she wanted to. More than anything, she wanted to throw her arms around him, drag his mouth back to hers so that she could reach for...whatever had seemed just out of her reach. But the messages from her brain didn't seem to be getting to her body.

"Well, well..." he said.

She blinked and then stared at him. *Well, well!* That's all he had to say? A joke from her childhood drifted through her mind as the anger brought strength to her body. *Well, well—the story of two holes in the ground.* With all her heart, she wished there were one nearby she could push him into. Her heart was still hammering, her breathing was still ragged, and he looked completely unmoved. At least he wasn't laughing. If he dared, she would make do with the lake and shove him into that.

"Why did you do that?" she asked.

"It was a mistake," Shane said.

She stared at him, appalled that she could feel tears begin to fill her eyes. She was not going to cry. She hadn't cried in a long time. Even Billy hadn't made her do that.

The thought gave her the strength to pull herself together. "Don't make it again," she said as she rose. Then she turned and moved toward the path.

The moment she did, Shane wanted to curse—her or himself, he wasn't sure which. And he wasn't sure why. All he was certain of was that it had been a mistake to bring her down here to the lake. In the moonlight, her skin looked as pale and delicate as the finest silk. He'd been wanting to touch it since he'd pulled that French fry from behind her ear.

But a moment ago, he'd wanted to do more than touch her, more than kiss her. For one frightening moment, his mind had drained of everything but her. He'd forgotten everything else, including his plan in bringing her down to the lake.

To find out about that damn letter.

Not only hadn't he gotten her to talk about it, but after what had just happened, his prospects didn't look good.

What in the world was she doing to him? Shane Sullivan always got his man. He'd never allowed a woman, any woman, to distract him before. Never.

If he wanted to catch Billy Rutherford, he was definitely going to have to find a way to handle Jodie Freemont.

But a woman had never driven him so wild with a kiss before.

It was something he thought about a long time before he followed her back to the house.

and forth?

JODIE OPENED her eyes and sat straight up in bed. She
must have dozed off. The illuminated face of the
clock on her nightstand told her that it was 1:50 a.m.
That meant she'd slept for twenty minutes.

What had awakened her? For a moment, she sat
perfectly still and listened.

Silence, except for the scrape of a branch against
her window. Out on the highway, the sound of a car
grew steadily louder, then faded. A board creaked.

Every muscle in her body tightened. Where had the
sound come from? Not overhead. Was someone
climbing the stairs? Fear tightened her throat as seconds ticked by on her bedside clock. Finally reminding herself to breathe, she inched her way back
against the headboard. She was overreacting. Old
houses were always creaking. Or maybe it was a case
of wishful thinking.

Jodie glanced up at the ceiling. More than anything,
she wanted to catch Billy Rutherford in her snare trap.
In her mind, she pictured him taking one step and
another and another—then the rope whipping around
his feet, jerking them out from under him and up until
he was swinging back and forth—

Another board creaked. This time it was louder and
she was sure it came from overhead. Excitement
mixed with panic as she wrapped her arms tightly
around her knees and watched her clock. The second

hand swept the face slowly. One minute…a minute and a half…two minutes.

She glanced up at the ceiling. Surely the trap would make some noise when it was triggered. Or Billy would certainly make some sound as the rope ripped his feet out from under him—a gasp, a shout, a curse?

Wouldn't there be some sound as he swung back and forth?

As if on cue, she heard a creak. Then silence. The second hand on her clock made another sweep.

Suddenly, she recalled Irene's comment. *I hope no one ends up hanging by their necks.*

Jodie felt her heart jump to her throat and stick. What if she'd killed somebody? Billy?

She had to know. Slipping off the side of the bed, she raced to the door. Another creak overhead stopped her dead in her tracks, and a completely different scenario filled her mind: Billy edging his way across the attic as close to the eaves as he could get. He would only trigger the trap if he actually walked directly across the attic floor.

Whirling, Jodie hurried to the fireplace and carefully lifted the poker from its stand. Then she frowned. What in the world was she going to do with it? She wasn't going to hit Billy Rutherford any more than she would have shot him if Hank Jefferson had sold her that gun. He might bleed. Even as she shuddered, the floor creaked again.

Straightening her shoulders, Jodie tightened her grip on the poker and whipped it in a wide circle. The great thing about a poker was that you could actually poke people with it—or at least threaten to. In her mind, she pictured Captain Hook. She would just *make* Billy walk across the floor to the spot where the rope would snap him up.

For a moment, Jodie stood still, visualizing her plan. Then shouldering the poker like a rifle, she walked to the door. Someone was up in the attic, and she was going to get him.

The moment she stepped into the hallway, the silence seemed to deepen. She waited for a moment, listening hard. The sound of a passing car couldn't penetrate this far into the house.

Overhead, there was silence too. Holding her breath, she edged her way down the hallway. When she reached the door to the attic stairs, it stood wide open. Once more, her heart jumped to her throat, fluttering there like a bird. She clearly remembered closing the door before she'd gone to bed. Could Billy have climbed in through the window and avoided her trap, then snuck down the stairs? Slowly, she turned. Was he even now lurking somewhere in the shadows?

This time the creak sounded like a shot. Letting out the breath she was holding, she whirled back to the stairs. He was still in the attic. Keeping to the very edge of the steps, she climbed them one by one.

The darkness only lessened a little as she approached the top. The moonlight that managed to push its way through the grime on the windows made little headway into the gloom. Pausing on the top step, she counted to ten as she listened.

Nothing. She stepped carefully onto the attic floor, and suddenly a hand clamped over her mouth, and an arm banded around her waist, immobilizing her.

As panic streamed through her, she ordered herself to think. *Billy?* She had to let him know it was her. But the moment she tried to move, she felt herself gripped even more tightly against a hard, male body. Mixed with the fear was a sudden awareness of how strong those arms were, how callused those fingers.

Not Billy's soft hands, she thought. And not Billy's scent. Suddenly the memory of what had happened earlier at the lake flooded through her. She recalled Shane's hand resting along the side of her face, Shane's mouth pressed lightly but firmly against hers until she couldn't think of anything, anyone but... It was *Shane!*

"The window." The words were barely a breath in her ear.

Narrowing her eyes, she peered through the gloom. Something seemed to be blocking what little light she'd noticed before. Wood scraped against wood as the window slid upward, and she could just make out a silhouette as it climbed into the room.

"Stay."

Shane released her so quickly she nearly dropped the poker. Because the shadow at the window was the only one she could make out, Jodie kept her eyes on it. A board moaned under the eaves. The shadow froze. Holding her breath, she counted to ten while the silence stretched. The moment the next board creaked, the shadow whirled toward it and suddenly there were two silhouettes locked together. The silence shattered as they pitched to the floor.

There was the sickening sound of a fist pounding into flesh and a series of grunts as the two figures rolled. A chair toppled and something rattled across the floor. Then the two figures rose again, blocking the light. She had to do something to help. Keeping as close to the eaves as she could, she edged her way toward the window. Glass shattered as they toppled a lamp. Poker raised, Jodie moved closer.

She dodged to the right when they rolled toward her. First one was on top, then the other. Which one was the intruder? Even as she hesitated, they rolled again, this time in the direction of the circle of rope.

The snare trap. Should she call a warning? Before she could open her mouth, a figure rose and staggered toward the window.

It had to be Billy. Shane wouldn't be trying to get away. In the time it took her to decide, the man had swung both legs over the sill and was gone. Jodie raced toward him.

Suddenly, there was a zinging sound, as if the string on a guitar had snapped. Out of the corner of her eye, she saw the other man suddenly pitch to the floor.

"What the—" Shane ended the thought in a grunt as he shot feetfirst toward the ceiling.

It occurred to her that it was just as she'd visualized it, then she threw herself at the other man who was halfway out the window.

"Stop." She grabbed at his arm as he reached for a tree limb. A shove sent her reeling into the eaves. As she scrambled to her feet, she saw Shane begin to swing forward, but the man was out of his reach when the rope pulled him back. She made it to the window in time to grab a foot. A mistake, she thought as it kicked her to the floor.

The rafters creaked ominously as she once more lunged toward the window. Leaning out, she saw the man, climbing along the limb of the maple tree. She threw one leg over the sill and leaned forward, reaching. A few more inches and…teetering, she stretched more and grabbed air just as a pair of hands clamped around her waist and jerked her back into the attic.

"Let me go. I can—"

"What? Break your neck?"

"I won't." She twisted one way, then another, but the hands gripping her were like a steel vise.

"You damn near toppled out that window."

"I almost had him. I can still…" Desperate, she tried to pry Shane's fingers loose. He relaxed his hold just enough to turn her around so she faced him. Jodie found that, even though he was hanging upside down, she was looking almost directly into his eyes. "Will you please let me go? He's getting away."

"Thanks to you. I'd have had him in handcuffs right now if you hadn't interrupted."

"I didn't interrupt. You interfered. If you hadn't, he'd have been swinging from his feet now instead of you."

"Let's postpone the debate until you get me down from this thing."

She tried backing away. His grip on her tightened. "I'll come back just as soon—"

"Forget it. Until you cut me loose, we're Siamese twins."

They might as well have been. They were so close, Jodie could feel his breath on her cheek and see the glint of anger in his eyes. But it wasn't fear that arrowed down her spine as her gaze moved to his mouth. All she could do was think—if he kissed her now, his lips wouldn't be soft and gentle as they had been down at the lake. And they wouldn't be patient. They would be demanding, hot and potent.

She felt his hands grow tighter, felt her own desire curl tight within her. But she wasn't going to kiss Shane Sullivan again. She couldn't. It wasn't possible to kiss a man while he was hanging upside down. Was it?

Perhaps, if he angled his head just right, and she angled hers…

Light flooded the attic. Footsteps thundered up the stairs.

"Jodie, are you all right?" Sophie led the way. Both she and Irene held their pokers at the ready as they crested the top of the attic steps.

"Good girl. Caught our prowler, I see," Sophie said, but she stopped short when she caught a glimpse of Shane. "You're not our prowler." She glanced at Jodie. "Let's get him down. Did Clyde show you how to unspring this thing or should I go back downstairs and get a knife?"

"There's a lever," Jodie said and decided to ignore the fact that Shane didn't release her as she walked toward it. The distrust between them was obviously mutual, and that suited her just fine.

"Brace yourself," she said as she threw the release lever. His grunt as he landed on the floor gave her some satisfaction. But the grin he shot her as the two ladies rushed to fuss over him cut it short. Sophie held one of his arms, Irene the other, as Shane rose to his feet.

"Are you all right?" Irene asked. "I knew that thingamajig wasn't going to work right."

"It worked fine," Jodie said. "If Shane hadn't interfered, I'd have caught our prowler."

"There *was* a prowler then," Sophie said. "I knew I saw someone climbing down that old maple tree in the backyard."

"That's how he got in, too," Shane said. "When I saw him start up, I used the key you ladies gave me. I thought I'd have a better chance of getting him if I came up here."

"Good thinking," Sophie said.

"Except that it cost us our prowler," Jodie pointed out.

Shane shrugged. "I would have had him if you hadn't interrupted."

Jodie strode forward until they were standing toe-to-toe. "I didn't interrupt. You interfered."

"Instead of arguing, the two of you ought to team up. That way you won't get in each other's way," Sophie said. "Right now, I think we'd better go downstairs and inform Sheriff Dillon we've had another break-in."

"And I'll make some of my famous hot chocolate. It's just the thing to calm everyone's nerves," Irene said, leading the way down the stairs.

"One taste and you'll wish we left you hanging," Jodie predicted in a low tone as she slipped past Shane and caught up with the two older women.

SHANE LEANED BACK in his chair and let the conversation hum around him. Across the length of the kitchen table, Dillon was jotting down information in his notebook. But no matter how cleverly or persistently the sheriff asked the question, no one was willing to say that the prowler in the attic had definitely been Billy Rutherford.

When it came right down to it, Shane wasn't certain himself. Thanks to the darkness and the fact that he'd been occupied dodging fists, he hadn't gotten a good look at the man's face.

Shane shifted his gaze to Jodie. Had she gotten a better look? She said not, and she could be telling the truth. In his mind, he could still picture her stretching out that window, still feel the fear that had twisted in his gut when he'd grabbed her and found that she was already more than halfway out, teetering. If he'd been a second later... Quickly, he pushed the image out of his mind and reminded himself that she'd had the full benefit of the moonlight while she was at the window. He studied her in the harsh, overhead glow of the kitchen light. Could anyone look that innocent and still be a liar? Part of him wanted to say yes. But there was another part of him... His gaze dropped to her mouth. It was soft, unpainted. She was sitting three feet away from him and he could almost taste her. Desire crept through him, leaving a dull ache in its wake.

He wanted her, and it was interfering with his judgment. The only thing he should be thinking about was whether or not Jodie had gotten a good look at the intruder. And if she had, was she lying to protect Billy Rutherford?

Deliberately, Shane shifted his gaze to Dillon. His best guess was that the sheriff wasn't sure about that, either. Otherwise the man would have beat a hasty retreat the moment he'd sampled Irene's special hot chocolate.

It was "special" all right. Her secret recipe had all the flavor of warmed-up mud. Lazarus had taken one sniff of the sample she'd poured into his dish and all but loped out of the room. Shane glanced down at his own full mug. In a minute he'd have to take another drink. His excuse that it was too hot was wearing thin. There wasn't a plant in sight, and there was no way to tip it up his sleeve since he was wearing a sweater.

When his gaze collided with Jodie's, he saw the amusement as well as the challenge. She raised her mug in a mock salute.

He reached for his, gripping the handle carefully as he lifted it. Then suddenly, he winced and the mug slipped through his fingers, spilling its contents as it rolled to the edge of the table and dropped to the floor. In the time it took him to grip his shoulder with his free hand, he read the expressions of everyone in the room. Jodie's was a mixture of admiration and envy, Dillon's was one of surprise, but the ladies' eyes were filled with worry and concern. He rubbed his shoulder, wincing again. "Sorry. I must have landed harder than I thought."

"Don't worry about a thing," Irene said as she hurried over with a cloth.

"I'll get you another in just a moment."

"Don't bother. I'll just help Jodie finish hers."

Dillon's eyebrows shot up. "Do you want a lift to the emergency room?"

Keeping his expression pained, Shane shook his head. "My shoulder seemed fine before. It must be stiffening up."

"Got just the thing," Sophie said, rising and moving toward the pantry.

"I'd better file this report," Dillon said, nodding to Irene and Jodie. "I'll send a patrol car by every hour or so. And if any of you hear from Billy, I want you to call me."

"It wasn't Billy," Irene said as she escorted Dillon out of the room. "Even as a little boy, he didn't like to climb trees."

"I've got something that will take care of that shoulder," Sophie said as she reentered from the pantry. "It works wonders for sore muscles and joints. Take off your sweater." Then turning to Jodie, she said, "You're going to give the lad a massage."

"Me?" Jodie asked. "I can't. I don't know anything about—"

Sophie snorted. "It isn't brain surgery we're talking about. It's a massage, and I can't do it because of the arthritis in my hands. C'mon, I'll talk you through it."

Jodie turned to Shane, and discovered there'd be no help from him. He just sat there, grinning from ear to ear. But the challenge in his eyes had her stepping up beside Sophie.

"There," Sophie said as she poured a dollop of oil into Jodie's palms. "Now, rub them together. There, that's good. Now, place your hands on his shoulders."

Jodie moved around behind Shane's chair. It was just a massage, she told herself. It wasn't...well, it wasn't a whole lot of other things. It wasn't as though she were kissing him again. Or feeling his body pressed close. As the warmth started to spread through her, she quickly pushed the other things she'd been thinking about doing with Shane Sullivan out of her mind. She could do this. People gave massages to other people all of the time. For some people, it was a job.

"Now, press down," Sophie said. "And release. That's right. Press and release. I told you, you could do it. It's as simple as breathing."

Right, Jodie thought. Except that it wasn't so easy to breathe anymore. The air around her seemed to have thickened slightly. *Think of something else,* she told herself. *Think of the grin on his face.* She drew in a deep breath and let it out.

"Now, move your hands closer to his neck," Sophie said.

She did as she was told and tried to block the sensations that had begun to move through her. Closing her mind to everything else, she focused on moving her hands over Shane in the rhythm Sophie was dictating. She'd never before realized how sensitive her fingers were. Incredible. They were absorbing everything—the prickly hairs on the back of his neck, the pulse beating at his throat.

"Press, release. Press, release."

Sophie's voice came from a distance, but it didn't matter because her hands seemed to have developed a will of their own. They were moving in a circular motion back to his shoulders, pressing and releasing, pressing and releasing. The feel of his skin beneath her hands was mesmerizing. The air seemed to be filled with the sound of her own breathing, her own heartbeat quickening. Beneath the musky scent of the oil, she could smell something much more intriguing, something dark and male.

Her palms recorded each separate sensation—the smooth, slick warmth of his skin, the taut muscles beneath that gave when she pressed. A feeling of power moved through her, and suddenly there were other places she wanted to touch. She stroked her hands down his spine, then moved them slowly up again. There was such heat here. It moved from his skin to hers and then spread until it burned deep in her center. She wanted to do more than touch him. She wanted to lean forward and press her mouth to the back of his neck. To taste him. To have him turn and...

His skin was only inches away from her lips when she paused. What was she thinking? Drawing back a little, she tore her eyes off Shane and glanced around the kitchen. It was empty. How long had she—

"Don't stop."

It took her a second to realize that he'd spoken, that it wasn't just the voice in her head.

"I can't. We can't." Before she could lift her hands from him, he snagged her wrist and turned to face her. The moment she looked into his eyes, they trapped her as swiftly, as surely, as his hand had. In them she could see exactly what she was feeling, and all she would have to do was lean forward. It wouldn't take much effort, because she felt as if she were caught by some kind of magnetic force that was pulling her slowly and inexorably toward him. And in another moment, everything she'd been imagining since the first time she met him would become reality.

Since the first time she met him... It was that thought that gave her the strength to pull herself free. She didn't know Shane Sullivan, not well enough to... She took three quick steps backward before she smacked into the refrigerator door.

"You—you know what I'm going to do? I'm going to fix myself a drink, something to get rid of the taste of that hot chocolate." If she could just keep talking... No, talking was not going to do it. She had to stop looking at him or the magnetic pull was going to get hold of her again. Turning, she found herself face-to-face with the latest motto of the day: Follow Your Passion.

Your passion is catching Billy, she reminded herself as she pulled the refrigerator open, *not making love to Shane Sullivan on the kitchen table.* She saw nothing but the bottle of milk that Irene had used to make the hot chocolate. Just the memory of it had her shutting the door and reaching for the overhead cupboard. "I think Sophie...yes, here it is, Sophie's cure for a head cold—a twenty-year-old, single-malt Scotch." Without glancing at Shane, she hurried on. "Care to join me?"

"Why not?"

"According to Sophie, it's good for what ails you," she said as she quickly filled two glasses, picked them up and turned. For a moment, just look-

ing at him was enough to have her nerves knotting
again. He was still naked from the waist up. He was
still beautiful. And she wanted him even more than
she had before.

She needed a drink. Holding the two glasses of
Scotch in front of her like a shield, she moved forward. "What shall we drink to?" she asked as she
set a tumbler in front of him.

"A pleasant day for the funeral," Shane said.

Jodie blinked. "What?"

"Even twenty-year-old Scotch can be lethal if
you're going to knock down eight ounces."

Jodie stared at the glass she'd filled to the brim as
Shane took it from her and carried it along with his
own to the counter. After carefully tipping most of
the liquid back into the bottle, he gave her back her
glass and lifted his own. "Why don't we drink to the
fantasy I was having a few moments ago?"

Jodie took a quick sip of her Scotch. Steadied by
the heat that burned the back of her throat, she said,
"It's going to remain a fantasy."

"I don't think so."

What she saw in Shane's eyes made her throat go
dry as dust again. It wasn't the easy humor she was
coming to expect. No, it was more like a threat—or
a promise. She took another sip of scotch. "We
can't... We don't even know each other."

His smile bloomed slowly. "It's not necessary to
know someone all that well to—"

Jodie raised a hand to stop him. "It's necessary for
me."

His grin widened. "Okay, ask me anything you
want to know."

There was a part of her that knew it was a trap.
But another part of her just couldn't resist. There was

more to Shane Sullivan than he was letting on. "You'll tell me the whole truth and nothing but the truth?"

"So help me, ma'am." He turned his chair around and straddled it. "Shoot."

For the first time in her life, Jodie thought she might have. If only she'd had a gun handy. Not the kind that Hank Jefferson had refused to sell her. Not a real gun. But if she'd had a water pistol handy, she would have taken aim and unloaded it just to wipe the self-confident grin off his face.

Setting her glass on the table, she sat down and said, "You're not really some distant cousin of Katie Dillon's, are you?"

Shane shrugged. "Well, in the sense that all of us are kin, I must be related in some way."

"Bull. You want to know what I think? I think you're a bounty hunter who's come here to track Billy Rutherford down."

For a moment, Shane didn't say anything. He didn't even move. Dillon was right. She *was* smart. The admiration he felt for her mixed with the annoyance he felt for himself. He'd been careless. And the reason for it was sitting right across the table from him. Instead of keeping his mind on getting his man, he'd been entertaining thoughts of… Ruthlessly, he pushed his fantasies aside.

"I'm right, aren't I?" Jodie asked.

"What tipped you off?"

"In the attic, you mentioned handcuffs. I don't think they're standard equipment for burnt-out corporate executives."

He recalled exactly when the words had slipped out, but he'd been hoping she wouldn't notice. He

rarely let his cover slip, but he supposed swinging
from the rafters by his feet was some excuse.

"Why are you a bounty hunter?" Jodie asked.

"The usual reasons, I suppose. It pays well and I'm
good at it. Why are you a librarian?"

"Inertia. I loved college, and applying for the job
at the library allowed me to stay right on campus."
She met his eyes squarely. "That makes me like my
mother. Afraid to try anything new."

"You must enjoy it," Shane said.

She shrugged. "Parts of it. I love books and I love
to research things and discover the answers, the secrets."

"It sounds a lot like bounty hunting."

"Except that I spend most of my time in front of
a computer screen, and lately…" Suddenly her eyes
narrowed. "Hey, I'm supposed to be asking the questions, not answering them."

"I've got a proposition for you. Why don't we
team up and track down Billy Rutherford together?"
The surprised look on her face summed up his own
feelings exactly. Where in the world had that question
come from? He always worked alone.

"No."

That one word should have flooded him with relief,
not disappointment. And certainly not annoyance
"Why not? Think about it. It makes perfect sense.
Especially if we don't want to stage another Keystone
Cops scene like the one we played out in the attic."

"I can't," Jodie said. "I want to catch Billy to
prove something—that I'm not like my mother. How
am I going to do that if I team up with a big-time
bounty hunter?"

"I can see to it that you get all the credit."

"But if you're the one who really catches Billy,

I'd know it. And if I'm going to change how everyone thinks of me, I think I have to convince myself first. So my answer is no.''

Shane watched in silence as she rose and turned away. He let her get to the door before he said, ''One more thing…''

She turned.

''Something very important you ought to know about me—I never take no for an answer. I'm going to persuade you to change your mind.''

5

"ALL I CAN SAY is that Albert wouldn't have to spend any money advertising his specials if he could just hire that man to sit in the window drinking cappuccinos every day." Having made this pronouncement from the doorway, Mindy Lou breezed into Jodie's office and settled herself comfortably in one of the chairs.

Shane, Jodie thought, but she asked the question just the same. "Which man?"

"Your handyman, of course," Mindy Lou stated with a beaming smile. "The man who convinced you to change from herbal tea to cappuccinos is also changing the drinking habits of most of the female population of Castleton."

"He didn't convince—" Jodie began, but Mindy Lou was on a roll.

"Nadine claims that cappuccino sales at Albert's have tripled since he came to town. And he doesn't have a date for the Mistletoe Ball yet." Mindy Lou leaned closer. "Nadine asked him if he was going, and she's very depressed because he didn't take the hint and ask her."

"I'm going to have to do something about that," Jodie said, jotting a reminder down on her desk calendar.

"Are *you* going to ask him to the ball?"

Glancing up, Jodie blinked at the expression of

astonishment on her assistant's face. "No. Of course not. What I meant was that I'm going to have a talk with Nadine and try to convince her to come back to school. Throwing herself at every good-looking man who comes into Albert's is not her only ticket out of Castleton." Then setting her pencil down, she said, "Why shouldn't I ask him? Not that I'm going to, because I'm not."

"You could certainly ask him," Mindy Lou said. "It's just that you never have a date for the ball."

"Because attending is part of my job. Angus depends on me to help him keep the names of the contributors straight. The money that's raised through the Mistletoe Ball keeps this library running." Why in the world was she defending the fact that she was dateless? Why did she sound like...*poor Jodie?*

Mindy Lou smiled. "If you did go with Mr. Sullivan, it would certainly distract Alicia Finnerty from her suicide watch."

"Please." Jodie dropped her head in her hands. "Don't tempt me. I'd do almost anything to get her out of my hair. I know she means well, but lately she's everywhere I go."

"She's probably trying to catch a glimpse of Billy Rutherford. Because of the reward and all."

"Reward?" Jodie asked.

"It's all over town that an insurance company is offering to pay $250,000 to anyone who can recover the money. And everyone in town is betting that Billy will contact you or one of his aunts."

"Great." With a sigh, Jodie leaned back in her chair. No wonder Billy hadn't made any move to contact her. If he did, someone was bound to spot him. And it wasn't just Alicia Finnerty keeping her under surveillance. She'd been running into Mike Buckley,

Sheriff Dillon's deputy, everywhere she turned, too. In the past two days, the only person she hadn't seen much of was Shane Sullivan.

"They'll catch him, you know," Mindy Lou assured her in a comforting tone. "Sheriff Dillon is meeting with your handyman right now."

"Dillon's meeting with Shane?"

"They were at Albert's when I stopped in to get you a cappuccino. I'm betting Billy Rutherford will be arrested and back in jail before you know it."

That was precisely what Jodie was beginning to fear. Picking up her notebook, Jodie rose. "Can you cover for me? I have a research project to finish."

"Sure thing," Mindy Lou said. "It's your break time anyway." Reaching into the paper bag she was carrying, she pulled out a foam cup. "Here you go. Enjoy."

Managing a smile, Jodie took it as she left the room. But the moment she had escaped into a stairwell, she frowned down at the cup in her hand. How was she supposed to enjoy it? If she didn't do something soon, Shane Sullivan was going to get credit for everything—from changing her beverage of choice to capturing Billy Rutherford.

Oh, he'd promised that he'd persuade her to change her mind and join forces with him, she thought as she climbed the stairs to the second floor. But in the past two days, he hadn't come anywhere near her except at dinner. He'd been too busy, she supposed. Even though she'd had trouble believing he'd been a burned-out corporate executive, she'd seen with her own eyes that he was pretty competent with a hammer and a paintbrush. Sophie and Irene were excited that one of the second-floor bedrooms was ready for guests.

Pushing through the door to the stacks, Jodie headed down one of the narrow aisles. From the time she was a little girl, she'd loved to go to the library. It was an escape, a place where she could relax and straighten out her thoughts. Pausing, she ran her hand along the spines of several volumes until she found one bound in leather. Opening it, she breathed in. Old books had a special scent that never failed to trigger the feeling of peace she'd always found in them as a child. Drawing in another breath, she leaned against the shelves.

She had to make up her mind. Should she go to Shane and accept his offer of a partnership or...what?

Billy was no idiot, and now with a reward posted, he'd be a fool to try to enter the house through the attic again. It would be equally risky for him to try to contact her. So what chance did she really have of getting the jump on a professional bounty hunter?

I never take no for an answer.

She only had to think of that massage she'd given him in the kitchen for the warmth to steal through her, thickening her blood, quickening her heartbeat, weakening her knees. She made herself breathe in, but this time, instead of the comforting scent of old books, she smelled the musky, male scent of Shane. It was almost as if she could reach out and touch him.

When she realized that she'd raised her hand, she snatched it back to grip the book she still held. Then she nearly dropped it as her gaze dropped to the title: *The Art of Erotic Massage.*

Quickly reshelving it, she hurried to the end of the aisle and turned into another one. What in the world was happening to her? No man had ever affected her this way. Certainly not Billy. She'd never imagined herself actually going to bed with Billy Rutherford.

Maybe that was her problem. Billy's approach to wooing her had been so…platonic. Maybe she'd become sex starved.

Or maybe it was just Shane. Perhaps he had this effect on all women. It seemed a likely possibility if he could inspire the entire female population of Castleton to drink cappuccinos.

She glanced down at the cup she still held in her hand. He hadn't inspired her. She'd decided to switch drinks before she'd even met Shane Sullivan. Removing the lid, she downed the contents and then tossed the container into the wastebasket at the end of the aisle.

She'd made her own decision then, and she needed to make another one now. Flipping open her notebook, she found the page where she'd listed every one of Sophie's calendar mottoes. She'd kept track of them since the first day they'd begun appearing on the refrigerator door. Perhaps one of them could help her. Visualize Your Goal, Take Action, There's More Than One Way to Skin A Cat, Go For It… Her gaze came to a dead stop. Follow Your Passion.

Closing her eyes, Jodie leaned back against the bookshelves. Everything seemed to lead back to having sex with Shane Sullivan. She wasn't just sex starved, she was sex crazed!

Suddenly she frowned. But what was her real passion? Massaging Shane Sullivan? Or capturing Billy and handing him over to the police? The image that filled her mind was the one she'd imagined on the front page of the local paper. She was standing with Billy and Sheriff Dillon, and the headline read: "Embezzler Captured by Local Librarian."

Opening her eyes, Jodie strode down the aisle. In the real headline, she'd make sure they used her name. In the meantime, she was going to figure out a way to work with Shane, steal some of his expertise, and then catch Billy by herself. After all, there was more that one way to skin a cat. Frowning, she shook her head to rid it of the disgusting image and, instead, summoned up the picture that was going to be on the front page of the *Castleton Bulletin*.

"WHAT'S SO IMPORTANT that you couldn't talk over the phone?" Shane asked the moment that Nadine had finished taking their orders and bustled away.

Dillon's brows shot up as he pulled a flat overnight delivery envelope out of his jacket. "You're the one who had this delivered in care of my office. I figured it was top secret."

"It is," Shane said.

"You going to open it?"

"Not here."

Dillon studied him for a moment. "When I said I'd cooperate by giving you a cover, you promised to keep me informed."

With a sigh, Shane glanced around the restaurant, then leaned closer to Dillon. "It's a two-headed coin. Sophie asked if I could get my hands on one, and the future of the bed-and-breakfast may depend on—"

"Enough." Dillon raised both hands. "As an officer of the law, I don't want to know any more."

"I didn't think so." Shane glanced at his watch.

"In a hurry?" Dillon asked.

"I don't like leaving the ladies alone at the house."

"Relax. I sent Mike Buckley out there to keep an eye on the place while you're gone. Not that I think there's much chance of Billy Rutherford paying his aunts a visit today. He's in Florida."

Shane stared at the sheriff. "He's in custody?"

Dillon shook his head. "Not yet. I got a call about an hour ago. Seems he flew in yesterday afternoon. The Miami police had been at the airport a few days before flashing his picture, and one of the gate attendants remembered it and called the police. Rutherford was long gone by the time they got there, but they're sure it was him."

Shane frowned. "He's laying a false trail."

"Maybe. But it could be the false trail led to here. First he makes sure that the search is focused in this area, then makes his escape to Florida."

"Without the money? I think not."

"Here're your drinks, gentlemen," Nadine said, then beamed a smile at Shane. "Is there anything else I can get you?"

Shane glanced at his watch. "I'll take one of your hamburger specials if you're serving lunch."

"Coming right up." Nadine was three steps away before she turned back. "Anything for you, Sheriff Dillon?"

"No, thanks," Dillon replied. As Nadine hurried off, he studied Shane curiously. "Eleven o'clock is a little early for lunch. Aren't they feeding you at Rutherford House?"

"Don't ask," Shane said.

After taking a long swallow of his coffee, Dillon said, "It's possible Billy's already got the money."

Shane shook his head. "He didn't have a chance to get anything the other night during the Keystone Cops fiasco."

"*If* that was him. Neither you nor Jodie confirmed that."

"She could if she wanted to, but she's bound and determined to catch him by herself, so she's not going to share any information."

"Why don't you get her to team up with you?"

Shane let out a frustrated breath. "I'm working on it."

Dillon drained his cup and rose. "I'd work a little faster."

"It's complicated."

Dillon smiled. "I never met a woman who wasn't. Why don't you try getting on her good side? You could always offer to escort her to the Mistletoe Ball tomorrow night. She usually spends the entire evening running around trying to make her boss look good."

Shane frowned as the sheriff walked away. Dillon wasn't the only one pushing him to ask Jodie to the Mistletoe Ball, although Sophie and Irene had been slightly more subtle. And he just might have considered it, if he hadn't realized that deep down inside he wanted to take her.

That scared him. He wanted her. And if it had been a simple case of desire, he would have handled it one way or the other. But there was something about her...or something about the way she made him feel...

When Nadine set the hamburger special in front of him, his frown deepened.

"Is there something wrong?" she asked.

"No, it's fine." He lifted a French fry, but the moment the waitress walked away, he dropped it back on his plate. Just looking at it made him remember how much Jodie had enjoyed the bag he'd smuggled in for her the other night. How she'd looked in the moonlight down at the lake.

This was ridiculous. He was starving, and he couldn't even enjoy his food. Worse than that, she was distracting him from the job he'd come here to do. Dillon was right. He had to convince her to work for him. Once he did, he would find out what was in that letter he was certain had come from Rutherford. And then he could get to the bottom of this case.

"You don't like the hamburger," Nadine said as she reached for his plate. "If you want, I can bring you today's special. Albert makes a mean lasagna."

"Lasagna," Shane repeated as a plan formed in his mind.

"I'll put in an order right away," Nadine said.

"No, I have to get back to work," he said, drawing out his wallet. "And do you think I could have a word with Albert?"

JODIE GLANCED at her watch as she walked across the library parking lot. Five o'clock on the dot. She was being predictable again. Come to think of it, ever since Shane Sullivan had promised to persuade her to become his partner, she'd reverted right back to her old ways—going to work at the exact same time, coming home, pretending to eat Irene's dinners, and waiting for Shane to take the initiative. That's what the old Jodie Freemont always did.

Reaching her car, she slid her key into the lock.

She saw it the moment she opened the door—a red rose lying on the passenger seat. It was wrapped in clear cellophane and tied with a green ribbon. Reaching for it, she noticed that a small bunch of mistletoe was tucked inside with the rose.

Shane was the word that tumbled through her mind. Turning, she leaned against the car door, unwrapping it enough to draw in the scent. How sweet. Her thoughts were drifting away when she spotted Alicia Finnerty gaping at her from the sidewalk.

When the idea popped into her head, it was just too perfect. She couldn't resist. Smiling, she raised the flower and waved at the woman. "It's from my new lover."

Then she turned and climbed into her car. There was more than one way to change one's image. And she couldn't wait to see what Alicia Finnerty would make of it. After carefully placing the rose on the seat, she fastened her seat belt and turned the radio up full blast. Then she backed the car out of the slot and waved again to the older woman as she shot out of the parking lot.

She was still laughing and the music was still blaring when she stopped at the corner for the light. And that's when she spotted him. Shane Sullivan was walking out of Albert's carrying a large box. Curious, she watched him as he walked to his convertible and loaded the box into the trunk.

It was only then that she heard a muffled shout and glanced into her rearview mirror. She had a brief glimpse of Alicia Finnerty waving frantically. Then her attention was completely riveted by the truck barreling down on her from behind. Fear streamed through her. Why wasn't he braking? Didn't he see the red light?

He was going to hit her. The instant the realization struck her, she jammed her foot down on the gas pedal and dragged the wheel to the right.

Tires squealed and glass shattered as the truck slammed into the right rear fender. The impact thrust her sideways into the door and her head whacked against the window. The car spun crazily in a circle, then skidded suddenly forward toward a parked car. She jerked the wheel, then heard the scream and crunch of metal pleating as she was thrown backward against the seat.

In the sudden silence, she opened her eyes. Stars

were still spinning in front of them when Shane appeared at the window.

"Are you all right?" he asked, pulling the door open.

"I...think so."

He reached across her to turn the key off and release the seat belt. Then he took her arm. "C'mon."

"Wait." She grabbed her purse and the rose, then allowed him to draw her out of the car. The first step she took, her knees buckled. Shane's arm tightened around her waist, and she leaned against him to negotiate the curb.

"Sit down."

"I'm fine." She would be in just a minute, she told herself as she sank onto the bench. It was then that she saw her car. It looked like an accordion. She felt the sting of tears behind her eyes and quickly blinked them away.

"Look at me," Shane said.

When she turned, there was no trace of the laughter she'd come to expect in his eyes. All she saw was anger, ripe and ready to leap out. Her stomach knotted.

"Your eyes look all right," he said shortly. "How many fingers am I holding up?"

"Two." She took a deep breath. "I'm fine. It's my car that was hurt."

"It will recover. You're insured. But you're going to have a headache soon." He paused to run a hand gingerly along her temple. When she winced, he drew back and rose. "I'll be right back. Don't move."

She was fine, Jodie told herself as she closed her eyes.

"What happened?"

She glanced up to see Sheriff Dillon hurrying toward her with Alicia Finnerty at his side.

"The truck didn't stop," Jodie said.

"The driver plowed right into her," Alicia said. "I saw everything."

"Tell me about the truck," Dillon said, pulling out his notebook.

"It went right on through the intersection," Alicia said. "It was a hit-and-run. But I got the license plate."

"Good work, Ms. Finnerty," Dillon said.

As they continued to talk, Jodie closed her eyes and prayed that when she opened them again, it would all be a dream.

"Here."

It was Shane's voice and she felt the cup he placed in her hand. The scent told her it contained herbs.

"Don't you know that all the women in Castleton drink cappuccino now?" she asked.

"The one thing you don't need is caffeine. I got you some aspirin, too. Take them."

Closing her eyes again, she popped them into her mouth and then took a swallow of the tea.

"Finish it so the aspirin will start working."

Jodie looked down at the pale-green liquid. "I'm doing my best to change my image in this town and you're spoiling everything." But she took another swallow, then managed a smile as Dillon joined them.

"Are you all right?" Dillon asked.

"She's as shaky as hell, and she's going to have a nasty headache." Shane said. "I want to take her to a hospital."

"I'm fine," Jodie insisted. "I saw two fingers, and my pupils aren't dilated. You said so yourself. I'm not going to a hospital. And you can't have me admitted unless I agree to it."

"Fine," Shane said. Then he turned back to Dillon. "When you pick up the driver of that truck, I'd like to have a talk with him. He was speeding."

"Did you get a good look at him?"

"Not good enough to be able to recognize him. But I have a hunch who it was."

Dillon studied Shane for a moment. "Alicia Finnerty says it was a young man, probably from the college. She would have recognized Rutherford."

Setting her cup on the sidewalk, Jodie rose. "You can't be thinking that Billy would do something like that."

"What I think is that driver intentionally wanted to hit you," Shane said, then turned to Dillon. "I want to see him when you pick him up."

"It's my job to handle the driver. I'll call his license plate into the state police, and I'll arrange to have someone from Tate's Garage tow her car. You take her home."

SHANE DROVE the first mile in silence. He didn't trust himself to speak. Not while the image of the truck hurtling toward Jodie's car was still clear in his mind. He'd been over a hundred yards away. There'd been nothing he could do to stop it. Nothing. Every time he thought of that, the anger and the fear bubbled up anew.

"I don't know why you're so angry," Jodie said.

He shot her a look and then returned his gaze to the road. "He was speeding, and he rammed his truck into you, then left the scene of the crime. You could be suffering from more than a bump on your head."

"It was an accident."

"I don't believe in accidents," he replied.

"You can't possibly believe that Billy is responsible for making that young boy run into my car. I mean, there's no reason. It's absurd."

"Billy might feel that the quickest way to get inside that house is to get you out of it."

"But Irene and Sophie would still be there," she pointed out.

"They might be next on his list," Shane said, downshifting as he headed the car up a steep incline.

Jodie turned to him. "If you're trying to scare me, it's not working. I don't believe it. Billy would never—"

When her voice suddenly trailed off, Shane glanced at her. "What is it?"

"In the letter he wrote me, he said that his life was in danger, that mine might be, too."

Cursing under his breath, Shane pulled the car onto the shoulder and stopped. Then he turned to face Jodie. "What letter?"

"It came the first day you were here. It didn't have a stamp."

"The one I picked out of the snow. Why didn't you turn it over to Dillon or at least mention it before this?"

"I wanted to catch Billy by myself."

Because he wanted to shake her, Shane fisted his hands in his lap. "What else was in that letter?"

Jodie recited it verbatim, then said, "I thought he was just trying to get my sympathy."

"Five million dollars is a lot of money. There could be other people after it. Or someone could be after the reward, and they could see you as competition. You could be in real danger. So could Sophie and Irene."

Jodie glanced down at the rose that she still held in her hand, then back at Shane. "If there's any chance that they could be in danger... I—I think you were right. About working together, I mean. If the offer's still open—"

"It's not."

Jodie stared at him. "What do you mean it's not? You just said—"

"That I think you might be in danger. Five million dollars in bait can attract all kinds of sharks, so I want you to tell me everything you know. Dillon and I will take it from there."

"No. No way." She poked a finger into his chest. "If you think—"

The moment he grabbed her wrist, he knew it was a mistake. They were close, so close that he could feel the heat that they seemed to create together. It nearly singed his skin. And she felt it, too. He could see it in the way her eyes darkened and feel it in the way her pulse began to pound frantically beneath his fingers.

"I told you that I intend to catch Billy Rutherford, and I will, with or without your help."

Her words were only a buzz in his head. He had to let her go. There were so many reasons why he had to let her go. But for the life of him, he couldn't bring one of them to mind.

To hell with it, he thought as he pulled her close and covered her mouth with his. He wasted no time tempting or teasing this time. Instead, he swept his tongue into her mouth, determined to savor everything he had missed the last time.

But this was nothing like the last time. In a heartbeat, her mouth was as hungry as his, as if she, too, had sampled a forbidden flavor that she'd been craving ever since.

Her taste was darker, richer than he'd remembered. He couldn't get enough. Her hands gripped his shoulders to draw him closer, and he didn't resist. Here was the passion that he'd sensed simmering below the surface, the fire he'd been wanting to ignite. Without warning, it raced from her to him with all the fury and searing heat of a backdraft. He had no time to think, to prepare, before sensations battered through his system—the scent of her hair, fresh as rainwater; the desperate touch of those slender hands; the sound of her voice breathing his name when he nipped at her lip.

He swept his hands down her, then around to cup her breasts, and she moved closer to fill his hands...perfectly. His mind emptied, then filled with the image of taking her right in the front seat of his car. He slipped his hand beneath her dress and found the smooth silk of her thigh.

A car raced by on the road. Three sharp, staccato blasts on the horn mixed with the blare of rap music.

Go away. The words barely formed in his mind when he heard the squeal of brakes and the scatter of gravel.

"Don't stop," she said when he withdrew his hand. "Don't—"

"We're on the highway," he said as he gently set her back in her seat. It was broad daylight, and he'd very nearly taken her in the front seat of his car.

Her hands were still fisted in his jacket, her lips swollen from his kiss, her eyes filled with him. Desire cut through him and twisted in his gut. He still wanted her more than—

There was a knock at the window.

Shane whirled to glare at the young man staring at them through the glass. He was eighteen or nineteen, clean shaven, wearing boots and a camouflage jacket and pants.

Shane rolled down the window. "What do you want?" he growled. The boy swallowed, his eyes shifting nervously from Shane to Jodie. "Miss Freemont, I—I thought it was you." The boy's gaze wavered to Shane for a moment, then he swallowed again and said, "Are you all right? Do you want me to—"

"I'm fine, Clyde," Jodie interrupted. "This is Mr. Sullivan. He's doing some work on Rutherford House. Shane, this is Clyde Heffner. He's a student at the college."

Shane exchanged a curt nod with the boy, meeting his eyes steadily.

"Well, I..." Clyde swallowed again, "I was just...I thought...I guess I'd better get going." Clyde took a backward step, then turned to walk quickly back to his truck. Shane waited until he'd started the motor.

"Damn. I'm sorry—" Turning back to Jodie, he stopped short, narrowing his gaze the moment he saw what was in her eyes. Not the embarrassment or anger he was expecting, but merriment. He watched it spread slowly across her features until her whole face was illuminated with it, and her laughter bubbled up, filling the air.

"Aren't you upset about what he saw? The two of us necking like..." His throat dried up at the thought of how far he'd nearly taken it beyond necking. "You do realize what he thinks. He thinks we're..."

"Lovers." Nodding, she burst into a fresh wave of giggles. "He thinks we're...lovers."

Shane's gaze narrowed even further. "And that amuses you?"

She managed another nod. Then pressing a hand against her stomach, she continued. "Don't you see? I've been trying so hard to change my image in this town. And now they'll think that you and I, that we... Oh, I wish I'd thought fast enough to introduce you as the gardener."

"The gardener? What the hell good would that have done?"

"Then I could be the Lady Chatterly of Castleton, New York." She paused to wipe the corners of her eyes. "Do you suppose that Clyde will think that I had him help me build that thingamajiggy in the attic to trap myself lovers?"

Shane felt a smile tug at the corners of his mouth. "Not a chance."

"Rats!" She grinned at him. "Well, I guess I have no choice but to catch Billy, with or without your help. Which will it be?"

"I don't—"

"Let's look at this logically. If you really believe that Sophie and Irene and I are in danger—" she picked up the rose that was lying in her lap and drew in the scent again "—it's important that we catch Billy as soon as possible. And two heads are better than one. Besides, I know Billy better than you and Sheriff Dillon do."

Shane stared at her, fascinated. Who was Jodie Freemont? He'd never met a woman who pulled and pushed at him in so many ways. In the space of less than thirty minutes, he'd been silly with fear for her, wild with lust for her. In one moment, he wanted to protect her. In the next, he wanted to... Even now, he wanted to drag her close and recapture those sensations that had been pouring through him when Clyde had interrupted.

And there she sat, running a rose along the side of her face, talking about logic. Did she have any idea what she did to him?

His gaze suddenly narrowed and focused on the flower. "Where did you get that?"

Her lips curved. "Right where you left it. In my car."

He stared at her for a moment before replying, "I didn't put that rose in your car."

6

"YOU DIDN'T leave this rose in my car?" Jodie asked. "Then who—"

"When did you find it?"

"Right after work. It was lying on the passenger seat. And my car was locked."

"Why did you think I left it?"

"Because..." Jodie felt the heat rise in her cheeks. Because she hadn't stopped thinking of Shane for two days? Because he'd promised to *persuade* her. Because she'd been waiting for him to kiss her the way he had just moments ago. All of the above and more... Dragging her thoughts back, she said, "Because...you're a magician. I guess I figured you'd have no problem leaving a rose in a locked car."

"It doesn't take magic to break into a car. Just the right tools."

"But who...?" Jodie began.

"Billy." They spoke the name in unison, and Jodie let the flower drop into her lap.

"Was there a note with it?" Shane asked.

"No. Just some mistletoe tied into the ribbon."

Unwrapping the rose, Shane carefully examined it. "It's in one of those little tubes of water, but I don't imagine it would last too long in this cold."

Jodie stared at the rose. "Are you saying that if I'd left work early, I might have seen Billy?"

"My guess is, he was probably banking on the fact that you never leave early."

"Of course." She threw up her hands. "Predictable old Jodie. People can set their clocks by me. If only I'd broken my usual routine—"

"What exactly would you have done? Made a citizen's arrest? Tried to talk him into giving himself up?" He waved the flower angrily. "Beaten him into submission with this?"

"I—I would have thought of something."

"You need a keeper," Shane said, shaking his head. "I'll tell Dillon that Billy's back in town, and then—"

"Back? Wait a minute. When did he leave?" Jodie asked.

"Billy was seen in Florida yesterday," he explained and quickly filled her in on what Dillon had told him earlier. When he was finished, he said, "This rose means I was right. The trip to Florida was just to make us think he's gone. I want you to tell me everything you know."

Jodie turned to face him. "Only if you agree that we're partners."

Shane couldn't begin to identify the emotions running through him. He only knew that when she looked at him that way, it melted something deep inside some small part of himself that he'd worked to keep rock solid. "This man is dangerous. Don't you get that? Even if he didn't hire someone to run into you, he's responsible for making you vulnerable like this."

"If we work together, we can catch him faster," she said.

All of a sudden her logic was flawless. He wanted to shake her for it. He would have if he'd trusted himself to touch her again.

"So, do I capture Billy by myself or are we partners?"

He didn't want to think of what might happen if she tried to trap Billy by herself. But he couldn't prevent the image from slipping into his mind—the truck speeding toward her, slamming into her and spinning her car around until it was teetering crazily on two wheels—

"All right, we'll work together," he said, taking her extended hand in his. "As long as you're aware that there are going to be certain complications. Things you might not be prepared for."

"I'm a quick learner," Jodie assured him.

"I'll keep that in mind." He studied her intently for a moment. "Because if we work closely together, I'm going to want to kiss you again, and more."

"Oh," Jodie said.

Her eyes were truly windows to her soul. He could see everything she was feeling—the flash of fear, the bright leap of delight, and ripe color of the passion that darkened her irises. The fast beat of her pulse beneath his fingers was nearly his undoing. But he wasn't going to kiss her again, not when he wasn't sure he could stop.

Very carefully, he released her hand. "Just so you know. Forewarned is forearmed."

Who the hell was he warning, and why did he think it was going to do either of them any good? Abruptly, Shane lowered his gaze to his watch, then shifted the car into gear and pulled out on the road. "We have to get back to the house."

"I think we should talk, establish some ground rules."

"We'll talk later, and you can show me that letter

Billy dropped off in the mailbox. Right now, we can't be late for dinner.''

Jodie pressed a hand against her stomach. "Don't remind me. Maybe I should have let you take me to an emergency room. Even hospital food has to be better then Irene's.''

Shane grinned. "Relax. I won the coin toss.''

She shot him a skeptical look. "You cook?''

His grin widened as he turned into the driveway. "With a little magic I do.''

Jodie rolled her eyes. "Now, I know I should have gone to the emergency room.''

Opening the door, he circled to the trunk and flipped it open. "A little sleight of hand here, a little sleight of hand there, and voilà! Lasagna. Albert guarantees it.''

"They wouldn't hear of letting me do takeout. How did you talk them into it?''

Shane shot her a grin as Lazarus loped across the lawn to greet them. "Must be my charm.''

JODIE KNELT at her window tracing patterns in the frosted glass. The sky was filled with stars, and a fresh dusting of snow seemed to magnify their light. If she leaned close to the glass, she could just see Shane's apartment over the garage. It had been less than half an hour since she'd seen him climb the stairs, but it seemed like more.

From somewhere in the middle of the house came the muffled sound of metal clanging, then the faint rush of water. Sophie and Irene were preparing for bed. Just as soon as their rooms were dark, Shane was going to signal her so they could meet and discuss their plans for catching Billy.

Rising, she crossed to the mirror. It was the third

time she'd checked her clothes. The sweats had made her look like a sausage, and the skirt had seemed too formal. But the jeans...turning sideways she checked her profile and then frowned. Maybe the jeans were a mistake, too. Slim-fitting, they made her legs looked too skinny. And her top...the clingy material and scoop neck made her feel too exposed. Then watching her image in the mirror, she moved her hand slowly from her waist, down over her hip to her thigh until it was resting on the spot where Shane's hand had been when Clyde had interrupted them.

It took only that to rekindle the memory of the sensations that his touch had caused. The melting warmth followed by the swift, stinging pleasure that had pierced right through to her core. On unsteady legs, she stepped closer to the mirror. Her face was flushed, her lips parted, moist. Raising her hand, she brushed her fingers across them and felt the ache in her very center grow sharper.

What had Shane Sullivan done to her? She'd never felt like this before. So needy, so... Could a kiss change a person that much? They did in fairy tales. One had changed a frog into a prince. Another had awakened the sleeping Aurora from a one-hundred-year nap.

But this was real life, she reminded herself as she clasped her hands together in front of her. And if she wanted to really change, she had to do more than kiss Prince Charming. Changing depended on how well her plan worked. And the first step was to meet with Shane.

There'd been no chance to talk during dinner. They'd been much too busy stuffing themselves with Albert's lasagna. And laughing. Jodie's lips curved as she recalled how much Sophie and Irene had enjoyed the meal. As soon as they'd sat down at the table, Shane had shifted the conversation from her accident to Gilbert and Sullivan operettas, one of Irene's favorite topics. He had an amazing ability to talk about a wide range of subjects. Two nights ago, he'd discussed one of Lee's campaigns during the Civil War with Sophie and held his own. Tonight, Irene had been impressed enough to invite him to join the Gilbert and Sullivan Society at the college.

Of course, he'd declined. He wasn't sure how long he'd be in Castleton. Jodie pressed a hand against her chest where a little band seemed to be tightening. Unlike Billy, Shane was being honest with them about his temporary residence. As soon as he found the money and Billy was back in custody, he'd be gone. Like his namesake in the novel, he'd ride out of town after saving the day. That was the real-life ending of fairy tales.

The sound of the knock at her door had her whirling. *Shane?* She hurried to open it, but it was Sophie who was standing outside, carrying a tray.

"I figured you wouldn't be sleeping yet," she said as she sailed into the room and set the tray on a table. "I fixed you something to drink." She handed a mug to Jodie, then lifted the other one in salute. "It's an old Rutherford remedy for what ails you."

Jodie eyed the older woman and took a sip. She felt the burn of the liquid as it made its way down her throat, and smiled. "It's Scotch."

"Guaranteed to cure anything that ails you," Sophie said as she tipped her mug back.

"Even a broken heart?" Jodie blinked and stared at her drink. Where had that come from?

Sophie scowled at her. "I thought you were over Billy."

"I am."

"Ah," Sophie said, her gaze narrowing. "Shane is nothing like Billy."

"Except that he's going to leave just as soon as—"

"Just as soon as he finds the money and sees that Billy goes back to stand trial?"

Tilting her head to one side, Jodie studied the older woman. "How did you know—about Shane, I mean?"

Sophie waved a hand. "Do I look like I was born yesterday? On the same day we just happen to run into a handyman with references from the sheriff's wife, we also learn that Billy, our embezzling nephew, has jumped bail. It doesn't take a genius IQ to figure that if Billy is back in town, it's because he stashed some money here, and a lot of people are going to be on his tail. Is Shane private or is he some kind of undercover cop?"

"He's private, and I'm helping him."

"Good for you. Tell him I'd like to help, too. But we probably can't count on Irene. She was really taken in by Billy."

"We all were," Jodie said.

Sophie sighed. "I know. I was the one who insisted that he stay in this room. It hadn't been used in years, not since our parents died. It annoys me that we let him stay here."

Jodie glanced around. "I didn't know Billy used this room."

Sophie frowned. "I didn't mean to mention it. I told Irene we shouldn't. It might make you feel funny. If you want to move out—"

"No." She moved to the fireplace and ran her hand along the mantel. "Maybe he hid the money somewhere in this room. In a secret compartment or something.''

Sophie glanced around skeptically. ''He'd need a pretty big space for five million in cash.''

''I'll have to tell Shane.''

''Good idea.'' Sophie said as she set her mug on the tray and started toward the door. ''The light's still on in his apartment. And the night is young.'' In the hallway, she paused, turning back. ''You don't have to repeat your mother's mistake.''

Jodie stared at the door for a full minute after Sophie closed it. Her mother's mistake had been loving a man who couldn't be tied down. Moving to the window, she rubbed her hand across the pane, erasing the patterns she'd made earlier and then stared out into the darkness. No, she thought with sudden clarity. The mistake her mother had made was hiding in that house and not following the man she loved.

A sudden flash of light grabbed her attention. Narrowing her eyes, she leaned closer to the glass. When it appeared again, she pinpointed it near the path that led down to the lake. *Shane.* He must be signaling her.

She moved quickly to the door, then down the stairs feeling like an adventurer. When she reached the foyer, she stepped over Lazarus and hurried to the closet to grab her coat. Then she crept out on the porch and closed the door quietly behind her. The moment her foot touched the snow, she thought of her boots, but she wasn't going back. Instead, she edged her way quickly around to the side of the house.

The moonlight didn't seem as bright as it had from her window, and she hesitated for a moment, searching the area where the woods began. She saw nothing but darkness. After glancing back at the upstairs windows, she started toward the path. That was where she'd seen the flashes of light from her room.

The farther she got from the house, the more quickly she walked. The snowfall had been feathery, and she felt it slipping into her shoes with each step. When she reached the trees, she could just make out footsteps leading in the direction of the lake. Pausing, she peered into the darkness. Where was he?

Ahead of her, the light suddenly winked once, then again, and she started forward. He was headed for the lakeshore where they'd walked before. That was it. They could talk in complete privacy there.

And that wasn't all they could do there. Shane's earlier words drifted through her mind. *Forewarned is forearmed.* She stopped in her tracks. Should she go back to the house?

Through the trees, she saw the light wink again, and she headed toward it. The moon was even less helpful with big chunks of overhead branches blocking it out. Stumbling, she grabbed for a nearby tree trunk, then slowed her pace. When the path forked, she paused again to peer into the darkness. Nothing. Overhead, an owl called. A twig snapped to her left. Slowly, careful not to stumble again, she followed the sound. As trees pressed closer to the path, she kept her arms raised in front of her to prevent herself from walking into one of them. With each step new questions slipped into her mind.

Why hadn't she thought to bring her flashlight? Why hadn't she worn her boots? Why hadn't Shane waited for her?

That question was foremost in her mind when she finally stepped out of the trees and saw the flat white stretch of the lake in front of her. In the pale, thin moonlight, she could see that Shane wasn't sitting on the log waiting for her. A quick look around told her that he wasn't anywhere else, either.

She was alone.

Pressing her hand against the quick flutter of panic in her stomach, she scanned the area again. The lake-shore was definitely empty. No light flickering any-where. Ordering herself to be calm, she drew in a deep breath. She hadn't imagined it. Someone had used that light to draw her here to the lake.

Was this the way Shane broke in a new partner? Or was this his method of getting rid of them?

If he thought he could scare her off...

It was then that the thought struck her. *What if she hadn't been following Shane?*

Her heart began to pound so hard she thought it might leap right out of her chest. Billy had said he'd be in touch. He'd left the rose in her car. Whirling, she let her gaze scan the woods that pressed in on the lake. Nothing seemed to be moving. Not a shadow shifted.

"Billy," she called softly. "Are you there?"

A light winked on in the trees about twenty-five yards to her right. She hurried toward it. There was no path to guide her there, so she made her way slowly, one step at a time. She was counting her fifth when hands grabbed her from behind and pulled her against a hard chest.

7

JODIE STOMPED DOWN hard on her captor's foot, and the moment she heard the harsh, muffled groan, she threw all her weight forward, hoping to break free. The arms held her fast, and they toppled together to the ground. Though her opponent took most of it, the impact jarred the breath out of her, and before she could recover, she found herself flat on her back beneath a crushing weight.

"Don't make a sound." The words were barely more than a breath in her ear, but recognition poured through her. It was Shane. The instant he removed his hand from her mouth, she whispered, "Billy's getting away!"

His reply was a barely audible grunt. In the silence that followed, she heard the sound of twigs snapping, footsteps pounding. The moment Shane rolled free of her, she sat up, wiping the snow from her face. He grabbed her by the shoulders. "Stay here! I'll be back."

Before she could reply, he sprang to his feet and raced into the woods.

Jodie drew in a deep breath. *Stay here? And let Shane catch Billy by himself?*

"Not bloody likely," she muttered as she scrambled to her feet and headed in the direction Shane had taken. The going wasn't any easier than it had been coming in. There was no path and very little light was making its way through the branches overhead. Stumbling, she pitched forward and landed on the ground. Ignoring the pain in her knee and the stinging of her palms, she scrambled to her feet again, then peered into the darkness and listened. The sounds of the two men running grew fainter as the flickering light was swallowed up by the darkness. Then all she could hear was her own harsh breathing. For the first time, she felt the wet snow melting down the back of her neck and the numbness of her feet. Glancing around, she saw nothing but trees, pushing themselves up from the snow. She had no idea where she was or where the lake was anymore. Pushing down the quick skip of fear, she moved forward again.

As the trees grew sparser, the moonlight fell in larger patches and she increased her pace until she could see clearly enough to run. Just as she began to pick up some speed, she slid on some stones and skidded hard into a tree. For a second she balanced herself against it, struggling for breath. Then she raced ahead. As the ground began to slope sharply upward, she doubled her efforts until her lungs were burning, her heart pounding. Finally, she burst through the last of the trees.

Ahead of her, the ground fell away until it reached a black strip of road that curved out of sight on either side. Drawing in deep gulps of air, Jodie glanced quickly to the right and the left, but there was no sign of Shane. Then above the sound of her own harsh breathing, she heard a motor start up. Headlights suddenly pierced the darkness, and a car appeared around the curve in the road to her right. She started down the embankment and immediately discovered she'd underestimated the steepness of the slope. Sliding and skidding, she grabbed for the skeletons of the sturdy weeds that still poked their way out of the snow. When her foot came down hard on a rock, her ankle twisted and slipped out from under her. She fell hard on her backside, then began to roll over and over, picking up speed until she finally came to a stop in the slush at the side of the highway.

For a moment she lay perfectly still, waiting for the sharpness of the pain in her ankle to fade. It would, she knew. Any minute now. She drew in a deep breath. The sound of the car gradually grew fainter, and she became suddenly aware of the icy wetness seeping into her jeans and her hair. Lifting her hand, she saw it was streaked with dirt. She moved then, rolling to her knees and using her good foot to stand. The moment she was upright, she placed her weight gingerly on her weak ankle. It held and relief flooded through her. Just then Shane appeared around the curve and ran toward her.

"I told you to stay put," he said as he reached her.

Lifting her chin, she looked him straight in the eye. "So you could run off and catch Billy by yourself? No way!"

Shane scowled at her. "That was *your* plan, wasn't it? Sneaking off to the woods to meet with him without telling me."

"I did *not* sneak—"

"Don't bother denying it," Shane interrupted. "I saw him signal you with that light, and I saw you sneak around the back of the house and follow him into the woods."

"I thought I was following you!"

"Me?"

"You said you'd give me a signal once Irene and Sophie turned off their lights. When I saw the light flash, I thought you wanted me to meet you at the lake." She took a step toward him, then winced as she leaned too much weight on her ankle.

"You're hurt."

"I just twisted my ankle. It's fine." But he was already on his knees, probing it with gentle fingers. "Really."

"I think it's swollen...and your feet are soaked...your jeans, too." Rising, he slipped out of his jacket and wrapped her in it, then put his arm around her. "C'mon, the house is just around the curve. Do you think you can make it?"

"Of course. It's fine." She took two careful steps at his side. "See?"

Shane said nothing until he'd managed to synchronize his step with hers. "Let me get this straight. You saw a light flashing, and you thought I was signaling you to join me down at the lake?"

"That's where we talked the other night, and I figured..."

As she continued to explain why she'd let herself out of the house and run into the woods, Shane kept his eyes on the road ahead and tried to block the image she was creating in his mind. It was as impossible as stopping the flood of emotions that had been pounding through him since he'd first seen her run toward the woods.

He'd been at his window talking with Dillon on the phone when he'd spotted her on the front porch. At first, he'd thought she'd grown tired of waiting and was coming to get him. But then he'd seen the flash of light at the edge of the woods, and she'd headed toward it.

To rendezvous with Billy.

The thought had sent a torrent of emotions pouring through him. Anger and fear had been the easiest to recognize. But the jealousy had stunned him. It had sliced into his gut and twisted. It was still rolling around there even now.

"Of course, when I got to the lake, and you weren't waiting for me, I began to suspect that you weren't the person I'd followed into the woods."

Dragging his thoughts back, Shane glanced at her. "Was anyone at the lake when you got there?"

"No."

"Then how do you know it was Billy you followed?"

"Because of the letter. He said he'd be in touch, and then he left the rose in my car. Who else would it be?"

"Maybe the same person who nearly ran you down today. Careful," he cautioned as they turned into the driveway. "From now on, you're not meeting with Billy or with anyone you even think might be Billy unless I'm with you."

Jodie stopped short and turned to him. "I thought we were partners. You're beginning to sound like a boss."

"You're the one who said we needed ground rules. I just laid down the first one."

HE WAS ANGRY. She could see it in the studied control of his movements as he'd closed the door to the hallway to block off any noise they might make. He hadn't spoken since he'd lifted her onto the counter and carefully removed her socks and shoes, but the anger had sprung hot and bright in his eyes right after he'd fingered the swelling on her ankle.

She was going to be fine. She'd opened her mouth to tell him so, but that one look he'd given her had dried the words in her throat.

She watched him locate a first-aid kit and set an Ace bandage on the counter.

"Tell me if it hurts," he said as he gently gripped her foot, his fingers on her sole and his thumbs lying on the base of her toes.

"No," she said.

Increasing the pressure of his thumbs and moving them a fraction of an inch toward her instep, he said, "How about this?"

"No."

"Does it hurt here?"

"No," she repeated again and again as he moved his thumbs slowly over the top of her foot. She couldn't take her eyes off them and their steady progress. Her calves had turned to water. How in the world could she feel any pain with the sensations that were slowly spreading through her?

"How about this?"

"No." How could she tell him that any discomfort in her ankle paled compared to the ache that was beginning to tighten and burn in her center?

He was cupping her heel in his palm while his fingers pressed against her anklebones. He touched her nowhere else, yet it seemed he was touching her everywhere. She wanted him to touch her everywhere.

"Shane..."

He glanced up at her quickly. "That hurt?"

"No...I..." What in the world was the matter with her? They were alone in the kitchen. She wanted him. He wanted her. Why couldn't she think of anything to say? What good were those mottoes if they couldn't help her at a time like this? *Go For It*.

"It's not black and blue, but there is some swelling. You should ice it and wrap it in an Ace bandage." He bent to release her foot.

Go For It. The motto drummed in her head as she placed her hands on his to keep it on her ankle. "Don't stop."

Her words were followed by a humming silence.

Shane simply stared at her. The anger that had been rolling around inside him since he'd gotten a good look at her foot suddenly drained completely away. In its place was something he couldn't even put a name to. Three nights ago he'd said the same words to her, and if she hadn't stopped, he'd have made love to her right here in this very kitchen. It would have been crazy and wonderful. But tonight…something had changed.

If he made love to her now, even more would change. He slipped his hand from beneath hers and took a step back.

"What's wrong?" she asked.

"Nothing. I…" As his words trailed off, he saw the sudden hurt leap into her eyes. "Jodie, I…"

She raised a hand to stop him. "I'm sorry. I just thought…I mean you said…I thought you wanted to…"

"I did. I do." Because he wanted more than anything to reach out and touch her, he stuffed his hands into his pockets. "It's not that."

"What then?"

He wished the hell he knew. And how was he supposed to find the words to tell her what he didn't understand himself? She was looking at him, waiting. He cleared his throat. "It should be simple. But it's not." *Brilliant.* "It's…different."

"How is it different?"

"Because—because we're partners now," he improvised. "It's one of those unwritten rules of any partnership. It wouldn't be good to become too emo-

tionally involved because…well, if we made love tonight, we'd want to again, and that could distract us.
We could lose sight of our goal, to catch Billy. And
we don't want that to happen.''

"No," Jodie said.

"There you go. That's why it's a rule." Before he
could change his mind, Shane started for the kitchen
door. Only when he'd unlatched it and stepped out to
the porch did he let himself look back at her. He was
immediately sorry. She looked frail and defenseless,
and more than anything he wanted to go to her. But
if he did… "Lock this door. Then you need to take
a hot shower, ice that ankle and then wrap the Ace
bandage around it."

Jodie slid off the counter onto her good foot and
hurried toward the door. Shane closed it and waited
on the other side of the glass until she'd slid the dead
bolt home. Then he turned and walked away.

She watched him through the glass until he had
climbed the stairs at the side of the garage. With each
step, she wished him back, willed him back. But he
didn't even turn around and wave before he disappeared into the apartment.

Men found it incredibly easy to walk away from
her. Her father, then Billy. But she was over the pain
of those rejections. This time she felt numb. Maybe
she was building up calluses. Or maybe she was just
too dumb to believe it yet. The light went out in the
garage apartment, and her heart contracted painfully.

Turning, she made her way through the kitchen and
down the hall to the foyer. Lazarus was sleeping in
his usual spot at the foot of the stairs. As she moved
closer, she wondered if she had the energy to step
over him. Perhaps, she would just lie down beside
him and—

Out of the corner of her eye, she caught a movement. Her heart flew to her throat as she whirled to see what it was. The mirror. Relief flooded through her. She'd caught her own movement in the full-length mirror that hung on the closet door. That's what it must have been. Just to make sure, she felt along the wall and flipped on the light. What she saw nearly made her jump out of her skin again. If she hadn't known better, she would have sworn that she'd just stepped into a fun house. Her hair stood up in little spikes all over her head, and her face was streaked with dirt. What on earth had she rolled into? She looked like the swamp thing.

And she'd just tried to seduce a man. *Perfect timing*. It was a wonder he hadn't *run* up those stairs to his apartment! Why hadn't she realized how she must have looked sooner?

Because she'd been too busy looking at Shane, thinking about him, wanting him. She pressed a hand against her stomach where the ache had begun to build again. What in the world was wrong with her?

"Face it," she whispered to the image in the mirror. "You were blinded by lust."

Lazarus lifted his head. "Rrrf."

"Shhh," she whispered over her shoulder. "I'm not talking to you." Then she turned back to stare at her reflection. It was then that the thought struck her. She was just as trapped as her image was in the mirror. Just as trapped as her mother had been in that house for all those years. She'd waited her whole life for men to make the first move. And they were always going to walk away from her unless she did something about it.

The dog lumbered to his feet, his toenails scraping on the parquet floor as he headed for the kitchen.

"Are you leaving me, too, Lazarus?"

The dog made no reply as he continued on his path to the refrigerator.

With a sigh, Jodie followed him. There'd been edible food for dinner, and she knew that he'd just keep banging his head against the refrigerator door until he got some. All the while she filled his dish with lasagna, she considered what to do next. She *had* tried to break out of her mold. Mentally, she listed the changes she'd made in her life.

She'd switched from herbal tea to cappuccino.

She'd gone late to work…once.

And she'd attempted to wear a seductive outfit to her meeting with Shane.

No, scratch that. You couldn't count a sexy outfit once it was camouflaged by a coat and destroyed by road slush.

All in all, it was a rather pathetic list. She was going to have to do more than that. The question was…what?

Lazarus butted his head into her leg.

"All right. All right," she said as she set the dish in front of him. Then she frowned thoughtfully. "For starters, I won't give up."

His only reply was to begin devouring his feast.

"Thanks for your support."

She reached into the freezer for some ice and quickly made a pack for her ankle, which she would bring upstairs. Returning the ice cube trays, the motto on the refrigerator caught her eye. Tomorrow Is Another Day!

She frowned again. That had been Scarlett O'Hara's plan when Rhett Butler had walked out on her at the end of the book.

A fat lot of good that was going to do her. Who

wanted to follow the advice of Scarlett—the woman who had fallen for a dufus like Ashley Wilkes when she had a man like Rhett Butler crazy for her? To top it all off, she'd let Rhett walk away from her. Moving to the refrigerator, she ripped off the motto and was about to crumple it up when she suddenly paused and read it again.

"Tomorrow is another day."

"Rrrf," Lazarus said, looking up from his empty plate.

"That goes for you, too. No more lasagna tonight."

"RRrrrf?"

"I know, boy," she said, grabbing his collar and urging him out of the kitchen with her. "It's either feast or famine around here, but there will still be some left tomorrow. I promise."

Tomorrow...? She paused on the bottom step. "Maybe Scarlett did have the right idea, boy."

After all, there wasn't a woman in the world who didn't believe that Scarlett eventually got Rhett back.

THROUGH THE screened door, Shane watched Jodie giving last-minute instructions to the Rutherford sisters as they settled themselves in their car. Conversation at the breakfast table had centered on the Mistletoe Ball. It was finally *B Day,* as Sophie had put it. Tonight the whole town of Castleton would turn out to celebrate the season and support the college library. Irene and Sophie were spending the day on campus, overseeing the final preparations, and Jodie had the day off since she had to assist her boss at the ball.

Shane smothered a sudden yawn. He'd been on the phone with Dillon before dawn, filling him in on the chase through the woods, and they'd come up with a plan. Dillon would make sure that someone kept an eye on the ladies, and it was his job to stick close to Jodie. Then they'd wait for Billy to make his next move. And when Rutherford did, Shane was going to make sure it was Jodie who got the credit for capturing him. It was the one gift he could give her before he left.

Still, he was frowning as he watched Sophie shoot the car down the driveway. The bases were covered, contingencies prepared for, and patience was a necessary component of any successful operation, so why the hell did he feel so...anxious? No, it was more than that. He felt...empty.

Jodie, on the other hand, looked perfectly relaxed, as if she had nothing more to worry about than making her boss look good tonight. He studied her as she turned and started toward him. Her walk was easy, her smile confident. There was no sign that she was favoring her ankle, no indication that she was any the worse for wear after her accident. And there was absolutely no trace of the hurt he'd seen in her eyes just before he'd walked out of the kitchen last night. He'd never wanted to hurt her. He didn't now. And he wouldn't, if he kept his distance.

His decision to do just that had seemed so logical in the middle of the night. Why in hell was he so tied up in knots?

"Have you changed your mind and decided to break your unwritten rule?" Jodie asked as she stepped into the foyer.

Shane stared at her, nonplused. It was the last thing he'd expected her to say.

She grinned suddenly. "I couldn't resist. You're standing under the mistletoe."

"Jodie," he said, taking a quick step back, then

following her as she moved toward the kitchen. "About last night, I—"

She turned back to him then. "Yes?"

Looking into her eyes as she waited for him to finish had the words fading and a need twisting fresh in his stomach. "I don't want to hurt you."

"I'm a big girl," she said as she turned and poured herself a cup of coffee. "And there's something I have to ask you. Partner to partner."

"What?"

She took a sip of her coffee and made a face. "How do you drink this stuff? I'm really beginning to develop a taste for cappuccino, but *this*..."

"Try it with sugar and milk. The more bitter the taste, the more you load in."

She reached for the sugar bowl, turning to the counter and ordering herself to be calm as she did so. Some of the sugar spilled as she ladled it into her mug. She prayed that he wouldn't notice. She'd rehearsed her speech and practiced it in front of the mirror. But it was difficult to keep her mind on her plan when he was standing right in front of her. Lifting her coffee, she took a quick gulp. She couldn't taste a thing. "Thanks. This is much better."

"So, what did you want to ask me?"

As she turned, she caught a glimpse of the motto on the refrigerator door. *Tomorrow* had become today. She took a deep breath. "After this is all over and we catch Billy, I'd like to know if you'd be willing to hire me on?"

Shane gave her a puzzled look. "I don't have much need for a librarian."

"I meant as a bounty hunter. If you think about it, I'm really sort of one right now, as your partner, and I was hoping you might have room in your firm for me. Of course, I'd be willing to start at the bottom and work my way up.''

"Wait a minute." He reached for the coffeepot, drained it into his mug, swallowed deeply. "I think I've missed a chapter here. You have a great job as a librarian."

"But I don't want to be one anymore. What's an entry-level bounty hunter's job like anyway?"

Shane ran a hand through his hair. "You live in your car and drink coffee that tastes like cold sludge. Believe me, it's not something that you'd enjoy."

"I'd get used to it."

"Why would you want to?"

"You like it," she pointed out. "I've been doing a lot of thinking about the excitement of being on the road, moving from town to town, the thrill of the chase."

As he listened, she continued to rattle off all of the things he'd always liked about his job, never being tied down, the things that had begun to wear thin lately. "You still haven't explained why you want to make this sudden career change."

"Because I want to change everything about me. I had this idea that if I could just catch Billy and get my picture on the front page of the newspaper, it would change my image in the town forever. So I've been doing these little things, taking baby steps— drinking cappuccino, going late to work. It was pretty pathetic really. And I've finally realized that I have to do more than that—I have to change everything about me."

"Why? You're fine just the way you are. If this is about not wanting to be like your mother, you're not."

Jodie lifted her chin. "I'm going to make sure of

that. I've decided I want to be like my father, instead. Some of my librarian skills will transfer to bounty hunting."

He shot her a skeptical look. "Such as?"

"C'mon, I'll show you." Walking past him, she led the way up the stairs.

When she turned into her bedroom, Shane stopped dead in his tracks. But even as he stood in the doorway, her scent reached out to him, wrapped around him. Without moving, he scanned the room. It was just as neat as it had been three days ago when he'd searched it. His gaze moved to the chair beside her bed. Draped across its arm was the short nightie she slept in. He'd picked it up three days ago and rubbed it between his fingers. He'd had no trouble imagining what she'd look like wearing it. He had an even better idea now. He could picture exactly where the lace would skim the tops of those incredibly long legs or how that thin, cream-colored silk would feel beneath his hands as he slid it down...

"Let's toss the place." Jodie said, turning back to face him.

"What?" Shane shook his head to clear it.

"Search the room. Look for clues."

"You think the money's here?"

Moving to the doorway, she took his hand and pulled him into the room. "I forgot to tell you something last night. Sophie said that this was the room Billy used when he stayed with them."

"I've already checked it out."

Jodie's smile faded. "You have?"

"I've been here three days and three nights. I've searched the entire place. That's my job."

She sank onto the foot of the bed, deflated. "So the money's not here."

He knew exactly what she was feeling. He'd been feeling the same way himself. "I'm saying that I haven't found it yet. I still think it's in the house somewhere."

"Well, then…" Pausing, she gazed around the room. "We have to look for clues. What about the mattress?"

"I looked there first."

"The fireplace?"

"I tapped and jiggled every brick."

Eyes narrowed, she scanned the room again. "There's got to be a clue. When you live somewhere, you leave behind something of yourself." Springing up, she hurried toward the bookcase built into the wall on one side of the fireplace. "Books."

"I upended and flipped through each one of them."

"Did you check the titles?" Jodie asked as she began to skim her fingers along the spines. "I looked at them briefly when I first moved in. Librarian's curiosity. But I didn't know that this was where Billy had stayed." She paused her hand. "And I don't remember seeing this one." Pulling it off the shelf, she tapped the spine. "These are call numbers. *Historic Homes in Central New York.*" Flipping it open, she stared. "It's from the Castleton College Library. But I didn't bring it here."

Shane walked toward her. "That was the one I found tucked behind some others. I thought I'd struck pay dirt, but there was nothing in it."

Jodie sank down on the floor and opened the book. "Why would Billy hide it unless it's a clue?"

As she flipped through pages, running her finger quickly down each one, Shane joined her on the floor.

"I don't see Rutherford House mentioned by name. But it wouldn't have been known as Rutherford

House when it was first built. It should be in here, though. Sophie told me that it was once operated as an inn where stagecoaches stopped. That's why her grandfather bought it. He got it for a song. Most of the tycoons who bought summer places in upstate New York wanted them to be right on the lakefront. But old Jake Rutherford was a skinflint. Look. This could be it!''

Shane studied the page she thrust at him. "I suppose."

"It has the same two windows across the front, the same circular window in the attic. It's just the landscaping that's different, and there's no garage." Pausing, she skimmed the page quickly. "This chapter is about houses that were 'safe places' along the Underground Railroad."

"Underground railroad? A stagecoach inn is hardly underground."

"It wouldn't have to be. The route that slaves took to escape to Canada wasn't all actually under the ground. A lot of the trip was over land or over water." She was running her finger down the page, skimming it, and suddenly she stopped. "Look, it says here that the houses along the route often had secret spaces that the escaping slaves could hide in. That has to be it. Billy found one of the secret spaces. Don't you think?"

"I think it's a good thing my partner is a librarian," Shane said as he rose with her.

Setting the book down on the bed, Jodie scanned the room again. "What do we do? Start tapping the walls?"

"No, first we'll pace off the outside of the house. Then we'll pace each room, add up the dimensions and look for a discrepancy."

IT TOOK THEM fifteen minutes to fall into a pattern. For the sake of consistency, Jodie did all the pacing and Shane kept track of the math. After that it went like clockwork, and by the end of an hour, they'd paced off every single room and found only one discrepancy—a two-by-almost-three-foot space behind the bookcase in Jodie's room.

"It has to be here. Billy would have had easy access to it," Jodie said.

The books lay in piles on the floor and Shane was carefully running his hands over every shelf looking for a spring that would make the bookcase swing forward. "*If* there's a way in, he'd have easy access. Otherwise…"

"There has to be. I just *feel* it."

Shane grunted as he used his knuckles to tap once more along the back of the bookcase. From her vantagepoint on the floor a few feet away, she watched as he ran his hand carefully over, then under the top shelf. Then slowly, carefully, he repeated the same procedure on the next one. She was itching to help, but she didn't want to get in his way. He clearly knew what he was doing. His fingers moved inch by inch over the wood, pressing, then releasing, pressing and releasing, competently, thoroughly.

She'd touched him just that same way. Though she tried, she wasn't able to block the heat that moved through her, nor the ache that it left behind.

For a second she closed her eyes. *Get a grip, Freemont!* Melting into a puddle of lust was not part of the plan she'd come up with last night. Today, she was going to convince him that she was a valuable partner, as competent—well, almost as competent— as he was. During a long, sleepless night, she'd had plenty of time to visualize her goal, two of them in fact. She wanted two men—in different ways, of course. Billy in jail. Shane in her bed. She'd spent time picturing both scenes in her mind, especially the latter.

Opening her eyes, she let her gaze move over Shane's lean, hard shape. It was becoming very easy to picture herself beneath him, her limbs tangled with his. And once the image was lodged in her mind... She switched her gaze to his hands. He'd made his way to the next-to-the-bottom shelf.

Suddenly she was picturing his hands on her, stroking her shoulders, her thighs, her— She had to say something! Anything. She went with the first thing that popped into her head. "What made you become a bounty hunter?"

He shot her a surprised look.

She managed a smile. "I'm a librarian. I have an inquiring mind."

He turned his attention back to the shelf. "I got into it through the back door when I resigned from the FBI."

Jodie blinked. "You were an FBI agent?"

"Yeah. I had some problems with the rules."

"I can understand that. But why bounty hunting?"

"I like the hunt," Shane explained as he turned himself on his back and began running his hands over the underside of the shelf.

"Have you ever discovered a secret room before?"

"Yeah," he said, shifting to his stomach and starting on the last shelf.

"What was in it?"

"A bronze sculpture stolen from a museum in Athens."

"Well?" she prompted. "Tell me everything. Inquiring minds want to know."

"Not much to tell. Except that when I discovered it, I also found I was locked in."

"How did you get out?"

He turned to look at her then. "The thief let me out after twenty-four hours."

Her eyes narrowed. "Who was the thief? Why did he let you out? Did you get the sculpture? C'mon!"

Shaking his head, Shane smiled as he leaned back against the bookshelves. "You ought to be thinking of asking Mark Dillon for a job, not me. You have a real knack for cross-examination."

"You're stalling."

He raised his hands in a gesture of surrender. "Okay. The thief was my father, he let me out when he was sure I realized I wasn't going to get out by myself, and I got the artwork after we negotiated a deal."

Jodie stared at him. "Your father is a thief?"

Shane nodded. "And my mother is a career FBI agent."

Jodie shook her head. "And I thought my parents were mismatched. How did they...get along?"

"They didn't. The only thing they had in common was an obsession with their careers, and that made it impossible for them to stay together. I only met my father that one time. He and my mother had split before I was born. I rarely saw my mother once I was old enough to be sent to boarding schools." Shane couldn't have said what it meant to him when Jodie slipped her hand in his and held it tight. He never talked about his family. He rarely even thought of them anymore. But he knew that Jodie's simple gesture of sympathy had eased a pain he hadn't known existed.

"I don't care how good they were at their professions, they're very stupid people. And I hope you got the best of the deal you negotiated with your father.''

His lips curved. "I got to take the sculpture back to Greece as long as I gave him my word I wouldn't come after him again."

Jodie studied him. "And you agreed?"

Shane shrugged. "They were my terms. He agreed to them. Since then, we've managed to avoid each other professionally."

"That's when you resigned from the FBI, wasn't it?" Jodie asked.

"How did you...? You're very good."

She smiled. "So are you. You found that sculpture and returned it."

"Yeah. But I would have preferred to get out of that room by myself."

"Exactly. I know just how you feel."

He studied her for a moment. "I think you do."

The moment their eyes met and held, the silence began to hum between them, just as it had before. Her hand was still clasped in his, and Jodie searched her mind for something to say. Anything. But it was Shane who finally pulled away and spoke first. "I can't feel any handle to pull, no button to push, and I've pressed and poked against every square inch. If there's a space back there, there's no way to get to it. The wall in Sophie's bedroom is solid brick, and I'd be willing to bet that what lies behind this bookcase is solid brick, too."

"I can't give it up." Pausing, she frowned. "You must have run into a lot of brick walls, figuratively speaking. What do you usually do?"

"I try to get inside the head of the person I'm hunting and figure out what they'd do."

Jodie closed her eyes. "Okay. I'm Billy and I've

just noticed this possible hiding place. Or maybe I
noticed it before when I spent time here as a kid. But
I could never find a way to get to it. This time I…go
to the library and try to find if anything's been written
on it.'' She opened her eyes then. ''He probably knew
the house was once a stagecoach stop. That's pretty
common knowledge. And I remember he came to
work with me one day and did some research. That's
when he must have found that book.'' Scrambling to
her feet, she moved to the bed and picked up the
book. ''And he didn't have a chance to return it because he was arrested. So he hid it behind some other
books, hoping no one would notice it.'' Flipping
through, she located the chapter and began to skim it
again. ''It has to be here somewhere. It says that often
the secret spaces were on the second floor, but…the
access was from the floor above.''

''The attic.'' They said the words together, but it
was Jodie who made it to the door first.

8

Jodie made it to the top of the stairs first, then paused. "Be careful. The trap is still set. Or—" she turned and pinned him with a look "—I hope it is."

"I reset it after I was through searching up here."

Turning, she edged her way along the eaves, bending low until she reached the brick chimney that came through the floor. "It has to be somewhere along here." She dropped to her knees. "It's dark."

Shane turned on his pocket flashlight.

Jodie glanced at him. "I suppose that's standard equipment for bounty hunters."

"Never leave home without it."

Even knowing where to look, they couldn't see it at first. The edges of the wooden slats on the trapdoor fit flush against those on the floor. Shane ran his fingers over the faint line, then slipped them into a niche that looked like a knothole. He lifted it to reveal an opening, barely two feet by three with a ladder attached to the bricks. His light made little headway into the darkness.

"I think I should go down first," Jodie said.

Shane's brows rose. "I think the privilege goes to the senior partner."

"Is that another one of your unwritten rules? For a man who doesn't like them, you certainly come up with enough. I think we ought to flip for it."

"Forget it. If it's the coin I think it is, we'll both be calling heads."

"Spoilsport." She sat back on her heels. "C'mon. I found that book. And I didn't give up when we couldn't find any other access."

He could feel the excitement radiating from her. In the filtered light that managed to slip through the attic windows, he could see that she nearly glowed with it. He'd experienced the same feelings himself, hundreds of times—the rush that came when everything was about to come together. But it had never seemed so sharp, so potent before.

"Please." She touched him, one urgent hand on his arm, and he could deny her nothing.

"Be careful," he said. But she was already over the side.

He heard the crack of wood first, followed by her startled yell and a thud.

"Jodie? Are you all right?" He leaned over the side and pointed the light into the darkness. He saw just the top of her head. "Jodie?"

When she glanced up, he could make out her features in the light. "Are you all right?"

"I think so. One of the ladder steps broke and I landed on something. It slipped out from under my foot."

"Get into the far corner," he warned. "I'm coming down."

"There's no room."

"Move." He waited only until he could see that she'd followed orders, then bracing his arms on either side of the opening, Shane lowered himself into the hole and used his arms and legs to create friction on the walls as he slid downward. Then he squatted and gripped her elbows to help her stand.

"Let me—"

"Ouch!" They spoke the word in unison as their heads smacked together smartly.

"Damn! There's no room in here," Shane said.

"Told you."

Shane gripped her shoulders. "You're really all right?" Saying the words helped, but the fear that had gripped him when he'd heard her yell was still streaming through him. "For a moment there, I—" He wanted to shake her. He wanted to... Pulling her close, he covered her mouth with his. It was a mistake. It was exactly what he'd promised himself he wasn't going to do. It was heaven.

He drew back only to take a breath. "You've been driving me crazy. Out of my mind."

"I know. Me, too," she said as she struggled to get her arms around him. "Ouch...the bricks."

He turned, shifting her so that his back was against the longer wall and every inch of her was pressed against him. "Better?"

"Mmm."

He held her, savoring the way her body molded perfectly to his. Just another moment, and then he would... When she moved against him, the thought slipped away. He had to taste her again. Brushing his lips over hers, he took them on a journey along her jaw to her throat. The pulse pounding there started a drumbeat in his head.

"I want you," Jodie said.

The words—three simple words—sent a jolt of need through him. Then the joy, sweet and surprising, filled him. It took all his strength to draw back. "Jodie, we have to stop. Let me—"

The moment he tightened his hands at her waist,

she scooted up, wrapping her legs around him. "Don't you want me, too?" she asked.

"Want you?" For a moment he rested his cheek against hers. "I want you so much it hurts."

"Make love to me." The words were a whisper in his ear and he felt his control slipping away, along with any will he had to drag it back.

"Kiss me. Please. Right now." And then her mouth found his, and he was lost…

This kiss was so different than the others. It was the one rational thought that swirled through her mind as his tongue teased and tormented and his teeth aroused. Should she have known there were so many ways to kiss? So many pleasures to discover? This time she tasted a desperation that was a perfect match for her own.

His lips scorched her throat, his hands singed the skin at her waist as they slipped beneath her T-shirt, then slid up to cover her breasts. She hadn't known it was possible to need this much. So much that her whole body burned and ached and pounded. Any minute now she was sure it was going to shatter.

He drew back, lifting her with his hands, shifting until she was pressed against the narrow, smooth wall again.

She dug her fingers into his shoulders and gripped him with her legs. "Don't stop."

"I won't." His hands were on her wrists. "Let go for a minute. Brace your arms against the walls." Then he was unfastening her jeans. He might have worked faster if her skin hadn't been so damp, so hot. He had to taste it. Salty, smooth, and it smelled of that scent that had been haunting his dreams. Starving, he followed the path of the jeans with his mouth, down her stomach, her thigh, her knee.…

"I can't hold on."

"Don't," he said, as he wrapped her legs around him again, then pressed her against the wall so that he could reach his zipper and the foil packet in the wallet in his back pocket.

All she could feel now was the heat building inside her so fast it was melting her. At any minute she might explode from it. "Hurry."

He entered her in one swift thrust. He could think of nothing but the sheer perfection of their union as he pulled out slowly and drove in a second time, going deeper still. He felt her tighten around him. As the tremors moved through her, his heart seemed to stop. He went perfectly still. Pleasure, passion, desire, he thought he'd known them all before. But nothing had ever been like this. And he had to have more. He began to move then, pushing into her harder, faster. This time she met him thrust for thrust until he was trapped, surrounded by her, filled with her. When he felt her tighten and begin to convulse around him, he surrendered to the madness and to her.

When he could breathe again, think again, he said, "Are you all right?"

"I'm not sure. I think I've shattered into hundreds of little pieces."

He felt his lips curve and was surprised they had the energy to do it. "Me, too."

"We must be crazy."

"Probably suffering the aftereffects of a concussion. Did anyone ever tell you that your head is as hard as a rock?"

"Sure. Blame it on me." When she felt him start to withdraw, she said, "Don't move."

"I'm not sure I can. But we can't stay this way forever."

Jodie opened her eyes then and looked around. Her back was still pressed against the wall, and the space seemed even smaller than before. "How in the world did we…?"

He grinned. "Told you I was a magician."

She could feel the laughter bubble up in him even as her own burst free. Tightening her arms around him for a quick hug, she winced when her elbow scraped against brick.

"Here," he said as he carefully disengaged her legs and set her down. "I'd better get you out of here."

"You're not that good a magician."

"Just put your foot in my hands. I'll boost you up."

"No way. We have to look for the money first."

"There's no room," Shane pointed out.

"We're partners. We do everything together."

"If we stay down here, there's only one thing we're going to be doing together, and I'm not sure that we can survive a second round." He gave her one searing kiss to drive home his point.

"Okay." Her heart was already pounding, her blood thickening. She lifted her foot and placed it in his clasped hands.

"Is this your good foot?" he asked.

"Picky, picky," she said. Placing her hands on either wall, she braced herself until her head was above the attic floor. Then she slipped her arms through the opening and hoisted herself up, swung up one leg and crawled out of the hole. On hands and knees, she peered back in. "Hey, I need my clothes."

The jeans landed next to her. Pulling them on, she said, "And can you see what I slipped on? A book, I think."

"Yeah. I got it."

"Don't throw it. Hand it up." She lowered her arm as far as she could into the space and closed her fingers around it. It was old all right. Very gently, she brushed away the covering of dust on the cover. "It's a bible. Someone must have left it behind."

"Do me a favor. Tip it upside down and flip through the pages. See if anything falls out." Shane said.

Jodie did as he instructed. "Is this standard bounty hunter procedure?"

"You'd be surprised what you find tucked away in books."

"Not to mention what you might find if you read them."

"Okay, okay. You did a good job with that historic homes book."

"Thanks, partner. I'm not doing so well with this one. Nothing's falling out."

"Figures. I've got more bad news. If this is where Billy hid the five million, it's not here now."

Setting the book down, Jodie peered into the space. "It has to be."

Shane glanced up at her. "The only thing down here was that bible. The floor itself is solid. No sign of a trapdoor. And the space is exactly what we figured—two feet by three. That doesn't leave any room even if I find a loose brick or two."

A few minutes later, Shane pressed his back against one wall, his arms and feet against the other and inched his way up until he could rest his forearms on the attic floor and lever himself out of the space. The look on Jodie's face summed up exactly how he felt. "You look like you just lost your best friend."

"I was so sure."

He put his arm around her shoulders. "This happens all the time in the bounty hunting business."

"What do you do when it does?" she asked.

"Usually, I have a beer."

Jodie glanced at her watch. "Ten in the morning is a little early for a beer."

"We bounty hunters are made of sturdy stuff. We can pretty much drink beer at any hour of the day. But it's especially helpful when you run into a dead end. It relaxes you. The idea is to get your thoughts off the immediate failure and clear your mind. Get a fresh perspective."

She couldn't prevent her lips from twitching. "You clear your mind with beer?"

"Absolutely. Of course, there *is* an alternative. But it takes two people. It works especially well when you have a partner."

"Oh?"

He placed his hand on her cheek, using his thumb to tip up her face. Then he brushed his lips against hers. "As the senior partner, I'd be glad to give you a personal demonstration. But to really maximize the results, I think we should go downstairs—"

The ring of his cell phone cut him off.

"Hold that thought," he said as he tugged it free of his pocket. "Yeah? Uh-huh. She's right here with me...." Pausing, he winked at Jodie. "We didn't answer the door because we're busy in the attic searching for the money. Okay. We can be there in ten or fifteen minutes." He was frowning as he pocketed the phone.

"Who was it?" Jodie asked.

"Dillon. Something's happened that he won't talk about on the phone. He sent Mike Buckley out to watch the house, and he wants us in his office pronto.''

IT WAS BAD NEWS. Jodie'd had plenty of time to decide that while she'd showered and changed. Otherwise, why couldn't the sheriff have told Shane over the phone? The grim look on Dillon's face as they entered his office had the fear knotting in her stomach. ''Sophie and Irene?''

''They're fine,'' Dillon assured her as he waved her into a chair. ''Unless you want to count a last-minute emergency with the amount of shrimp ordered for tonight's ball. The state trooper who's keeping an eye on them is young and very enthusiastic about his work. I get detailed reports every hour, on the hour.''

''What's up, then?'' Shane asked. ''Has Billy been arrested down in Florida?''

Dillon glanced at him. ''What happened to your theory that his trip to Miami was just a smoke screen?''

''I'm at a point where I'm starting to reevaluate all my theories about this case.'' Quickly he filled Dillon in on Jodie's discovery of the secret hiding space and the fact that it had turned out to be a dead end.

''Interesting.'' Dillon tapped a pencil on his desk, then said, ''So you're more open to the idea that Billy may have already collected his ill-gotten gains and left town?''

''It's one possibility,'' Shane said.

''Then why did he write me that note, asking me to help him?'' Jodie asked. ''And who was that in the woods last night?''

''None of it seems to make sense,'' Dillon said, leaning back in his chair. ''Unless those incidents are the real smoke screen designed to make everyone believe Billy's still in town.''

"But that means he has to have a partner," Jodie said, "someone who's helping him out."

Dillon looked at her. "That's right. When Shane first came to me, he had a theory—one that I didn't buy—that Billy had staged the whole scenario of romancing you and then jilting you to make sure that no one would suspect that he'd left the money in your care until he could get back here for it. I told him he was dead wrong."

"I was," Shane said. "If you're thinking that Jodie *is* helping him, you're dead wrong now."

Dillon shifted his attention to Shane. "Maybe. But what if the break-ins and even the car accident are a series of staged events—to give Billy time to retrieve the money and get out of the country?"

Shane studied the sheriff for a moment. "What's happened to make you think that?"

"Yes, what?" Jodie demanded.

"Harry Tate called me from his garage about an hour ago and told me he'd found a lot of money packed into the spare tire well in the trunk of your car. He estimates about ten thousand dollars. Do you have any idea how it got there?"

Jodie simply stared at the sheriff. She could feel Shane looking at her. And she knew how it must look because her mind was doing an instant replay of everything that had happened since he'd come to town. Images flashed into her mind. Dropping the letter Billy had written so that Shane could see it. She could have planned that to distract him, to make him think that Billy was around. And then there was the flower, the same day that Billy had been spotted in Florida. And then she'd caught him in that trap. She pictured

Shane swinging back and forth by his feet. He'd probably think she'd planned to rendezvous with Billy and sprung the trap on him so that Billy could escape. Then she'd led him into the woods last night and to the secret hiding space this morning. More distractions. More scenes staged to convince him that Billy was still in town.

And then she'd seduced him. How was she ever going to convince him that she wasn't, she never could be——?

"She's not Billy's accomplice," Shane said.

Turning, she stared at him, but he was looking at the sheriff, his expression unreadable.

"You got any evidence?" Dillon asked. "Or are we talking hunches?"

"Someone led her into the woods last night. I saw the guy drive away. And there *was* an intruder in the attic the other night. I tangled with him."

"Somebody could be helping her," Dillon pointed out.

"True, but if she knew that money was in the trunk of her car, why would she arrange to be hit and take the chance that it would be found?"

Dillon nodded. "Good point."

"You're right about one thing, though. Billy's got an accomplice. And someone is definitely trying to make us believe it's Jodie."

"But why would they do that?" Jodie asked.

Shane turned to her then. "My guess is that they want you out of the way. They've rammed into your car, lured you into the woods, and now they're trying to get Dillon to arrest you."

Dillon frowned. "Ten thousand dollars is a lot of money to use to get her out of the way."

"Not compared to five million," Shane countered.

"If you're right, the money's still in the house," Jodie said. "And someone wants us very much to believe that it isn't."

Shane glanced at Dillon. "She's good."

"You've searched?" Dillon asked.

"Everywhere I can think of. Unless there's more than one secret hiding space."

"Sophie and Irene might know," Jodie said. "Maybe it's time we talked to them and laid it all out. They've lived in that house all their lives. If anyone knows where the rest of the money could be, it's one of them."

"Why did you do that?" Jodie asked the moment that they were out on the street.

"What?" Shane opened the passenger door and closed it once she'd settled herself inside.

"You talked Dillon out of believing I'm Billy's accomplice."

"I wouldn't go that far. Dillon has a way of making up his own mind. He's about as sharp as they come."

"I know. I was worried there for a minute until you came to my defense. Why?"

He flashed her a grin as he climbed behind the wheel. "What kind of a partner would I be if I didn't back you up?"

She laid a hand on his arm when he turned the key in the ignition. "No, I really want to know. I was sitting in there listening to what Dillon was saying and I started thinking of everything that's happened in the past few days. You came here believing that I'm Billy's accomplice. When I think of all the things that have happened since you got here, I don't know why you've changed your mind. Especially now that ten thousand dollars has turned up in my car. In your shoes, I don't think I could be so sure."

He studied her for a minute. "I'm sure."

"Why?"

Because I'm in love with you. The words popped into his head without warning. They stunned him. He practically had to bite his tongue to keep from saying them out loud. Not because they weren't true, but because he needed time to think about them, to make sure... He stared at the way her eyes had darkened with seriousness. With very little effort, he could make them darken even more. All he had to do was lean over and kiss her. He put his hands on the wheel and gripped it hard.

Oh, he was in love with her all right. It was what had sent him running out of the kitchen the night before babbling about the unwritten rules in a partnership.

"I'm waiting," she said. "Partners tell each other the whole truth. I think it's another one of those unwritten rules."

Shane prayed that lightning wouldn't strike him dead. "I can't really explain it. When you're a bounty hunter long enough, you develop this instinct, a sort of gut feeling about certain things. It tells me you're not working with Billy."

"But when you came here, didn't you have a gut feeling that I *was* working with Billy?"

"Yes." He started the car and pulled it out of the parking place.

"So, what changed your mind?"

"You couldn't make love with me and still be helping Billy at the same time."

He shot her a glance as he turned the corner and headed the car across campus toward Slocum Hall where the Mistletoe Ball would be held that night. She was mulling his answer over. He could almost hear the wheels turning inside her head. The answer he'd given her was true enough, but he wasn't sure it was the whole truth. He loved her for her honesty, loyalty and intelligence. Did his certainty about her innocence arise out of his knowledge of these qualities? Or did he believe in her because he was in love with her? A lot of fools had been led down that garden path.

When he'd pulled into a free parking spot and they'd climbed out of the car, she turned to him and said, "I made you break one of the unwritten rules of any partnership. What makes you so sure I didn't seduce you just to distract you?"

He grinned at her. "That's easy. Because you didn't seduce me. I seduced you."

"Ha," she said. "This from the man who practically ran out of the kitchen last night. I seduced you! I lured you into that secret space and I—"

Reaching out, Shane wrapped his hand around her neck and pulled her mouth to his. It was the quickest way he could think of to shut her up when he spotted Alicia Finnerty hurrying toward them. Hopefully, she hadn't been close enough to catch what they were arguing about. But whatever his intentions were, once her lips parted beneath his, he forgot all about them. One taste was all it took to have his heart pounding and his blood draining from his head.

"You *are* having an affair with Mr. Sullivan!"

Jodie drew back from Shane the moment she recognized the voice. Turning, she tried to summon up a smile. "Miss Finnerty. Nice morning."

"How could you do this to me?"

"I don't understand." Jodie frowned. "What did

I—?'' She let the question fade off because instead of looking the way she usually did—as if she'd just swallowed a canary—Alicia Finnerty looked as if she'd just lost her best friend.

"You're having an affair with Mr. Sullivan. When I heard the rumor this morning, I told everyone Clyde Heffner was just trying to make mischief. He swore he'd seen you kissing in this very car. And he was right, wasn't he?"

Stepping forward, Jodie took the older woman's hands in hers. "It's like this…. I…we…" She cast a desperate look over her shoulder at Shane.

"When you waved that rose at me yesterday and told me it was from your new lover, I thought you were just trying to throw me off the scent. I thought it was from Billy and you just didn't want anyone to know." Alicia pulled one of her hands free and fumbled in her pocket for a tissue. "My reputation will be ruined. How could you do this?"

"Miss Finnerty…" Jodie began.

"Clyde didn't have the whole story," Shane continued, putting his arm around Jodie and drawing her close. "It's more than an affair we're having."

Alicia Finnerty sniffed into her tissue. "It is?"

"It's much more serious than that," Shane assured her.

Alicia Finnerty stared at them. "You're not engaged! To a handyman?"

"She is trying to convince me to become a gardener," Shane said.

Jodie swallowed the laugh that threatened to bubble up. "No, we're not engaged."

"Well, not officially," Shane said. "Not yet, anyway. I haven't had time to get a ring." Raising Jodie's hand to his lips, he kissed her fingers. "You're the first to know, Miss Finnerty. Tell her, darling."

When Jodie said nothing, merely stared at him, he continued, "She's still getting used to the idea. So am I. But she literally swept me off my feet. Just this morning—"

Jodie stomped down hard on his instep, then turned to Alicia Finnerty. "Don't pay any..." The words faded away the moment she saw that the despair in the woman's eyes had turned to hope. "We...that is..."

"I was thinking that we might make an announcement tonight at the ball," Shane added.

"Oh, my," Alicia said. "Oh, my. Oh, my. I have to go. I have a lot to do before the ball tonight."

Jodie waited until the woman was out of earshot before she turned to Shane. She wanted to shake him. But she wanted to hug him more, so she went with the latter impulse and threw her arms around him. "You are the most exasperating, surprising, outrageous, kind, sweet man. Thank you."

"I was expecting a left hook or a right cross."

Leaning back, she smiled at him. "That's the second time today you came to my rescue. Did you see the look on Alicia's face? I never realized that she...I mean, she's so annoying at times. I never stopped to realize how important her image in the town is to her."

"Most people's are."

"When you leave—" The moment she said the word, Jodie found she couldn't finish the sentence. For a few humming seconds, it just hung in the air between them. She felt his fingers tighten on her hand. But it was the band of pain tightening around her heart that kept her from speaking. It was only when Shane opened his mouth that she quickly raised a hand to stop him and said, "Don't worry. I'll think of something and make sure that she gets the scoop. In the meantime, we did come here with a plan, I believe."

She'd taken three steps toward Slocum Hall when Dillon's car pulled up behind theirs.

"What's up?" Shane asked when the sheriff climbed out.

"I just got a call from the state trooper who's watching the ladies. He says that Sophie just had a close encounter with a potted poinsettia. It missed her only by inches."

9

"YOU CAN'T KEEP US from attending the ball," Irene said, setting her bag down on the kitchen table and turning to face Mark Dillon. "Sophie and I have to be there to see that everything runs smoothly. And if Jodie's not there, Angus Campbell will probably fire her."

"Not to mention that putting us under house arrest violates our constitutional rights," Sophie declared.

Dillon stared at them. "House arrest? Where did you get that idea?"

"You escort us home and your deputy is parked in our driveway. My sister and I weren't born yesterday," Sophie said.

Jodie very nearly smiled when Mark Dillon sent her a pleading look. Together, the Rutherford sisters presented a very formidable front. But how could she possibly smile when she was still picturing in her mind the shattered poinsettia plant only inches away from where Sophie had been standing?

"We want to call our lawyer," Sophie said.

Dillon turned back to the women. "Ladies, that won't be necessary. I just want to ask you a few questions."

"Not until we seek the advice of counsel," Sophie insisted.

"All right." Dillon threw up his hands in surrender. "If I give you my word that you can go to the ball, can I talk to you without waiting for your lawyer to show up?''

The two sisters exchanged looks, then turned back to the sheriff. Sophie nodded, and Irene said, ''I'll make a pot of tea.''

''No.'' Shane and Jodie spoke in unison.

''I could go for some coffee,'' Jodie added quickly.

''I'll fix it.'' Shane moved toward the counter. ''You ladies sit down and relax. You have a big evening ahead of you.''

''The point I want to make very clear,'' Dillon said as he glanced around the table, ''is that you all might be in serious danger.''

''Because a pot of flowers almost fell on me?'' Sophie asked.

''No. Because it's possible someone dropped that plant on purpose, just as someone might have rammed into Jodie's car yesterday on purpose.''

''That wasn't an accident?'' Sophie asked.

''Probably not,'' Dillon said.

''Why would anyone want to hurt Jodie?'' asked Irene.

Frowning thoughtfully, Sophie took her sister's hand. ''They think Billy hid the money he embezzled here in this house. If Jodie and I were out of the way, he might think he could convince you to help him get it out.''

''Or Irene could be next on his list,'' Dillon added.

Her color rising, Irene drew herself up to her full height in her chair. ''Billy would never hurt us.''

''It doesn't have to be Billy,'' Jodie said. ''It could be someone who's after the reward and wants to get us out of the way.''

''Or it could be someone else who's after the five

million dollars and doesn't care who he has to hurt to get it," Shane said.

"Even Billy could be in danger," Jodie added. "That's why we need your help."

For a moment, neither of the sisters spoke. Finally Sophie said, "They're right, Irene. Five million dollars is a lot of money. There could be people out there who might hurt Billy to get their hands on it. The best way to protect him would be to cooperate with the sheriff."

"All we want is some information. Do either of you have any idea where Billy might have hidden the money?" Dillon asked.

"Shane and I found a secret space behind the bookcase in my room," Jodie said. "But the money wasn't there. Do you know of any other secret spaces in the house? Or can you think of any other places where the money might be?"

Sophie shook her head. "I didn't even know about the space behind the bookcase. Did you, Irene?"

"No, and you didn't find any money," Irene pointed out. "So you have no proof that Billy stole anything. He's innocent just as he said he was."

"Irene—" Sophie began.

"I'm not going to listen." Clamping her hands to her ears, Irene rose from the table. "If you'll excuse me, I think I might just have time for a nap before I have to dress for the ball tonight."

Sophie waited until Irene had left the room before she rose with a sigh. "I'll try to talk some sense into her, but you can see what I'm up against."

When the two ladies had left, Shane passed out the three mugs of coffee he'd poured. "Those are two very loyal women."

"And stubborn," Dillon said.

"I don't think that they want to play any part in handing Billy over to the police," Jodie said. "Especially Irene."

Shane took a long drink of his coffee and began to pace. "We're right back where we started. We believe the money is in this house, but we don't know where. Rutherford wants to get it, but so far he can't. We think he's going to contact Jodie again, but so far he hasn't. It's a standoff. We have no idea what his next move will be. And in the meantime, Sophie and Jodie and perhaps even Irene are in danger."

For a few minutes, there was silence in the kitchen except for the sound of Shane's shoes wearing a path between the table and the door. Jodie took a sip of her coffee and watched him lean down to pick something up off the floor. *Mistletoe,* she thought as she watched him tuck the sprig back into the bunch over the kitchen door. In the few days since he'd hung it up, it had dried and begun to drop like rain all over the house. And then suddenly it struck her. "Mistletoe."

When the two men turned to stare at her, she said, "There was mistletoe tucked into the rose that Billy left in my car. Maybe it meant something."

"A mistletoe message?" Dillon asked skeptically.

Leaning forward, Jodie looked at Shane. "You said that a good bounty hunter tries to think like the man he's tracking. I'm trying to think like Billy would. If he leaves me a note, I might take it to the sheriff. But *mistletoe?* It's not anything concrete. Look at the reaction I'm getting."

"Go on," Shane said. "What do you think it means?"

"Maybe he intends to contact me at the ball tonight."

Dillon frowned. "Someone would be bound to see him."

"Right," Shane said. "But I don't think he intends to show up there. He'd just like us to believe he's going to. Jodie may be right. He might have planted that mistletoe in the hopes that it would convince us. A note would have been too obvious. In any case, he has nothing to lose by trying to focus our attention on the Mistletoe Ball on a night when this house will be empty."

"You're going to be at the ball?" Dillon asked.

"I'm taking Jodie," Shane said. "And thanks to Alicia Finnerty, everyone in town should know it by now. Do you have enough men to stake out this place tonight?"

Dillon nodded. "I can round up a few. But won't Billy suspect a trap?"

"We'll have to set it very carefully. Jodie, you and I will have to make an entrance at the ball, make sure we're seen," Shane said as he glanced at his watch. "I'll have to run a few errands, see if I can find a tux. I'm assuming you'll be there, too?"

Dillon made a face. "Monkey suit and all. Everyone in town turns out for this thing."

Shane nodded. "Once the ball is in full swing, we'll duck out and come back here."

"Me, too," Jodie said.

"It'll look too suspicious if we all disappear," Shane said.

"We're partners—"

"You'll *both* stay at the ball," Dillon said. "That's the only way we'll convince anyone that the house is really empty. Besides, I don't have enough men to wait in the woods and protect Sophie and Irene, too. If Billy's playing all the bases, they could still be in danger. I'll assign Mike Buckley to bodyguard them at the ball, and I'll put out word that it's his official assignment after the 'accident' this afternoon. That will be some explanation for why he's not out here sitting in the driveway in case Billy notices his sudden absence." Rising, he said, "I want your word that the two of you will stay at the ball."

"You've got it. Cooperating with law enforcement officers is another of those unwritten rules for all good bounty hunters," Shane said to Jodie before he followed Dillon out onto the porch.

"I hate rules," Jodie muttered.

SHE DIDN'T LOOK like a librarian.

Jodie took one hesitant step toward the mirror. The dress—what there was of it—was black. Reaching up, she fingered one of the thin straps at her shoulder, then turned sideways. The silky sheath molded every single curve of her body until it stopped at her ankles. But the slit in the side ran up to midthigh.

She'd tried it on in the store six months ago when she'd bought it for the cruise Billy had promised to take her on, but she hadn't remembered it clinging quite so...provocatively. Nor could she recall that much leg being revealed. She took a step toward the mirror. Her makeup was different, too. The gray shadow she'd applied with a liberal hand made her eyes seem enormous.

Whether it was the dress or the makeup, she didn't look anything like Jodie Freemont. And she didn't feel like her, either. Slowly Jodie smiled, and the image in the mirror smiled right back at her. She wasn't going to be Jodie Freemont anymore.

Tonight she would make sure that the whole town would see her in a brand-new light.

More importantly, Shane Sullivan was going to see her that way, too. Lifting her hand, she touched the sprig of mistletoe she had tucked in her hair for good luck.

At some point while she was getting herself ready, she'd come to terms with the fact that she wasn't personally going to capture Billy. She didn't even care about that anymore. The only thing that really mattered to her was Shane.

And once Billy was captured, Shane wouldn't have any reason to stay in town anymore.

Moving closer to the mirror, she studied her reflection. It was a clear case of wanting her cake and eating it, too. She wanted Billy behind bars, but she didn't want to lose Shane. No, it was more than that. Deep in her heart, she wanted the story he'd made up for Alicia Finnerty to be true. As she watched, she saw shock register on the other Jodie Freemont's face and felt a ripple of panic. Had she fallen in love with Shane Sullivan? Was that why she felt an arrow of pain pierce her heart whenever she thought of him leaving?

Straightening her shoulders, she said, "I'm not going to let him walk away from me."

She jumped and whirled around at the knock on her door.

"How do we look?" Irene asked as she fluttered her fan and sailed into the room.

Jodie stared at the two women. They were dressed in costumes from an earlier age, long satin dresses with hooped skirts.

"All the committee members are coming as characters out of *A Christmas Carol*. And Albert is dressing all his catering staff in Victorian costumes, too.

It was my idea,'' Irene explained as she spun in a circle. "What do you think?"

"We look like fools," Sophie grumbled. "Tell us the truth."

Moving toward them, Jodie gave them each a hug. "You look wonderful."

"Liar," Sophie muttered so only Jodie could hear.

"We have an extra costume if you'd like to borrow it," Irene said.

"Leave her be," Sophie said. "She looks great the way she is. Besides, Shane is waiting downstairs in the foyer. She can't keep her date waiting."

"Shane's here?" Jodie felt another ripple of panic in her stomach. It was one thing to formulate a plan and quite another to carry it out.

"Go for it," Sophie said softly as she nudged Jodie toward the door.

SHANE WAS PACING back and forth in the foyer. As soon as he realized what he was doing, he stopped. Lazarus, his head on his paws, was staring at him curiously.

"Nerves," Shane explained. "It's probably the tuxedo. I don't get to wear one as often as James Bond does."

Lazarus blinked once, then continued to stare.

"Yeah. It's not just the tux," Shane admitted with a frown. It was the woman who was going to walk down those stairs at any minute. He hadn't had this many butterflies flapping around in his stomach since...sometime back in his teens. Glancing down, he saw that he was in danger of crushing the flowers he'd brought for her. Drawing in a deep breath, Shane made himself relax his grip. Roses. He'd made sure that Alicia Finnerty had seen him buy them. And she'd followed him to the jewelry store, too. The box with the ring in it was burning a hole in his pocket. Miss Finnerty would have her scoop. And Jodie would have her wish.

After tonight, no one in town would ever think of her in the same way again.

Shane began to pace again. And once the ball was over and Billy was in jail, all he'd have to do was convince Jodie that the ring was for real, that he really wanted to marry her. He'd known when he was speaking the words out loud to Alicia Finnerty that it was what he wanted. And just thinking about it made his nerves tighten into hard knots.

If only he could make the evening absolutely perfect for her, but she wasn't going to be able to capture Billy. If he could have changed that, he would have. He'd spent the afternoon sorting through the possibilities, and there were several alternatives he might have pursued on his own behind Dillon's back. But he couldn't. He wouldn't take the risk with Jodie at his side.

"Shane?"

He looked up and when he saw her, the breath simply left his body. He opened his mouth to say something. Not a sound came out.

Then she was standing in front of him. He was vaguely aware that Sophie and Irene had followed her down the stairs, but he couldn't take his eyes off of Jodie. With an effort, he handed her the flowers. It took even more concentration to say, "You're... going to need a coat."

"It's in the closet," she said as she lifted the roses and drew in their scent.

He didn't move. Neither did she.

"I'll just put these in water," Sophie said.

"C'mon, Irene. Help me find where you've hidden all the vases."

"You look…lovely," Shane said.

"You don't look like a bounty hunter," she said, smiling up at him.

It was the smile, the laughter as it reached her eyes, that began to ease the paralysis gripping him. He started to reach for her, but held himself back. He had a plan, and he was going to carry it out.

"They've left us alone so that you can kiss me," Jodie said. "We're standing under the mistletoe."

Shane nearly groaned. "Jodie, I…" Taking her hands he raised them to his lips and kissed each palm. "This will have to do for now. If I really kiss you, we'll be late for the ball." Though it took great effort to release her, he kept his eyes steady on hers. "In fact, we won't make it at all."

"It's time to go," Irene announced as she led her sister back into the foyer.

"Yes," Shane murmured, moving to the closet to assist the two sisters and then Jodie with their coats. "After you, ladies."

Jodie stopped short the moment she stepped out the door and saw his car. "You put the top down!"

"It's the only way to ride in a convertible," Shane said.

"You'll freeze," Irene warned, as she took out the keys to her car.

"Santa always has the top down on his sleigh."

IRENE AND SOPHIE had done an amazing job turning Slocum Hall into a Christmas wonderland. In the afternoon, it had been tired looking, the peeling paint and dulled marble flooring only hinting at the glory of an earlier time. But tonight, it presented an entirely different image to the world.

Standing behind Jodie in the reception line, Shane let his eyes wander down the length of the wide foyer. Tiny Christmas lights twinkled everywhere. They glowed from the tree, wound their way up the railing of the curved staircase and cascaded from the balconies on the mezzanine level. Poinsettias banked each pillar and circled a raised platform at the far end of the room where a string quartet played old English carols. Wandering among the guests, waiters dressed in Victorian costumes offered champagne and hors d'oeuvres.

Mark Dillon was on the dance floor with his wife, making sure he was seen. He'd be leaving shortly, Shane figured as he shifted his gaze back to Jodie. The last arrivals were making their way through the line.

She'd been smiling and talking nearly nonstop for over an hour now, shaking hands and adeptly making sure that each one of the guests was introduced by name to her boss, a pompous bore named Angus Campbell, and a studious-looking bookworm type who was the newly elected president of the college.

It had taken Shane barely five minutes to be impressed at how good she was at her job, which currently consisted of making the two men at her side look good. Then he'd spent the past fifty minutes wondering why she underestimated herself. Or why the whole town did for that matter. Couldn't they see how competent she was? How beautiful?

Maybe they would after tonight. In spite of the fairy-tale transformation of the hall, it was Jodie who'd been catching everyone's eye since she'd arrived. It had been exactly what he'd wanted. And exactly what he didn't want, he realized as he watched the bookworm take her hand and lead her out onto the dance floor.

He'd taken one step after her when his arm was grabbed firmly. "You'll have your chance," Sophie said. "But I'd like a moment of your time if I could." Taking his arm, she marched him to a small alcove behind one of the pillars. Once there, Sophie pitched her voice low. "Alicia Finnerty says you went into a jewelry shop this afternoon."

Shane barely kept himself from reaching into his pocket and bringing out the box. "Yes."

"The way she's telling it, everyone is going to believe that you bought Jodie an engagement ring this afternoon. I'd like to know where she got the idea that you and Jodie were engaged. Jodie hasn't said anything."

Shane nearly wiggled in his seat. He hadn't felt this guilty since he was a kid. "I'm afraid I told her that."

"You…" Sophie let her sentence trail off and simply stared at him for a moment. "Then you're really engaged to Jodie?"

"Not exactly," Shane said, wanting very badly to loosen his collar. "It's…a long story."

"Hmm," Sophie said, studying him closely. Then suddenly she gave him a curt nod. "I'll trust you to make sure it has a happy ending."

"Yes, ma'am," Shane said, rising as she did and watching her charge back to join her sister. He could only hope that Sophie's trust wasn't misplaced.

FOR THE FOURTH TIME in as many minutes, Jodie found herself scanning the crowd to find Shane. He was still where he'd been sixty seconds earlier, dancing with Kathy Dillon. That meant the sheriff had made his getaway. At least one part of the evening was going as scheduled.

On the other hand, her plan to make this night with Shane unforgettable was hitting some rough spots. Shifting her gaze to Angus Campbell, her boss, she watched his lips move and dragged her attention back to the conversation. He was still droning on and on about how someone had donated some rare books to a downstate college library by accident. It had allowed them to build a new library.

Wonderful! It was just like Angus to obsess over something like that. As for herself, she was obsessing about the tall, handsome man in the tuxedo who was currently dancing much too close to his cousin, several times removed. And it wasn't jealousy she was feeling, she assured herself. It was frustration. It had been two hours since they'd arrived at the ball and she hadn't had a minute alone with Shane.

She hadn't even danced with him. Quickly she stifled the impulse to race out on the dance floor and drag him away from Kathy Dillon. She'd have to be a linebacker to do it since she was completely surrounded by rather large men. Hal Richardson, one of the college's most generous alumni, blocked her path from the front, and President Willman and Angus flanked her on either side. Then there were other men who were standing just outside the circle, and they seemed to be hanging on every word that Angus was saying.

"...don't you think, Miss Freemont?"

The moment Jodie heard her name, she tried desperately to dredge up the rest of the question in her mind. It was Hal Richardson who'd asked it, and he'd made several very generous donations to the library in the past. It wouldn't do at all to offend him. "I'm sorry," she said, flashing him her best smile. "My mind was wandering a little. What was it you asked?"

The large man smiled at her. "Nothing important, little lady."

"Mr. Richardson was just saying that if someone left our library a couple of million dollars worth of rare books, it would rob us all of our annual Mistletoe Ball," Angus said, frowning at her.

"Not to mention the company of this very lovely young lady," Hal said. "And we're boring her to death, gentleman. May I have this dance, Ms. Freemont?"

"I would love to dance with you." Jodie beamed another smile at him as he led her to the dance floor. Escape was only a dance away.

"SHE'S THE BELLE of the ball, isn't she?"

Shane shifted his gaze from Jodie to the waiter who stood at his side, holding a tray of flutes brimming with champagne. It took him a second to recognize Nadine in the Victorian costume. "You sound surprised."

"She was always the quiet, mousy type. The dress makes a difference, but still…"

"What?"

She shook her head. "I don't understand how a man could be so totally smitten by her."

Was it that obvious, Shane thought with a frown. Or was she referring to Hal Richardson who was holding Jodie altogether too close on the dance floor? He took one step forward before he caught himself.

"Don't tell me she's got you caught in her net, too?" Nadine said. "Have some champagne."

Shane raised the glass he was holding. "I still have some."

"It's flat by now." Nadine nipped the glass out of his hand and replaced it with a fresh one. "Enjoy. There's plenty more where it came from."

The sound of Jodie's laugh snatched his attention back to the dance floor. So she found millionaires with silver threaded through their hair amusing. In about two more minutes, he was going to take great pleasure in wiping that smile off Hal Richardson's face. And then he was going to find the courage to do what Sophie had trusted him to do an hour ago.

"HE'S A VERY LUCKY MAN."

Jodie stumbled, then felt her foot come down hard on her partner's shoe. "Mr. Richardson, I'm so sorry."

"Hal, please. Any woman who steps on my toes more than once while we're dancing *must* call me by my first name. It's one of my rules."

Jodie smiled at him. "Hal, I'm sorry for the other times I stepped on you, too."

"No need. As I said, he's a lucky man, and you don't have to worry your head about that blonde he's talking to."

As he swung her around, Jodie caught a glimpse of Nadine just turning away from Shane.

"She doesn't have a chance," Richardson said. "The whole time we've been dancing, he hasn't taken his eyes off of you except to occasionally glare daggers at me."

"Really?"

Hal winked at her. "I think you ought to go over there right now and ask him to dance before he invites me to step outside."

Jodie glanced quickly over to see if Angus was watching her. He was.

"I'll take care of your boss."

"You're a sweetheart," Jodie said, beaming a smile at him before she turned and threaded her way across the dance floor.

"Care to dance?" she asked, lifting the flute from Shane's hand and taking a long swallow of champagne. The fizz tickled her nose, then bubbled at the back of her throat. She took another drink.

"Enough." He took the glass and set it on the tray of a passing waiter.

"You're wasting very good champagne," Jodie protested. "Irene only orders the best, and I haven't had a chance to sample it because I've been so busy talking."

"We can steal a bottle when we leave. I don't want anything clouding your senses when I finally get you alone."

She felt the quick skip of pleasure move through her, then grow as he threaded his fingers through hers and placed his other hand at the small of her back. "I wish we could leave now. I wish..." But she couldn't tell him what she truly wished. What if he didn't feel the same way? What if he—

"Soon," he murmured. She felt his lips brush her temple, and as he drew her steadily closer, until she was pressed close against him, Jodie became aware of how every one of her senses was heightened. The lights draped from the balcony overhead brightened, the scent of the Christmas tree grew sharper. And the violins, so muted before, rose clearly above the chatter of the crowd. The string quartet was playing a popular Christmas tune, but the title seemed to be just out of reach. Shane swung her in a circle, and her head began to spin pleasantly. When he drew back slightly, she moved forward, unwilling to give up the sensation.

"Is that mistletoe you're wearing in your hair?"

"I thought you'd never notice," Jodie said.

"I'm glad that man you were dancing with didn't. I might have had to put him out of commission."

"Hal is a very nice man," she murmured. When the room seemed to spin again, she found a place to rest her head right in the crook of his shoulder.

"Hal? It was Mr. Richardson in the reception line."

"You have to call him Hal after you step on his toes more than once. It's one of his rules."

"I'm sure it is."

"I think I like his rules better than yours."

"I think I *will* have to put him out of commission."

"You're jealous." She lifted her head from his shoulder, and was surprised at the effort it took. "Hal said you were."

"It might be healthier for *Hal* if you broke his rule and went back to calling him Mr. Richardson."

Jodie started to laugh, but a sudden wave of dizziness swept over her. The sound of the violins faded and her vision seemed to gray.

"Jodie?" The grip of his hands was firm on her arms.

"I'm fine," she assured him. "I was just dizzy for a second." But he was already steering her to the edge of the dancers. "I don't want to stop dancing."

"I'm going to get you some fresh air and some food."

"Mr. Sullivan."

"Buckley? Is that you?" Jodie asked. He was dressed in the same kind of Victorian era costumes the waiters were wearing.

Sheriff Dillon's deputy cleared his throat. "Yes, ma'am. I'm working undercover tonight." Then he turned to Shane. "I'm acting under orders, sir. Sheriff Dillon told me that I was supposed to report to you before I left."

"Why are you leaving?" Shane asked.

Mike Buckley cleared his throat again. "There's been a big traffic accident on Route 20, east of the village. Several cars piled up when a tractor-trailer jackknifed. The state police have already summoned Sheriff Dillon to the scene, and I'm to tell you that he had to call a few of the men in from Rutherford House to help out. He said you'd know what to do."

"Thanks, Buckley," Shane said.

"What *are* we going to do?" Jodie asked the moment the young deputy walked away.

Shane steered her toward a set of French doors that opened to a terrace. "First, I'm going to get you some fresh air and a plate of food, and then I'll leave for Rutherford House."

"I'm going, too." Jodie insisted as a second wave of dizziness washed over her. She stumbled, and only Shane's grip on her prevented her from falling.

"You're not in any condition to come with me," Shane said as he slipped off his jacket and draped it over her shoulders. "Besides, someone has to be here to keep an eye on Sophie and Irene."

"I'll be fine in a minute," Jodie said. "And if Billy is falling for our trap, then he could be at Rutherford House even now. Sophie and Irene should be safe, especially here in this crowd."

Shane sighed. "Jodie, I…"

She moved toward the balcony that framed the terrace, careful to put one foot in front of the other.

''See, I can walk a straight line. I just had half a glass of champagne on an empty stomach.''

''I'm going back in to get you some food. Then, we'll see.''

Jodie waited until Shane disappeared through the French doors before she sank onto the nearest bench and dropped her head into her hands. Champagne had never made her this dizzy before. Pressing her hands against her temples, she fought against the whirling sensation.

''Jodie?''

The voice seemed to come from far away. Jodie struggled against the grayness that was pressing in on her as she felt strong arms go around her, drawing her to her feet. She had to convince Shane that she was all right. Slipping her arms around his neck for support, she prayed that she'd be able to fake it long enough to convince him. But when she opened her eyes, it wasn't Shane's eyes she was looking into. It was...

''Billy?''

10

"AT YOUR SERVICE, sugar," Billy said.

"But you—you're not supposed to be here." Too late she realized what he must be thinking about the fact that she'd thrown her arms around him. He had drawn her closer until her body was pressed against his. She moved her hands to his shoulders, but before she could prevent it, his mouth was on hers and another wave of dizziness hit her. Her head seemed to be filled with swirling champagne bubbles.

"Whoa, wait a minute, sugar," Billy said as he drew back and settled her on the bench. "I never used to make you swoon when I kissed you. Did you miss me that much?"

"I had some champagne on an empty stomach," Jodie said, struggling to clear her mind. The surge of adrenaline that had moved through her the moment she'd recognized him was helping. He was wearing a Victorian costume, just as all the waiters were. Between that and the black wig, it was no wonder no one had recognized him. But she'd come to know and despise his smug good looks too well not to identify him immediately.

She knew she had to try to keep him talking until Shane came back... "What are you doing here?"

"I sent you a message." Taking her hands, he drew her to her feet. "I was almost sure you'd understand the mistletoe. And I thought you'd be happier to see me."

"Billy, I—" A sudden increase in the volume of violin music alerted Jodie to the fact that the terrace doors had opened again. *Shane...*

"Whoever it is, get rid of them," Billy whispered before he shifted to the side.

"Miss Freemont?"

Jodie blinked as Alicia Finnerty stepped onto the terrace. "Miss Finnerty—"

"I just had to know. Has he done it yet?"

Jodie shook her head to clear it. "Has he... Has *who* done *what?*"

"Mr. Sullivan. Has he popped the question?" Alicia asked.

"No," Jodie said, praying that she could find the right words before they spun away on puffs of air. "But...he's coming back any minute."

"Ohhh, I'm so sorry." Alicia hurriedly backed toward the door. "I'll be waiting just inside."

The moment the woman closed the terrace doors, Billy was pulling her toward the steps. "Is she right about that? Is this Sullivan guy popping the question?"

"No," Jodie managed. "No, he made that up for Miss Finnerty...because...her feelings were hurt.... Wait." They were halfway down the stairs before she finally managed to stumble against him and halt his progress. *Stall.* It was all she could think of to do. Shane had to be coming back any minute.

"What's the matter with you? Are you drunk?" Billy asked.

Jodie shook her head again. "I told you. I just had a half a glass of champagne on an empty stomach. Shane went to get me some food. He'll be—"

He frowned at her as he grabbed the lapels of her jacket to steady her. "Forget him. He won't be back."

She gripped his wrists. "Why not? What have you done to him?"

Billy frowned. "There *is* something going on between you, isn't there? Nadine told me, but I didn't believe her."

"Tell me what you've done to Shane!"

Billy drew her closer. "I could make you forget him. I never lied to you, Jodie. I couldn't contact you these past months. If I had, someone might have suspected that I'd hidden the money here. But the feelings that I had for you were…different. We could still—"

"What have you done to him?"

Slowly, Billy dropped his hands. "Nothing. That's Nadine's job."

"Nadine? What's Nadine got to do with this?"

"She's my partner, and tonight she's handling your handyman. Not that she'll have any trouble after the drug takes effect."

"Drug?"

"In his champagne. I imagine it was starting to kick in about the time he brought you out to the terrace. By now, he ought to be felled like a tree."

"But Shane didn't—" Jodie bit down hard on her lip before she blurted out the rest of the sentence. What was the matter with her? She didn't want Billy to know that Shane hadn't drunk the champagne Nadine had given him. And she was almost sure he hadn't. Concentrating very hard, she tried to picture exactly what she'd seen when she'd been dancing with Hal Richardson—Nadine handing Shane a glass, then walking away. The glass had still been filled to the brim when she'd taken it from him and…

Jodie blinked as she felt one of the swirling champagne bubbles pop in her head. *She* was the one who'd been drugged, not Shane. And she couldn't let Billy know that. The thought had barely spun through her mind before she stumbled and felt herself pitching forward. The snowdrift was reaching out to her, beckoning her into its softness when, suddenly, Billy's arm jerked her back against him.

"I've never seen you like this. You *are* drunk."

Jodie drew in a deep gulp of air. How much of the drug had she swallowed? How long would it take to fell *her* like a tree? Where was Shane?

"If you're stalling in hopes that Sullivan will come racing out here, the way he did last night in the woods, forget it. Nadine's got a syringe ready to pump more into him if she didn't slip enough into that drink."

As the fear twisted tight and cold in her stomach, Jodie willed the gray fog pushing at the edge of her mind to recede. "I slipped. I'm not drunk, and I'm not waiting for anyone to race out after me. I can take care of myself."

Billy's eyes narrowed. "You've changed."

When he began to pull her along the path once more, Jodie glanced down at her feet and concentrated on watching them make slow, steady progress. It seemed to help. *Visualize Your Goal.* Don't think about Shane, or the syringe. All she had to do was put one foot in front of the other until she got to the car, and then she could sit.

"Here we are," Billy said.

Jodie shifted her gaze from her shoes to the car— Shane's red convertible.

"What in hell is the top doing down in this weather?" Billy asked.

Jodie slapped her hand down on the top the moment he started to raise it. "Santa always rides with the top down."

"Santa?"

"Have you ever seen him put the top up on his sleigh?"

"What the hell are you talking about?"

"It's one of Shane's unwritten rules. He has a lot. If we're taking his car, we have to stick to them."

"Fine," Billy said as he opened the door and settled her in. "We'll do it your way. Maybe the cold air will sober you up." Climbing into the driver's seat, he fished under the seat to retrieve the keys. "Valet parking simplifies everything."

"Why are we taking Shane's car?"

"So whoever the sheriff has staked out at Rutherford House will think it's Sullivan bringing you there."

"Aha." Very carefully, Jodie reached for the seat belt. *Visualize Your Goal.* Wrapping her fingers around the strap, she pulled, and inserted it into the slot. Excellent. If she just pictured each little movement she had to make in her mind, she would be fine. What next? She glanced around and felt another wave of dizziness. Quickly, she closed her eyes. The motion of the car, the purr of the motor were so soothing. She rested her head against the seat. For just a moment. The gray fog was all around, ready to swallow her up. She snapped her eyes open and began tapping her feet. Then she reached for the radio and began punching buttons at random.

"Would you stop that? I don't remember you being such a fidgeter before," Billy said.

Jodie snatched her hand back. What else could she do? *Visualize Your Goal. There's More Than One Way to Skin A Cat.* Drawing in a deep breath, Jodie prayed that she hadn't recited the slogans out loud. If she couldn't move, she'd have to talk. Turning in her seat, she concentrated on Billy's profile and said the first thing that came into her head. "Where did you hide the money?"

Billy glanced at her, then back at the road. "Not so fast, sugar. I haven't come this far to spill the beans before I get my hands on it."

"Does Nadine know where it is?"

"I'm the only one who knows where it is."

"But it's somewhere in Rutherford House, isn't it?"

"You could say that."

"I just did. Say it, I mean."

"But you don't know where. And you should. Thanks to you, I discovered everything I needed to hide that money right in your college library."

This time the wave of dizziness seemed stronger. Jodie rested her head against the seat again as images, phrases and scenes from the evening began to swirl in her head, much the way the bubbles had earlier. Shane was dancing with Kathy Dillon again and she had to get to him. Only Angus Campbell held her back, droning on and on about rare books. Then suddenly she could see Nadine, stalking Shane, getting closer and closer with a three-foot syringe raised over her head. Finally, as if a shutter clicked, all she could see was books swirling around her. Old ones with faded leather bindings whirling around and around, blotting out the lights...

Jodie snapped her eyes open. She knew exactly where the money was.

"THIS IS IT, ISN'T IT?" Alicia Finnerty asked, fluttering her hands as she stepped into Shane's path.

"Yes," Shane said. What he wanted to say was, *It's the last straw.* Alicia Finnerty was the third person to get in his way since he'd made his way through the line at the buffet table. First it had been Irene, insisting that he add some shrimp to Jodie's plate, then it had been Angus Campbell, wondering where Jodie had disappeared to. Drawing in a deep breath, he prayed for patience.

"She's waiting for you," Alicia said.

"Yes," he repeated as he glanced past the Finnerty woman's shoulder to the French doors that had been his goal for the past twenty minutes. The woman he'd waited all evening to propose to was outside on the terrace, possibly freezing to death. "If you'll excuse me, Miss Finnerty."

"Oh, of course," Alicia said, backing away. "Good luck."

Shane took three steps and found his path blocked again, this time by Nadine.

"We have to talk," she said.

"Not right now," Shane said. "I have to save a lady from hypothermia."

"You may have to save her from more than that. Billy Rutherford's got her."

"HOW'S YOUR HEAD?" Billy asked as he stopped the car in the driveway of Rutherford House.

"Fine," Jodie said and prayed that she could fight off the next dizzy spell.

"Be very sure of that," Billy said, gripping her shoulders and turning her so that she had to meet his eyes directly. "I have a gun in my pocket, but I don't want to have to use it."

"No," she said. "You might have an accident."

Billy gave her a little shake. "I know how to use it, and I will. Do you understand?"

The fear that sprinted through her helped to clear her head.

"Do exactly as I say. There's someone approaching the house now. When I let you out the passenger side, I want you to wave and tell him that we've come back to get the check Irene is going to present to the library tonight. Tell him that she left it in her room by mistake. We'll only be a minute. Have you got that?"

Jodie nodded, then let out the breath she was holding when Billy released her and climbed out of the car. Surely Sheriff Dillon wouldn't be fooled by such a lame excuse. She had to hope that—

"Now," Billy said as he drew her out of the car. "Make it convincing. Unless you want me to shoot him."

She felt something hard jab into her side and she immediately waved a hand at the man who was still about fifty yards away from the house. "We've just come back for the check. Irene forgot it, and we can't end the ball without it."

"We'll only be a moment," Billy prompted.

"We'll only be a moment." Then she watched in dismay as the man waved and turned to head back the way he'd come.

It was going to be up to her. Billy Rutherford was going to get away with the money if she didn't stop him.

"C'mon," Billy said, nudging her forward with the gun.

Visualize Your Goal. Jodie repeated the words in her mind like a chant as she moved toward the house.

"Visualize your goal," Billy said as he followed her into the foyer. "It's good advice."

How many times had she said it out loud? Jodie wondered. She was going to have to be more careful.

Lazarus suddenly growled, rising from his prone position at the foot of the stairs. Jodie watched in horror as Billy aimed the gun at the dog.

"No." She sagged suddenly against him. "Please. He won't hurt you."

Slowly, Billy pocketed the gun. "Make sure he doesn't interfere."

Still leaning heavily against Billy, she said, "Lazarus, it's all right. Good dog." Just like the man outside, Lazarus took her at her word, dropping to the floor and settling his head on his paws.

"Let's go," Billy said, keeping her between himself and the dog as they started up the stairs.

Visualize Your Goal. This time she didn't allow herself the luxury of chanting it. Instead, she began to construct an image in her mind of what her goal had to be: to catch Billy in that snare trap before he discovered that the money wasn't where he'd left it. By the time they reached the second floor, she was imagining him walking toward the center of the attic. The rope was just circling his feet when he suddenly stopped in front of her bedroom door.

"There's a book in here I'd like to show you," Billy said with a smile.

Jodie felt her heart plummet right down to her toes. He knew. Somehow he knew exactly—

"It's too bad we don't have time," he said, urging her along the hall toward the attic door. "I checked this book out of your library and discovered the perfect place to hide the money."

The moment she started to climb the stairs, another

wave of dizziness hit her. Stumbling, she fell forward, her hands slapping hard against the steps.

"Get up," Billy said.

Head spinning, she willed herself to grip the railing, then used it to pull herself up the remaining stairs. Was the drug finally going to win? It couldn't. She wasn't going to let herself even think it.

Gathering all her strength, she concentrated on the picture she'd formed in her mind earlier: Billy standing in the middle of the attic floor, the rope snapping tight around his ankles, yanking his feet from under him and snatching him upward.

The sudden, sharp jab of the gun in her back had the image fading to black.

"Over there," Billy said, poking her with the gun again. "Walk along the eaves over to that chimney."

For the second time since they'd entered the house, Jodie's heart plummeted to her feet. Billy wasn't going to go anywhere near the middle of the attic. She wasn't going to be able to catch him in her trap, after all.

SHANE WAS CURSING HIMSELF as he reached the parking lot. Why hadn't he envisioned this possibility? He'd never underestimated an opponent before. Why in hell had he left her alone on the terrace? Because he was so besotted that he hadn't been thinking straight all day. And now Jodie... The fear that he'd been holding at bay washed over him in a wave.

"My car's gone." Even as he spoke the words, he struggled for control. He didn't have time for fear. Pulling his gaze from the empty space, he searched the lot for an alternative.

"C'mon, we can use Albert's van. Billy took yours," Nadine explained as she urged him toward the back of Slocum Hall. "He knew that he could because of the valet parking. He wants whoever is at the house to think you're just bringing Jodie back to pick up Irene's check."

"I'll drive," Shane said when they reached the van. The moment he got behind the wheel, he focused his attention on getting out of the parking lot and off campus. If he allowed himself to think of Jodie, of how much danger she might be in, the fear would rush in and paralyze him. When he had to stop at the traffic light in town, he glanced at Nadine. "You seem to know a lot about Billy's plans."

"I should. I helped him make them," Nadine said.

"Of course," Shane murmured. "You were working for Jodie at the library last summer. You helped him research the house."

"He asked me to check out the books on my way home from work. That's all. He never let me read them. He never even told me about the money until he knocked at my door a few days ago and told me he needed my help." Pausing, Nadine glanced at him. "Not because of the money, if that's what you're thinking. Last summer, when he was here, we saw each other a few times. He told me that I meant something to him. And after he was arrested, he kept in touch. He told me that as soon as he was cleared, he'd be back and we'd go away together. That's why I quit college. I believed him. And all the time, it was really Jodie he was coming back for."

"How do you know that?" Shane asked as he took the turn onto the highway and pressed his foot down hard on the gas pedal.

"I saw them kissing on the terrace just a few minutes before I ran into you. He told me that he only got engaged to her because he had to make sure that no one would suspect he'd hidden the money here. He said he was just using her, but he was using me."

"Do you know where the money's hidden?"

"Somewhere in that house. That's all I know. And he's getting desperate."

Even as the fear once more sprinted through him, Shane concentrated on keeping his foot steady on the gas pedal. The van was already doing eighty-five, and he didn't want to risk ending up in a ditch.

"How desperate?" he made himself ask.

"Desperate enough to hire one of the kids at the college to run his truck into her. And he nearly went nuts when he wasn't able to meet her in the woods last night. He made me sneak into Tate's garage and plant ten thousand dollars in her car. I think he'd do anything to get that money."

Shane tried not to think of all the things Billy might do to Jodie. He'd get there in time. He had to. "What's the plan tonight?" he asked.

"My job was to slip you a drug in a glass of champagne. But Miss Freemont took it right out of your hand."

How much of it had she swallowed? He tried to recall exactly how full the glass had been when he'd taken it from her.

"I was trying to find Billy to tell him about the mix-up when I saw him kissing her on the terrace. And that's when it hit me," Nadine said. "Miss Freemont was right. You should never depend on a man for your financial security." She shook her head. "After all this blows over, I'm going to go back to school."

"Miss Freemont is often right. It's one of her most endearing and annoying qualities," Shane muttered as he took a curve on two wheels and gave in to the urge to floor the gas pedal.

DON'T PANIC. JUST THINK. Jodie repeated the words together like a chant as Billy nudged her along the eaves toward the chimney. Stumbling again, she gripped one of the beams. "I can't see."

"Feel your away along. If we turn on the light, that man outside will know we're not just here to get the check for Irene. And I would prefer not to have to shoot anyone."

Jodie shoved down the quick skip of fear, peering into the darkness as she inched her way along. Moonlight was pushing its way through the grime on the windows, but it wasn't enough for her to make out exactly where the rope lay along the floor. When they reached the chimney, Billy leaned down and lifted the door.

"It's a secret room. Down you go," he said.

Jodie felt her head begin to spin. "I can't."

Billy motioned impatiently with the gun. "All you have to do is throw your feet over the side and drop. It's not very far."

"Far enough that you didn't want to risk it that first night you broke in. The ladder broke, didn't it? That's why you didn't get what you came for."

"How do you know about the ladder?"

How much should she tell him? Jodie thought frantically.

"It's going to hurt when I shoot you in the leg."

Everything. She felt a surge of adrenaline, or fear. Whatever it was, it had the dizziness receding. "What you want isn't down there anymore," she said.

"That's impossible. No one could possibly—"

"Be as clever as Billy Rutherford? I found your bible and I took it out."

For a moment Billy simply stared at her.

She didn't need anything else to tell her she was right. "The only thing I can't figure out is how you intend to convert it back into cash. It's not as though you can take out an ad in the paper."

"Of course not. But the nice thing about being in the investment business is that you meet people who invest in things besides the stock market. I happened to have a client who needed cash in a hurry, and I have at least three possible buyers for that bible lined up in South America. It's a rare first edition of the St. James version. By the time they finish their little bidding war, I intend to at least double my investment. Now, I think it's time you told me where it is." He moved steadily closer until the gun was pressed against her throat.

Jodie swallowed. "I...carried it over there to the window so I could get a better look at it."

"Show me," Billy said, grabbing her arm and pushing her ahead of him.

As she took the first step, Jodie tried to picture exactly where she and Clyde had spread the circle of rope that night. All she had to do was lead Billy close enough, but not too close, or she'd be caught. Two steps, three. Crossing her fingers, she fell to one knee and threw herself sideways.

"Get up."

"My ankle...I twisted it in the woods last night. The book's right over there." She pointed at the light filtering through the window. "See. On the table."

"It better be," Billy muttered as he stepped around her.

He'd taken two steps, and her heart was sinking

when she finally heard the sharp whistling sound of the snare.

"What the—!"

A sharp explosion drowned out the rest of Billy's sentence.

The gun. He still had the gun. Frantically, Jodie felt along the floor for something, anything. Where was a fireplace poker when you needed one? The second that her fingers closed around the leg of a chair, she scrambled to her feet, lifted the chair and swung. Then she felt the rush of air as Billy swung past unharmed.

"Cut me down!" he shouted.

It seemed darker suddenly. Someone was at the window, blocking the path of the moonlight. *Shane?*

The gun exploded again. Glass shattered.

Fear sprinting through her, Jodie positioned the chair over her shoulder and swung with all her might. She connected with something hard enough to send the pain singing up her arm. She heard the sound of the gun smacking against the floor just before she followed suit and the gray fog swallowed her up.

"SHANE." The moment she managed to murmur the name, the fear shot through her, pushing away the gray fog she'd been trapped in. Opening her eyes, she discovered she was in her bed. What had happened to Shane? She could remember the glass shattering...

Sitting up, she stared at the wavy patterns the sunlight was making on her bed as she tried to remember more. But everything was so gray after that...she couldn't see...

Suddenly the door of her room swung open and Sophie and Irene breezed in.

"Good. You're up," Sophie declared with satisfaction as she set a tray on the nightstand.

"Where's Shane?" Jodie asked. "Billy shot at him. I heard the glass shatter."

"Shane is just fine. He climbed up the maple tree and had to break the window to get in the attic. But you'd already taken Billy out with the chair. The doctor says he's suffering from a concussion. Shane's staying at the hospital until he can hire a private security firm to take over guard duty. He thinks Billy's faking it."

"He probably is," Irene said with a sigh. "He faked everything else."

Jodie and Sophie turned to stare at her. Then moving quickly to take her sister's hand, Sophie asked, "Are you all right?"

Irene raised her chin. "I'm fine. I had a long talk with Nadine before the sheriff took her away. She told me how Billy has been two-timing Jodie—or her—depending on your point of view. I guess I just didn't want to believe Billy would steal our life savings. Because if I believed that, I'd have to believe they were really gone, that we have nothing...."

Jodie reached for Irene's other hand. "None of us wanted to believe Billy could do something like that. We were all fooled by him."

"And we're going to be fine, Irene." Sophie put her arm around her sister. "We've still got each other. And we've got Jodie, too. Plus, this bed-and-breakfast thing is going to be very good for us. It'll give us something to do now that the Mistletoe Ball is over for another year."

"And there's the reward for finding the money. Your share will replace at least part of what Billy..."

She let the sentence trail off when she noticed the two ladies were staring at her. "What?"

"They didn't find the money," Sophie said.

"Didn't Billy tell them?" Jodie asked.

"He was out like a light," Sophie said.

"No matter." Jodie waved a hand. "I know where it is." Then suddenly, she frowned. "At least I did." Raising her hands, she pressed them against her temple and felt the bandage for the first time. "What happened? Did Billy shoot me?"

"You bumped your head when you fell," Irene said. "The doctor says you'll have a headache and probably a black eye."

"Nice of him not to mention the amnesia."

"Amnesia?" Shane asked as he stepped into the room and crossed quickly to the bed.

"Shane, you're all right?" When he took her hand, she held on tight. He was here.

"Well, at least you remember me."

"She knows where the money is, but she can't remember," Irene explained.

"She will." Shane turned to the two ladies. "In the meantime, I seem to have brought some company. They followed me from town."

"Who?" Sophie asked.

"Alicia Finnerty and Zach Reynolds. He's here to get Jodie's picture for the front page of the *Bulletin*."

"My picture?" Jodie asked. "I must look horrible."

"You should see the other guy," Sophie said.

"I can't get my picture taken. I'm not dressed."

"He'll wait," Shane assured her. "So will Alicia Finnerty. She brought her knitting and her cell phone." He glanced at his watch. "I'm sure they want to join their families for Christmas dinner, but that still gives you more than twenty-four hours to spruce yourself up.''

"I'll fix them some tea," Irene said, hurrying toward the door.

"Not on your life," Sophie said, elbowing her sister out of the way as they burst into the hallway.

"Do you have something against my tea?" Irene asked.

"Irene, you and I are going to have a little talk," Sophie said as she closed the door behind them.

"I thought they'd never leave," Shane said.

"I..."

The moment Shane saw the tear roll down her cheek, the panic surfaced in him. With it came all the fear and the rage he'd felt last night when he'd finally climbed through that window and seen her lying there lifeless on the floor. Ruthlessly, he shoved the memory away, then struggled to control the emotions pouring through him. He tightened his grip on her hands. She was here. She was fine. He'd made sure of that before he'd ridden with Billy in the ambulance to the hospital. "Don't. Please don't cry."

"I can't...help it."

"You've got everything you wanted. You caught Billy single-handedly in your snare trap. You're going to get your picture on the front page of the *Castleton Bulletin.* No one in town is ever going to think of you in the same way again."

"But I can't remember where I put—"

"Will you stop worrying about the money? Billy will tell them. He'll have to this time if he wants to make a deal."

"But he doesn't know. I took it out of the attic, and if I can't remember where I put it, you'll never hire me as a bounty hunter."

Shane stared at her. He wanted to shake her. "Is *that* what you're crying about?"

When she nodded, he very nearly did shake her. "Well, you can stop right now. I have no intention of hiring you as a bounty hunter."

"See," Jodie sniffed. "You don't think I'm good enough."

The dejected look on her face had his anger fading and the panic rising again. "It's not that. Jodie, I—" All of a sudden the words that he'd rehearsed faded from his mind. He'd planned it all out so carefully on the drive back from Syracuse. He'd even stopped in Castleton to make sure that the Finnerty woman and Zach Reynolds would follow him to the house. Desperate, he released one of her hands and tugged a small box out of his pocket and set it on her lap. "This isn't going the way it's supposed to. None of my plans work when I'm dealing with you."

Jodie stared down at the box.

"Open it." It gave him some satisfaction that her hand was shaking when she reached for it and lifted the lid. Then she raised her eyes to his.

"You want me to wear that for Alicia Finnerty. So she'll think you popped the—"

Shane clamped a hand over her mouth. Suddenly the nerves and the panic that had been bumping around in his stomach settled into a hard knot. "No. I want you to wear that because I love you. And because you want to marry me as much as I want to marry you."

"For real?" she asked when he freed her mouth.

Shane framed her face with his hands as he searched for the words to convince her. "I came here to Castleton because I was feeling restless. Empty. I thought that working on a case, getting back into the field, would help. But I stopped feeling empty the moment I met you. I think I really came here looking for you, Jodie Freemont. Did I get you?"

For a moment, Jodie didn't say a word. She couldn't. Instead, she threw her arms around Shane Sullivan and poured herself into the kiss.

When she could think again, breathe again, she found herself snuggling on Shane's lap. "Did I answer your question?" she asked.

"I'm not sure. Maybe you ought to say it again."

Jodie started to laugh, and Shane was drawing her closer when she suddenly placed both hands on his chest. "The money! I remember. It's not money at all. It's the bible we found in the secret space. It's a rare edition, and I put it in the drawer of my nightstand."

"You put a book worth five million in your nightstand?" Shane asked.

"That's where the Gideons always leave theirs."

"Good point," Shane said as he ran his hands over her in one possessive stroke and then shifted so that she was beneath him on the bed.

"Now will you hire me as a bounty hunter?"

"If I hold out a little longer, will you persuade me?" Shane asked as he slipped a hand beneath the edge of her nightie.

"What about Zach Reynolds and Alicia Finnerty?" Jodie asked with a laugh.

"I sat them on the couch under the mistletoe. Maybe they'll get lucky."

"I love you, Shane Sullivan," Jodie said as she drew his mouth down to hers.

"Forever," he murmured as he kissed her.

Epilogue

"THAT'S NOT ME."

Jodie stood in her room at Rutherford House pointing at her reflection in the mirror. The woman pointing back at her wore an ivory-colored silk sheath that fell to her ankles. A headband of white roses and mistletoe held a mist of veil in place. It was nearly midnight on New Year's Eve, and she could hear the muffled sound of the musicians practicing Mendelssohn's "Wedding March."

"Of course, it's you. You're lovely," Irene said as she fluffed out the veil. "And it's almost time. Just about everyone in town has turned out for this wedding."

"Oh, my," Jodie said, pressing a hand to her stomach. "I don't think I can go through with it."

Sophie started for the door. "Bridal jitters. I'll get the Scotch."

"No," Jodie said as she continued to stare at the mirror. The only thing she could recognize about the woman staring back at her was the fear in her eyes. "You don't understand. Shane is marrying the wrong person. And he's hired the wrong person to work in his firm." She pointed to the mirror again. "He's in love with her, not me. She's the bounty hunter."

"Nonsense." Sophie moved toward her and took one of her hands.

Irene took the other one. "You're the one who caught Billy."

"What if that was a fluke?" Jodie asked. "What if I can't do it again? And now that Shane has given me a position in his security firm, I could go down in history as a bounty hunter who could only catch one man."

"That's not true," Sophie said. "You caught Shane."

"That's number two already," Irene added.

Sophie patted the hand she was holding. "Remember today's motto: Step Into the New Year as a Whole New You. The woman you see in the mirror *is* the new you—Mrs. Shane Sullivan."

Jodie shot a quick look at the door.

"If you're thinking of making a break for the attic and climbing down that tree, forget it," Sophie advised. "He'd catch you."

"You love him, don't you?" Irene asked.

Jodie nodded. That was the one true thing she could hold on to. Flanked by the two older women, the bride in the mirror was beginning to look a little more familiar. As the butterflies in her stomach settled, she could almost recognize herself. Blinking back a tear, she said, "I'm going to miss you."

"No, you're not," Sophie said firmly. "Shane has already booked this room one weekend a month for the next year."

"He has?" Jodie asked.

"Said he didn't want you to get lonesome, but I think he wants to supervise some of the renovations we're making with that reward money. If you ask me, he's developed a taste for being a handyman."

A knock sounded on the door, and the two women quickly stepped in front of Jodie.

"Shane Sullivan, if that's you…" Sophie began.

"It's just us," Shane's father said as he opened the door and drew Shane's mother into the room. Jodie had made sure that Shane invited them to the wedding. Tall and debonair, Alexander Sullivan reminded Jodie of Sean Connery right down to his Scotish accent. She'd felt at ease with him from their first meeting. It was Miranda, Shane's mother, who had her nerves bubbling up again. At first the two of them had seemed surprised and a bit uncomfortable meeting each other. But in the four days they'd spent living in the close confines of Rutherford House, they'd grown more at ease.

Alexander cleared his throat. "I've got a message from Shane. He's giving you two more minutes to walk down those stairs."

Miranda sighed. "He was always so bossy. It's part of being a Sullivan, I think. We came up to see if we could help."

"Irene and I will get the Scotch," Sophie said as she led her sister out to the hallway.

There was a moment of awkward silence, and then Miranda walked toward Jodie. "There's something we want to give you."

Jodie glanced down at the pearl earrings in the older woman's hand.

"Alex and I picked them out today. We want to thank you for marrying our son." She shot a shy glance at Alexander. "And for making sure that Shane invited us to the wedding. Not only has it given us a chance to spend time with our son, but coming here and seeing how happy you and Shane are…it seems to be contagious. Alex and I have decided to see one another again.''

"I think it's the mistletoe strung up in every room," Alex said.

"You can blame that on Shane," Jodie said.

Miranda smiled sadly. "He never cared much for Christmas as a child. I think he wanted his father to be there, too. It is a time for family."

"I have a feeling his new wife is going to change all that," Alex said, moving closer to put his arm around Miranda. "She managed to get us both here for the wedding."

Jodie reached for the earrings. When her hand shook, Miranda helped her fasten them in her ears.

"Welcome to the family, my dear," Alex said.

"It's a rather strange one," Miranda added. "But we intend to work on it."

"Jodie."

As Shane burst through the door, Miranda stepped quickly in front of Jodie. "You can't see the bride before the wedding. Tell him, Alex."

"I have to talk to her," Shane said. "I'm not leaving until I do."

Alexander took Miranda by the arm. "C'mon, dear, they'll be along shortly. We'll let the musicians know."

In the time it took for them to leave the room, all the butterflies returned to Jodie's stomach. She could see the fear in Shane's eyes, the hint of panic. It was the perfect match to the emotions swirling around inside her. "You've changed your mind. I understand. What else could you do?" She gestured toward the mirror. "She's a complete fake."

"What are you talking about? I came up here

to—'' He tossed the boxes he was carrying on the bed and moved toward her. "Sophie said you—''

She raised a hand. "No, let me finish. I wanted to change my image, and now everyone thinks I'm some kind of wonder woman. I'm never going to be able to measure up."

"What the hell are you talking about?" Shane asked.

"I haven't changed. I'm still the same person inside that I've always been."

"Thank heavens," Shane said. "Because it's the real Jodie Freemont I fell in love with."

"You couldn't have. You're not listening."

He took her hands. "I fell in love with the woman I saw trying to convince Hank Jefferson to sell her a gun. The woman who can't be late for work. The woman who resurrects stray dogs and who loves driving with the top down in the winter. And it's that woman I want at my side—at home, in the office, forever."

Jodie stared at him. "You do?"

"Yes." Raising her hands to his lips, he kissed them.

"I love you, Shane Sullivan." Saying the words was enough to send the rest of her doubts flying away.

"Then we're going to go through with this?"

Holding his hands tightly, she nodded. "Together."

Shane smiled at her. "Sophie sent up some new calendar mottoes she ordered, just in case I couldn't convince you." He drew her toward the bed where he'd tossed them. "Take a look."

Jodie glanced down at the titles. "*365 Ways to Keep Your Man Happy in Bed. 365 Days to Become the CEO of Your Company.*"

"I know which one I vote for," Shane said.

"Maybe I'll use them both."

Shane threw his head back and laughed. "I can't wait."

From below came the first strains of the "Wedding March."

"I'll get my father," Shane said.

"No. Let's walk down the aisle together. It may be the last chance I get to give Alicia Finnerty something to talk about."

"I don't believe that—not for a minute."

They were both laughing as, hand in hand, they descended the stairs."

Santa's Sexy Secret

LORI WILDE

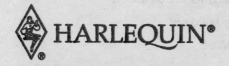

HARLEQUIN®

TORONTO • NEW YORK • LONDON
AMSTERDAM • PARIS • SYDNEY • HAMBURG
STOCKHOLM • ATHENS • TOKYO • MILAN • MADRID
PRAGUE • WARSAW • BUDAPEST • AUCKLAND

Dear Reader,

What better way to spend a day than making people laugh? My father, who writes comedy songs, taught me this at an early age. My endearingly goofy husband, who creates the most hysterical answering machine messages you'll ever hear, reinforced this lesson, too.

My father was forever telling jokes and singing silly ditties. I grew up thinking all dads went around the house wearing a chicken hat and blacking out their teeth just to make their kids laugh.

I suppose it was little wonder that on our first blind date four years ago, my future husband won my heart when he met me at the zoo wearing a pair of huge rainbow-colored sunglasses and warning me not to mistake him for a baboon.

These two wonderful men have given me so much joy and love over the years that I felt compelled to write a romantic comedy to honor them.

I hope you love reading *Santa's Sexy Secret* as much as I loved writing it. I'm so thrilled to be able to share with you this story of a reluctant Santa and the heartwarming elf who teaches him what love and laughter are all about.

Happy holidays!

Lori Wilde

To my father, owner and CEO of Windmill Music,
who taught me everything he knows about writing,
and to his own creation, Tin Panny Lou.
Daddy, I love you.

1
_____

THE DRATTED Santa suit itched.

A lot.

In fact, Sam Stevenson realized with dawning horror, the suit was infested with fleas. Vigorously, he scratched an ear. He had to get out of this blasted thing before the merciless bugs flayed his meat from the bone. He did not intend to let children sit on his lap and risk passing the torture on to them.

"I gotta go," he muttered to the slender elf standing on the podium beside their sleigh, which consisted of an elaborately painted cardboard-and-plywood structure.

"Go?" The young woman blinked at him. "What do you mean? The store opens in two minutes and a mob of kids are waiting outside to see Santa. You can't go anywhere."

If he wasn't so uncomfortable he might have taken the time to admire the way her short, ginger-ale-colored hair curled about her sweet gamin face. A face for which she had obviously been hired, but Sam could think of nothing except stripping off his britches as quickly as possible.

"Listen, lady, I've got something I have to take care of. The kids will just have to wait." Sam started for the exit.

Miss Pixie sprang forward, arms outstretched, blocking his way. The jingle bells on her red-and-white striped elf hat jangled merrily as she moved. "I'm sorry, but you're not leaving."

"Excuse me?" Sam scratched furiously at his neck. What was this woman's problem? He was certain the department store wasn't paying her enough to act as his warden. "Are you telling me what I can and cannot do?"

"I know what's going on here, and I want to tell you that I don't approve." She sank her hands on her hips and frowned. Stern condemnation glistened in her olive green eyes.

Sudden apprehension rumbled through Sam. Could she have somehow guessed his secret?

"What are you talking about?" Sam clawed at his beard. The buggers were eating him alive. He had to get out of this vermin-plagued costume. Now.

"I know what's going on and I can help. My mother is a social worker."

"I don't care if your mother is Margaret Mead, get outta my way."

"Margaret Mead was an anthropologist," she corrected. "Not a sociologist. An anthropologist studies mankind. A sociologist studies social groups."

"Who gives a rat's patoot?"

"Anger." She shook her head. "A classic symptom."

Openmouthed, Sam paused long enough to stare at her. The woman was certifiable.

He tried to sidestep around her but she anticipated his move and went with him step for step as if they were waltzing.

"It's nothing to be ashamed of," she continued earnestly.

Okay, maybe having fleas was nothing to be ashamed of but Sam didn't wish to announce his plight to the entire world. In that moment he remembered a particularly humiliating experience that had happened to him in fourth grade when his favorite teacher, Miss Applebee, had discovered lice in his hair.

Sam cringed at the uncomfortable memory. The suit had to come off. Not only because of the fleas, which were indeed reason enough, but because the besieged costume reminded him of his poverty-stricken childhood.

He raised a finger and wagged it under her nose. "Get out of my way, sweetheart, or I swear I'll walk over you."

"The children are depending on you. You represent something pure and honest and wonderful. How can you shatter their dreams? Don't those little kids mean more to you than alcohol?"

"Alcohol?"

"I know a lot of the store Santas who've been hired this season are down on their luck. Men who can't hold regular jobs because they have drug and alcohol problems. Men who just need a helping hand and someone to care about them. It's not your fault that you're an addict but it *is* your responsibility to stop drinking."

Sam threw his hands in the air. "You're a lunatic, you know that? I'm not an alcoholic."

"Denial!" she crowed triumphantly. "Another classic symptom."

Swiveling his head, Sam searched for redemption from this verdant-eyed zealot, and got none.

Instead, the sight of at least three-dozen shoppers and their ardent offspring bearing down on him at warp speed assaulted his eyes.

"Santa. Santa," the children chanted.

Yikes! He had to escape. Sam faked left, then went right and sprinted past the pixie.

"Hey," she cried, "you can't expect me to face these excited kids alone. They want Santa."

People in hell want ice water. The phrase ran through his head, but he didn't say it.

The elf woman chased after him and grabbed the tail of his Santa jacket before he could bolt through the door marked Employees Only.

"You're not going anywhere, Santa," she growled out and dug in her heels. "And if you do, I'll report you to the store manager, Mr. Trotter."

Sam bared his teeth and willed the fleas to jump onto her. He tried to shake her off, but she held on with more tenacity than carpet lint on a wool jacket.

"Look, Mommy, that elf is trying to hurt Santa," a childish voice said.

Oh great. Now they had an audience.

"Let go," Sam demanded through gritted teeth.

"No." She narrowed her eyes and clung tighter.

Sam grabbed the corner of his jacket and jerked hard, intending on dislodging her. Instead, he ended up dragging her closer to him.

He saw a dusting of freckles across the bridge of her cute little nose, a tiny half-moon scar on her otherwise flawless forehead. Another time, another place and he would have admired her tenacity. But not here, not now, not with fleas feasting on his flesh.

"Mommy, Mommy, make that elf leave Santa alone!"

"You're scaring my daughter," a woman in the crowd protested.

This wasn't right. He shouldn't be drawing attention to himself. The whole point of this stakeout was to hide behind Santa's jovial facade. His boss, Chief Timmons, would have Sam's hide if he blew his cover on the very first day.

Sam had known this was going to be an awful assignment. Chief Timmons made it clear that this stint as Santa was punishment for blowing up the mayor's brand-new Lexus during his last undercover duty, never mind that it had been an unavoidable accident.

The fleas were gnawing as if they hadn't had a meal since last Christmas. Sam couldn't help wondering if Carmichael's, the famed Dallas department store, had stowed the mangy suit at a dog kennel. He couldn't take any more of this. Something had to be done.

Sam clamped his hand over the pixie's wrist and pried her fingers loose. Then, before she had time to get another hold, he bolted through the door.

Once in the vacant storeroom, he ripped the beard off and scraped his face with the vigor of a poodle scratching at full throttle. Next, he snatched the bedraggled felt hat from his head and flung it to the floor.

His fingers grappled with the big black buttons on the front of his suit, fleas hopping in all directions. He jerked off the padding strapped around his waist to simulate Santa's bulk, kicked off his boots and shucked down his pants, his mind on one thing only.

Relief.

What he hadn't counted on was that relentless, do-gooding female elf with the persistence of an Attica prison guard.

She burst through the door, catching him standing there in nothing but his briefs.

SHE'D CAUGHT Santa with his pants down.

Edie Preston came to a screeching halt. Her mouth

dropped. She had no idea that Santa was so muscular, so manly, so gosh-darned sexy. And she certainly hadn't expected to find him almost naked in the storeroom.

What she had expected was some flabby, middle-aged drunk sucking whiskey from a flask or popping a handful of pills, not a young, vital hunk-among-hunks in a very compromising position.

He snapped his head around and deep sapphire eyes sliced into hers forcing Edie's gaze to the floor.

"What is it?" His voice cut like slivered glass. "What do you want from me?"

"I—I—" Her gaze hitched a ride from his sturdy ankles to his hard firm buttocks. Her face heated hotter than a curling iron on the highest setting. She could not seem to find her tongue even though she was sure it lay in its usual place on the floor of her mouth.

"If you've gotten your eyes full could you leave me in peace?" He turned toward her.

"I—er—didn't mean…" she stammered, unable to wrench her gaze from the spectacular sight of Santa's washboard abs.

What was a man like this doing playing Santa at a mall department store? He should be modeling underwear or playing professional sports.

"What am I supposed to do about those children?" She gestured helplessly toward the door.

"Don't know, don't care." He reached an arm over his head and clawed the back of his neck.

"Could I ask a question?"

"I have the feeling you're going to ask it no matter what I say." He sighed. "So go ahead."

"Why did you run in here and take off your clothes?"

"Fleas."

"Excuse me?"

"Fleas." He scratched his chest; bright-red welts dotted his skin.

"You have fleas?"

"The suit did." He nodded at the discarded garments scattered across the cement floor.

Edie slapped a hand across her mouth. "Oh my, and I was giving you a hard time."

"Yes," he said. "You were."

"I'm so sorry. I had no idea. See, I've worked with store Santas before and I've had some unpleasant experiences."

"Are you always so quick to stereotype?" The smirk on his face told her he enjoyed her embarrassment.

"No. Listen, I'm very sorry. Let me make it up to you. I'll go find the manager and tell him about the suit." Edie felt as small as a popcorn kernel. She usually prided herself on being nonjudgmental but her reputation was riding on Santa's sobriety.

It had taken her a week of tall talking to get Mr.

Trotter to agree to hire men from the local halfway house for seasonal employment and that was after she'd already gotten approval from the store owner, J. D. Carmichael himself. Her argument that the men worked cheap was what swayed him, not her speech about community responsibility.

If Santa got soused, Mr. Trotter would hold her personally accountable. That's why she'd jumped to conclusions about his desire to run away and she was ashamed of herself.

"Before you go, would you mind doing me a favor?" he pleaded.

"A favor?" Oh heavens, what did this sexy man want from her?

"Could you scratch right here?" He twisted his arm around his back. "Right below my left shoulder blade. I can't reach the spot, and it's driving me crazy."

"Uh..." Touch this man? Her fingers ached to obey his request but her brain urged her legs to run right out the door.

"Come on, lady, have a heart."

"It's Edie."

"What?"

"My name's Edie. Edie Preston."

"That's great."

"What's your name?"

"Sam. Could you be a doll, Edie, and help me out here?"

She started to chew a fingernail but stopped herself. She'd almost broken the habit except when she was under a great deal of stress.

"Please," he begged.

"Well…"

"If you don't want to touch me then find me something to scratch with. A stick, a coat hanger. Have mercy, ma'am. Please."

Please. The magic word Edie could never resist. He certainly seemed sincere. She took a deep breath.

"Okay, I'll do it." She stepped forward and tentatively reached out a hand.

His flesh was taut and warm. He arched his back. "Higher," he instructed.

Edie splayed her fingers over his warm skin. An odd shiver zipped through her system.

"A little to the left."

Her heart thumped. She was actually touching this incredible man. Unbidden, her gaze slid down his back to the curve just above the waist band of his underpants.

What she saw was so delightful Edie snapped her eyes away and focused instead on a tower of boxes stacked in the corner.

"No," Santa turned Greek God said. "Too far. Back, back. Ah! There, that's the spot."

Edie raked her hand back and forth, keeping her eyes firmly averted.

"Harder," he said, his voice guttural. "Faster."

Geez, she needed a flame-proof suit to combat the fire building inside her.

"Yes!" He groaned. "Don't stop."

Sam bent forward slightly. Edie stood right behind him furiously scratching his naked back.

"You got it, baby!"

At that moment the storeroom door flew open. Edie and Sam turned in unison to see Mr. Jebidiah Trotter, standing in the doorway, a gaggle of rowdy kids visible behind him.

"Just what," Mr. Trotter demanded, "is going on in here?"

"I can explain," Edie said.

Mr. Trotter slammed the door behind him, crossed his arms over his chest and leveled her a condescending stare. "I suggest you begin immediately, Miss Preston, and tell me why I shouldn't fire both of you this very minute." He threw a disdainful glare in Sam's direction.

Edie raised her palms, then pulled them downward in a calming gesture. "You've got a store full of kids waiting to see Santa. If Santa doesn't appear, their mothers will take them to another department store and you'll lose business," Edie said, appealing to his mercenary side.

She didn't care for Carmichael's new manager, but she prided herself on getting along with most anyone. However, Mr. Trotter was difficult to please and wielded a heavy-handed management style, preferring punishment over positive reinforcement.

Trotter tilted his nose upward. ''Be that as it may, I will not have you and your *Santa* playing sex games in my storeroom. Especially when you're suppose to be working.'' He tapped the face of his wristwatch.

Sex games with Santa? Edie darted at quick glance at her nearly naked partner-in-crime and gulped. Until today she had never considered Santa Claus the least bit sexy, but Sam had changed all her preconceived notions about the Christmas icon.

Sam stepped between Edie and Mr. Trotter, a thunderous expression on his face. ''Listen here, Trotter, your Santa suit was infested with fleas. That's why I'm in my underwear. That's why I have welts on my body, which Miss Preston was so kindly scratching for me. If you don't get me a new suit pronto, and lay off threatening the lady, I'll be forced to report this incident to the public health department.''

''You wouldn't dare.'' Trotter sniffed.

If she squinted just right in the glare of florescent lighting, Trotter looked exactly like the Grinch who stole Christmas—snooty nose, sour expression, virtually hairless—with an attitude to match. Edie slapped a palm over her mouth to keep from giggling.

''Try me,'' Sam growled, leaning forward in a menacing stance. How anyone could appear menacing in his undies, Edie didn't know, but Sam was pulling it off with the pugilistic aplomb of a heavyweight boxer. "Oh, and I believe you owe Miss Preston an apology."

"An apology? What for?" Trotter's brows plunged together in an angry V.

"Insinuating that she's the type to have a sordid affair in the storeroom."

Trotter snorted. "I will not apologize."

The two men stared each other down, eye to eye, toe to toe.

Sam clenched his hands.

Trotter's Adam's apple bobbed.

Neither blinked.

Edie's heart skipped a beat, her tummy tightened. Sam was standing up for her! No one had ever championed her like this before and while she found it thrilling, she was also terrified Trotter would fire them both. She needed her job to pay for next semester's tuition and she was certain Sam hadn't taken the position as store Santa simply for the fun of it. She had to smooth things over.

"It's all right, Sam," Edie soothed. "I know how things must have seemed—with you in nothing but your B.V.D.s and me running my hands along your..." She hesitated on the word *body*. "Why don't I go out and entertain the children before we lose customers?"

"Are you sure, Edie?" Sam asked.

"Yes." She turned to the manager. "Mr. Trotter, I give you my word, that nothing of a...er...sexual nature was going on between Sam and me, nor will it ever. I was simply trying to help him with his unfortunate flea problem.''

Mr. Trotter cleared his throat. "Well," he said, "you have been an exemplary employee until now. I guess I can give you another chance."

He wagged a finger under Sam's nose. "But if I even get a whiff that there is hanky-panky going on between the two of you, then you are both out on your ears. Is that understood? Carmichael's has an image to uphold."

Edie forced a smile. "Yes, sir, thank you. You won't regret your decision."

Sam said nothing, just kept glaring at Trotter with a wicked stare that sent goose bumps up Edie's spine. Sam possessed the same volatile edginess of Mel Gibson's character in the first *Lethal Weapon*—one of Edie's all-time favorite movies. An edginess that appealed to the nurturer in her. She had an unexpected desire to pacify him.

"Let me see if I can find another Santa suit," Trotter said. "Wait here, Stevenson. Miss Preston, back to work." He made shooing motions at her.

Edie ducked her head, scurried around Trotter and through the door, the bells on her hat jangling merrily. She breathed a sigh of relief, but it was only temporary. Yes, she had managed to hold on to her holiday job, but in the process she had promised to keep her hands off sexy Santa Sam.

And as luck would have it, he was the most intriguing man she'd met in years.

2

"JINGLE BELLS" jangled from the store's sound system for the nine zillionth time, as a pair of twin toddlers sat crooked in the corners of Sam's elbows, toothily drooling over his hands in surprisingly coordinated unison. He was going hoarse from too many boisterous ho, ho, hos, and his backside still itched like the dickens.

All around their little North Pole island, shoppers bustled, pushing and vying for bargains at the sales racks. The perfume counter was two aisles over, and Sam was beginning to believe the scent of rose petals was permanently imbedded inside his nostrils.

Mistletoe and holly hung from the ceiling above them, and the numerous Christmas lights strung throughout the entire tableau twinkled merrily off and on. Periodically, a nasal-voiced announcer would break in over the PA system to declare a sale on gold-plated back scratchers in bath accessories or nativity-scene decorated finger bowls in fine china.

Chief Alfred Timmons knew how to torture a guy. And surely, punishment was all this assignment amounted to because Sam didn't have a spare moment to watch the employees in order to figure out who was behind the recent rash of store thefts. Most of his investigative efforts would have to be concentrated after hours when he finished with the Santa gig every day.

He sighed. That meant twelve- and fourteen-hour workdays. Most of it spent in this red-and-white get-up. Okay. Timmons had made an impression. Sam had learned his lesson. He would never blow up the mayor's car again.

"You all look so adorable." Edie grinned. "Santa and the twins."

Sam shot her a dirty look. The woman was *way* too perky for her own good.

"Smile," instructed the twins' mother, standing off to one side.

Sam faked a smile for the kids' sake.

"Say 'fruitcake!'" Elf Edie sang out gaily, as she bent slightly to peer through the camera mounted on a tripod and clicked the shutter.

Sam blinked against the flash. At the rate he was going he'd have third-degree retinal burns by the time this day was finished. He'd already endured a litany of more than a hundred, "Santa, I wants" over the course of the last two hours. Nobody seemed to care that *Santa* wanted a potty break, a double-meat cheeseburger and a thick chocolate malt.

The twins were no more enamored of the infernal flashbulb than he. They both broke into instant tears.

"Ho, ho, ho." Sam jostled the babies, trying to quiet them. They stared into his face, then looked at each other and sobbed harder.

"I'll take them off your hands." Their mother stepped forward and relieved him of his charges.

The young mother had his complete admiration. How she dared to brave the mall alone the day after Thanksgiving with two eighteen-month-olds in tow was beyond his comprehension. The mother loaded her kids into their stroller then went over to pay Edie for the photos.

Despite his best intentions to keep his lingering glances to himself, Sam found his gaze straying down the curve of Edie's well-shaped thighs encased so enticingly in forest-green tights. She wore a red tunic sweater that just barely covered her equally well-shaped bottom.

Knock it off, Stevenson, he chided himself. *You can't get involved with her no matter how enticing the view. Don't get mixed up with people you work with. Remember Donna Beaman?*

How could he forget Donna? He'd been assigned to guard the leggy supermodel after she received death threats for testifying against a murder defendant Sam had arrested.

She'd seduced him and he'd fallen for her hook, line and sinker, to the point where he went to political functions, dressed in tuxedos and even took elocution lessons to please her. When Donna dumped him for a millionaire polo player, Sam's ego had been crushed.

What a complicated mess that relationship had become with the upshot being that one, he made it a personal policy never to get involved with co-workers or witnesses or informants, and two, he didn't get mixed up with anyone who couldn't accept him for himself, faults and all. And especially no woman who wanted to turn him into something he wasn't. He'd had enough of that from his Aunt Polly.

Still, despite his mental declaration to the contrary, he couldn't seem to stop his eyes from roving. Nothing wrong with looking at the menu, after all, just as long as you didn't order anything.

Sam tilted his head and boldly admired how the wide black belt nipped in neatly at Edie's slender waist. Sneaking peeks at this fetching, camera-wielding elf made the job tolerable.

"Got a nice tail on her don't she, Santa?"

What? Sam looked over at the next kid standing in line.

The boy was about eight with a cynical oh-yeah? expression on his freckled face. He leaned against the thick velvet rope with a cocky stance, arms crossed over his chest, legs wide apart, defiant chin in the air. The kid had no parent in attendance.

Uh-oh.

Sam had seen that same truculent stance too many times in the mirror not to recognize trouble when he spotted it. Twenty years ago he'd been the one to stand in line for the joy of heckling Santa. Paybacks were hell.

"Aren't you a little young for such talk?" Sam asked dryly, mentally casting himself back to that age.

Whenever he had acted outrageously he'd done so for one reason—attention. It had been tough growing up with an absent father and a mother who worked two jobs to make ends meet. His mother had been unable to control his rambunctious nature, and he'd run wild. Then, his mother had died of kidney failure when he was twelve. Angry at the world, he'd turned to shoplifting and petty vandalism in order to alleviate his emotional pain.

He had craved discipline, and Aunt Polly had shown up to adopt him and rescue him from himself. And while his aunt's efforts had kept him from ending up on the wrong side of the law as an adult, no matter how hard he had tried to please her, he'd always fallen short of his goal. Since his mother's death no one had loved him unconditionally.

Sam motioned to the boy. "Come here."

The kid shook his head. "No way. For all I know you're some old pervert."

"I'm Santa, kid."

"There's no such thing as Santa. You're a fraud, a fake. I'll even pull off your beard and prove it." Quick as lightning, the kid vaulted over the rope and onto the plywood sleigh. He reached out to snatch at the artificial beard but before he could grab it, Sam's fingers locked around the boy's wrist.

Sam stared him in the eye. "I'm guessing Santa didn't bring you much last year."

The boy looked startled. "There is no Santa."

"That's where you're wrong."

"Oh, yeah? Then why didn't you bring me the bike I asked for last Christmas? Why didn't you bring my daddy back home?" The boy's voice broke just a little on that last question.

"So that's what this is all about," Sam murmured. He put his arm around the boy's waist and lifted him onto his lap. The boy did not resist. "You want to tell me about it?"

The boy ducked his head and shrugged. "Nothing to tell. My dad left me and my mom. He never calls, never sends presents. My mom works real hard cleaning rooms at a motel, but she doesn't have much money. You know what I got for Christmas last year? Underwear and socks and then she took me out to a fast-food restaurant."

"That's not going to happen this year," Sam told him. "Santa's going to see to it personally. You go over there and give that pretty elf your name and address."

The boy looked at him. "Really?"

The expectant hope in his eyes hit Sam clean to the bone. He knew what it was like to be poor and unwanted. "Really."

"Gee, thanks."

"But Santa's got one request of you."

The boy rolled his eyes. "I knew there'd be a catch."

"It's not a catch. It's common courtesy."

The boy sighed. "What is it?"

"Watch your mouth and mind your mother."

"Okay." He shrugged. "I guess I can do that."

"Promise?"

"Bring me a bike and I'll do it."

The kid drove a hard bargain. Sam handed him a candy cane and watched him scurry over to Edie. A warm feeling sprouted in his chest. He had helped that boy feel better about himself and Sam would make sure the kid had a very special Christmas this year.

Edie talked to the boy, then turned to smile at Sam, an expression of awe on her fresh face. That look struck him like an arrow to the heart.

Maybe, Sam thought, *this assignment wasn't going to be so crummy after all.*

THE MORE SHE SAW OF Sam Stevenson, the more impressed and confused Edie became. He was handsome and lord, was he in great shape. He had a killer smile and infinite patience with crying babies. He'd stood up to Mr. Trotter for her, and he'd done a very nice thing giving special attention to that unhappy young boy.

So why was a guy like him playing mall Santa?

Curiosity gnawed at her.

From previous years as an elf at Carmichael's, a seasonal position she'd held all through undergraduate school and while getting her Master's degree in psychology, she knew that usually two types of men took the job. One, men so down on their luck they could only get temporary, minimum-wage work, or two, retired grandfathers who liked being around kids.

With his looks and skills Sam could easily have found a better job.

Unless he was in some kind of trouble. He denied being an alcoholic, but what about drugs? What about a gambling addiction?

Edie cast a speculative glance at him. He chatted with a little girl who wanted to know what reindeers ate so she could leave something for Rudolph and the other reindeers on Christmas Eve along with the requisite cookies and milk for Santa.

As a child, Edie had been the same, always worried about everyone and trying to make sure they were all taken care of. Her father had told her that reindeers ate Cheerios. Funny, she had thought at the time, that Cheerios was Dad's favorite cereal, too.

Sam told the little girl that reindeers loved oatmeal because it made them fly higher and faster.

What a great imagination.

Edie's inherent curiosity kicked into overdrive. He

was such a paradox. She had to know more about him and why he was working at the store.

Who knows? Maybe he is like you. Maybe he just loves Christmas. Or maybe he is going to school and needs money for tuition.

Thank heavens it was time for their prescheduled break. And maybe she would take him to lunch and sate her curiosity. She took the stand-up cardboard sign that had the face of a clock printed on it and moveable plastic hands. It said Santa Will be Back at

Edie set the time for two o'clock and posted the sign at the end of the line.

"Ready for a break?" she asked him a few minutes later after the last child had gone through.

"You read my mind."

"Not exactly." She grinned. "My stomach's been growling for over an hour. Would you like to grab a bite to eat at the cafeteria?"

"Dressed like this?"

"Of course not. You'd be mobbed."

"Do we have time to change?"

"We've got an hour." Edie pointed to the sign.

"You're an angel." He disembarked from the sleigh, alighting beside her graceful as a panther.

She peered at him, wondering why her heart was pounding so hard and why she had an irresistible urge to break into song. "You've got something on your cheek."

"Where?" He raised a hand. "Ick. Something sticky."

Edie stood on tiptoes to inspect him closer. "Looks like kid gunk."

"A lollipop-chomping little girl decided to kiss me."

"I've got some moist towelettes in my pocket. When you're working around kids you never know when one will come in handy." She retrieved a small flat package from the pocket of her tunic and tore it open. "Hold still."

Then she reached out and ran the towelette over his cheek. Her fingers trembled slightly and she felt a sudden light-headedness. She crumpled the towelette in her hand. "There. All gone."

He stared at her. Edie caught her breath. He had such beautiful blue eyes. It was strange for a dark-haired man to possess such arresting azure eyes. She was more captivated than ever.

"You've got really beautiful skin," he murmured.

"Th-thank you."

"Flawless."

"You should see the stuff I slather on my face at night." She laughed nervously.

"Now that is a tempting thought."

The idea of Sam seeing her in pj's sent a flood of heat swamping her body until she felt as if she were standing in a pool of melted butter.

MAN, but it was hot in here.

Sam gazed into those beguiling emerald eyes and knew he had to get away from Edie.

Fast.

Or he would be breaking his own rules about getting involved with people he worked with.

And that wasn't good. Not good at all.

He turned his head, and to his dismay saw a small-potatoes thug he'd arrested numerous times, coming down the luggage aisle and headed right toward him.

Freddie the Fish.

So called on the streets because he had pop eyes, fleshy folds of skin around his neck that flapped like gills when he got excited and he had such a penchant for sardines he always kept a can in the front pocket of his shirt.

Why was Freddie the Fish at Carmichael's? Freddie had been arrested, convicted and done time in prison for stealing from department store warehouses and fencing the stuff with his cousin, Walter the Weasel. Could Freddie be in cahoots with the whomever was stealing from the store?

The evidence he'd been given pointed to an inside job. The thefts had been going on for about a week. So far dresses, lawn equipment and Christmas decorations totalling ten thousand dollars had been stolen. Someone who knew the store and knew it well was smuggling the stolen items right out from under the manager's nose. No wonder Trotter was so foul tempered. Since he'd only been manager for a month, his reign was not off to a good start.

Sam frowned. It wasn't a good idea to assume anything about Freddie. For all he knew the man was merely doing his Christmas shopping.

Freddie swaggered closer.

Crud! The last thing he needed was to be fingered by Freddie the Fish.

Do something, Stevenson.

Desperate to hide his identity, Sam locked gazes with Edie, pulled her to him and dipped his head. Her sweet little mouth rounded in a startled circle.

Sam's lips were already on hers before he realized belatedly that Freddie probably wouldn't recognize him in the Santa suit.

OH! OH! His touch was incredible.

Rough, masculine fingers tenderly grazed Edie's delicate, feminine skin. Hot, firm lips scorched her mouth. Their lips interlocked like matching puzzle pieces.

Sam was kissing her!

It was probably sheer coincidence, not destiny at all but in that moment the store stereo system began playing, "I Saw Mommy Kissing Santa Claus."

Immediately, her senses zoomed into overload. *Tilt! Tilt!* The smell of him, the pressure of his body flush against hers, the intense thudding of her heart.

Her mind disengaged from her surroundings. She

forgot she was standing in the middle of Carmichael's, forgot about the multitudinous, post-Thanksgiving shoppers flowing past them, forgot about everything but Santa Sam and his dangerous kiss.

And what a kiss it was. Long, lingering and full of promise. What things would he have done with his tongue if they'd been alone?

Her stomach swooned, her cheeks flamed, her nipples tightened.

Cease and desist, Edie Renee! There will be absolutely no bursting into spontaneous combustion!

But her body completely ignored her mind's admonitions as Sam's kiss morphed her from a mild-mannered elf into a human incendiary device.

"Look Mommy, Santa Claus is kissing an elf," a child cried, pulling Edie back to reality.

"Hey, you two," a smart-mouthed teenager shouted. "Get a room."

"For shame, Santa. What would Mrs. Claus say?" someone else chimed in.

Gulping, Edie stepped back but couldn't take her eyes off him. "Wh-why did you do that?" she whispered, perplexed.

He pointed at the ceiling. "Mistletoe."

Edie looked up and sure enough, she was standing under a sprig of mistletoe. "Oh." A tree parasite had caused him to kiss her. Nothing else.

Sam took her hand. "Come on, let's get out of here. We're drawing a crowd."

Heedlessly, she allowed him to drag her into the employee lounge. Once there Edie changed in the ladies' room, Sam in the men's.

Sam emerged a few minutes later wearing a wide grin, black denim jeans and a black turtleneck sweater. His hair was combed back off his forehead, giving her full access to his gorgeous features. The man had to be the best-looking Santa Claus in the annals of department store history.

All she'd done was take off her elf hat and Merry Christmas apron, exchanged the elf shoes for brown patent leather loafers, brushed her hair and put on some lipstick. She felt as nervous and excited as a fifteen-year-old on her first date.

Calm down, Edie. You don't know anything about this guy.

Yeah, but that was the point of taking him to lunch.

"You ready?" he asked.

"Uh-huh." It was the most she could say.

He held the lounge door open for her and as they stepped into the corridor, Edie caught a glimpse of Trotter lecturing Jules Hardy, a sales clerk from cosmetics.

"Go back, go back." She turned and ran smack into Sam's chest which was solid as a brick wall.

"What is it?" Sam asked, taking her hand.

"Trotter," she said. "After what happened this

morning, I don't think it's a good idea for him to see us together.''

But it was too late to disappear back into the lounge, Trotter half turned toward them. One more second and he'd catch them holding hands.

Sam gave Edie a light push. ''You go left, I'll go right. We'll meet at the cafeteria.''

Nodding, Edie ducked down and disappeared behind a carousel of maternity dresses.

THE MINUTE she slipped away, Sam realized he'd sent her up a blind alley. She was trapped in the corner of the store with no way past Trotter.

He would have to divert the man's attention.

Sam aligned himself with a pillar decorated in red-and-white crepe paper, and stood with his arms plastered to his side, his knees clamped together. Quickly, he darted his head around the corner for a peek.

Trotter preened before a three-way, full-length mirror, licking the fingers of one hand, then combing down the few strands of hair he wore too long in a pathetic attempt to disguise his balding pate.

Turning to the other direction, Sam searched for Edie. He saw a rack of dresses ripple with movement, then spotted the top of Edie's curly head as she scurried on all fours, headed for the lingerie department.

Sam clamped a hand over his mouth to hold back the laughter.

Trotter pulled his eyes from his own reflection and

tilted his head. A frown creased his high forehead. He pivoted on his heel and walked to where Edie crouched behind a barrel of sale-priced underwear. His shoes squeaked with every step.

Creak. Creak. Creak.

Sam had to do something. He couldn't let Edie bear Trotter's disapproval alone. Stepping from behind the pillar, he called, "Mr. Trotter. May I speak to you for a moment?"

The store manager halted. "What do you want, Stevenson?"

Think, Sam. Think.

"Er…"

"Yes?" Trotter snapped. "Speak up."

Sam peered over Trotter's shoulder, searching for Edie. This was her chance to get out of the store. Where was she? "I'd like to ask about the employee discount."

Trotter frowned. "You don't get a discount. You're here to work off a community service obligation, not for a pay check."

At that moment, Edie suddenly popped to her feet about two yards behind Trotter. She waved her arms and mouthed the word, *"Go"*.

Sam shook his head at her.

"What's going on here?" Trotter demanded and snapped his neck around.

Quick as a jack-in-the-box, Edie ducked out of sight.

Trotter turned back to Sam and narrowed his beady eyes. "You're up to something, Stevenson. I've got a very bad feeling about you."

"Who, me?" Sam smiled innocently.

"Yes, you. Get back to your department." Trotter clicked his heels. "Right now."

"Uh, sir, I sorta got turned around. Could you show me where my department is?"

"Oh, for heavens sake." Trotter snorted. "Follow me."

When Trotter led the way out of ladies' wear, Sam breathed a sigh of relief. He might have looked like an imbecile but at least he'd bought Edie some time.

Why he should care, Sam couldn't say. But something about that sweet little pixie plucked heavily on his heartstrings.

3

COMMUNITY SERVICE?

Edie crouched behind the barrel of half-priced undies and pondered what Trotter had said. Sam was working off a community service obligation? She started to nibble a fingernail but stopped herself.

Peeking around the top of the panty barrel, she saw that Sam and Mr. Trotter had disappeared. A quick glance at her wristwatch told her they only had twenty-five minutes left for lunch. Now, with her curiosity about Sam stoked to high intensity, she simply had to speak to him.

"Miss Preston!"

Startled by Trotter's rapid-fire pronunciation of her name, Edie leapfrogged a foot into the air.

"Explain yourself, Miss Preston, just what are you doing on the floor in ladies' underwear?"

"Hi," Edie said perkily, peering into Trotter's unwavering stare as if for the second time that day the store manager hadn't caught her in an embarrassing position.

"Don't give me that goody-goody smile of yours. What are you doing here?"

"I'm on my break." Edie scrambled to her feet.

Trotter rested his hands on polyester-clad hips. "Haven't you read the new policy I posted on the bulletin board in the employees' lounge this morning?"

"New policy?" Edie kept a pleasant smile on her face.

"Employees are not to roam over the store. You either stay in the lounge or in your own department. No visiting with your girlfriends in housewares, no gossiping in shoes."

"What?" Edie straightened herself to her full five-foot-two and stared the man straight in the eyes. She couldn't believe this latest outrage. According to some of the other managers, Trotter had instituted policies since he'd become manager that seemed to have no purpose beyond alienating the employees. "That's utterly ridiculous."

"Not so ridiculous, Miss Preston, when one considers that over ten thousand dollars worth of merchandise was pilfered from the store two nights ago."

"Why are you punishing the employees for shoplifters?"

"I have every reason to believe that the thieves are employees."

"You've got to be kidding." She blinked at him.

"I'm deadly serious. In fact, I'm beginning to wonder if those men from the halfway house that you talked Carmichael into hiring are behind the thefts.

They've been here a week and that's exactly how long the thefts have been going on. And, if it turns out that they are involved, I'm afraid I'll have to ask for your resignation.''

Edie opened her mouth and started to protest, then realized it was pointless arguing with the man who obviously had his mind made up. She didn't think any of the three guys she'd met during her last clinical rotation at Hazelwood Treatment Center were involved. She had truly believed in them and they had wanted so badly to go straight. That's why she'd begged first Carmichael and then Trotter to hire them. Then again, one never knew for sure.

Pensively, Edie left the department store and headed down the mall, zigzagging around the gift-laden shoppers to Lulu's Cafeteria. She hung around the door, scanning the lunchtime crowd for Sam.

"Hi," he murmured in her ear.

Edie whirled to face him. She hadn't heard him come up behind her. The man was as sneaky as a cat on the hunt.

"Hi yourself."

"Hungry?" He took her by the elbow and guided her toward the line, a medley of delicious aromas scenting the air.

"Starving." *For information.*

Edie tried not to be dazzled by Sam's strong fingers but her body possessed a mind of its own. Her elbow heated, then her forearm, then her shoulder and the next thing she knew every nerve ending burst, enkindled.

"Whew," she said, twisting her arm from his grasp. "It's awfully warm in here."

"Probably the heat lamps."

No, that wasn't it. What made her skin catch fire and sizzle like bacon on a hot griddle was the enigmatic Sam Stevenson.

"Here you go." He handed her a green plastic tray that was still warm from the dishwasher and smelled of industrial strength soap, and silverware rolled up in a red cloth napkin.

"Thanks."

He smiled and her knees melted. She barely managed to load her tray with tossed salad, iced tea, baked halibut, green beans and cherry pie for dessert. At the register, she fumbled in her pocket for change but Sam beat her to it. Leaning over, he paid the cashier for their meals.

"Oh," Edie protested. "I can't allow you to pay for my lunch."

"And why not?" His blue eyes danced merrily.

"Because I invited you," she argued, plucking a twenty-dollar bill from her pocket. "I'm paying."

She felt guilty letting him spend his money on her. If he was working out a community service obligation it probably meant he didn't have another job or extra cash to spare.

The cashier had already rung up their purchases and passed Sam his change.

"Wait a minute, I'm paying," Edie insisted.

"Hush, Edie, it's taken care of."

She didn't need him to take care of her. He was the one down on his luck, not the other way around. "But I insist."

"You're holding up the line." Sam picked up his tray and headed into the dining area, leaving her standing with her hands on her hips. "You can pay for lunch tomorrow," he called over his shoulder.

Lunch tomorrow? Edie thrilled to the thought. They would be having lunch together tomorrow?

Pulse slipping through her veins like high water through a dry creek bed, she picked up her tray and followed him to a table in the far corner. When she arrived, he pulled out the chair for her.

What a gentleman.

Okay, Edie Renee Preston, slow down. So he is the most fascinating, handsome man you've ever met. So he pays for your lunch and pulls out your chair for you. So he is good with kids and has the most amazing tush. He has also done something bad. Not terribly bad, of course, or he'd be in jail, but he is walking down the wrong road.

But Edie, with her abundant curiosity and her heartfelt desire to rescue anyone and anybody in need, was about to change that.

She eased into the chair. Sam leaned over to re-move the plates and bowls from her tray.

The festive scent of his cologne teased her nose. He smelled like Christmas—gingerbread cookies and peppermint sticks and evergreen trees. His shoulder, encased in that nubby wool sweater, grazed softly against her cheek, and she drew in a deep breath.

The memory of their kiss in the midst of the crowded department store sent a shiver of pleasure angling through her.

Ack! What was this strange, new desire over-whelming her?

Edie tipped her head and peeked up at him. Her eyes focused on his lips. Darn! Why wasn't there a nest of mistletoe hanging from the ceiling of Lulu's Cafeteria?

After Sam put their trays away, he came back and sat across from her. She watched with fascination as he spread his napkin in his lap, stirred sugar into his tea and added ketchup to his French fries.

"I want to apologize again for my behavior this morning," she said, flattening her own napkin in her lap. "I completely misunderstood what was happen-ing. You know, with the Santa suit and the fleas."

He swallowed a bite of his cheeseburger before re-plying. "No harm done."

Sam possessed perfect table manners. Unlike the last disastrous blind date Edie had been on.

That guy had talked incessantly the entire time he'd

chewed his food, bragging how rich he'd become managing fixed-income portfolios. Edie wasn't even sure what a fixed-income portfolio manager was, but at the time it struck her that getting rich off people on fixed incomes was inappropriate. Not to mention that she'd had to repeatedly dodge the food particles he'd liberally sprayed across the table at her.

"I have a tendency to get carried away sometimes," she said. "My mom tells me to be careful, that it's easy to let enthusiasm turn into zealousness. It's something I'm working on."

"I don't think you're overzealous. Just passionate."

Edie beamed at his compliment. "Why, thank you."

This guy was the stuff of dream dates. Except for that community service thing.

"So are you really going to buy that boy a bicycle for Christmas?"

"Sure." Sam shrugged.

"Why?"

"Why not?" Their eyes met.

"It's a lot of money and effort. Why that boy?"

"He said his father left the family, that his mother couldn't afford to celebrate Christmas. I felt sorry for him. Is that a crime?"

Sam sounded defensive. He didn't fool Edie for a moment. She knew he didn't like showing his soft side. Many men didn't. They were afraid that feelings made them vulnerable.

"May I ask you a personal question?"

"If I don't have to answer."

"How come you're working as a store Santa? I mean you don't seem the type."

Sam leaned back and draped one arm over his chair. He narrowed his eyes, quirked a smirk like a very naughty boy. "Are you sure you really want to know?"

Edie nodded.

"Even if it portrays me in a less than favorable light?"

He was going to tell her the truth. She had to give him points for honesty. "Yes."

"Court-ordered community service," he said.

"You committed a crime?"

He nodded and winked, suddenly appearing very dangerous in those dark clothes.

"What on earth did you do?" she whispered, her heart thudding a thousand miles an hour as she waited for his answer with bated breath.

"I BORROWED A CAR without permission." Sam gave her the official story supplied by Chief Timmons to Mr. Trotter.

It wasn't far from the truth. Last month, he had taken the mayor's car because he had been in hot pursuit of a drug dealer. It was his bad luck that the high-speed chase had ended when he crashed the car into a gasoline tanker truck and blew the Lexus sky high. What the mayor and Chief Timmons kept forgetting, however, was that he had nabbed the drug dealer and no one had gotten injured.

"You stole a car?" Edie stared. He hated dashing her high expectations of him. Why her opinion mattered, he couldn't say. But oddly enough, it did.

"Well, I intended on returning the car. Let's say it was something of a joy ride."

"That's not so bad."

"And then I sort of…accidentally destroyed it."

"Was the car expensive?"

"A sixty-thousand dollar automobile."

Edie winced.

"Yeah."

"Why'd you do it?" She leaned forward, fascinated by his story, her cherry pie completely forgotten.

"Boredom I guess. The judge gave me a choice. Sixty days in the county lockup or make restitution on the car and spend a hundred and twenty hours playing Santa. Not a difficult decision."

Edie shook her head. "But why did you steal the car in the first place? You've got everything going for you—looks, charm, brains. Why would you jeopardize your future for a costly joy ride? And at your age," she scolded. "It's not as if you're a misguided teen."

A certain look came into her eye. The same look he'd frequently seen on his dear old Aunt Polly's face when she'd given up her life as a missionary in the South Pacific to come home to the States and take care of him.

The ardent look of a saint intent upon saving the sinner.

"Uh, how did your wife take the news?" she asked.

He grinned, amused. So this attraction he felt was not one-sided. He'd guessed as much when he kissed her. She was fishing about his marital status. "I never made that particular mistake," he drawled, reminding himself that he would not make a mistake by acting on feelings she aroused in him.

"You consider marriage a mistake?"

He almost said for policemen, yes, but bit his tongue in time. What was it about her that made him want to spill his guts? "The divorce rate is fifty percent."

"But that means that fifty percent of the couples make it," she said.

"That's true." Edie was a glass-half-full kind-of-gal, no denying it.

She studied him a moment. "I can help you, Sam."

He leaned back in his chair and stared at her. That gorgeous mop of curly honey-blond hair, those trusting green eyes, that round, determined little chin. Sam groaned inwardly.

"Oh? I wasn't aware that I need helping."

"I have my master's degree in psychology and I'm working toward my doctorate. I do know a bit about border line personality disorders."

He couldn't suppress his smirk. "Are you diagnosing me?"

"Well, no, of course not. I don't know you well enough to do that. You've got so much going for you, and yet you do something dumb like steal a car. Why?"

"Maybe I'm just rotten to the core."

"Oh, piffle."

"Piffle?" He raised an eyebrow. "Is that some sophisticated psychological jargon?"

"You're making fun of me," she accused.

"Maybe a little." She was fun to tease; so earnest was she in her campaign to regenerate his image.

"What do you do for a living when you're not playing Santa?" she asked.

"This and that," he hedged. He didn't like to lie, even though it was often a necessary ingredient of his job. "Never could settle on one career path."

She nodded. "I suspected as much."

It was all he could do to keep from bursting into laughter. Her seriousness was genuine. She really thought she had him pigeonholed.

The woman was a reformer.

To the core.

And he was attracted to her.

That added up to serious trouble. In his current situation, Sam could not imagine a worse scenario.

The very last thing he needed was some do-gooding woman following him around telling him just how she planned to turn him into the man of her dreams—nice, respectable, home every night.

A man who looked good on paper but had no spunk, no spine, no backbone. Edie was the type who simply assumed that everyone shared her notion of the ideal home life. She was his Aunt Polly all over again—forever intent on rescuing the heathens from themselves.

He would bet a thousand bucks Edie had never done anything naughty in her entire life.

Sam knew without asking that she'd never gone skinny-dipping in the lake under a full moon. She'd never skipped school in favor of playing hooky at the local pool hall, nor had she toilet-papered the neighbors' houses on Halloween.

And Edie thought she could help him! He almost laughed aloud.

In reality she was the one crying out for life lessons. That's why she was such a crusader—taking on the flaws of others because secretly, deep inside, she was afraid to face her own rebellious nature. Which he suspected, from the kiss he'd given her, she kept tightly under wraps. She wanted to let loose, but she didn't know how.

His groin heated at the memory of their kiss. In her

lips he'd tasted so much untapped potential that he had wanted so badly to excavate. He wanted to be the one to show her just how thrillingly wicked the act of making love could be.

Unfortunately, he would not have the chance. Much as he disliked this assignment, he *was* undercover and he would not put either the investigation or Edie in jeopardy by starting a romance that he could not finish. He would not do that to either one of them. And after the investigation was over and she discovered he'd lied to her would she still be interested in him?

She reached out and placed her hand atop his. "I'm serious. I'm getting my doctorate in psychology. I can help you."

He lowered his eyelids and gave her his sexiest, come-hither stare, hoping to scare her off with raw sexuality. "Yeah?" he said in a low, husky voice. "And what if I pulled you down to my level? What if I like my life exactly as it is? What if I don't want to be saved?"

His approach paid off, rendering her to helpless stutters. "I...er...well...what I mean is..."

Reaching out, Sam stroked her jaw with a finger. She blinked, wide-eyed but did not draw back from his touch. She was so soft, so perfect. She deserved a man with a safe job, a quiet mind and a heart empty of old hurts.

"I know you mean well," he said, "but I'm way past saving."

"No one's past saving."

He wasn't the petty criminal she thought he was, but he did have his rough, wild side. A side no woman had ever been able to tame. With him, Edie was in way over her head and the cute thing about her was that she didn't even know it. Armed with a sincere smile and good intentions she marched straight into the heat of battle, never realizing she was more vulnerable than a Girl Scout in Vietnam.

From his research into Carmichael's Department Store, he already knew Edie had talked Mr. Carmichael into hiring workers from the local halfway house. Those three guys, Kyle Spencer, Harry Coomer and Joe Dawson, were his prime suspects in the thefts because they had started at Carmichaels on the very same day the first thefts occurred.

Kyle Spencer had already served a previous stint in prison after robbing a liquor store to pay for his drug habit. Harry Coomer had been on and off the wagon for years, and hung with an unsavory crowd. A DUI conviction had landed him in the halfway house. Joe Dawson had once been a decent family man, but his addictions had driven him to embezzle from his company. Any or all of them could be involved.

Why Edie had so ardently championed these three men with Carmichael and Trotter, he had no idea.

From what he'd seen of her, he didn't think Edie Preston was dumb, but boy, was she too trusting. He could tell her stories that would straighten her hair.

But why would he seek to spoil her innocent naïveté and destroy her obvious belief in her fellow man, even if he thought her deluded?

Sam looked across the table at Edie. His breath caught in his lungs. Unruly apricot curls corkscrewed around ears so delicate they appeared molded from finest porcelain. Her complexion was as smooth as creamed butter with the warm undertones of summer peaches.

And those lips! Firm, full, sweet as hand-dipped chocolate. Thanks to Freddie the Fish, he knew first-hand how incredibly kissable they were.

"We better head back," he said, before he did something really stupid like kiss her again. "We've got just enough time to change."

"Yes," She dropped both her gaze and her smile. "You're right. It's time for me to mind my own business."

Damn! Why did he feel like a schoolyard bully who'd broken the news to a five-year-old that there was no such thing as Santa Claus?

"DR. BRADDICK?" Edie rapped on her advisor's door at nine o'clock on Monday morning following the Thanksgiving holidays. She had just enough time to get her idea approved before heading to Carmichael's for another day of photographing tots and gazing into Sam's amazing blue eyes.

An idea so exciting that it had kept her awake most of the night.

The gray-haired, bearded man looked up from his desk. "Edie." He broke into an instant smile. "Lucky you caught me. I was about to leave for a conference."

"May I come in? I don't want to interrupt."

"Sure, sure." He waved at a chair. "Have a seat. You don't mind if I pack while we talk?"

"Oh, no, sir. Go right ahead."

He had an open briefcase on his desk and was filling it with books and papers. "What can I do for you, my dear?"

Edie settled her hands in her lap and cleared her throat. "I've decided to change my dissertation topic, and I need your blessing."

"Really?" He pushed the briefcase to one side so he could give her his full attention. "But I thought you had already done significant research on the subject I suggested. The long-term chemical effects of pharmacology in the psychotic brain. I even planned on including an excerpt from your work in my new book of critical thought."

"I know." Edie twisted her fingers. How to tell her instructor that his topic was...er...deadly boring to her. "But then this wonderful opportunity to do field research opened up to me."

"Wonderful? Do tell."

She met his gaze. "Dr. Braddick, I'm tired of spending my time cloistered in libraries and psychiatric hospitals and rehab centers. I'm more interested in helping ordinary people improve their daily lives than in deviant psychology."

"Since when?"

Since the beginning, Edie suddenly realized. Her admiration for her teacher's reputation had allowed her to get caught up in his vision.

"For some time now," Edie replied.

"Oh."

The dean looked so disappointed Edie had to quell the urge to rush ahead and tell him it was okay, that she would work on the dissertation he wanted her to do.

But it wasn't okay. She didn't want to write about chemicals and drugs and the tragically mentally disturbed. She wanted to study regular people who had problems that she could actually solve and without an arsenal of drugs. So she took a deep breath, plunged ahead and told him about Sam.

"I have to know why he behaves the way he does," she concluded.

Dr. Braddick sniffed. "Other than your obvious fascination with this person, what do you hope to achieve by doing a case study on him?"

"To prove that if appropriate intervention occurs at the right time in an individual's life, it can make all the difference," she said, her excitement growing at the thought. Edie knew she could help Sam.

"Intervention? Explain yourself."

"Enhance his self-image through positive reinforcement. I believe I can turn him from the wrong path and show him how to reach out and take hold of the wide wonderful world that's waiting to embrace him. Hold a psychological mirror to his face, show him what he really looks like to others."

"Do you have any idea how simplistic that sounds?" Dr. Braddick's lips puckered as if he'd sucked on a particularly sour lemon.

For the first time Edie noticed that the bald spot atop his head had an amazing resemblance to an aerial map of Florida. Hair disappeared around Miami and didn't show up again until near Tallahassee. A large brown mole sat near Tampa.

"You think you can transform this man," her advisor said bluntly.

"No," she denied, focusing on Tampa to keep from losing her temper.

"You're a psychologist, Edie, not a missionary." Dr. Braddick shook his head, and a few errant strands of hair fell haphazardly across Jacksonville. "I had expected much more from you."

"What's that supposed to mean?" Edie frowned, irritation rising inside her. Dr. Braddick was miffed because she wasn't going to help write his book for him.

"Classic," he mumbled. "I don't want to hurt your feelings, but this is a very adolescent tendency."

"What is?"

"The eternal female need to tame the bad boy. It's the basis for romance novels, and the myth plays a prominent role in young girls' fantasies. But it has absolutely no foundation in scientific reality. Ergo, the bad boy can't be tamed."

Ergo? Who used words like *ergo* and when had Dr. Braddick gotten so darned pompous?

"I never expected you to make such broad generalizations, sir."

"And I never expected my top student to fall for a chest-thumping Neanderthal."

"I have not fallen for anyone," she denied hotly. "I merely found a subject that interested me more then the assignments you've been spoon-feeding me for the past two years."

Edie had never argued with her professor. She had been so busy groveling at the feet of Dr. Braddick's illustrious reputation, that she'd never considered that he didn't have all the answers.

They stared at each other across the desk that had become the widest chasm between student and teacher.

"Fine," Dr. Braddick said at last, the muscle in his jaw twitching with suppressed anger. "I'll allow you enough rope to hang yourself. Go ahead, engage in your case study. But don't blame me when things fall through and it costs you a wasted semester."

Edie exhaled. "Thank you."

"But before I approve this, there have got to be some ground rules."

"All right."

"Firstly, you absolutely, positively cannot become romantically involved with this man. In any way, shape or form. If you do, your research will be tainted and you must scrap the project. Is that understood?" He peered down at her over the tops of his reading glasses.

She nodded. "You don't have to worry about that."

"Secondly." Dr. Braddick narrowed his eyes. "This man cannot know he is the object of your study. You must observe him in secret. Otherwise, he'll alter his behavior and your results will be skewed."

"I can do that."

"And, I want a preliminary proposal on my desk the first day class resumes in the new year."

"All right."

"And, I want you to show a clear correlation between your study and how you expect to apply the results to future cases. In other words, I need to know that this project is not simply an excuse for you to get close to this man. I need concrete evidence that the interventions you use with this subject can in turn be used with other subjects to elicit constructive improvements.''

"Yes, sir." Edie got to her feet. "I promise, I won't disappoint you."

Dr. Braddick made a noise of disbelief.

She shook his hand, wished him a good trip, then left his office. As she walked through the deserted campus, past oak and pecan trees bare of leaves, a broad smile spread across her face.

"Woo-hoo," she shouted to the overcast sky and clicked her heels. Thanks to her interest in Sam, she'd finally had the courage to question her advisor. If just knowing him for a few days could bring this much of a change in her, what would a lifetime do?

4

Subject continues to work out court-appointed community service as Santa at Carmichael's Department Store. He plays the part well, remaining jovial and patient despite some minor disturbances. Including a three-year-old who unexpectedly sprung a leak on Santa's knee, and a recalcitrant elf who forgot to put film in the camera, forcing Santa to endure a half dozen do-overs.

IN HER NOTATIONS Edie did not mention that *she* was the elf in question. She closed her notebook, capped her pen and slid both into her purse.

She sat in her car outside Carmichael's with her engine idling, waiting for Sam to depart through the employee entrance. She had raced from the store ahead of him without changing clothes, hoping to get into position before he emerged.

Her heart was doing this strange little number that

oddly resembled the rumba. *Thud, thud, thud, thud, thud—thump. Thud, thud, thud, thud, thud—thump.*

What if Sam spotted her when she followed him? Where would he go after work? What would she do when he got to where he was going? These questions circled her brain like hungry vultures searching for roadside victims.

Before she had time to work herself into a full-blown frenzy, Sam exited the store looking sensational. He wore snug blue jeans that sculpted his gorgeous behind, black running shoes and a baseball jacket.

To Edie's consternation, he wasn't alone. Joe Dawson walked beside him, and they were talking animatedly.

What was Sam doing with Joe? Not that she had anything against Joe. He was a good guy when he wasn't drinking. Edie had met him in her clinical externship at the Hazelwood Treatment Center's drug and alcohol rehabilitation program. After ending up in prison for embezzlement, Joe had been serious about turning his life around and he had seemed truly grateful to Edie for getting him a job in the accounting department at Carmichael's.

Nevertheless, Edie knew that Joe was still too close to the edge, too near temptation to be hanging out with bad influences.

Like Sam?

Fretting that Sam and Joe might have too much in

common, Edie tugged off her elf hat, and tossed it aside as she watched the two men cross the parking lot and get in Joe's car.

Joe started his car. Edie put her trusty little Toyota in gear and inched after them.

Joe drove a half block and switched on his left-turn signal. Up ahead was a small shopping center that contained a liquor store, a drugstore, a hair salon, an insurance agency and a flower shop.

Don't go to the liquor store, she mentally pleaded.

Although she had no personal experience with alcohol abuse, as both a psychology major herself and the daughter of a social worker and a Presbyterian minister, Edie had met people with substance abuse problems.

The experiences had made an impression on her. She had never touched a drop of alcohol in her life. Not that she thought any less of those who did take a drink now and then. Plenty of people could imbibe and be none the worse for it. But not Joe Dawson.

And Sam?

Edie's gut tightened.

Joe stopped the car outside the drugstore. Edie allowed herself a relieved sigh, then immediately wondered what they were buying and decided to follow them into the building.

The two men got out of the car.

Edie parked a safe distance away and watched them disappear inside.

Well, she wasn't going to find out anything lurking in the car but what if she followed them in and they spotted her?

So what? It was a free country. She didn't owe them any explanation. She could shop in the drugstore just as readily as they.

Her mind made up; Edie left the car and scurried inside.

The heat in the overcrowded building stifled her senses. Edie wished she'd left her coat in the car. She glanced down first one aisle and then another.

No Joe. No Sam.

Rats.

She walked past first aid supplies, past cosmetics and soaps. She dodged a group of gray-haired ladies arguing over which was the most flattering color of Miss Clairol and skipped around a clutch of uniformed schoolgirls giggling about the nine hundred varieties of blemish cures.

She caught sight of Sam standing at the pharmaceutical counter at the back of the store. Edie screeched to a halt and turned her back to him. Ducking her head, she walked backward to the end of the aisle one baby step at a time, until she stood just a few feet away. Luckily, she remained hidden from view behind a cardboard cutout of some famous athlete extolling the virtues of his favorite brand of jock itch cream.

She was out of Sam's sight, but within hearing

range. The suspense was killing her. What kind of prescription was he getting filled?

The pharmacist mumbled something.

Sam laughed.

Edie cocked her head to one side. Straining, she leaned farther back.

Her heel caught the athlete's life-size cutout, and he began to totter. Desperate to keep out of sight, Edie reached to steady the grinning cardboard effigy.

And lost her balance in the process.

Her elf shoes skidded on the waxed floor. One knee buckled and the leg went shooting out beneath her.

Flailing, she desperately grabbed for a shelf in a vain attempt to remain standing and wrapped her fingers around the metal rack.

For one miraculous instant the rack held.

Then, just when she thought she had everything under control, the smug, artificial athlete slowly toppled onto her shoulders.

The straw that broke the camel's back.

Edie's remaining leg gave up the battle. The thin rack collapsed under the full brunt of her weight.

She sank to the floor, crushing Mr. Jock Itch underneath her.

The contents of the shelf showered down. Boxes and boxes of condoms.

A dozen different brands. Viking. White Knight. Sir Lancelot.

Color condoms. Ultra-thin condoms. Ribbed-for-her-pleasure condoms.

A clerk shouted in dismay.

People rushed over.

Edie felt a blush heat her cheeks and spread to tingle her scalp. Looking down, she saw she held a box of condoms in her hands.

Neon. Bargain count—fourteen for the price of twelve. Jumbo size.

"Edie? Are you all right?"

She heard Sam's voice and wished at that moment that she was naked on Interstate 12 doing the tango with a dancing gorilla. It would have been far less embarrassing.

"I'm fine," she managed to say.

"You're sure?" he insisted, helping her to a sitting position. His hand lay pressed against her back and all she could do was wish him away.

"Great. Never been better. I wreck drugstores all the time. It's a little hobby of mine."

She tried not to look at him, but he cupped a palm around her chin and she found herself gazing into those compelling blue eyes.

"Well then, sweetheart," he said, gently prying the box of condoms from her hand and tugging her to her feet, "if you're planning that big of a Christmas party maybe you should have these things delivered."

HE HADN'T MEANT to tease Edie about the condoms.

If Sam was being completely honest with himself, he would admit he was jealous.

Who was she buying those condoms for?

What was more important, why did he care?

She wasn't married. Joe Dawson had told him that. Another thing that had irritated Sam was the admiration evident in Joe's voice when he spoke about Edie. He had been lauding her virtues since they'd left the drugstore. Clearly, the guy had a major jones for her.

That knowledge didn't improve Sam's mood much.

"Turn right," he told Joe.

"Sylvan Street?"

"Uh-huh."

They drove past an odd combination of houses in the ethnically mixed neighborhood of Jameson Heights. Hundred-year-old, multifamily Victorians sat on lots next door to newly built adobe structures. This house had a tile roof, that one had pink flamingoes in the yard.

Sam had grown up here at a time when the area was rough-and-tumble. He liked the cultural diversity. On warm evenings in the summer, one could walk down the sidewalk and smell dinners cooking in an exotic mix of spices: curry and cumin, anise and fennel, garlic and oregano.

From one window would come a throbbing salsa beat, from another the wail of a blues guitar. There might be a low-rider parked in one driveway, a Harley in another, a brand-new Volkswagen Beetle in a third.

"Here's my place." Sam pointed to the frame house built in the fifties that he had recently renovated himself.

Joe pulled into the driveway. "Do you need a ride to work tomorrow?"

"No, thanks. My car should be out of the shop."

Joe nodded. "Hey, maybe you'd like to go out with me and Kyle and Harry a week from next Saturday night. Harry's girlfriend is headlining at a gentleman's club over on Ashbury. You interested?"

Sam pricked up his ears. This is what he'd been angling for when he'd befriended Joe the afternoon before, then asked him for a ride to work. "Sounds like a fun time," Sam said, as he got out of the car with the bag of prescriptions he'd picked up at the drugstore for his Aunt Polly.

"See ya at work." Joe put the car in gear and backed from the driveway.

Sam waited a moment then walked across the street to his Aunt's house. He rang the bell. "Got your pills," he said, when she opened the door.

Even in her early seventies, Aunt Polly still possessed the same military posture from her youth. She reached out and took the sack. "Good boy, Sammy," she praised.

When he did what she wanted, his aunt lauded him with compliments but let him step out of line and she lashed him with the sharp side of her tongue. Even now, at age twenty-nine he was unable to escape her chiding. He'd learned to live with it. He loved her after all, in spite of everything.

"I always knew if I chewed on you long enough you'd turn out to be a good boy. Course it took a whole lot of chewing." She chuckled. "You certainly had a mind of your own. Always had to do things your way, and the rules be damned."

"How's the arthritis today?" he asked, not all that interested in cataloguing his faults.

She made a face, held up her gnarled fingers. "Don't ask. You want to come in? I've got soup cooking."

"Thanks for the invitation, but I've got work to do."

"Work, work, work. When are you going to settle down and get married?" His aunt shook her head. "If you don't give me grandnieces and grandnephews soon, I'll be too old to play with them."

"Ha! That'll be the day."

"I'm serious, Sam, you need somebody to watch out for you."

That was the last thing he needed. "I promise." He leaned over to kiss his aunt's dry cheek that smelled of lanolin. "When and if I decide to get married, you'll be the first to know."

After bidding her goodbye, he trotted back across

the street to his house. The place seemed unnaturally silent, unusually empty.

To heck with self-pity. Sam turned the television on a bit too loud, trying to drown out his loneliness.

Marriage. Aunt Polly seemed to think that was a cure. Never mind that she'd never married herself.

Truthfully, he was too busy for marriage. He often worked long, dangerous hours. He'd seen too many police officers' marriages fail for those very reasons. Sam had decided maybe he wasn't the marrying kind. Why should he surrender his independence?

A lump formed in Sam's throat. Yes. It would take someone pretty darn special to get him to the altar. His fantasy woman would have to accept him for who he was, a stomach-scratching, bad-joke-telling, junk-food-loving caveman. She would not try to force him into some ridiculous mold the way Donna had.

An old embarrassment flared in him. Why had he allowed Donna to manipulate him? When in love, his self-respect seemed to fly right out the window.

No more.

In the past love had twisted him into shapes he didn't fit. He wasn't a hunk of pasta dough ripe for the press of some woman's choosing. He wasn't fancy. No rigatoni or farfelle or mafalda. He was elbow macaroni, slightly bent, but down to earth.

And then, for absolutely no reason whatsoever, he thought of Edie Preston.

Sweet Edie with the face of an angel and a ditzy,

interfering, endearing personality that made you want to hug her and swat that round little bottom at the same time.

Right now she was probably making love to her boyfriend.

Sam ground his teeth.

Damn. He had a job to focus on. Thieves to catch. A penance to pay so he could return to real detective work. Some pixie with a smile that rocked his world, wasn't going to distract him.

Too bad she had the most stellar pair of legs he'd ever seen and a chest that could rivet any man's gaze. Too bad she possessed eyes as green as deep summer. Too bad she was so innocent.

She deserved some socially conscious, human rights activist to a world-weary guy whose life revolved around dangerous criminals, perilous risks and touchy situations.

Unlike Edie, Sam had no illusions about changing the world. He was a cop because he enjoyed seeing justice done, not because he was out to save humanity.

If he ever fell in love he wanted a tall, muscular woman who could protect herself. A practical-minded woman who accepted the world as it was and didn't expect him to be something he wasn't. Not a bit of fluff who tried to change his basic personality at every turn.

Unfortunately Christmas was still over three weeks

away. Could he resist her until the twenty-fifth? Or better yet, could he solve the thefts before then?

Tomorrow, he'd go into the store early. Chief Timmons had gotten him a key from J. D. Carmichael. He would snoop around, and see if he could unearth anything on his own time. Playing Santa wasn't getting him anywhere, especially since he couldn't seem to keep his eyes off a certain charming elf.

If he didn't watch himself, if he didn't keep his guard piled higher than the Great Wall of China, Sam feared he could fall for Edie Preston.

Fall hard enough to shake the plaster on his rebellious self-image.

For a man who had spent his entire life trying to prove that he was too tough for mushy stuff like love, that would never do.

THE WAY Sam had called her sweetheart. In that deep sexy tone. Edie sprinted around the upper level of the mall, unsuccessfully trying to focus on anything but Sam and the previous day's humiliation. She'd spent the entire night tossing, turning and thinking about Sam. Around dawn she had come to one conclusion. She still wanted to do a case study on him. He was her sphinx. The riddle she had to solve. The enigma she must crack. If she could come to understand the real Sam Stevenson, Edie felt she could understand anyone.

How she was going to face Sam again after yesterday's fiasco at Serve-Rite Drugs?

Edie cringed.

He would look at her and think—Glow in the dark condoms. Jumbo size. Then, just like any virile, red-blooded American male, that thought would lead to another and his mind would ride the sensual track, only a mental hop, skip and jump to picturing her naked.

Her face flamed.

Head down to cover her impending humiliation, she pumped her arms and legs faster, propelling herself around the mall's upper level, desperate to outrun her folly.

She approached a side entrance near Carmichael's, and from the corner of her eye, caught a glimpse of someone striding through the door. She tried to slow up and put on the brakes but it was too late.

She slammed into the back of a tall, broad-shouldered man.

''Whoa, there.''

A hand reached out and wrapped around her waist, holding her close, holding her safe.

That voice. That touch. That unique masculine scent.

It couldn't be. She looked up and blinked.

But it was.

Talk about Murphy's Law. Talk about being in the

wrong place at the wrong time. Talk about the fickle hand of fate.

She was cursed. Doomed to continually disgrace herself whenever she was around him.

Sam. Standing before her, big as day and twice as nice.

Inwardly, she groaned, as if he didn't already consider her the world's biggest klutz. He was probably beginning to think she had some kind of medical condition.

"Edie?"

"Sorry about rear-ending you," she blabbered, then realized how that sounded.

"Try keeping your head up when you're power walking," he said, chucking a finger under her chin, and sending a fissure of pure sexual energy sizzling through her. "It'll cut down on mishaps."

"Th-thanks," was all she could stammer in return.

"Don't mention it." He smiled and she found herself lost at sea in his eyes.

"What are you doing here so early?" Edie glanced at her watch. "The store doesn't open for another hour."

"Uh…" Sam hesitated and dropped his gaze.

In that instant, Edie knew he was about to lie to her and her heart plummeted into her sneakers.

"Er…I'm meeting someone."

If he'd been Pinocchio, his nose would be punching her in the chest right about now.

"Someone?"

"Joe Dawson. He gave me a ride home last night. My car is in the shop and in return I told him I would help him with his, um…"

"Yes?" Edie could see him searching his mind for a plausible excuse. His deception upset her.

Why Sam, why?

"His taxes."

"Joe's an accountant," she pointed out.

A desperate expression crossed his face. "Uh, I know but I have an investment he's interested in as a tax shelter."

"You don't have to lie to me, Sam," she said softly. "If you don't want me to know something, tell me that it's none of my business."

"Edie…" He reached out to her but she stepped away.

"It's okay. For whatever reason you feel compelled to steal cars and lie. I'm not judging you. I'm just curious as to why you feel the need to do things that are detrimental."

"I'm sorry," he said. "You're right. There are things I can't explain to you."

"You don't owe me any explanations but you do owe it to yourself, Sam, to question your own behavior."

"I'm not what I seem to be."

"No," she replied, "you're not."

That was why she found him so mesmerizing. Was

Dr. Braddick correct? Was she under the spell of nothing more than a woman's age-old desire to tame the bad boy? Was she so gullible as to believe she could change this man who oozed potential and yet seemed so eager to throw it all away in the pursuit of macho thrills?

Nonsense. She would prove to both herself and Dr. Braddick that Sam was worth saving and she was just the psychologist to do it.

EDIE COMPLETELY unnerved him.

The expression of disappointment in her eyes sent him hurtling back to his childhood when he'd had to face Aunt Polly after being collared by the store detective for shoplifting a screwdriver at Bunson's Hardware.

What had begun as a humiliating experience had in the end turned into an interest in police work. The officer who'd come to the store had a long talk with him about right and wrong and in the end Sam had joined the afterschool, community basketball team sponsored by local law enforcement. Because he had admired and respected the officer so much, Sam had become a policeman himself.

Unfortunately, he couldn't explain that to Edie. What troubled Sam was how badly he wanted to tell her that he was an undercover cop, not a two-bit criminal serving out court appointed community service as she believed. But he could not because it put her in jeopardy.

Forget her, Stevenson, and get on with your job.

It was bad enough he'd been thinking about Edie

so intently that morning, that he'd accidentally locked his keys in the car. Why couldn't he get the woman off his brain?

Today, he planned on befriending another man from Joe's halfway house, Kyle Spencer. Kyle, a mechanic by trade, had been hired at Carmichael's as a maintenance worker one week ago, and he was currently dating fellow employee, Jules Hardy.

Besides using his investigative skills in an attempt to discover if Kyle might be involved in the thefts, Sam hoped the man had a Slim Jim he could borrow to break into his locked vehicle.

He tried to concentrate on his work, both as Santa and as undercover cop. He bounced kids on his knees, all the while keeping his eyes on the crowd. He skipped lunch and instead hung around the parking lot talking to the employees who sneaked out for a smoke, surreptitiously asking questions about their colleagues.

Yet no matter how hard he struggled to keep his mind on track, time after time Sam felt his attention irresistibly drawn to Edie. He loved the way she smiled at the children, and the way she hummed Christmas songs under her breath. He adored the way she smelled like warm chocolate chip cookies fresh from the oven and the way she made his groin tighten whenever she occasionally brushed against him.

His desire for her was nonsensical and he knew it. Pure animal attraction had never overwhelmed him

like this before, but he would not succumb to this
driving urge to nibble those full cherry lips again. He
would not.

He could resist.

At that moment, Edie dropped a roll of film not
two feet from him. She bent over to pick it up favoring him with an up-close-and-personal view of the
world's most spectacular behind.

Sam gritted his teeth. He could resist.

Well, he *could!*

Case Study—Sam Stevenson
Observation—December 8

   Subject hangs around the department store
long after his shift has ended. Why? Today, a
thousand dollars worth of tools were discovered
missing from the hardware section. Early this
morning, subject was seen in that area of the
store, clearly violating the new store policy
against loitering in other departments. Could
there be a connection between subject and the
missing tools?

EDIE NIBBLED on the end of her pen, then crossed out
the last sentence. Conjecture had no place in an ob-
jective case study; yet, she couldn't help wondering.
Was Sam involved with the stolen tools? She didn't
want to believe it, but something told her he was not
all that he seemed.

Little things gave him away. The furtive manner in which he kept glancing around the store at the oddest times as if he expected a burly policeman to tap him on the shoulder. The way he would suddenly disappear leaving Edie to entertain the waiting children until he returned.

One thing was clear; she had to follow Sam again.

Feeling like a cast member from *Mission Impossible,* Edie mentally played the theme song in her head as she sat slouched in the front seat of her Toyota Tercel, waiting for Sam to appear.

A shiver ran through her and she snuggled deeper into her coat. She thought of letting the engine idle and running the heater, but she'd just bought a book called, *How to Find Out Anything About Anybody.* The author suggested when tailing someone it was best to remain as unobtrusive as possible and that meant not running your car engine despite the cold.

She glanced at her watch. Over forty minutes had passed since the end of their shift.

Joe Dawson came and went. Still no Sam. Just when she'd decided to call it quits, Sam emerged from a side door and headed for a classic red Corvette parked in a far corner. He hesitated a moment, casting a furtive glance first left, then right. Then he pulled something from his hip pocket.

What was he doing?

Edie twisted around and grabbed the binoculars

resting on the back seat. Bringing the field glasses to her eyes, she studied him.

He held a straight metal object in his hand and he was feeding it alongside the car window and down into the driver's side door.

Her heart catapulted into her throat.

No! No! He couldn't be stealing that red Corvette. Not right before her very eyes.

But it seemed that he was.

In less than a minute he had the door open, then he quickly glanced around again before climbing inside. He bent his head low over the dash so that she could barely see the top of his head.

She watched cop shows. She knew he was hot-wiring that car.

"For shame, Sam Stevenson," she lectured. "Haven't you learned anything from your stint in community service?"

Apparently not.

The Corvette roared to life, a puff of exhaust shooting from the tailpipe. He slipped the car into gear and pulled out of the parking lot.

Oh! He was getting away.

Edie tossed the binoculars into the seat beside her, started her own engine and took off after him.

Hang on Sam! I'll help you!

She gunned the Toyota, whizzed past a station wagon filled with startled nuns, changed lanes and slid in behind Sam, careful to keep two cars sand-

wiched between them. They chugged along at seventy
in a fifty-five-mile-per hour zone.

Going so fast set Edie's teeth on edge. She obeyed
the laws of the land. She didn't speed, she didn't litter
and she certainly didn't steal cars.

She did like helping her fellow man, and if saving
Sam from himself meant a few measly traffic viola-
tions then she would accept responsibility for her actions.

Just when she was thrilling to life in the fast lane,
Sam took the Jameson Heights exit ramp and pulled
into the driveway of a white-frame house, circa
1950s, with green shutters on curtained windows. No
lights shone through. Edie pulled over to the curb
where she was, three houses down from him, and
parked.

What was he doing here? Whose house was this?
She feared the answers to those questions. Mostly, she
feared what dark things she might discover about this
mysterious man.

He got out of his car, walked up the steps, reached
in his pocket for a key, opened the door and went
inside.

Did he live here?

Hmm.

Had he stolen this car only to bring it home?

Edie frowned and experienced a strange letdown.
What had she expected? That he would take it to a

chop shop? Drive to the Mexican border? Meet Joe Dawson somewhere in a clandestine exchange?

Yes. Yes. And yes.

Maybe he was stopping off to pick up something and would be on his way in a few minutes.

A light came on in the house. Edie put the binoculars to her eyes. She couldn't see much from this distance. Through the half-opened curtains she spotted a couch, caught a glimpse of a television set.

A shadow passed before the window.

Sam.

And he'd taken his shirt off.

His bare chest glistened in the muted lighting. It looked as if he were heading for the shower.

Edie inhaled sharply and almost choked on her breath. She coughed, gasped. Even from this distance the man had the power to disrupt her oxygen supply.

Resolutely, she turned her mind and her eyes away from the sight of his naked torso. As Edie sat pondering the question of what to do next, she happened to glance in her review mirror. A patrol car rolled slowly down the road toward her.

Her heart scaled her throat.

Don't panic. Don't assume anything, Edie told herself, but her palms were suddenly sweating enough to fill a ten-gallon bucket.

And in her heart, she knew. Someone had reported the red Corvette stolen. Someone had witnessed Sam stealing it from the mall parking lot.

The police were on to him.

The car inched closer, passed Edie. The driver was a Denzel Washington look-alike, his gaze trained on Sam's house. On the red Corvette.

Edie's pulse leapt like a tiger lunging at the bars of its cage. She had to warn Sam. So determined was she on helping him, she didn't stop to consider the consequences of her actions.

She stumbled from the Toyota, raced down the property line of the house beside her and into the backyard. She couldn't let the patrolman see her.

Darn! There was a six-foot privacy fence between this house and the one next door.

Edie drew a deep breath and got a running start at the fence. Someone inside the house pushed open the sliding glass door and yelled at her but she was already over the fence and into the yard next door.

She was still two houses away from Sam, separated this time by a chain-link fence and a really big German shepherd lying on the back porch.

The animal lifted his head and uttered a low, menacing growl.

She yelped and sprinted forward.

The dog charged.

The chain-link fence clanked nosily as her feet found toe holes.

The dog lurched.

Edie squealed and felt teeth sink into her rear end.

She heard a loud ripping noise when she pulled free and tumbled over the fence.

She fell and scraped her palms, but she didn't take time to assess her wounds. Thankfully, this last house had no fence. She could see Sam's backyard from here.

Her breath coming in short, quick gasps, she turned her head toward the street, and saw that the patrol car had pulled to a stop beside Sam's house.

Hurry. Hurry.

On winged feet, she flew up the stone steps and pounded on Sam's back door with both fists. "Sam, Sam," she shouted. "Get out here, now."

He didn't answer.

Oh, no! Had the cop already taken him away?

She pounded again. Harder this time. "Sam!"

The back door jerked open. Edie tumbled inward to see Sam standing dripping wet and totally naked save for the narrow strip of towel wrapped around his waist.

His eyes widened. A smile curled at the corner of his lips. "Edie? What are you doing here?"

The front doorbell rang.

It had to be Denzel.

And Sam was nearly naked in thirty-degree weather. Oh, no!

She grabbed his hand and tugged him out the back door. Never mind his undressed state. She would get him to the car, and crank up the heater to warm him.

She'd take him to her house. They could talk and decide how to extricate him from this mess.

"You've got to get out of here. Now."

"Wait. Slow down. What's going on? I just got out of the shower." He looked completely perplexed.

Despite the urgency of the moment, Edie couldn't help noticing how the terry cloth towel clung damply to his tanned, muscular body, nor could she keep her eyes from tracing the whorl patterns of dark chest hairs. Heck, even his long bare toes were cute.

Stop this, Edie. You can't let physical attraction deflect you from your purpose. Forget Sam's good looks. Remember that he's your dissertation project. Professionals do not become involved with their subjects.

"What's going on?" he repeated, dragging her back to the present moment.

"A policeman is at your front door. You're about to be arrested," she said, still yanking on his arm. "Come with me. My car's parked out front. We'll have to go the back way, and I can tell you from experience that German shepherd in house number two is a real meanie. If we hurry. I can get you out of this. At least for the time being."

He stared at her as if she'd stepped off a spaceship.

Maybe she'd been talking too fast and he hadn't understood the urgency of the moment.

The doorbell pealed again.

"Excuse me, Edie." He turned and started back into the house.

"No!" She clung to him like super glue. "Not unless you want to go to jail."

"Go to jail?" His eyes were laughing but he kept his mouth perfectly straight. He thought she was joking. "For what?"

"For stealing that red Corvette parked in your front driveway."

Sam's mouth twitched, then he tossed his head back and the sound of laughter rolled from him like gathering thunder.

Edie frowned. "What's so funny?"

"That's my car."

"Don't you lie to me, Sam Stevenson. I saw you break into it. I saw you hot-wire the thing in the parking lot."

He wiped tears from his eyes with the back of a hand and chuckled that much harder.

Edie sank her hands on her hips. She didn't understand this man. Not one bit. "You won't be laughing when that Denzel Washington look-alike cop on your front step has you in handcuffs. This is serious."

"So it's my neighbor Charlie at the front door? Come on in. Close the door. Have a seat. I'll be right back." Sam twisted the towel tighter around his waist then padded down the hall to the front door.

Confused, Edie stepped inside and pulled the door

shut behind her. It wasn't a figment of her imagination. She *had* seen Sam break into that car.

Muted male voices were discussing something in the hallway.

Edie tiptoed forward and tilted her head, hoping to overhear their conversation.

The front door clicked closed.

Footsteps sounded.

Edie darted back to the kitchen table and plunked into a chair.

"Yeow!"

She shot to her feet, her hand at her backside. Her pants were ripped, her skin nipped. That German shepherd had nicked her and she'd been so intent on warning Sam, she had forgotten all about it.

"What's wrong?"

Sam's tall frame filled the doorway, concern for her etching his face.

She swallowed. Hard. She forgot all about the dog bite. Her gaze traveled from his broad shoulders, down his impeccable chest to where the dark hairs on his belly disappeared into a V where he kept his towel closed with a mere thumb and forefinger.

Sucking in a deep breath, Edie realized only that thin scrap of terry cloth stood between her and glory. If Sam's fingers were to slip…

"What did Denzel want?" she asked, moistening her lips with the tip of her tongue.

A smile tugged his mouth upward. "To invite me to his Christmas party."

"Oh."

"I heard you cry out in pain just now," Sam said. "Is something wrong?"

Edie fingered her torn pants. "I sort of had a run-in with your neighbor's German shepherd."

One eyebrow shot up on his forehead. "Snookems?"

"Two houses over." She poked a thumb in the direction she'd come from. "I think he won the argument."

"Let me see."

Edie's gaze flicked to his towel once more. "Maybe you better put on some clothes first."

"Yeah," he said and darn if his voice didn't sound husky. "I'll be right back."

"Take your time."

He wasn't gone for long but it didn't take many minutes for Edie to feel foolish. In her mind's eye she retraced her steps, relived her mistakes.

She dropped her face into her hands. He probably thought she was nuttier than a pecan tree at harvest time.

Then she realized she was missing a prime opportunity to get to know him better. Tidy kitchen. No dirty dishes in the sink, no toast crumbs on the counter like at her place. The color scheme was masculine, black and white and chrome. Black-and-white

checkerboard pattern on the tile floor, black counter-
top, white cabinets, chrome appliances.

Getting up, she opened the refrigerator door as quietly as she could and took stock. Ah, now, here was
proof a rebel lived here. One can of beer, ketchup, a
carton of Chinese takeout.

Nosily, she opened the carton of Chinese food.
Beef lo mein. Her favorite.

"Hungry?" Sam asked. "I can call for a pizza if
you want me to."

"No." She shook her head and put the lo mein
back on the shelf. "I've got to be going." Before she
did something totally idiotic like jeopardize her dissertation.

He wore blue jeans and a Dallas Cowboys sweat-
shirt. In his hand he held a bottle of hydrogen peroxide, antibiotic ointment and a box of adhesive ban-
dages. "Let's take a look at that wound."

This was humiliating. Edie turned and favored him
with a view of her bottom.

Sam stepped closer and squatted level with her
backside. "The pants are goners, I'm afraid."

She felt his fingers touching her skin through the
tear. Closing her eyes, she fought back her natural
feminine responses to being touched by a man she
found very handsome by reminding herself repeatedly
that she was a psychologist. Sam needed her help. She
would not compromise either her case study or his

future mental health for the sake of a little physical attraction.

"The bite's not bad. Hardly any blood at all. Snookems barely broke the skin, but I imagine you're going to have a bruise in the morning. Good thing I know the dog's had his shots."

"Good thing," Edie echoed.

"Could you bend over the table so I can doctor this?"

"Uh, sure."

"This might sting."

The hydrogen peroxide was cool, countering the sudden heat in the room. Next came the ointment, then the bandage. It seemed an eternity passed before he said, "There. All done."

She straightened, and spun away from him as quickly as she could. "Thank you."

"No. Thank you."

"For what?"

"Risking life and limb to warn me."

"You're not angry that I thought you were stealing another car?" She peeked at him.

His eyes crinkled at the corners when he smiled. "A natural mistake. What impresses me is that you cared enough to follow me home and then endangered yourself for my sake."

She shrugged, feeling guilty. She couldn't tell him ulterior motives had possessed her to shadow him.

"I'd hate to see you get into any more trouble," she said. That was certainly true. No lies there.

He took a step toward her. "I'm not a project, Edie."

Project? Had he guessed that she was using him as a case study? But how could he know that?

She laughed nervously. "I never said you were."

"I can see it in your eyes. You're like my Aunt Polly, just like my old girlfriend. You take one look at me and see a 'fixer-upper'. Well, I'm not some run-down house, lady. I'm a man." He took another step. The floor creaked beneath his weight. "With both strengths and flaws."

"I never…"

"Shh." He raised a finger, pressed it against her lips. "I've seen a lot of life. A lot of ugly things I pray you'll never see."

Edie gulped.

"Your bright, optimistic outlook on the world is one of the things I like about you. But Edie, you've been too sheltered. Yes, maybe you spent your life helping out at homeless shelters and counseling alcoholics but it's always been secondhand. You could perch a safe distance away and give out advice without having to get your hands dirty."

"I resent that." Her temper flared. Who was he to judge her?

"Come on, admit it. You've never done anything bad, have you? You don't break the rules. You never

came in late after your parents' curfew. You've probably never even gotten a parking ticket."

"Well, Mr. Smarty, you'd be wrong. I did something bad once."

"Oh?" He smirked, irritating her even more. Just
because she didn't lie and cheat and steal didn't mean
she hadn't lived. "What terrible crime did you com-
mit?"

"I forgot to return a library book. They sent me a
notice that said if I didn't pay for it they were going
to issue a warrant for my arrest," she confessed.

Sam threw his head back and laughed at her for
the third time that evening. Long. And hard.

Edie bristled. "It wasn't funny!"

"I'm sure it wasn't to you. And I'm also sure you
burned rubber getting to the library as fast as you
could to pay that fine."

"You're not being fair."

"No, Edie, you're the one who's not being fair.
Until you've walked a mile in my shoes, don't assume
anything about me and don't try to save me, okay?"

She stared at him. He was right. The outside world
hadn't really touched her. Because of her parents and
their occupation, because of her own chosen field,
she'd always been the one to give advice, to lend a
helping hand. But in all honesty did she really know
what she was talking about? Who was she to give
him advice? She'd never been poor, never gone without food, never lived without a roof over her head.

"Before you're ever going to relate to your patients, before you can ever really understand people, you're going to have to take a walk on the wild side, Edie Preston."

"A walk on the wild side?"

"Face your temptations. Acknowledge your demons."

This didn't seem the time to point out she had no demons. No temptations.

Except one.

The urge to help others exorcise *their* demons.

She studied him. This sexy, dangerous man with a steel jaw and the ability to excite her like no other. In that moment Edie knew there was another temptation in her life. One she had been avoiding for a very long time.

6

SAM TOOK a step toward her.

Edie backed up, until she bumped flush against the kitchen wall, her eyes widening.

He had one goal on his mind.

Kiss those lips. Kiss her silly. Scare her off. Make her go away. Before she interfered in his investigation. Before she interfered in his life.

Already, she was coming too close. Following him, warning him about the cops, trying to psychoanalyze him.

The woman was nothing but trouble. She looked at him with bright, admiring eyes. She saw him as a knight in slightly dented armor. Armor she aimed to polish to a high shine.

He'd seen the look. Once a crusader, always a crusader. He couldn't change her any more than she could change him. Not that he even wanted to change her. Her earnestness, sincerity and concern for others captivated him, but being attracted to a woman like Edie and living with one were two very different things indeed.

One way or the other he had to get rid of her and

kissing her seemed the most pleasant method to achieve his purpose.

"I could teach you to walk on the wild side," he murmured, coming closer and resting his forearm on the wall above her head. If his most forward moves didn't make her run for the hills, nothing would.

Edie blinked.

He lowered his head along with his voice, and never took his eyes from hers. "I'd enjoy teaching you." He reached out a hand, softly traced a finger around the neck of her blouse. Her body trembled at his touch.

She squared her shoulders, took a deep breath and drew herself up tall. "At this juncture in your life, don't you think it would be more constructive if you concentrated on changing your self-defeating behavior patterns rather than trying to seduce me?"

"Do you?" He dipped his head lower still until their lips were inches apart.

"Yes." She nodded her head vigorously. "I do. You're using sexual overtures as a way to avoid dealing with your own shortcomings."

"Am I?"

"Yes."

"How do you know I'm not just hot for you? Sometimes doctor, a cigar is only a cigar."

"Are you trying to intimidate me with your sexuality?"

Yes.

"You mean like this?"

Then he wrapped his arms around her waist, pulled her to his chest and kissed her like he had been aching to kiss her since his lips had brushed hers that very first day at Carmichael's.

Man, did she ever taste good. Like honey and dew-drops and sweet, sweet sin. Her breath hammered in his ear, her soft scent curled in his nostrils.

He shouldn't have kissed her. Not even to scare her off. He was rock hard and growing harder by the moment. His veins filled with heated tension. It had been a long time since he had made love to a woman and his body was well aware of that fact.

You can't make love to Edie, he told himself. *You're an undercover cop, and she thinks you're a hapless screwup. You're too set in your ways to be reformed. You're rough-cut, she's fine china. There's a hundred million reasons this can't continue.*

"Sam," she whispered into his mouth.

"Yes, sweetheart?"

"Please get your hands off me. Please stop kissing me."

It was a plea, not a request. From her responsive lips he knew she wanted him as much as he wanted her, but the tone in her voice told him that she knew, just as he did, that their pairing wasn't right.

Slowly, gently, he disengaged his mouth from hers and let his hands fall to his sides.

Her green eyes drilled a hole straight through him

and he dropped into the luminous depths. He feared he was in jeopardy of losing his very soul.

He almost kissed her again.

And then the phone rang. The damnable, blessed telephone.

"Excuse me," he said to her, and moved to pick up the receiver. "Hello?"

"Samuel O'Neil Stevenson, do you have a woman in your house?"

"Aunt Polly."

"Don't you Aunt Polly me. Virginia Marston just called. Apparently some crazed woman climbed her fence, sprinted across her backyard and ran into your house. Are you up to your old shenanigans?"

"No, Auntie." Sam rolled his eyes to the ceiling.

"You know the road to hell is paved with S-E-X."

"I thought you wanted me to give you grandnieces and nephews." He couldn't resist the urge to tease his aunt.

"Not like that," she sputtered. "The regular way. Get married first."

"Well, I can put your mind at ease, Auntie, I'm not having sex."

At least not right now.

Sam glanced over at Edie. She was studying him like a scientist at a microscope. He pressed the receiver against his chest. "My Aunt Polly," he told her.

"Sam? Sam?" Despite being muffled by his sweat-shirt, Aunt Polly's voice rang out across the kitchen. "Did you say something to me? Are you still there?"

Letting out a long-suffering breath, Sam returned the receiver to his ear. "I'm here."

Edie silently mouthed, "I'm leaving. See you at work tomorrow."

Sam ached to tell her not to go. He wanted her to stay but at the same time he wanted her as far away as possible. Hell, he didn't know what he wanted. The woman muddled his brain, skewered his thinking, scrambled his good intentions.

"We can't have strange women climbing over fences to get to you," Aunt Polly droned in his ear.

"No, ma'am." He watched Edie turn and walk away. His gaze fixed on the hole in her pants, her round, firm buttocks peeping through and felt himself grow hard all over again.

Damn Snookems for biting her.

Damn Aunt Polly for interrupting.

But most of all, damn himself for wanting Edie Preston more than he had ever wanted any woman in his life.

IF DR. BRADDICK knew what had gone on in Sam's kitchen, he would force her to abandon the project. If he knew the feelings raging in her heart he would probably kick her out of the doctoral program all together. Edie groaned and sank lower into the tub.

What was she going to do?

Edie drained the water from the tub, got out and wrapped a towel around herself.

Her attraction to Sam threatened to ruin her dissertation project, but if she gave up her case study, what chance did she have of actually helping him and others like him?

More than anything, she needed to prove that Sam was worth saving. In order to accomplish her goal she had to keep her sexual feelings on a short leash. No matter how she might desire him, she simply could not act on those desires.

But one thing he'd said stuck in her brain and refused to let go.

How could she hope to understand her patients if she herself had never succumbed to her darker urges?

Take a walk on the wild side, he'd dared.

Sam was absolutely correct. She had no idea what it was like to let loose and really live. Despite being halfway through her Ph.D., Edie's education had been sadly lacking.

But if she did decide to broaden her horizons, it could not be with Sam.

Edie slipped into her bathrobe, ran a comb through her hair and was padding to the bedroom when the telephone rang.

Sam, she thought immediately. But why would he call her?

Snagging the cordless phone on the second ring, she perched on the edge of the bed. "Hello?"

"Edie?"

"Yes?"

"This is Jules. Jules Hardy from the department store."

"Hey, how are you?"

Jules Hardy was a busty, bubbly redhead who worked in cosmetics. Jules never lacked for dates and always had wild tales to tell about her adventures and misadventures as a young, single woman living *la vida loca* in the twenty-first century. Now if Edie ever wanted to take a walk on the wild side, this was the woman to teach her how.

"Listen, I'm in a bit of a pickle, and I heard you were studying to be a head shrinker."

"Psychologist. Yes, that's true." Edie tucked a strand of wet hair behind one ear. "What can I do for you, Jules?"

"Well, I'd rather not get into the details over the phone. It's kinda personal and involves my new boyfriend, Kyle Spencer. In fact, Kyle is the one who told me to call you."

Edie tightened her grip on the receiver. Kyle Spencer. One of the men from the halfway house she'd gone to bat for with Carmichael. She gulped. "Is Kyle in some sort of trouble?"

"Kinda. It's involved."

Letting out her breath in one long expiration, Edie lay back on the bed. "Legal trouble?"

Was Kyle mixed up in the store thefts? Was that what worried Jules?

"I need to see you face-to-face. This is rather private. Can we meet somewhere?"

Edie glanced at the bedside clock. Ten minutes after ten. She usually went to bed at ten-thirty. But someone needed her. Someone was in trouble and she could help.

"Well…"

"Oh, please," Jules said. "I really need your expertise."

"All right."

"Can you meet me at the coffee shop on Wayfarer Lane in an hour?"

"I'll be there."

"Thank you, Edie. You're the greatest. I appreciate this so much."

"You're welcome."

"See you then."

Jules rang off and Edie hung up the phone, wondering what in the heck she'd just committed herself to.

SAM ARRIVED AT Carmichael's before dawn and slipped around the back to the freight entrance as he had every morning since starting this assignment. The security guard went off duty at 4:00 a.m., and the dock workers didn't arrive until six. For two hours the inside of the store remained unguarded. If anyone wanted to steal a big shipment of goods, this was the time to do it.

After secreting himself in the shrubbery to the left of the loading dock, he pulled a doughnut from his jacket pocket. It was a little worse for the wear, squashed flat, the chocolate glaze sticking to the waxed paper wrapping, but he was too hungry to care.

He wished for a cup of strong coffee because he hadn't gotten much sleep either, thanks to one Edie Preston.

Edie, of the impish face and infectious grin. Edie with the short, curly hair that made him think of fizzy ginger ale—light, bubbly, refreshing. Edie, who tended to stick that cute little nose of hers in where it didn't belong for all the right reasons. She cared about people. Truly cared. Sam could honestly say he'd never met anyone quite like her.

Darn the woman. Why couldn't he get her off his mind and out of his dreams?

He waited.

A battered brown Chevrolet cruised by.

Sam narrowed his eyes. It looked a lot like Harry Coomer's car. He sat up straighter. He knew that all the workers from the halfway house, Joe, Kyle and Harry, had a strict curfew. They had to stay in from midnight to 6:00 a.m. If that was Harry, then he was out of the halfway house illegally.

The car turned around at the far end of the mall parking lot and looped back. It looked a hell of a lot like Harry's car. The vehicle slowed as it neared Carmichael's. The light from the street lamps swept over the front of the car as it drove past, and caught the glint of something metal swinging from the rearview mirror.

Harry had a rabbit's foot on a metal chain dangling from the mirror of his car.

It had to be Harry Coomer's vehicle. Whether Harry was in it or not, Sam didn't know.

He held his breath and waited. The car looped around the parking lot once more, then disappeared.

Time ticked by.

Fifteen minutes. Twenty. Half an hour.

The car did not return.

Sam stifled a yawn and shifted on the ground, his buttocks growing stiff from the cold.

And speaking of buttocks, he wondered about Edie's dog-nipped fanny.

Her compact female tush dominated his fantasies with irritating regularity. For a few wonderful minutes yesterday evening, he'd held that dainty fanny in his palms.

"Knock it off, Stevenson," he growled under his breath when his fantasizing about Edie began to cause an unexpected stirring below his belt. He was on stakeout for crying out loud; he could not afford this distraction.

But he could not prevent his masculine imagination from exploding. He saw her. In his house. On his bed.

Naked. The glory of her exposed for him alone. Her sweet lips pressed to his; her soft body held close.

Sam gulped.

Then, as if his dream had sprung to life, he saw her. Not in his mind's eye. Not in his fantasy. Not in his lingering memories.

There. In front of him. Not ten yards away from where he sat hidden in the bushes.

Edie Preston. With some big-chested, red-haired girl he recognized from Carmichael's cosmetics counter.

They were standing at the loading dock entrance, fumbling with the key code to the alarm system.

Sam rubbed his eyes. Surely, he must be seeing things. What was Edie doing here at this time of morning hanging out with a girl who possessed a questionable reputation at best? And why were they attempting to gain unauthorized entry into Carmichael's?

"OKAY," Jules said, punching in some numbers on the keypad outside the freight entrance. The heavy metal doors jerked and rolled upward with a loud clang. Edie winced against the noise and cast furtive glances over her shoulder.

"When we get inside," Jules continued, "there's another control panel on the right wall that mans the security cameras storewide. All we have to do is deactivate them, and we're free to roam about the store undetected.''

''And you have the security code to that, too?''

Jules nodded.

''How did you get these codes?'' Edie whispered, tip-toeing in behind Jules who had switched on a flashlight.

They found themselves standing on the loading dock surrounded by towers of boxes. Jules hit a lever mounted at the wall and the door fell closed behind them with a loud rattle.

''I used to date the manager before Mr. Trotter. Dave Highsmith. He gave me the codes so we could meet in the store after hours.'' Jules slanted Edie a glance.

''I'm worried that when Trotter reviews the security tapes he's going to notice the time lapse and figure out someone shut off the camera for ten or fifteen minutes,'' Edie said.

Jules shrugged. ''It's a risk we'll have to take. He has no way of knowing it was us.''

Edie shook her head. ''Let's just get this over with and get out of here.''

She hadn't slept a wink. She had been with Jules at the all-night diner on Wayfarer Street planning this excursion and waiting for 4:00 a.m. to roll around. Jules knew that the store's indoor security guard's shift ended two hours before the first dock worker arrived at six. After hearing Jules's story, Edie knew they had no recourse but to break into the store. Not if they wanted to keep Kyle out of jail and Jules from getting fired.

Apparently, on the previous evening, Jules had hidden in the rest room until the store closed, in order to rendezvous with Kyle, whose shift in the maintenance department ended an hour after closing time. According to Jules, they had made wild passionate love on the cosmetics counter completely unaware that a new security camera had just been added to that department in the wake of the thefts.

When he got back to the halfway house, Kyle had learned from Joe, who'd seen the invoices, about the new cameras and he'd called Jules in a panic. Since the security cameras were reviewed first thing every morning by Mr. Trotter, it was essential that someone get into the store before dawn and steal the incriminating tape.

Kyle couldn't help because he was unable to leave the halfway house after curfew. A tape of Jules and Kyle in the store alone after hours was enough to raise suspicion about their involvement in the thefts. Kyle could be sent back to jail on parole violation and Jules would be fired. And no doubt Edie would lose her job, too, since she'd laid her reputation on the line when she'd vouched for Kyle.

Edie groaned inwardly at the thought, which had been circling her head since Jules had poured out her tale of woe.

No job. No Sam. No dissertation subject.

She'd been awfully fortunate that Jules had come to her. Otherwise…Edie shuddered at the thought.

But before Edie and Jules did anything, they had to shut off all the security cameras so they wouldn't be taped sneaking into the store. With only a pencil thin beam of light to guide them, they made a beeline for the camera control panel.

Of course, if they got caught, it would mean much more than being fired.

What if her arrest got on the news? Dr. Braddick would have a cow. She envisioned her parents sitting around the television set sipping their nightly herbal tea. She could hear the reporter. "Now, for this late-breaking story. Former Girl Scout and doctoral student breaks into Carmichael's Department Store at North Hills Mall amidst allegations of thefts. What made her do it? Details at six."

Edie pictured herself behind bars, wearing a black-and-white striped prison uniform and cringed. She couldn't go to jail! Stripes made her look hippy.

"Jules," Edie whispered, struggling to keep the tremor from her voice. "Maybe this isn't such a great idea after all. Maybe we should just go to Trotter, come clean about what happened between you and Kyle and let the chips fall where they may."

"You don't seriously think Trotter would be that forgiving, do you? He's been looking for any excuse to can Kyle and me. And he'd love to try and pin the thefts on us.''

"You're probably right about that." Edie had to agree.

"We don't have any choice. You can't back out on me now."

No, she couldn't. Edie had promised and she never broke her promises, but this still felt wrong.

"Psst." Jules had already moved through the warehouse. She waved the flashlight beam at Edie. "This way."

Before Edie could protest, Jules opened the door from the loading dock into the department store. Light spilled in, illuminating the darkness and steadying Edie's nerves somewhat. She scurried after Jules.

In a flash, Jules located the small camera mounted on the back wall, and climbed up on the counter. After fumbling with the camera for a few minutes, she ejected the tape and stuck it in her pocket.

"Got it," Jules crowed triumphantly.

Edie inhaled sharply and took a step backward.

And a cold, bony finger pointed her in the back.

Edie let out a shriek and immediately clamped a hand over her mouth.

Who was jabbing her in the lower back with an unknown object?

Freaked out beyond sensibility, she leapt to one side, her arm raised reflexively in self-defense. She swung around hard to strike the man behind her.

Except it wasn't a man.

It wasn't even human.

Edie stared owlishly as a scrawny mannequin in hot pants and a halter top—would department stores ever stop putting out summer clothes in the winter?—clattered to the floor, her head and limbs disengaging in the process.

One arm whizzed over Edie's head. A leg struck her on the thigh. The head rolled like a bowling ball down the bedding aisle and disappeared under a bed draped in a cute floral print comforter Edie had been considering buying herself for Christmas.

To Edie's ears the resulting cacophony was deafening. She cringed and waited for mall security to show up with the police in tow.

"Jules?" she whispered loudly, but her new *friend*, did not answer.

Oh crud, what now?

Then from the darkened aisle a man appeared. Edie's heart galloped and her mouth grew so dry she could not speak.

This is it, she thought. *I'm going to be arrested.*

Now, she would walk that mile in Sam's shoes. Now, she would be able to relate to him. Now, she could empathize.

She could only pray her punishment would be as lenient as his had been. Her bottom lip trembled as she struggled to ward off tears. Thrusting her hands over her head, she said, "I'll go quietly officer."

"Edie?"

Her heart leapt. It wasn't a policeman or mall security.

"Sam?"

From out of nowhere he had appeared before her like a superhero to the rescue.

Sam stepped from the shadows and she saw his dear, sweet face. He could use a shave, she noticed, a heavy five-o'clock shadow graced his jaw, but he was the most wonderful sight to ever greet her eyes.

He bent down, stuck something in the top of his boot before whispering, "Are you all right? I heard a scream and came to investigate."

"I'm fine. I just knocked over a mannequin."

"What are you doing here?" he asked.

"I was about to ask you the same thing."

Sam swallowed. Edie watched his eyes. "Um…I was driving by and saw that the freight entrance door was open a crack. Considering the thefts I figured I better see what was going on."

"Rather than call the cops?"

"I don't like talking to the cops."

"What were you doing driving by at five in the morning?" Edie asked, a sinking feeling settling deep inside her. She knew he was lying. What she did not want to face was the real reason he was in the store.

"I had a wicked case of insomnia." He winked. "After you vaulted over fences to warn me, I couldn't stop thinking about you."

She wasn't going to let him sidetrack her with that charming grin. "Weren't you worried about stumbling across the thieves?"

"What is this? Twenty questions? How am I supposed to know you're not the thief?"

She narrowed her eyes at him. "I don't owe you any explanation, but I will tell you why I'm here so you don't think I've got anything to do with the stolen merchandise." Quickly, she told him about Jules and Kyle and the ruinous security tape.

"So you two turned off the security cameras?" he asked when she finished.

"Uh-huh."

He breathed a sigh of relief. "That's good to know we're not on camera right now."

Then a sudden, horrible thought occurred to her. What if she'd been set up? What if Jules and Kyle and Sam were all in on the store thefts and they were using her as an alibi? It made perfect sense. The cameras were off. Sam was distracting her. Jules had disappeared. For all she knew Kyle had sneaked out of the halfway house. Good grief! Joe and Harry could be involved as well. At this very moment, they could be loading stolen goods into a van bound for Mexico.

Edie brought a hand to her head. How gullible was she to have fallen for Jules's story? She was too trusting, too eager to help, too darn unsuspecting.

Don't assume anything, Edie. See if you can get to the bottom of this.

"I better help you clean this up." Sam pointed at the dismantled mannequin. "The lady sorta went to pieces."

A hysterical giggle born of fear and embarrassment erupted in Edie's throat. "Poor girl lost her head."

"Flipped her wig." Sam bent and picked up a mop of fake hair.

"She doesn't have a leg to stand on." She shouldn't be laughing but she couldn't seem to help herself.

"This tragic lady reminds me of a song I wrote when I was in high school," he said picking up mannequin spare parts.

"You write songs?" Edie swallowed her laughter and ended up hiccuping.

"Not really. I only wrote this one to rebel against my Aunt Polly who forced me to join the Glee Club. She thought it would keep me out of trouble."

Edie pushed a strand of hair from her eyes and studied him in the thick shadows. There. He'd just told her something personal about himself.

Great. He picks this time and this place to bare his soul when at any moment they risked discovery.

"How does the song go?" she asked.

Sam picked up the mannequin's torso and tucked it under his arm. "Let me see if I can remember."

"I once had a robot girlfriend," Sam sang, his rich baritone voice filling the store, putting her at ease.

"With a pretty, mechanical smile. She wasn't very romantic, until I turned her dial."

He picked up the mannequin's errant leg and attached it to her body. "When I switched on her power and energized her soul, her tiny tin lips would open and her blue plastic eyes would roll. I got her at a bargain, from a strange mail-order place. She came to me disassembled and packed down in a case. I studied her schematics, then put her arms in place, wired up her circuits and bolted on her face."

Their eyes met. He grinned.

"I kept her in my closet, standing in her case," Sam crooned. "So somebody wouldn't see her and say 'Oh what a disgrace'."

He attached the other leg, then crammed the headless mannequin back on her pedestal. "But then one morning early, I found a little note, when I decoded the symbols and read what my darling wrote."

Dramatically, Sam clutched a hand to his chest. "My head then started spinning, and I with anger turned green. For my little robot girlfriend had eloped with a pinball machine."

Edie collapsed on the floor, laughing. "You're a poet," she managed to wheeze between the helpless giggles. "A true artist."

Chuckling, Sam sat down beside her, and pulled his knees to his chest. "Aunt Polly wasn't too happy when the Glee Club decided to perform 'Robot Girlfriend' at the spring recital."

Edie gazed into his eyes. He was such a fascinating, complex man. Now she knew for sure that doing a case study on him was the right thing. "Who broke your heart?"

"Me? Who says anyone broke my heart?"

"I'm a psychologist, remember? That song is a dead giveaway. You might have thought you were composing it to irk your Aunt Polly, but whether you knew it or not, you had an ulterior motive."

An emotion she couldn't quite identify flitted across his face and she knew he was about to deny that anyone had ever hurt him, then unexpectedly, he confessed. "Head cheerleader, Beth Ann Pulaski. She wanted me to be something I wasn't. Clichéd story. Rich girl, poor boy from the wrong side of the tracks. In the end when she realized she couldn't make a silk purse from a sow's ear, she dumped me for the first-string quarterback."

Edie reached out and touched his hand. "It still hurts, doesn't it?"

He shook his head. "Nah. I'm not that goofy kid anymore. But I did learn something from Beth Ann and I guess that's reflected in my song. Birds of a feather flock together. You can't be something you're not and there is no point in pursuing a relationship with a woman who can't accept you for yourself."

His eyes drilled into her.

She and Serenading Sam were alone, except for the erstwhile Jules, illegally, in a department store that had been experiencing a rash of thefts, and for all she knew, he was in on it.

She wouldn't jump to conclusions. She would not. She'd made a mistake over the Corvette, assuming Sam had stolen it. She wasn't about to make a fool of herself for the second time in as many days by accusing him of being in the store for nefarious purposes.

But why else was he here? She didn't buy his insomnia story. Not for a moment. She needed to get out of here and away from him as soon as possible. She needed time to think, to decipher her confusing feelings for him.

Edie gulped. "Can you help me find the mannequin's head? When last seen it was rolling for freedom down the aisle of the bedding department."

"Ah, Marie Antoinette lives."

"You're so funny."

He reached out for her hand. "Hold on to me, I don't want you to slip and fall in the darkness."

Hesitantly, she placed her hand into his and allowed him to guide her toward the bed where the mannequin's head had disappeared.

"Which way did she go?"

"Under there." Edie pointed to the bed in question.

Sam dropped to all fours, lifted the dust ruffle and peered underneath the bed.

Edie didn't mean to take a long, lingering gander at his bottom wagging so enticingly in the air but she just couldn't help herself. She admired the way his blue jeans molded to his muscles, enjoyed the thrill that exploded in her belly.

A few minutes passed while he tried to dislodge the hapless mannequin's head. He cursed under his breath, then got to his feet.

A cobweb dangled from his hair.

"Hold still." Edie rose up on her toes and brushed the web away with her hand.

Their eyes met.

She could feel his breath on her skin.

"Thank you."

"How about the mannequin?" she asked, anxious to alter the chemistry between them before something happened.

"Wedged between the wall and the headboard. I think I can reach it from the top." He turned and climbed onto the bed.

"Let me see." Edie sat beside him and they both peered down the back of the headboard. Sure enough Marie Antoinette stared sightlessly up at them.

"What can we dislodge her with?" he mused.

"Curtain rod?"

"Excellent idea."

Edie scooted off the bed and retrieved a curtain rod from the next department. She returned, brandishing it like a sword.

"En garde," she said, feeling like she needed to do something to keep the mood light, to keep herself from dwelling on the reason why Sam had shown up out of nowhere.

"Okay, Zorro, calm down." He reached for the curtain rod. Their hands touched, kindling the growing spark between them.

Edie jerked her hand away.

Sam dropped his gaze, and resumed his position on his knees in the middle of the bed.

Neither of them commented on the power surge of emotions that resulted every time they touched.

He slipped the curtain rod behind the headboard. "It's really stuck," he said after a few moments. Using the curtain rod like a fulcrum, Sam shoved with all his strength. The head gave way, throwing him off balance.

He fell backward. Onto Edie. His large body covering hers.

Quickly, he shifted.

Edie looked up. Sam peered down.

And then he kissed her. Softly at first, then harder.

Edie's world tilted, whirled. She was lying on a bed in Carmichael's, the most incredible man in the world spread out on top of her. A man with lips of pure gold. At any moment they could be caught and arrested. Any moment they could be discovered. By kissing him here, now, in this way she was jeopardizing everything she held dear.

"We better stop this," she said, her voice shaky. What was she thinking? Hadn't she warned herself repeatedly after that incident in his kitchen that she would keep her physical distance from him? He was a man who needed the benefits of her clinical expertise. He was not, under any circumstances, a potential mate.

Sam sat up.

One of his pant legs had risen up on a shin. Edie glanced down, saw something poking from his boot.

She caught her breath, raised her head, met his eyes.

Why was the butt of a handgun protruding from the top of his boot?

7

SAM'S EYES followed Edie's gaze. He leaned over and with a quick flick of his wrist, pulled his pant leg down to conceal the gun-toting boot. Calmly, as if nothing had happened, he straightened and stared her in the face.

"Why don't you let me take you to breakfast?" he asked.

He has got a gun!

But he is not pointing it at you.

Yes, but why did he have a gun in the first place? Only policemen and criminals hid weapons in their eel-skin Justins.

And she knew he wasn't a cop. He'd told her he was working out a community service obligation.

I will not jump to conclusions. I will not jump to conclusions.

Unfortunately, the conclusions were jumping onto her. What other explanation might there be for his behavior?

"Breakfast?" he asked again.

"I can't." She waved helplessly at the cosmetics counter. "I've got to find Jules."

Sam leaned close, and whispered in her ear. "Sweetheart, it might be a good idea if you and your friend left the store."

Was he warning her off because something was about to go down? Wasn't that how criminals referred to their heists?

"Yes. That's probably a good idea. Thank you."

He just kept looking at her. Edie's stomach dove to her feet. Why did she possess such a need to help him? How had he ensnared not only her curiosity but her desire as well?

She should stay away from him for so many reasons. For the sake of her dissertation, for the sake of her job, for the sake of her sanity. Before meeting Sam Stevenson, she had never considered doing something this crazy.

He wasn't good for her.

Not at all.

He stood, retrieved the loose head and rested it back on the mannequin's body.

"Hey, Edie. Who's this?" Jules popped from behind a panty hose display. "Oh, wait a minute." She snapped her fingers. "You're Santa. Did Edie call you and tell you to meet her here or something?"

"There you are!" Edie exclaimed. "Where have you been, Jules?"

"Actually, at first I thought you'd gotten nabbed by mall security. When you screamed I dove for cover. Then I heard talking. When bedsprings started creaking, I figured you two were taking advantage of the cameras being turned off and needed your privacy.''

''It wasn't like that,'' Edie protested.

Jules smirked. ''No? Then how come he's got lipstick on his collar?''

Sam rested a hand at his collar as Edie turned to see her lipstick smeared across his white shirt. She felt embarrassed heat rise to her cheeks.

''Well, it's been nice chatting with you, Sam,'' Edie said as if they were at a cocktail party instead of locked after hours in a department store. ''But we've got to go.''

''Allow me to walk you ladies to your car,'' Sam said, then looped his arms through theirs and guided them back out the way they'd come.

''STEVENSON,'' Chief Timmons growled over the phone. ''I want some answers and I want them now.''

Bleary-eyed, Sam rolled over and stared at the clock. Seven-thirty. He'd gotten back from Carmichael's less than an hour ago. He'd thought he would catch a few hours of much needed sleep before he had to be back at the store by ten for another day of Ho, Ho, Ho.

''What's the matter?''

''I just got a call from J. D. Carmichael and he is fit to be tied.''

Sam swung his legs over the edge of the bed. "What for?"

"Last night, while you were supposedly staking out his store, over five thousand dollars worth of perfume was stolen from the cosmetics department."

Last night? Cosmetics? Sam groaned inwardly. Jules and Edie had been in the cosmetics department.

But he'd left with them. They couldn't have hidden five-thousand dollars worth of perfume on their persons.

That didn't mean they hadn't stolen the items before he had gotten into the store and hid them somewhere to be picked up later by an accomplice.

Except Edie would never steal. She was too honest and aboveboard. Too unerringly good. Besides, she was simply too smart to do something so dumb.

But he had witnessed her entering the store with his own eyes.

Could she possibly be a thief?

No way.

How well do you really know her, Stevenson? Some of the sweetest faces can hide the most treacherous hearts.

His mind balked. He could not believe that of Edie. She'd come to his house to warn him; to save him from the police. She was a reformer, a rescuer, a crusader. She didn't know the first thing about criminal offenses.

But Jules Hardy had free reign of the store while

Edie and he had been otherwise occupied. Had there been another accomplice secreted somewhere? That would explain the male voice he'd heard coming from Trotter's office. Say Jules's boyfriend, Kyle Spencer? Sam had a strong suspicion the story Jules had given Edie was false. What had really been on that security camera tape? Jules stealing perfume?

"And that's not all," Timmons continued. "When Trotter and the security team reviewed the tapes this morning they discovered that the cameras had been turned off for twenty-five minutes."

"You don't say."

"Do you know anything about that?"

"Not really," he hedged. He hadn't been the one to turn the cameras off.

"What have you got to say in your defense, Stevenson?"

"It's under control, Chief."

"Is it really? Are you aware that more items have disappeared since you started working at Carmichael's than before?"

"I promise, I've got a handle on it." Sam scratched his jaw and yawned.

"What's your next move?"

"Believe it or not I'm going to a strip club on Saturday night with the three guys I suspect might be behind the whole thing. Harry Coomer was out past curfew. I saw him driving around the mall." He also had concerns about Kyle Spencer but if he voiced those to his chief he'd be forced to explain about finding Jules and Edie in the store and he wasn't ready to come clean about that.

"This better be all business, Stevenson."

"It is. You know I'm not the strip club type." Unless it was Edie undressing herself for his eyes only.

The chief's voice changed. "I'm worried about you, Sam."

"Worried about me, sir? Whatever for?"

"This assignment was supposed to help you focus, instead you seem distracted."

"I'm not distracted," Sam denied.

"Just solve the case. And please try to wrap it up before anything else is stolen." Then the Chief hung up without saying goodbye.

Case study—Sam Stevenson
Observation—December 10

Yesterday subject was found to possess a firearm—reason unknown. Today, subject is his usual jovial self when dealing with children. Subject offered no explanation for his appearance in the store after hours on December 9. The fact that more merchandise turned up stolen during this same time frame causes this observer to wonder if the subject might have been involved.

EDIE PAUSED and stared at the wall. She was sitting in the employee lounge on her lunch break, catching up on her notations. What else could she say about Sam?

Sam remained an enigma despite having revealed a small part of himself to her when he'd sang her the robot girlfriend song.

He was kind, handsome, good-natured, understanding.

But he stole cars and he carried a gun. And maybe he was responsible for the department store thefts.

Never mind that he wrote songs about teenage heartbreak at the hands of the head cheerleader. Sam possessed a darker side that she must uncover.

She had to find out more about him. About his personal life. Who his parents were. How he'd been raised. Who was Aunt Polly?

Genetics and environment. Those clues held the keys that unlocked behavior. She would find her answers in Sam's past.

Yet how did she go about getting this information without quizzing him directly?

It wasn't as if she could get him to croon to her in the darkness again. Unless…

What better way than a date? You were supposed to reveal all that getting-to-know you stuff on a first date.

Yet did she dare get that close to him again given the fact she had very little control over her emotions when she was in his presence? Even working beside him at the store was torture. On a date he would expect more kisses. Kisses would only lead to trouble. Before she embarked on this endeavor she had to be sure she could handle any sexual overtures.

And, would Dr. Braddick approve of her dating him even if it was the only real way to obtain in-depth information?

Edie toyed with a strand of her hair, twisting it around her index finger before making up her mind. She pressed her pen to the paper.

Problem—obtaining information without appearing obvious.
Solution—meet subject in a casual social situation.
Plan of action—ask subject out on a date.

THREE DAYS LATER, on Saturday afternoon, she finally worked up the courage to ask Sam out. Her palms were so sweaty she had to wipe them against her pant legs. She'd never asked out a guy before. It was more difficult than she thought it would be.

Throughout the day, she'd cast furtive glances his way. He looked so jovial in that Santa suit, smiling and joking with the children, but Edie knew what lay beyond the padding and the fake beard. Yards and yards of lean, muscular male. Even now, watching him give the last child in line a candy cane, tingles bubbled inside of her.

Santa, you can come down my chimney any time.

Immediately she mentally chastised herself for that dangerous thought. Much as she might like getting close to Santa on a physical level, she could not. This relationship must remain strictly aboveboard. No more stolen kisses. No more lying underneath him on Carmichael's bedding. No more late-night fantasies about what might have been.

Sam met her gaze, his eyes twinkling mischievously as if he could read her mind. "Ready to call it a night?" He stepped down from the sleigh and turned to leave.

Edie gulped. "Sam."

He stopped and favored her with a grin worth committing a carnal sin for.

"What is it, Edie?"

"I was wondering…" She couldn't even look him in the eye. Edie stared intently at her hands. This would be easier if he wasn't wearing a red suit and artificial whiskers.

"Yes?" His voice was soft, enticing.

Just say the words, Edie.

"I was wondering, if you're not busy, would you like to go out tonight?"

He crooked a finger under her chin, raised her face to meet his. "I'd like that very much, but I'm afraid I've got plans tonight."

"Plans?" she repeated like an idiot.

"I'm going out with Joe and Kyle and Harry. We've had this planned for two weeks and…"

"That's okay." She pulled away from him, her heart sinking into her shoes with disappointment. He was spending his evening with the guys. Not even a date with her could cancel his plans. What did that mean? Would Sam rather be with them than with her? "No problem."

"But I'd be happy to go out with you tomorrow night."

"Really?" Her pulse leapt joyously. Was she pathetic or what?

"Sure. You can pick me up at eight."

"Great." Edie smiled and watched him walk away.

Then it dawned on her. He was going out with the three worst guys in the world for him to be with.

Where were they going? Edie thought about the store thefts. Might they be involved? All four of them in on it together, maybe even Jules, too? She grimaced. She hated to believe the worst about any of them but the facts were staring her in the face. Sam in the store without reasonable explanation. Joe was good with money. Kyle knew the store security codes. Harry had underworld connections. Were they planning on fencing the items or whatever it was that thieves did with stolen merchandise?

She had to know for sure if Sam was involved in the department store thefts. She had to put her mind at ease once and for all. Like it or not, she had to follow him again.

THE FOUR OF THEM crowded into Joe's compact car and headed for the strip club masquerading under the guise of a gentleman's cabaret.

Harry talked nonstop about how his sexy girlfriend was going to wow their pants off. Sam couldn't help thinking that no matter how well put together the woman might be, she couldn't hold a candle to a certain little elf. An elf that had taken up permanent residence in his head.

Sam couldn't stop thinking about Edie and their impending date. This wasn't good. This wasn't right. He should be concentrating on the job at hand. He should be finding out if the men in the car with him were stealing from Carmichael's Department Store. What he should not be doing was pining over a woman who wanted nothing more than to reform him. To mold him into the man she yearned for him to be.

Wincing inwardly, he recalled the early-morning hours on that bed in Carmichael's Department Store with Edie's hot little body crushed beneath his. Even now his lower region tightened with the memory of her wriggling beneath him.

He had been out of his ever loving mind telling her about Beth Ann Pulaski and singing her the robot girlfriend song. Why had he revealed so much about himself to her?

A weak moment. It was his only excuse. His sudden loquaciousness had nothing to do with her delicious scent or her wide green eyes or the way her little giggle thrilled him to the bone.

Why couldn't he stop thinking about the taste of those sweet red lips, the feel of her satin soft skin, the sound of her breathy voice?

No woman had ever dominated his wakefulness like this. Not even Beth Ann and he'd been a randy teenager at the time.

Edie.

Innocent and feisty. Determined and loyal. Caring and kind and considerate.

She had no place in his life, nor he in hers.

But he wanted her.

With a fierceness that scared him.

When had he become so vulnerable to her charms? How had he allowed this to happen?

Sam was so busy berating himself he hadn't realized they'd pulled into the club parking lot until Joe shut off the engine.

Neon lights flashed—Girls, Girls, Girls. On top of the building was a lighted caricature of a voluptuous female wriggling out of her G-string. The bump and grind music from inside the building throbbed so loudly they could feel the vibrations through the floorboard of the car.

''Ready boys?'' Joe asked.

Harry and Kyle cheered. Sam forced a noise of enthusiasm.

Okay, he told himself. *Get on the ball. The sooner*

*you solve the case the sooner you can quit being
Santa.*

And the sooner he could get away from Edie Preston and her bewitching spell.

8

THEY WERE GOING to a strip bar! Edie watched from the parking lot of Sinbad's Gentlemen's Cabaret as Joe, Harry, Kyle and Sam walked in the front door.

She sighed. Men.

For Harry, Kyle and Joe, she knew the temptation to drink would be strong. For Sam, Edie wasn't sure what would tempt him the most. Drink or naked feminine flesh.

Did she really want to find out?

The words Sam had spoken to her in his house the day she'd suspected him of stealing the Corvette rattled in her head.

Before you're ever going to relate to your patients, before you can ever really understand people, you're going to have to take a walk on the wild side.

Yes. She wanted to know. What was it about the wild side that so gripped Sam?

She parked in a far corner of the lot and sat there a few minutes collecting her courage. She could do this. All in the name of science. This was for her dissertation. Nothing personal. Right?

Taking a deep breath, Edie got out of the car. Rain

had fallen earlier in the day and cool humidity permeated the night air. She pulled the collar of her coat tightly around her neck and eased up to the door.

The sound of Donna Summer's "Hot Stuff" blasted.

Edie slipped inside and stood in the darkness of the entry way, taking in the sights before her.

Three near-naked women danced and twirled on a stage in the center of the room while a fog machine occasionally belched out clouds of smoke. Strobe lights gyrated.

The place was so dark Edie could barely see in front of her. She inched forward, and took an empty chair at a table in the back.

She hadn't located Sam and his friends. She slipped from her coat, removed her mittens and rubbed her palms together.

"What'll ya have?" A waitress with a Pamela Anderson figure wearing a barely there outfit fashioned after a tuxedo, hovered near Edie's elbow.

"I'm fine thanks." Edie smiled.

"There's a two-drink minimum," the waitress had to shout to be heard above the noise.

"Oh, well, in that case I'll have a cola."

"It'll cost you seven-fifty."

"Seven dollars and fifty cents!"

"Or you could get an alcoholic beverage for the same price," the woman suggested with a shrug.

Edie had never consumed alcohol before but it seemed extravagant to pay seven-fifty for a cola.

Take a walk on the wild side.

"Okay," she said. "I'll have a drink."

The waitress looked at her expectantly.

"You want to know what kind of drink?" Edie asked.

"That'd be a start."

"Uh, well, what do you suggest?"

"Beer, wine, mixed drink. Mixed drink's are the best bargain for the money."

"All right then, I'll have a mixed drink." Edie folded her hands together on the table.

The waitress sighed. "What kind of mixed drink?"

"You choose."

"How about a Slow Comfortable Screw?"

"Beg pardon?"

Was the woman suggesting some sort of kinky sexual proposition? Fear clinched her stomach. She was in way over her head.

"Don't panic honey." The woman laid a hand on her shoulder. "I don't want to take you to bed. A Slow Comfortable Screw is a drink."

Edie felt her face flame in the darkness. She wanted the woman to leave as quickly as possible. "Yes, bring me two of those comfortable thingies."

"Why do I get the feeling I'm not going to get a tip out of this one?" the woman muttered under her breath and sashayed away, hips swinging like a pendulum.

Embarrassed at her ignorance, Edie plucked a twenty from her purse and left it on the table. She'd show that waitress that she indeed knew how to tip.

The music changed. Now they were playing "Bad Girls."

Edie studied the men sitting around the stage. They were whistling and clapping and waving bills at the women. The dancers would come over and shake their groove things in the guys' faces and relieve them of their money.

What did it feel like, Edie wondered, to strut your stuff like that? Capitalizing on men's desires to see women naked. It sounded frightening and exhilarating and bizarre.

The women strutted and flaunted their bodies. One swung around a pole as if she were a world-class gymnast. Another did the splits. A third did very strange things with a banana.

Oh, dear!

The waitress brought her drinks, whisked up the twenty and pranced over to a table full of rowdy men in cowboy hats.

Edie took a sip of her drink.

Sweet. Fruity. And it warmed her straight to her toes.

Nice. Very nice.

She took another sip and finally spotted Sam. He

and the other fellows were sitting at a table not far from the stage. Sam had his back to her, his attention riveted on the dancers.

Sadness washed over her.

Was this what he found attractive? Blatant exhibitionism? Naked female flesh swinging and twisting and cavorting under colored lights?

Apparently so.

Humph.

Edie took the thin red cocktail straw in her teeth and sucked hard.

Gosh this thing tasted good.

She fished out the cherry and chewed on it. What was that saying Jules had related to her? If you could tie a cherry stem with your tongue that meant you were good in bed.

After she swallowed the cherry, Edie sat nibbling on the stem, her gaze welded on Sam and company. He was laughing at something Joe had said.

Ha. Ha.

Still giving the cherry stem hell with her teeth, Edie took a notepad and pen from her purse. She squinted in the almost nonexistent lighting.

Case Study—Sam Stevenson
Observation—December 14

Subject has entered a strip club with three male co-workers. He seems very entertained by the more basic aspect of the male-female relationship. The stripper offers him a look at her body. He deposits money into her skimpy garter.

Edie watched Sam do just that, and she experienced a sudden urge to cry. What in the heck was the matter with her? She was simply observing him for her dissertation. She shouldn't care if he chose to visit Hugh Heffner at the Playboy Mansion. She was a scientist. A professional. Her emotions had no place in the case study.

She slammed the notebook closed, jammed it in her purse and sat trying to do the impossible—tie that silly cherry stem into a knot with her tongue.

Minutes later Edie realized she would never be good in bed. The mutilated stem fell to pieces in her mouth. She spit the shreds into a napkin and took a big swallow of her drink.

This time a warm fluffy cloud enveloped her body. Her head swam muzzily and she had the strongest urge to sing. Who invented this drink? It was wonderful.

The dancers were hoofing it to "You Sexy Thing," when Edie realized she had to go to the bathroom. She pushed back her chair. The wooden legs screeched against the floor.

"Shh." Edie put a finger to her lips and rose to her feet.

Whoa! Why did her knees feel like overcooked noodles?

Was she tipsy?

Edie giggled. This wasn't so bad.

Now, where was the potty?

She managed to find the bathroom and on her way back to her table, she bumped into a tall, burly man with arms that bulged around the sleeves of his tight black T-shirt. He looked as if he spent a lot of time at the gym. He had been pacing in front of the door, something lacy and very skimpy clutched in his hands.

"There you are!" he said, when she jostled his elbow.

"Oops. I'm sorry."

"Okay, so you're late. Don't worry about. Just get dressed. Your set starts in seven minutes." He thrust the lacy thing at her. "And put on some more makeup."

"Makeup?"

He narrowed his eyes at her. "Mac sent you, right? Vera called in sick and Mac was suppose to send someone over."

And then it hit Edie what this man was saying. He thought she was a relief stripper come to fill in for his ailing dancer.

A wicked little voice whispered inside her head. *Take a walk on the wild side.*

She could go up on stage and dance. She could find out firsthand what it was like. It would be a perfect sidebar to her case study on Sam. She would explore his world, analyze it and use her analysis to draw conclusions about him.

She could have men ogling her and wanting to take her home.

She could have Sam's undivided attention.

The last thought cinched it.

"Yeah," Edie said. "Mac sent me."

The guy raked his gaze over her. "Mac's got good taste, I'll say that for him."

"Thank you." Edie fluttered her eyelashes at the guy, feeling more sexy and seductive than she'd ever felt in her life. It didn't hurt that she was fueled by a Slow Comfortable Screw. "Where do I change?"

The guy pointed to a door. "Through there."

"Thanks."

Pulse quick and thready with excitement, knees weak, Edie pushed through the door. She could do this. She would do this. Then Sam couldn't say she'd never done anything bad. She'd gotten drunk and now she was going to perform a striptease.

She found the dressing room easily enough. A blonde and a redhead sat in bathrobes applying a fresh round of makeup, a third woman lounged in a bean-bag chair leafing through a copy of *Real Confessions* magazine.

"Hi," Edie greeted them. "I'm new."

"Good for you," the one in the beanbag chair said without looking up.

"Mac sent me," Edie explained.

"You better quit gabbing and get dressed," the blonde at the mirror said. "You're on in five minutes."

"Oh, okay." Edie shrugged out of her coat and hung it on a rack.

"Come on, honey," the redhead said, "move it."

Hands trembling, Edie took off her clothes and slipped into the tiny outfit. A glittery gold G-string and a gauzy see-through bra.

I can't go on stage dressed like this.

But before she could back out, the redhead pushed her into a chair. "Here, I'll help you with your makeup, but just this once."

"Th-thank you," Edie stammered.

The woman slathered her in so much mascara and eyeshadow Edie feared she'd come off looking like a circus clown. But when she looked into the mirror she couldn't believe the creature that peered back.

She looked exotic, worldly and very desirable.

Her fears evaporated. She was going out there and she was going to dance for no one but Sam.

A statuesque brunette appeared from behind a curtain, perspiring and wiping her face with a towel. She turned to Edie. "You're on."

"Wait," the redhead said, slipping off her own six-inch heels and tossing them to Edie. "You'll need these."

Edie slipped on the heels and teetered before the

curtain. She took a deep breath and sucked in her tummy.

"Go on." The redhead shoved her through the curtain and Edie found herself on stage with two other women.

And she simply stood there.

"Brick House" blasted from the stereo system.

"Hey, baby," some guy from the audience leered. "Shake it!"

The stage lights blinded her. She couldn't see the audience but she could hear them out there—breathing.

Her courage slipped and she almost turned and ran.

And then she remembered Sam.

Slowly, Edie began to rotate her hips.

Sam's watching. Show him what you've got, her inner self urged. *Show him you can strip with the best of them.*

Then for his benefit alone, she danced.

EDIE?

Thunderstruck, Sam's mouth dropped open.

It couldn't be.

He rubbed his eyes with both fists. That woman had been on his mind so much he was imagining she was up there dancing on the stage for him in the most incredible little getup ever created.

Blinking, he looked again.

She was coming closer, moving gracefully as a

swan, arching her back, circling her hips, giving him a come-hither smile.

It *was* Edie!

But how? Why?

For a second, he sat frozen, stunned by her mesmerizing beauty and her unexpected act.

Then he realized that every lecherous eye in the place was trailing down her fine, firm body and a surge of hot, red jealousy shot through him.

In an instant, he was on his feet, pulling his coat from the back of his chair and heading straight toward her.

SAM WAS COMING AT HER, a grimly determined expression on his face—his jaw set, his blue eyes blazing fire.

Edie squealed and backed up.

He didn't look happy. Not a bit.

In one long-legged stride he stepped on the bottom of an empty chair next to the stage, then onto the tabletop and from there, onto the stage itself.

"Come here," he commanded.

Edie raised her palms. "What are you doing?"

"No woman of mine is going to parade herself naked in front of a bunch of slobbering strangers."

"I'm not your woman," she declared, planting her hands on her hips and staring him in the eyes. She stood up to him, defied his high-handedness, but her heart was pit-patting like the revved-up rhythm section of a world-class band. She had inspired this macho performance in him.

And he'd said that she was his woman.

Why should that make her feel so warm and happy and terribly afraid she was going to screw things up?

Customers were booing, yelling at Sam to get off the stage. From the corner of her eye Edie saw a man approaching from the back of the darkened room.

Sam stalked after her like John Wayne pursuing Maureen O'Hara in *McClintock!*.

Edie turned to run.

But the six-inch heels were her undoing. She misstepped and teetered precariously at the edge of the stage.

"Gotcha," Sam said, snaking an arm around her waist and throwing his coat over her body.

His breath was warm against her cheek, his lips oh so close, his brow pulled together in a deep, disapproving frown.

He looked mad enough to take her over his knee and spank her bare bottom.

Damn her for being thrilled about that.

Instead of spanking her, however, he picked her up as if she were no heavier than whipped cream and tossed her over his shoulder.

"Put me down," she insisted. She wasn't into this Neanderthal, me-Tarzan-you-Jane scenario. She was a modern, independent—if somewhat sheltered—

woman and if she chose to dance at a strip club that was none of Sam Stevenson's business.

Apparently, however, he was making her his business.

Edie squirmed against his shoulder, but he held her firmly in place with one hand pressed to her back.

The crowd, from her upside-down vantage point, looked weird. Their faces a mix of displeasure and laughter. Male voices whooped and hollered and then another man hopped up on the stage and went after another dancer.

Chaos ensued.

Men shouted. Tables tipped. Glass shattered. Women screamed.

"Call the cops," someone yelled.

Never missing a step, Sam calmly carried her off the stage.

Only to find his passage blocked by the burly man who'd mistaken Edie for a stripper. He had his hands folded over his massive chest.

Edie peered around Sam's shoulder. Uh-oh. The guy—who resembled a large chunk of granite—looked really mad.

"Put her down," the burly man insisted.

"Out of my way, buddy," Sam growled.

"Look what you caused." Granite-chunk swept a hand at the discord around them. "You can't touch the strippers."

"She is not a stripper," Sam said. "She's my girl-friend."

First she was his woman and now she was his girl-friend. Hmm. If she kept upgrading at this rate the next thing she knew she'd be his wife.

And unfortunately, that wasn't an entirely unpleas-ant thought.

"Put her down. I don't want to have to tell you again." Granite-chunk moved closer.

"Get out of my way," Sam said. "I'm taking her home."

Edie was getting nervous, with her fanny sticking in the air, these two massive men standing nose to nose, within seconds of duking it out.

Holding her as he was, Sam was at a disadvantage. When he tried to sidestep around Granite-chunk, the guy doubled up a powerful fist and punched Sam sol-idly in the eye.

Sam's head shot back. His knees wobbled. Edie gasped.

He let her slip to her feet.

Edie turned on Granite-chunk. "You big bully! You didn't have to hit him."

"Hey," Granite-chunk said. "Don't start with me. I was only doing my job."

Swaying slightly, Sam placed a hand to his eye, which was swelling rapidly.

"Don't just stand there," Edie snapped at Granite-chunk. "Get me an ice pack."

Dumbfounded, the guy blinked at her.

"Go on."

He moved away.

Edie turned her attention to Sam. She pulled up a nearby chair. "Sit."

He shook his head. "Not until you put on my coat."

The coat he'd wrapped her in when he'd carted her off the stage had fallen to the floor.

"Okay." Edie shrugged into the coat. It smelled of him. Musky. Male. Nice. "Now, sit down."

He obeyed.

The music had stopped and the shouting had started to die down, but Edie didn't notice.

Tenderly, she touched his eye. "You're going to have quite a shiner."

"That hurts," he complained.

"Ah, poor baby."

Sam glared at her. "Hey, I'm the one who rescued you."

"I never asked you to save me. I'm not some helpless damsel."

"Why is that, Edie? Because you're the only one who can rescue people? What's the deal, don't *you* ever need anything from anyone?"

"Hush," she admonished.

Joe Dawson came over to them. "Wow, Sam. That was so cool the way you went up on stage and dragged Edie off."

She lasered a chilly gaze at him. "Don't encourage this sort of behavior, Joe."

"When did you start dancing, Edie? If I'd known you did this on the side I would have come in here a long time ago." Joe wriggled his eyebrows.

"Shut up, Joe. Before you're sporting a shiner to match this one," Sam growled.

In the distance they heard sirens. The police were on their way.

"Maybe you and Kyle and Harry should get out of here," she suggested to Joe.

"You're probably right. But how will Sam get home?"

"I'll drive him."

One eyebrow went up on Joe's forehead. "You sure?"

"I'll be fine," Sam said.

Joe raised a hand. "Okay then, see you tomorrow, caveman."

Edie rolled her eyes.

Then, to her surprise Granite-chunk appeared with an ice pack. She thanked him nicely and pressed the pack to Sam's eye.

"We better get out of here too," he said.

"No, we'll just explain to the cops what happened."

"I don't really want to talk to the cops." He shook his head.

Right. Sam had secrets she knew nothing about.

"Let's go out the back way," he suggested.

"Yes, I need to pick up my clothes and purse."

Edie took his hand and led Sam through the back entrance. The club patrons had already cleared out considerably, leaving a huge mess behind. Once in the dressing room, Edie was dismayed to find a man and a woman locked in a passionate embrace on top of her clothes.

"Oh, excuse me," she said.

They ignored her completely.

She cleared her throat. How was she going to get her clothes out from under them?

The sirens wailed louder, sounding as if they were almost in the parking lot.

"No time to waste." Sam said, and scooped her into his arms.

"What are you doing?"

"You can't walk in those damned shoes."

"But what about my things?"

"We'll worry about that later." He carried her out the back door, Edie trying to keep the ice pack pressed to his eye.

He staggered into the parking lot.

"I'll drive us," she said.

"No way, sweetheart. That's alcohol I smell on your breath."

"I only had one Slow Comfortable Screw," she protested.

"Oh, so that's what got into you." He grinned and

despite his battered eye, or maybe because of it, he looked damned sexy. Was this guy rugged or what?

"I don't even feel tipsy any more. I can drive," she insisted.

"Hush. I'm assuming your driver's license is in your purse back there in the dressing room, so you're not even legal in that respect."

She looked up into those blue eyes and felt the pull of something inexplicable inside her. How could a man who cared enough not to let her drive while inebriated be a bad guy? Still, he seemed desperate to avoid law enforcement authorities. Why? She didn't really want to know the answer.

What did that mean? Would she ever understand him?

"I see a taxi," Sam said. "Wave your hand and flag him down."

He stepped out into the street carrying Edie, at the same time two patrol cars screeched to a stop in the club parking lot. He whistled loudly at the cab driving slowly down the street. Edie frantically waved her hand.

The taxi pulled over and they tumbled into the back seat at the same moment the police stormed into the strip club.

"Whew." Sam breathed, lolling his head against the back seat of the cab and closing his eyes. "That was a close call."

"Where to?" the taxi driver asked.

Edie leaned forward and gave the man Sam's address.

Sam opened his good eye and stared at her. "We're going to my house?"

"Yes," she said. "Someone has to tend that eye of yours."

9

THEY WERE GOING to his house.

Edie and he.

Together.

Alone.

She in that devastatingly skimpy outfit, covered only by his overcoat.

Sam swallowed a groan. He didn't think he could take much more of this.

He wanted her.

With a rampant fierceness that scared him.

She settled against the seat and glanced over at him. "Put the ice pack back on your eye."

"It's cold."

"Are you always so whiny?"

"Only when I think it will get me attention." He gave her his most endearing grin.

She wasn't impressed. "Ice. On your eye. Now. Before it blows up as big as the Goodyear Blimp."

"Yes'm. Anybody ever tell you that you're sexy when you're giving orders."

"Ice pack," she threatened.

"Okay, okay."

He pressed the heavy pack to his tender eye. Ouch. He didn't know whether his muzziness was due to the warmth of the cab's heater or the comfort of Edie's nearness but leaning back with his eyes closed, Sam must have fallen asleep. It seemed as if mere seconds later the cab pulled to a stop outside his house and Edie was nudging him with an elbow.

"Pay the man, Sam. All my money is in my purse back at the strip club."

"Oh, yeah." He shook his head and the ice pack plopped wetly into his lap. "Sure."

He fumbled in his wallet, paid the driver then got out with Edie.

"Where's your house key?" She stood on his front sidewalk, shivering in the damp night air. He wanted to put his arms around her, hold her close, warm her up.

He removed the key from his pocket and handed it over to her.

She trotted up the steps ahead of him, her skyscraper high heels striking the cement with a provocative *click-clack* noise. Even in his damaged state Sam couldn't help admiring her legs in those dangerous shoes. Her gams went up and up and up until they disappeared beneath the hem of his coat.

Damn, but she looked gorgeous wearing his clothes.

He would love to see her in one of his long-sleeved, white dress shirts. Or a pair of his silk boxer shorts. Or his cowboy hat and nothing else at all.

Unlocking the door she pushed it open, then stepped over the threshold and flicked on the light. She stood illuminated in the doorway like some otherworldly sprite, crooking a provocative finger at him.

"Come in where it's warm."

He obeyed, following her inside and kicking the door closed with his foot, his heart hammering so hard he feared it might spring from his chest.

Physical desire for her crashed over him in an unstoppable tidal wave. He couldn't take his eyes from her. He admired the way her bottom swished beneath the stiff fabric of his coat, envisioned the sweet, naked body beneath.

Soft curving breasts. A tiny high waist. Hips that sloped like gently rolling hills.

Mama mia! He needed hosing down with a fire extinguisher.

Every sexual fantasy he'd ever had about a woman was rolled up into this one compact, exquisite little package. And it seemed as if he'd been waiting for her his entire life.

WITH TREMBLING HANDS, Edie washed up in Sam's bathroom sink. Raising her head, she peered at herself in the mirror and catalogued her features.

Wide green eyes made even larger by an overuse of mascara, mussed amber hair, lips painted the most blatant color of scarlet, cheeks shaded with excess rouge.

A real hottie.

A fox.

A babe.

Nouns she'd never applied to herself. She didn't recognize this woman.

The lady in the mirror was a sexy siren. The type men did crazy things for—like marching onto a stage and slinging her over their shoulders. This woman was a naughty femme fatale.

Where was good girl, Edie Preston?

She looked down at Sam's coat and the towel in her hand. For the first time in her life, she felt confused about her identity.

Shaking off the sensation, Edie dried her hands and stepped from the bathroom. She had to get out of here as soon as she could. She was having some very unprofessional thoughts about Sam and if she lingered she feared what might happen between them. She'd stay just long enough to make sure that he was going to be all right and then she'd call another taxi.

She found Sam where she'd left him, sitting on the living room couch, the ice pack clutched to his right eye. She sat beside him, reached up and removed the ice pack. The room seemed very small and intimate. She had never been so aware of proximity to another human being.

"I'm sorry," she said.

"For what?"

"Causing this."

He shook his head. "You didn't cause anything."

"Just the blackening of your eye and the destruction of a bar."

"May I ask you a question?"

She shrugged. "Sure."

"What were you doing at the club tonight?"

Edie didn't answer.

"You were following me again, weren't you?"

"Yes," she admitted.

"Why?"

"I was worried about you. Hanging out with Joe and Kyle and Harry. They've all three been in prison. I know they're trying to turn their lives around, and I'm struggling not to be judgmental. But a strip club is hardly the place to start. I'm sure you're aware that by simply being in that place they were violating their parole. I'd hate to see you get involved in something unsavory."

He opened his eyes and stared up at her. His gaze so intent it robbed her of breath. "You really care what happens to me?"

"Yes," she whispered.

"Why were you up on that stage?"

"I wanted to see what it was like to take a walk on the wild side. You were right. Tonight I discovered I really haven't lived."

He reached up and wrapped a hand around her

wrist. Instantly, her pulse quickened. "No, Edie, I was wrong. You don't have to get into trouble yourself in order to be a good psychologist."

Sam swallowed hard, his Adam's apple bobbing. When he spoke again his voice was husky. "When I saw you on that stage, taking off your clothes for those barbaric guys, I lost it."

"I wasn't taking my clothes off for those men. I was taking my clothes off for you. I sat in the audience for a while, watching you watch those other women and I got jealous. Then when the guy that punched you in the eye mistook me for a stripper, I decided to go along with it."

"You were taking your clothes off for me?" He smiled.

"Duh!"

"But why?"

"Because I wanted you to want me."

"I do want you, Edie." He reached over and took her hand. "What I can't figure out is, do you want me because I represent a project for you or do you want the real me? Warts and all."

Guilt zinged through Edie. What would he think if he knew she was doing a case study on him?

His face glistening in the lamplight, hovered so close to hers.

His strong hands spanned her waist and he pulled her into his lap. "I've been fighting my desire for you," he whispered. "I know it's wrong. You deserve someone better. Someone college educated who can give you the moon."

"You're as good as any man alive, Sam Stevenson, don't let anyone tell you otherwise. And I don't want the moon."

"What do you want?" His breath smelled like peppermint and his eyes shone with a fevered gleam.

At his question, a profound heat built between her legs, a heat so vehement she lost all words for speech.

"Do you want me to kiss you?"

"I can't." She shook her head.

"Can't or won't?"

"Shouldn't."

"Then why did you come back here with me tonight?"

"To make sure you were going to be okay."

"Is that the only reason?" He tilted his head and brushed his lips lightly against the nape of her neck.

Edie moaned low in her throat. A low guttural sound she couldn't believe she had uttered.

Oh, how she wanted him.

Wanting him wasn't smart or rational. Not only was he a co-worker, and possibly a thief, but he was her dissertation project. Dr. Braddick had warned her about getting involved with him on a personal level.

But common sense didn't figure in where passion was concern. The novelty of her emotions made Edie desperate to explore him while at the same time afraid of moving forward.

Sam sensed her dilemma. "We don't have to do anything you don't want to do, sweetheart."

Sweetheart.

She loved the way he said that word. His soft intonation made her feel special in a way no man ever had. She had never allowed anyone to get this close to her before. She'd always been too busy with her studies and her efforts to help others. For many years her own needs had been put on the back burner. Now, she was blindsided by the depth of her desire.

She wanted him to make love to her. So very much.

But she could not.

Sam began to nibble on her earlobe, right and wrong muddled into a beguiling stew of hungry, aching need.

When Sam ran his tongue against the underside of her chin, caution leapt out the window leaving her shaken to the core. She didn't care about her dissertation or her job. Tomorrow loomed far in the hazy distance.

What mattered was now.

Sam's arms tightened around her and his fingers began to explore, unbuttoning the coat and running his rough callused fingers over her smooth silky skin.

He seemed to know exactly where to touch—stroking and rubbing, licking and caressing. The living room spilled into a kaleidoscope of sensation—the sight of his Christmas tree in the corner, lights merrily winking. The feel of the leather couch beneath them, the scent of Sam's hair, the taste of sin in her mouth.

With him, she danced on the wild side. Excited and exciting. Letting loose. Letting herself go free. Letting the flow take her into uncharted territory.

His coat fell away from her shoulders. His teeth nipped lightly at her exposed flesh. He buried his face in her hair and inhaled sharply.

"You smell so good," he murmured softly. "Like a Christmas angel."

His hands were at her breasts, covered only by the gauzy thin strip of material she'd worn while dancing onstage. He flicked the material out of the way with his thumbs, then bent his head to draw one perky nipple into his mouth.

His tongue was liquid fire. She writhed beneath him.

He raised his head. Their eyes met, melding into something deep and ancient.

His mouth captured hers stealing all her senses. Shivering, Edie surrendered to temptation.

HE TOOK HER to the living room rug, laid her down and gazed upon her with marvel in his heart.

The gauzy material around her breasts clung wetly to her nipples where he had just suckled. Her skin glowed in the sparkling of Christmas tree lights.

Sam caught his breath. She was so beautiful that he ached whenever he looked at her.

He held her, caressed her, kissed her. She was the rarest treasure and he wanted their first lovemaking to last a long luxurious time.

Edie came alive beneath his fingers. Her responsiveness stirred him. Her little moans sent shafts of pure desire lancing through him.

He drowned in the scent of her, exalted in her womanhood. She was the most incredible creature he'd ever met.

"Open your eyes, Edie," he murmured in her ear. "Open your eyes and see what you're doing to me."

Her eyes flew open then, and widened with wonder.

Slowly, gently, he touched her between her legs, working her to a fevered pitch.

She arched her back, called his name repeatedly.

"Do you want me, Edie? Do you want the real me, faults and all? I'm not an enchanted frog waiting for your kiss in order to turn into a prince. I can't be changed, or healed by your love," he whispered into her ear. "But tell me it doesn't matter. Tell me that you want me and me alone. Tell me that I'm enough for you."

Edie stopped moving. He propped himself up on his elbow and peered down at her. A serious expression eclipsed her previous pleasure.

"Sam." She reached a hand for him but he shied from her touch.

"You can't promise me those things, can you?" A heavy sensation dropped into his gut. She couldn't promise to take him as he was because she was just like Donna. She wanted him to be something he wasn't. She couldn't love him for himself.

"It's not that, Sam." She sat up, pushed a mop of curls from her eyes.

"What is it then?"

She snagged her bottom lip between her teeth. "I can't...there's something...it's just that I don't know the real Sam Stevenson."

"No." He had to acknowledge the truth. "You don't." How could he expect her to give him the answer he so badly needed to hear when she suspected he was a petty criminal serving out a community service sentence?

"But you could talk to me." She placed a hand on his shoulder. "You could tell me all about yourself."

He wasn't some puzzle for her to piece together. Nor was he an outlaw to be reformed, but a flesh-and-blood man with both strengths and weaknesses.

But he could not tell her these things. Because of his job, he'd been forced to lie. About himself. About his motives. This was wrong. No matter how right it might feel.

He shook his head, draped his elbow across his knee. "Maybe it would be best if you went home."

She stared at him a moment, then drew in a long breath. "Perhaps you're right."

"Just because we have this animal magnetism going on between us doesn't mean we have to act on it.''

She nodded. "Exactly."

He got to his feet, held out a hand to her. "I'll call you a cab."

EDIE STARED OUT the rear window as the taxi pulled away from Sam's house, her heart wrenching in emotional pain, her body still aching with suppressed need.

He stood bare-chested in the doorway, waving goodbye, a sad expression on his face. Edie watched until the car went around the corner, then she turned to face forward.

She pulled his coat tightly around her shoulders, brought the collar to her nose, inhaled the scent of him and very quietly started to cry.

She shouldn't have been so disappointed in the way things had turned out, but she was. Miraculously, Sam had saved her from making a terrible mistake, rather than taking advantage of her during a vulnerable moment. If she had made love to him she would not only have irrevocably ruined her dissertation but she would have lost her power to help Sam.

For in her heart Edie knew that if they had consummated their simmering attraction, she would have lost what shred of objectivity she had left.

She would have lost her head as well as her heart.

It was better this way.

Much better.

She had chosen the correct course. She'd done what was expected of her. She had been a good girl. She hadn't completely sacrificed her dissertation. She'd done the right thing.

If that was true, why did she feel so empty inside?

Nothing made sense anymore. Not her education or her job. Not her need to help others.

The only thing in her life that made sense was back there in that house on Sylvan Street. The one thing that she could not have.

10

HE HAD FALLEN in love with her. That realization shook Sam to his very essence.

A week had passed since they had almost made love at his house. A week filled with tortured thoughts and sleepless nights. A week of struggling to focus on his job with miserable results.

He could not stop thinking about her, no matter how hard he tried.

When he sat in his kitchen, he could see her bent over the table, her fanny in the air, her blue jeans ripped. When he went to the drugstore to pick up prescriptions for Aunt Polly, he saw her sprawled out on the floor covered in condoms. When he sat on the couch and pressed the sofa pillows to his nose, he could smell her sweet lovely scent.

And at work, his eyes followed around the room like a lost puppy dog.

Somewhere, somehow, despite his best intentions to the contrary, he'd fallen for her.

Did he dare trust his feelings? He thought he'd been in love before but Donna had only loved him when he did what she wanted.

Being in love again was the last thing he wanted.

Especially with Edie. They were an impossible match. The bad boy and the crusader. The cynic and Miss Merry Sunshine.

Except he wasn't all that bad any more and hadn't been for a long time. Not counting blowing up the mayor's Lexus.

But too many women had tried to change him in the past, seeking to mold him into the image they wanted. First Aunt Polly, then Beth Ann Pulaski and finally Donna Beaman. In the end, he'd resented their interference.

He never wanted to resent Edie.

Every time he looked at her, his heart melted a little. *Give it a try.*

But he was afraid. The little boy who'd had to fend for himself on the street was still buried inside him. The child who'd never experienced unconditional love and wasn't even sure such a thing existed.

He wasn't ready for this. Not while he was still playing Santa. Not while he was under strict orders not to reveal his identity to anyone.

Chief Timmons had no idea how grueling a punishment this assignment had become.

There had been no more thefts, and he'd managed to rule Joe and Kyle out as suspects. After talking with them, he'd discovered they both had air-tight alibis for each time something had turned up missing from the store.

Harry, however, was another story. As was Jules. Neither of them could adequately account for their whereabouts during several crucial incidents, and Harry's lie detector test had been inconclusive.

And there'd been that night when Sam had seen Harry in the mall parking lot. The same night Jules and Edie had broken into the store.

In the back of his mind, however, Sam was beginning to suspect someone else entirely. Someone previously beyond reproach. His suspicion had started that night in the department store. The night he'd heard someone in Trotter's office.

While he weighed the evidence and plotted his next course of action, Sam still worked side by side with Edie, playing Santa to her elf.

She kept her distance from him and she'd lost that familiar sparkle in her eyes. It hurt him to know he was the cause of her sadness.

But there was no way he could redeem himself. Not now. Not yet. Not until he knew for sure who was involved with the robberies. Once the case was solved, once she knew his true identity, maybe then they could start over.

TEARS WELLED IN Edie's eyes as she loaded film into the camera. It took her a minute to collect herself before she could look up and tell the next mother in line to put her child on Santa's lap.

She was tired of the silence between her and Sam. Ever since that night at his house things had been strained. He barely spoke more than he had to throughout the course of the day, and he spent a lot of time away from the sleigh. She no longer believed he was slipping off in search of booze or pills, but she couldn't help wondering where he went.

She glanced at Sam, but he avoided her gaze as he had all day long.

Now, she wished she had not pleaded with Dr. Braddick to let her do a case study on him. She was involved. She was hooked, addicted, enslaved by his kisses, desperate for more.

So what if he was working out his community service obligation as a store Santa? So what if he carried a concealed weapon in his boot? Obviously the stolen car incident had been a fluke, a one-time thing. And as far as her suspicions about his being involved with the store thefts—ludicrous! But it was almost Christmas and if she didn't do something soon, she'd probably never see him again.

Sam wasn't a thief. She'd bet her life on it.

That left her with one course of action. She'd tell him how foolish she'd been. How she'd been spying on him for her dissertation. She'd come clean. Hopefully, he wouldn't be too angry with her. Hopefully, this wouldn't get in the way of their budding relationship.

Tonight. She'd tell him tonight.

And let the chips fall where they may.

"MAYBE WE COULD grab a cup of coffee, Sam. I really need to talk to you," Edie said when the operator announced over the PA system that the store was closing in ten minutes.

"Uh, I have business with Mr. Trotter," he said. "I'll catch you later."

Her face fell, and he knew he'd hurt her yet again. Damn. This wasn't what he wanted. Not at all.

Edie gave a brave little shrug to show she didn't care but the wounded expression in her eyes branded him with guilt. "Sure. Later." Then quickly, before he could say something to smooth things over, she scurried away.

A notebook fell from her pocket.

"Wait," he called to her but apparently, she didn't hear him for she just kept walking. Sam bent to retrieve the notebook.

He never meant to read it, but it lay open on the floor and when he looked down, his name leapt out at him.

Case Study—Sam Stevenson
Observation—December 23

He is not a bad boy at all. It's just a persona he hides behind to protect himself. He is good and kind and caring. He is tender and just and concerned about the feelings of others. This observer is certain he is not involved in the recent thefts at Carmichael's Department Store. Problem— Due to inappropriate behavior on the part of this observer, the case study has been compromised. Dissertation subject will have to be changed. Approval pending Dr. Braddick.

Sam's hands felt at once fiery hot and icy cold. He flipped the pages, started at the beginning and read how Edie had followed him, studied him.

Betrayed him.

He was her dissertation project.

Hard, bitter anger rose inside him. Edie was no different from Aunt Polly or Beth Ann Pulaski or Donna Beaman. He was nothing to her but a psychological endeavor.

And to think he'd thought he was falling in love with her!

Anger, hurt and resignation all ran through him. He tucked her notebook in his pocket. Well, that would teach him to care about someone. Sam plunked down in the sleigh, too stunned to move.

Then, from the corner of his eye, something caught his attention.

Freddie the Fish.

In the luggage aisle. The same place he'd been the first time Sam had kissed Edie.

Freddie was pushing past shoppers, his gaze scanning the room. Then from a side door Mr. Trotter appeared and motioned Freddie over. They talked together for a moment, heads bent, then Freddie followed Trotter back through the closed door that led to the warehouse.

Sam narrowed his eyes, and ducked down behind the sleigh. His instincts told him something was up.

What was Freddie the Fish doing with Trotter? The

suspicions he'd been entertaining for some time now expanded.

He climbed down from the dais and stalked through the crowd.

Children called to him. Shoppers waved as they lined up at the checkout stands. Sam forced a smile and walked faster. A few beard hairs flew into his mouth. His artificial belly shifted, throwing him off balance. Sam waddled to the door Trotter and Freddie had disappeared through. He lay his ear against the door and listened.

Nothing.

Taking a deep breath, he pried the door open and stepped through.

Except for the usual boxes of merchandise, this section of the storeroom was empty.

He cocked his head and listened intently.

No voices.

He squeezed past the boxes, turned a corner. His boots echoed in the hollow stillness.

They had disappeared awfully fast.

He kept walking.

Trotter and Freddie could have gone down any corridor; disappeared behind any door.

Damn.

Frustrated, he stopped, sank his hands on his hips and turned around.

He was in the main part of the warehouse now. The loading dock was a hundred yards to his left. It was after closing time and the place was deserted.

Sam scratched his head and leaned against a packing crate labeled Waste Materials.

What was happening to him? He was losing his edge. So what if Trotter was talking to Freddie? They could be related. Just because Trotter was consorting with a known thief that didn't mean the man was crooked.

He was letting Edie get to him. She was blowing his mind, messing with his head. She and her case study.

Sam kicked the crate.

The wood cracked, tearing the plastic wrapping beneath.

And revealing a box of brand-new radios that didn't look anything like waste materials.

WHERE WAS SAM GOING?

Edie had come back to the sleigh to look for her notebook and caught sight of Sam in his Santa suit as he disappeared through the door into the storeroom.

Because of the thefts, Trotter had warned all unauthorized personnel to stay out of the warehouse. Sam was violating store policy.

Why?

She no longer thought he was involved in the robberies but she wanted to get him alone and this was a good opportunity.

Yes. She had to speak to Sam. She couldn't stand

not knowing how he felt about their relationship, about her. Especially since she'd decided she had to abandon her dissertation. Despite her best intentions, she'd fallen in love with him. She could not objectively do a case study on him. Dr. Braddick had been right.

Trotter or no Trotter, she was going after Sam.

Taking a deep breath to fortify herself for whatever might happen, she slipped through the empty store as "Blue Christmas" played on the stereo system.

"Sam," she called timidly, stepping around a stack of boxes.

Nothing. No one.

Hmm. She had seen him come in here. Couldn't mistake that Santa suit.

Nor the gorgeous man wearing it.

She trudged through the warehouse, alternately calling out his name, then stopping to scan the area for him.

A few minutes later, she heard a noise and turned the corner into the main warehouse.

And saw Sam digging in a large crate marked Waste Materials.

Except it wasn't waste materials in the box but electronic equipment. Radios, DVD players and computer components lay on the ground around him.

Edie looked at the merchandise and gulped.

Oh, Lord, don't let it be true after all!

"Sam," she said sharply, "what are you doing?"

"EDIE!" He felt his face flush a deep crimson beneath his white beard. "I—I—this isn't what you think."

"Are you trying to tell me you weren't stealing this equipment?" She waved a hand at the crate. The disappointment in her eyes was more than Sam could bear.

"You don't understand."

"Oh," she said. "I understand too well."

He ached to tell her that he wasn't a thief. But he couldn't blow his cover. Not now. Not when he was so close to finding out who had placed the items in the crate. And not when her own life could be at risk if she knew the truth.

He had only one choice. He had to lie to her.

Sam hung his head. "All right. You caught me. I'm the one who's been stealing from Carmichael's."

Her cry of dismay clawed him straight down to the bone. "Oh, Sam! How could you?"

He thought of her notebook in his pocket, pulled it out and handed it to her. "Seems you're not above a little deception yourself, Edie."

She stared at the notebook. "You read it?"

He nodded.

"I can explain."

He raised a hand. "Don't bother. Seems you were right about me from the first. I am a bad boy. Rotten to the core."

"No," she whispered. "Even after all this I can't believe that about you."

"Believe it," he said even though it killed him to

utter those words. "Just as I have to deal with the fact that I was nothing more to you than a research project."

"Sam, that's not true. Be fair."

"You be fair, Edie. You followed me, used me, spied on me. What am I supposed to think?"

Her bottom lip trembled.

Ah, damn.

"You've got to turn yourself in to Mr. Trotter, Sam. It's the only way to make this right."

"I can't."

"Yes, you can. I'll go with you. I'll stand beside you. We'll get through this."

"We?"

"Yes. Together. That is if you want me to help you."

He shook his head. "Can't resist meddling, can you sweetheart?"

"I'm not meddling."

"You're so damned sexy when you're righteous." He took a step toward her. Her hands trembled slightly but she held her ground.

"Wh-what are you doing?" she demanded.

"This." He had to test the depth of her feelings for him. Did she love him as a man? Or was he simply a project for her? Someone to reform. He needed an answer.

He took her in his arms and kissed her. He had to have one more taste of those irresistible lips before she disappeared from his life forever. Had to inhale her scent one last time. Had to feel the soft crush of her breasts against his chest.

And she didn't resist. She went limp in his arms for a moment, and then she flung her arms around his neck and kissed him back.

I'M HELPLESSLY HOOKED.

For the first time in her life, she understood the meaning of addiction. Edie felt crazed with emotion and wildly out of control.

She was addicted to his touch, his smile, his easy drawl. She needed him as desperately as flowers needed sun and rain and carbon dioxide.

Surely this relationship couldn't be healthy. She was falling for a criminal. Yet how could loving him be so wrong when it felt so perfect?

His kiss took her down, down, down in the torment of exquisite pleasure. He had no right to make her feel so good.

The sound of approaching voices killed the kiss. Sam pulled back.

"Someone's coming," she said. "You're going to have to give—"

Before she could say the words Sam clamped a hand over her mouth. "Shh, don't utter a sound."

Oh my gosh. Her breath rattled in her lungs like a loose shutter in the wind.

He grasped her around the waist and dragged her behind a ceiling-high shelf. He crouched low, taking her with him and shielding her head with his body.

Sam, don't do this, she mentally begged him and tried to squirm from his grip.

He held her firm, pressed his lips next to her ear. "Please, Edie," he whispered. "Don't fight me. Please, please just trust me."

Trust.

How could she trust a thief?

But oh, how she wanted to believe in him.

She'd counseled so many women who had done foolish things for the love of a man. Edie had sat in her psychologist's chair, passing judgment on people, offering her opinion on something when she'd had no real idea what she was talking about.

Now, she knew the power of love. At this moment, she could have forgiven Sam anything. Like a mother for her child, she loved him unconditionally. He didn't have to be a model citizen to earn her trust.

The voices grew louder. Two men were in the warehouse with them. Edie, who'd had her eyes tightly clenched, opened them and peered through a small hole in the boxes around them. She saw trousered legs and shoes.

She recognized one of the voices. Trotter.

Sam moved, letting her go and duck walking to the end of the shelf. In his hand he held the gun she'd seen the night they picked up the mannequin and he sang her his song.

The sight of the gun horrified her. What should she do?

"Someone's been in the crate!" the second man exclaimed.

Trotter cursed. "Get it loaded. Quickly. The truck is here."

Edie frowned. What did this mean?

Sam motioned for her to stay down.

"I told you the cops had someone undercover in the store."

"Shut up," Trotter said. "This is the last shipment. We won't be caught. I've planted some of the merchandise in the lockers of those men Carmichael made me hire from the halfway house."

Mr. Trotter was behind the thefts?

Dumbfounded, Edie's mouth dropped open. Well, if Trotter and his accomplice were the ones who'd been stealing from Carmichael's, who then was Sam?

The loading dock doors rolled up. Edie peeked around Sam's shoulder to see a large Carmichael's delivery truck backed against the platform.

"What's going on?" she whispered.

"Shh. Stay still."

But the more Edie thought about it, the madder she became. Trotter had stolen from the store, and now he was trying to blame it on Kyle, Harry and Joe.

Red-hot anger shot through her and before she had time to consider her actions, habit took over. She was not the type to let an injustice go unpunished.

Edie rose to her feet and marched forward. Sam grabbed for her ankle but missed. She rushed Trotter who was standing on the loading dock. He looked very startled to see her.

"Miss Preston," he exclaimed.

"You—you—creep! How dare you blame innocent people? How dare you steal from the store? This is inexcusable." Edie shook a finger at him.

Trotter's mouth dropped open, but only for a second. His eyes narrowed. He lunged for her and grabbed Edie by the hand.

"You're going to regret that speech, my dear," he said and pressed the cold, rude nose of a pistol flush against her temple. "Now, get into the back of the truck."

11

DAMN HER SWEET, wonderful, impulsive hide.

He'd wanted to follow Trotter and Freddie, see where they were taking the stolen goods to fence. Now, his cover was about to be blown. They had his woman, and he would die before he let them leave the premises with her.

But Trotter had a gun pressed to her head.

Sam's gut roiled.

He stood, moved past the shelf and around the boxes. He raised his gun in both hands. "Police. Let her go, Trotter. It's not worth dying over."

"Police?" Edie's words echoed in the building. "You're a cop?"

Sam's eyes met hers. And darn if she didn't grin as big as a kid in a cotton-candy factory.

Trotter swung his gaze to Sam and cursed vehemently. Freddie the Fish was still tossing electronic equipment into the wooden crate. He stopped what he was doing and blinked. "Santa?"

"Sorry, Freddie, I'm afraid a sack of coal is all you're going to find in your stocking this Christmas. Get your hands over your head."

Sam turned the gun on Freddie. The man kept staring at him as if he couldn't believe he was being arrested by Santa Claus. Sam stepped over, relieved him of his gun and ordered him onto the ground. He cuffed Freddie, then trained his duty weapon on Trotter.

Trotter remained at the loading dock entrance, Edie clutched in his arms.

But the woman didn't have the presence of mind to be afraid. She kept haranguing him with words. Sam almost smiled.

"You should be ashamed of yourself," she lectured. "Didn't your mother teach you that it's not nice to point?"

"My mother's dead," Trotter said.

"Oh, I'm sorry."

Trotter shrugged. "That's life."

"Well, stop and think a moment. What will your wife say?"

"She left me. Ran off with an insurance executive. I didn't make enough money to please her," Trotter responded bitterly.

Sam watched Edie's face. He could see her mental cogs whirling. What was she up to?

"A man of your standing." Edie shook her head as if she didn't have a pistol against her temple. "Why would you do this?"

From his position on the ground, Freddie the Fish snorted. "He doesn't make enough to pay off his gambling debts. He's into my boss to the tune of two-hundred grand.''

"For shame!" Edie scolded and Sam prayed Trotter wouldn't blow her away just to shut her up. "And to think I had so much respect for you."

Trotter blinked. "You did?"

"Yes, but that was before I found out about this. How on earth do you expect to earn back my trust?"

The girl was nutty as a Christmas fruitcake, Sam concluded. He'd suspected this about her the moment they'd met when she'd tried to block him from stripping out of his flea-bitten Santa suit. Lucky for her, he was very fond of fruitcake.

Most women in the same predicament would sob or faint or freeze. Any of those responses would have been normal reactions.

But Edie Preston certainly was not normal.

Not by a long shot.

Her unconventional approach was one of the things he liked most about her.

"Well?" Edie demanded. "How do you expect to redeem your reputation?"

Trotter seemed confused. Sam used the opportunity to creep closer.

"What do you mean?" Trotter asked, sweat beads popping out on his broad forehead. "There's nothing to redeem. I'm going to kill you and Santa, then I'm going to load those electronics onto this truck and drive away."

"Hey," Freddie protested. "What about me?"

"You've set me up with the fence. You've served your purpose," Trotter said. "Maybe I'll shoot you, too. Place the gun in your hand. Make it look like you murdered them, then shot yourself out of remorse." Trotter paused to consider his new scenario. "Yes. It just might work. After all, as the girl said, I do have a reputation. Who would believe I was robbing the store?"

"It's not going to happen, Trotter. Put down the gun and let Edie go," Sam said tightly.

"You're in no position to be issuing orders, Stevenson."

Sam stared at Edie, peered deeply into her eyes. Silently, he sent her a message and prayed mental telepathy really worked. *Duck, run, move your head, anything to give me a clear shot at him.*

She didn't seem the least bit scared. Imperceptibly, she nodded. Had she understood what he wanted?

"This has gone on long enough, Mr. Trotter." Her voice was firm.

Then with a quick one-two action, she came down hard on his instep with her heel and drove her elbow backward into his gut.

"Ooph." Trotter's face darkened and he loosened his grip on her.

Run Edie, run.

But instead of moving out of the way, Edie turned inward, grasped Trotter's gun-toting wrist and bit him.

"Yow!" he yelped.

His gun clattered to the cement.

"Serves you right," Freddie the Fish mumbled from his low-level vantage point.

Sam didn't waste a second. He covered the ground between him and Trotter in two long-legged strides. He took the man by the collar and held on for dear life, his duty weapon pushed against Trotter's cheek. Let him have a dose of what he'd just dished out to Edie.

Pride for her welled inside him. "Are you all right?" he asked.

"Yeah!" She feigned boxing moves at Trotter, hopping from one foot to the other. Jab, jab, uppercut. "That'll teach you to mess with Santa Claus, you big bully."

The woman was too much. Sam grinned. "You made a mistake when you took this one as hostage, Trotter."

"Tell me about it." Trotter glowered. "I should have fired you both when I had the chance."

"Edie," Sam commanded. "Get the cell phone out of my hip pocket. Dial 911. Get them to patch you through to Chief Alfred Timmons. Tell him that Santa's got a surprise package waiting for him in Carmichael's warehouse."

SAM WAS A COP, *Sam was a cop.* Edie mentally chanted, grinning. She should have known her instincts about him hadn't led her astray. She hadn't made a mistake by falling in love with him.

She'd been waiting on a bench in the busy police station for over three hours. She'd already given her statement to one of the officers who'd arrived to help Sam cart off Trotter and his unhappy accomplice.

Now, she was waiting for Sam to wrap up the details of the arrest. They had a lot to discuss.

Like what the future might hold.

An eager excitement fizzed inside her and Edie struggled to quell her nervousness.

When Sam finally emerged from behind closed doors minus the Santa suit, his dark hair combed back off his head, a gun holster at his hip, a badge pinned on his chest, Edie's heart tripped.

He was so handsome. So forceful. So manly. He was chatting to another officer and he hadn't seen her yet. She gulped and held her breath.

Her nervousness transformed into something much more palpable.

Fear.

A million what-ifs rose to her mind. What if he didn't want her? What if she had somehow screwed things up between them?

She pushed aside her fears. Edie wasn't one to sit and wonder. For better or worse, she was the type to grab the bull by the horns and demand answers.

He finished his conversation and started across the room. Phones rang, computer keyboards clacked, voices hummed but Edie could scarcely hear anything over the steady pounding of her heart.

Rising to her feet, she moved toward him.

"Sam."

"Edie." He stopped.

Anxiously she studied his face, searching for a sign.

"You're still here."

"Yes."

"I thought you'd be long gone." He smiled faintly. A smile was a good thing. Yes?

"I wanted to talk to you."

"That's good. I needed to talk to you too."

"You do?"

His features turned serious. "Do you have any idea how foolhardy you acted today?" He shook his head. "I can't believe you simply charged over to Trotter and started lecturing him."

"He had it coming." She notched her chin upward.

"Edie, he is a dangerous man, he had a gun. Didn't you think about that?"

"I could only think about one thing," she said.

"And what was that?"

"How he was trying to frame the other guys. Blame them for his wrongdoings. He had to be held accountable. I couldn't sit by and do nothing."

"Fools rush in," Sam muttered and shook his head. Her heart knocked painfully against her chest. He thought she was a fool.

"Did you learn anything from this?" he asked.

"What do you mean?"

"About rushing into situations without enough information."

"Now that you mention it," she admitted. "I was pretty scared."

A smiled crooked one corner of his mouth. "I never would have guessed. You were cucumber cool. And you really threw Trotter off guard. When we were interrogating him, he kept saying 'that girl wouldn't stop lecturing me.'"

"Really?"

"You've got high expectations of people, Edie Preston."

She couldn't mistake the twinkle in his eye. That was a good sign.

Right?

"Do you need a ride home?" He angled his head.

"I thought you'd never ask."

"This way." He placed a hand to the small of her back and guided her to the door and into the night.

Edie gnawed on her bottom lip, wished desperately she'd had her makeup kit with her so she could freshen up. Unfortunately, she was also in her elf suit with the darned jangling jingle bells.

Please, she thought, *just let me survive the drive home. Let me find the right words to tell him how I feel about him.*

When they reached the parking lot, he stopped beside his car and took her hand.

"Listen, Edie, I want you to know that I've had a great time these past five weeks playing Santa with you."

Oh, no. Here it comes. You're a great girl but...

"Me, too," she whispered, her gaze scanning his face, searching for answers.

"You're a great girl."

Her stomach roiled. Her hands trembled. Tears gathered behind her eyelids.

So much for taking a walk on the wild side.

"You're a wonderful guy." She blinked. Willed away the tears.

"I know I'm not good enough for you. I grew up the hard way, on the streets. I spent my youth rebelling against authority. If it hadn't been for my Aunt Polly..." He shook his head. "But I digress. I'm a cop. I see the dark-and-dirty side of life. You're an optimist. You're clean and pure and innocent. I'm afraid..." He stopped.

"Afraid of what?" she urged.

He took a deep breath. Were those tears glistening in his eyes? Her heart stuttered.

"If we start dating that I'll ruin what I love most about you."

What he loved most about her? Her pulse quickened.

"Your inherent belief in the goodness of your fellow man."

A lock of hair had fallen across his forehead. She raised on tiptoes, patted the strand back into place.

"Shh," she said. "Don't be silly. We're perfect together. I need your cold-eyed realism just as much as you need my cockeyed optimism. You've taught me so much about life, Sam Stevenson, in such a short time.''

"Same here.'' His voice was gruff.

"For so many years I've been like everyone's kid sister. Guys don't make passes at me. Construction workers don't whistle at me on the street. I'm the good girl. But you make me feel like a real woman. Alive, sexy, sexual. You've given me the courage to take risks, to really experience life. I can't tell you how good that feels.''

"Really?''

She nodded.

He actually blushed. Big, tough cop didn't know how to take a compliment. "Well, you make me feel pretty sexy, too. The last thing I ever expected was to fall in love with you.''

Emotions knotted in her throat. "You're in love with me?''

"Hell, yes,'' he said gruffly. "Why do you think I was trying to break things off with you?''

"Is that what you usually do when you're in love? Run away?''

"I'm scared I can't live up to your expectations. I was worried you'd pass judgement on me. That I wouldn't measure up to your expectations. Aunt Polly wanted so much from me. So did my last girlfriend. I can't offer you anything more than what you see right now, Edie. Take me as I am. For better or worse.'' He held his arms wide, exposing himself to her.

Instinctively, she knew this was a very difficult thing for him to do—lay himself bare.

"And if I say yes?"

"Then I'm taking you back to my place."

"Yes," she said. "Yes, yes, a thousand times yes."

Embracing the exhilarating insanity of the moment, Edie climbed into the Corvette beside him and snapped her seat belt into place. He drove through the light traffic to his quaint house in his eclectic neighborhood.

I'd love living here, she realized, in this melting pot of cultures.

Sam pulled into the driveway and leapt from the car, hustling around to the passenger side to help her out.

He ushered her up the steps and across the threshold, both their breaths coming in sharp, hurried gasps. He positioned her on the couch, then turned on the stereo.

"Walking in a Winter Wonderland," issued forth.

He joined her on the couch and pulled her into his lap. "Christmas will always be our special time," he whispered, his warm breath feathering the hairs back from her ears.

"We won't be able to hear a Christmas song without thinking back on this moment," he continued.

"Or see a sprig of mistletoe without remembering the first time you kissed me."

"You mean like this?" Sam kissed her softly, gently, repeatedly.

"More like this," Edie said, introducing her tongue into the mix.

"Whew." He pulled back a few minutes later.

"When you take a walk on the wild side, you really take a walk on the wild side."

"I learned from the best." She grinned.

"I love the way you smile," he said.

"I love the way you smell." She buried her nose against his neck. "Like pine cones and peppermint and gingerbread."

He caught her chin in his palm, turned her face to meet his eyes. "And I love you, Edie Preston, with all my heart and soul."

"I love you, too, Sam," she whispered. "More than you'll ever know."

He rose to his feet, Edie clutched firmly in his arms. Her giggle echoed in the room. "Where are we going?" she demanded.

"To the bedroom."

"Ah."

"Got a problem with that?"

"No. Not at all. But I do have one request."

"And that is?"

"Do you still have the Santa suit?" she whispered. "Because I've always had this wild little fantasy..."

You're not going to believe this offer!

In October and November 2000, buy any two Harlequin or Silhouette books and save $10.00 off future purchases, or buy any three and save $20.00 off future purchases!

Just fill out this form and attach 2 proofs of purchase (cash register receipts) from October and November 2000 books and Harlequin will send you a coupon booklet worth a total savings of $10.00 off future purchases of Harlequin and Silhouette books in 2001. Send us 3 proofs of purchase and we will send you a coupon booklet worth a total savings of $20.00 off future purchases.

Saving money has never been this easy.

I accept your offer! Please send me a coupon booklet:

Name: _____

Address: _____ City: _____

State/Prov.: _____ Zip/Postal Code: _____

Optional Survey!

In a typical month, how many Harlequin or Silhouette books would you buy <u>new</u> at retail stores?

☐ Less than 1 ☐ 1 ☐ 2 ☐ 3 to 4 ☐ 5+

Which of the following statements best describes how you <u>buy</u> Harlequin or Silhouette books? Choose one answer only that <u>best</u> describes you.

☐ I am a regular buyer and reader
☐ I am a regular reader but buy only occasionally
☐ I only buy and read for specific times of the year, e.g. vacations
☐ I subscribe through Reader Service but also buy at retail stores
☐ I mainly borrow and buy only occasionally
☐ I am an occasional buyer and reader

Which of the following statements best describes how you <u>choose</u> the Harlequin and Silhouette series books you buy <u>new</u> at retail stores? By "series," we mean books within a particular line, such as *Harlequin PRESENTS* or *Silhouette SPECIAL EDITION*. Choose one answer only that <u>best</u> describes you.

☐ I only buy books from my favorite series
☐ I generally buy books from my favorite series but also buy books from other series on occasion
☐ I buy some books from my favorite series but also buy from many other series regularly
☐ I buy all types of books depending on my mood and what I find interesting and have no favorite series

Please send this form, along with your cash register receipts as proofs of purchase, to:
In the U.S.: Harlequin Books, P.O. Box 9057, Buffalo, NY 14269
In Canada: Harlequin Books, P.O. Box 622, Fort Erie, Ontario L2A 5X3
(Allow 4-6 weeks for delivery) Offer expires December 31, 2000.

PHQ4002